BOMBS AND BANDWIDTH

BOMBS AND BANDWIDTH

THE EMERGING RELATIONSHIP BETWEEN INFORMATION TECHNOLOGY AND SECURITY

ROBERT LATHAM, EDITOR

PROJECT COORDINATED BY THE

SOCIAL SCIENCE RESEARCH COUNCIL, NEW YORK

THE NEW PRESS

NEW YORK
LONDON

Published in the United States by The New Press, New York, 2003
Distributed by W. W. Norton & Company, Inc., New York

LIBRARY OF CONGRESS CATALOGING-IN-PUBLICATION DATA

Bombs and bandwidth : the emerging relationship between information technology and security / Robert Latham, editor.
p. cm.
Includes bibliographical references and index.
ISBN 1-56584-867-5 (hc)—ISBN 1-56584-862-4 (pb)
1. National security—United States. 2. Information warfare. 3. Military intelligence. 4. United States—Military policy. 5. World politics—21st century.
I. Latham, Robert, 1956-

UA23.B6 2003
355'.033073—dc21
2003043616

The New Press was established in 1990 as a not-for-profit alternative to the large, commercial publishing houses currently dominating the book publishing industry. The New Press operates in the public interest rather than for private gain, and is committed to publishing, in innovative ways, works of educational, cultural, and community value that are often deemed insufficiently profitable.

The New Press
38 Greene Street, 4th floor
New York, NY 10013
www.thenewpress.com

In the United Kingdom:
6 Salem Road
London W2 4BU

Composition by dix!

Printed in Canada

2 4 6 8 10 9 7 5 3 1

CONTENTS

ACKNOWLEDGMENTS

In the late fall of 2001 Craig Calhoun, president of the Social Science Research Council, asked that I think seriously about the connections between September 11 and the transformations under way in the relationship between information technology and security. That initial important intervention by Craig Calhoun led to this volume. While September 11 and its aftermath is a central theme that runs through the chapters, each author takes a wider view in an effort to provide insight into the important transformations under way in this area.

The ability to bring together such an outstanding group of experts to probe this issue owes a great deal to the Ford Foundation, which generously has supported work on IT, international cooperation, and global security at the SSRC. Saskia Sassen, as chair of the program steering committee, lent her support for the project, recognizing that this is a crucial set of issues to address in a fast-changing global security environment.

Thanks go to Deborah Matzner, who initially helped bring these authors together into a collective. Marcela Sabino took over from Deborah and has done a superb job of moving the pieces from drafts to the final, published chapters you see before you. I am grateful for her watchful eye seeking clear, accessible language and concepts. Finally, Paul Price deserves thanks for his aid throughout the entire process, from initial conceptualization to final publication.

EDITOR'S NOTE

This book went to press as events surrounding the U.S. invasion of Iraq were unfolding. Many of the issues we have addressed here are deeply intertwined with these and other evolving international security developments. We will continue to address these in a range of venues, including the Social Science Research Council website, www.ssrc.org.

INTRODUCTION

ROBERT LATHAM

The relationship between information technology (IT) and security is as old as society itself. Ancient societies, like modern ones, sought information about the intentions and actions of real or imagined enemies (what we now call "intelligence"). Their technology was not the telegraph, radio, or satellite but the tower, smoke signal, and horse. In between the modern use of sophisticated electronic technologies and the ancient use of physical and mechanical technologies lies a long history of change in the relationship between IT and security.[1]

Our purpose here is not to trace that history but to focus on and critically assess contemporary changes. We believe we are in the midst of an important period of transformation. States, militias, firms, nongovernmental organizations (NGOs), social movements, and ethnic groups the world over are increasingly making advances in digital IT—associated with computers and networks such as the Internet—a central factor in their strategies of action and choices about how they organize themselves. Compared to the past these social entities are now far more self-conscious about IT as an instrument of action and means of organization. This heightened awareness does not stem simply from the high level of attention IT has received in mass media. Far more important is the ability of groups to be directly involved in designing and applying IT for their own uses, as desktop computers and local, organization-specific, digital networks (e.g., Ethernets) become increasingly widespread.

The transformation began before the attacks of September 11 (or "9/11"). But that event has galvanized and deepened attention to the relationship between IT and security, as many chapters in this volume show. Far more than earlier fears of large-scale computer failure associated with the year 2000 (Y2K), September 11 has prompted a host of questions that raise issues that extend beyond technology per se. Policy makers, journalists, activists, and citizenries around the world have become preoccupied with issues such as the development of worldwide systems of electronic surveillance; the effectiveness of such systems versus the cost in loss of privacy they may entail; the implications of terrorist organizations' use of electronic communications—from cell phones to the Internet—to coordinate their operations; the potential of the Internet to fan the embers of hatred and violence or help the cause of peace; the perceived vulnerabilities of digitally dependent vital infrastructures of developed countries—from electric power systems to financial markets—not only to error but to purposeful electronic disruption; and the attempts of military forces to exploit innovations in IT.

These issues were probed prior to 9/11 but not with anything like the same urgency or interest, as any follower of news about the United States effort to build a system of Homeland Security can readily recognize. If the current period of transformation described above is based on changes in perceptions and strategies of action involving IT, then 9/11 must be counted as pivotal, as so many organizations, from militaries to NGOs to corporations, are treating it as an important occasion to redefine missions and approaches.

The chapters in this volume offer the reader an opportunity to develop an informed perspective from which to better understand the nature of and response to IT-related threats, the new structures of power emerging around IT, and the ethical-political implications of transformations in this area of human endeavor.

THE IMPORTANCE OF SOCIETY

These broad concerns suggest that when thinking about the relationship between IT and security it is not enough to focus on war and military organization: society is also important. It matters in four basic ways.[2] First, protecting the institutions (economic, political, and social) and resources (material and human) that make up a society has historically been understood by states to be one of the fundamental goals of security (the other, closely related goal being the survival of the state itself). For centuries, that meant protecting a society (its cities, population, national economy, form of life, and natural resources) from attack: armies could invade, ships could bomb, spies could sabotage. As contemporary developed societies increasingly rely on complex information and communication-based systems to operate, there emerges an entirely new layer of perceived vulnerability to invisible enemies attacking the systems from half a world away. Finance and commerce, electric power, health care, and city services are among the areas that depend on digital networks in the developed states and societies of the global North. If these networks are sabotaged by electronic intrusion—perhaps originating halfway around the world—it is assumed that the systems they manage would fail.

The very notion held by states that a society can be secured by strengthening national borders is challenged if entrance to its digital networks can be gained from anywhere, anytime. Concepts of national security and global security—bearing in mind that some systems like financial markets are global in scope—

are being rethought in nonterritorial, virtual terms, as the chapters by Bendrath, Denning, Gray, Libicki, and Yould suggest.

Society matters, in the second place, because social groups are the predominant users of IT and many of their applications have security implications. Most prominent today are the applications of IT by social groups that produce what are viewed as security threats. Groups associated with global terrorism, ethnic and nationalist violence, and transnational crime use IT for their own purposes: either communicating and distributing resources within their own networks (see Nordstrom and Rohozinski) or penetrating and disrupting the information systems in the developed world as just described above. (The identification of social, nonstate actors as producers of threats does not displace states as sources of threats via IT. As Bendrath points out, both types of actors are on the radar of the U.S. government.)

Of course, societal groups of this sort have always managed to communicate—whether it be via ships or landline telephones—but digital IT offers a number of opportunities: utilizing, as the chapters by Nordstrom and Deibert and Stein point out, an increasing range of communication options (from Internet cafés to satellite phones); exploiting the large amount of information on the World Wide Web to carry out operations (attacks or smuggling can be coordinated via published information about systems of transportation); reaching out to new recruits or passive supporters (providing financial or other aid) around the world who might otherwise be difficult to contact; pursuing a form of "public relations" through websites that make an online case for a cause on one side of a violent conflict. While much attention is now given to international threats, such as Al Qaeda, any given society may, as the chapters by Nordstrom and Rohozinksi demonstrate, contain individuals or domestic groups dedicated to violence or crime that can exploit IT against their own social institutions and population.

At the same time, it is important not to overemphasize threats as the only form of IT use relevant to security. As opposed to applications that produce threats, there are also applications that are associated with the reduction of violence and the possibility of greater peace. Relevant are the exchanges online (sometimes in chat rooms) between individuals from across lines of conflict, which might otherwise never take place (see the Kadende-Kaiser chapter on Burundi). Also relevant are the attempts of activist organizations and NGOs to bring to the fore questions about the human dimensions of conflicts such as the status of refugees or the basic human rights of women (see the Dartnell chapter on Afghanistan). Although many claims over the last decade have been made about the Internet as a force for peace and human development, the chapters by

Dartnell, Kadende-Kaiser, and Rohozinski show that there is no obvious or automatic relationship between IT, peace, and development.

A third way that society matters is as a realm of IT-related innovations that can be applied in the pursuit of security, especially by states and their militaries. Perhaps the most well known form of innovation is in the realm of organizational style and strategy. For over a decade, transnational corporations have been organizing themselves into multi-firm networks linking their production and marketing resources worldwide. IT has been central to these networks in that it allows firms to share up-to-the-minute information as well as knowledge about markets and production.[3] Such applications and innovations have inspired the U.S. military to attempt to organize itself into networks across and within various units (a part of what is called the Revolution in Military Affairs, discussed in the chapter by Gray). In such networks military resources, from individual soldiers and tanks to miniature surveillance robots, are linked, communicating and sharing access to data such as live action images of enemy positions. While such military networks can operate in large-scale wars, they also can be applied against threats from flexible, diffusely organized terrorist networks—striking anywhere, anytime (see the chapter by Deibert and Stein).

The application of IT-related innovations to security does not rest solely on borrowing organizational strategies from the private sector. It can also involve long-term partnerships between industry and the military. During the Cold War the U.S. government was the main force stimulating IT innovations. Sometimes the government directly undertook research and development (R & D), as in the case of the Internet (developed through the Defense Advanced Research Projects Agency [DARPA] and National Science Foundation);[4] other times it just sponsored R & D in corporations and universities, as in the case of the mainframe computer.[5] Over the last decade, the boom in private-sector IT development has shifted the balance of innovation closer to industry. This has opened up an opportunity for U.S. security agencies (from the military to intelligence) to exploit private-sector innovation, as well as continue to sponsor R & D itself. It has also led to new forms of public-private partnership reminiscent of the Cold War military-industrial complex, which allowed firms such as General Dynamics to cater to military-industrial needs for warplanes, tanks, and ships. The chapter by Lenoir documents how both the military and the entertainment industry are collaborating to generate innovations in one particularly interesting area: electronic simulations of battle—"wargames"—used by the military for training and strategic development and by the industry for the production of game products for mass entertainment. Intricate partnerships between the entertainment industry and the military in this area are developing rapidly and suggest that the relationship between society, security, and IT will continue to evolve in unanticipated—and often disturbing—ways in the near future.

A fourth way that society matters is as a source of ethical and political considerations that raise questions about the purpose of security. To gain the hypothesized protections that greater surveillance affords—learning of planned crimes or terror attacks, for example—how much privacy are citizens willing to surrender? How closed are societies willing to be as they attempt to strengthen their borders to keep out groups and individuals viewed as potential threats? How much global spying are foreign states and societies willing to tolerate as they contemplate violations of their national sovereignty? The chapter by Rotenberg reviews what is at stake for privacy in the United States in recent changes in surveillance practices and regulations, as symbolized by the USA PATRIOT Act passed after 9/11. Libicki's chapter deals with the various logics and possibilities for tightening the U.S. border, especially through various forms of IT. And in her chapter, Landau provides an overview of the infrastructure and institutions, anchored in the United States, that are available to carry out surveillance on a global basis. All three chapters should prompt readers to weigh more accurately the balance between surveillance, human rights, and sovereignty.

Whose Security?

The above discussion of the ways that society matters opens up two questions. One question is: what is the perspective from which we are making claims about security? Whose security is at stake (that of the U.S. state, that of an ethnic enclave's, or that of the worldwide community of states and societies)? And are we talking about policies (on the part of the U.S. military, the United Nations, or the European Union) or conditions of security (war, conflict, attack, threat, peace)? This volume starts from the assumption that the U.S. state is a central force in shaping global security, particularly as it relates to IT. And that the U.S. state pursues security not only to make itself as a state and its society secure, but also to make secure the entire international system, a system within which the United States has tremendous stakes as the largest economy and as the most powerful actor. The uses of IT by the United States to organize its globe-ranging military forces (see the chapter by Gray); to construct capacities for global surveillance (see Landau); and to strengthen national borders (see Libicki) are among the crucial factors that shape the overall structures of global security. The point is that while the United States is not the only state pursuing information-warfare capabilities (China and Russia are also doing so quite vigorously), the U.S. effort is likely to have the broadest effects by virtue of its global military system.

We can see U.S. policy and practice as one critical window into understanding this important period of transformation in this area, but not only as it applies to the international realm. Policies bearing on the domestic realm are also relevant because the reach of IT-based domestic security policies extends beyond U.S. national territory. Homeland Defense is, as the chapter by Yould shows, at its core about the interaction of the international and domestic realms, driven by the fear that internationally networked threats are present and operating domestically. It also remains to be seen to what extent U.S. policies regarding IT are becoming models for the policies and practices of other states around the world.

This volume also assumes that policies and conditions of security are deeply intertwined, as the forces put in place by policy makers to achieve security (the deployment of mobile, electronically networked military units, for example) help determine the conditions of security, contributing to the nature of war, threats, and even peace.

But no matter how important U.S. policy is to this area, it is not the only factor shaping conditions of security. The actions and policies of groups outside the United States are also important: whether that means the policies of developing world states, the pursuits of NGOs (see Dartnell) or the actions of ethnic groups in local conflicts (see Kadende-Kaiser and Rohozinski). And when it comes to considering who or what is to be made secure, the focus should be not only on the United States but on all the countries and communities around the world. Thus, we use the term "global security" to refer not just to the global structures of security and the national policies that bear on them. We also use the term to refer to the many contexts (local, national, or regional) around the world where security is a major issue due to war and long-standing conflict.

IS SECURITY CHANGING?

The second question suggested by the discussion on why society matters is whether and how security is changing. As implied in the above discussion, there is nothing new per se about the protection of society, socially generated threats, private and public technological innovation, or ethical implications to security policies. These factors obviously take a different form in the twenty-first century, as indicated by the chapters in this volume that discuss new policies, new practices, and even new types of threats. The question is, do these changes and their twenty-first-century context point to any overall transformation in security?

This question offers no easy answer and requires a more lengthy consideration. Security has—at least since the beginning of World War II—been a complex affair, pursued across three basic dimensions: physical space (territory, atmosphere, ocean), infrastructure (networks and systems that determine how societies are organized), and ideas (norms and perceptions that shape social action). If security is transforming, then we would expect to see changes in the way states and societies are organized to achieve security through space, infrastructure, and ideas.

Physical Space

The dimension we most closely associate with security is physical space: that is, land, sea, and atmosphere. Physical space is generally organized into territory. Territory is an expanse of land (or geographical area)—and often the abutting waters—that is under the jurisdiction of a political power. Today the political power of relevance is the state. Throughout history, armies have been deployed across territories and bodies of water—whether they were provinces, kingdoms, countries, or whole empires—in order to defend their own land or lay claim to other lands (in the name of security or national aggrandizement). Territory remains important to security because people, places (such as cities), and resources (such as oil, factories, or even computer networks) exist in physical space. As societies are organized today, cyberspace and cyber threats ultimately matter because they have implications for life that occurs in physical space. A cyberattack on a computerized electrical system matters in security terms because it may disrupt life in a city by threatening social order, economic life, or basic human services.

Land is not the only real, spatial dimension relevant to security: atmosphere is as well. Sovereign control over territorial airspace goes along with the control of territory and is sanctioned by international law. The stakes of control are significant. Ever since World War II the dominance and use of airspace has been critical to military conflict. (The recent armed interventions in Bosnia, the Persian Gulf, and Afghanistan reinforced the importance of control of the air, as large-scale air campaigns were central to the Allied effort.) In addition, the capacity of radio and television broadcasters to send signals into a territory across its airspace limits the state's control of the information circulating in its society.

But the airspace abutting territory is not the only aspect of the atmosphere that is relevant: "outer space," lying at and beyond the boundary of the atmosphere is important as well. This is where satellites circle in orbits above the earth, outside its atmosphere, receiving and sending signals (data, pictures, voice) for telephone systems and data networks around the world. Outer space has had an important place in security affairs ever since the first satellites began to be launched in the late 1950s and early 1960s. Developed countries' militaries—

especially that of the United States—use satellites for their own communications and to spy via long-range cameras and listening mechanisms (see the overview provided by Landau).

Similarly, the sea is a space that has always had a close connection to security. Like the atmosphere, it can be separated into its territorial form (i.e., the waters that lie within twelve miles of national territory, to which states can lay sovereign claim) and its nonterritorial form, the oceans and seas beyond the twelve-mile territorial water limits that are a sort of global commons. Oceans allow vessels to move about and deploy themselves in faraway places. They thus represent a space from which threats can emerge as forces, large and small (e.g., terrorists), might use waterways to attack or infiltrate a society. It is also the space from which cyber-threats are likely to emerge because submarine cables are a major conduit not just of telephone traffic but of Internet traffic. Access to the depths of the oceans to disrupt cables or tap them for surveillance purposes—something the United States has more or less monopolized—will remain crucial to security for years to come.

As long as humans remain corporeal beings, spatially based transformations in security—whether IT-related or not—will be of great importance. We are deeply anchored in space, and physical threats to our bodies, homes, communities, and "nations" understandably continue to preoccupy us. Perhaps the best-known hypothesis about a transformation under way suggests that—at least for the most developed societies—the capture of territory is no longer a motive for war, since today, wealth increasingly depends on knowledge-based businesses (from software development and data management to high finance) rather than land-based agriculture or heavy industry (such as steel production).[6] The growing prevalence of information networks (such as the Internet) as a means to conduct business only reinforces that view, as transactions occur on computer screens and data are transmitted in cyberspace.

Whether or not land as a reason to go to war is less relevant, states—even in the developed world—are still organized to fight wars across territory and to seize and hold it if necessary (if not in the name of permanent gain—such as a colony—then in the name of less permanent security—such as a temporary occupation or no-fly zone). We also cannot discount the prospect that states may be willing to go to war to defend global or national infrastructure (that is not simply cyber-attacked but physically attacked). On one level the current U.S. military intervention in Afghanistan is exactly this: a response to an attack on infrastructure of government, finance, and aviation.

Since militaries have not shifted significantly away from territory-based war yet, looking for space-related transformations by focusing on war motives may miss some important changes afoot in how states and societies—especially the United States—are organized for security. In particular, it would miss transformations associated with the way that states pursuing security perceive and represent physical space through digital forms of IT.

In the past, physical space was known through physical survey (through scouts and surveyors) on the ground and later in the air, and as represented through drawn maps or photographs. The emergence of detailed scale-drawn maps was important to three major transformations bearing on security: they enabled a) political powers to fix sovereign borders and identify how they might be violated; b) military forces to move about and conduct battle in a more organized and precise way (also allowing for the identification of enemy forces); and c) explorers to chart voyages around the world and change the face of history through empire for the rest of the millennium. With the advent of the scale map, forces large and small, on land or sea, could be fielded and coordinated across time and space.

While two-dimensional scale maps are still in use, today there is a new form of representation and knowledge about physical space that is emerging around IT. It is actively being pursued by the U.S. military as well as civilian organizations, ranging from high-tech land surveyors offering their services to businesses, such as surface mining firms, to environmental NGOs tracking the loss of forests and other natural habitats. This new form of representation is based on satellite imagery (high-resolution images of the earth's surface), a global satellite navigation system that allows those who access it to discern their exact position or the position of others being tracked (called the global positioning system or GPS); and on computer systems that put all geographical data together to produce in-depth digital maps of terrains and that can portray the life that exists on such terrains, such as cities and even specific buildings (called geographic information systems or GIS). In the military sphere three other elements can be added: a) the simulations (see Lenoir's chapter) mentioned above that create digital renditions of real spaces, based in part on GIS, within which actors or players can move about and make strategic choices; b) the correlation of intelligence data from global surveillance (see Landau's chapter) with GIS to produce socio-geographic portraits of places; and c) the formation of digital infospheres equipped with consoles, keyboards, and other interfaces in zones of conflict and military deployment (that is, "battlespaces") through an array of flying drones, satellites, and sensors, for use by combatants.

From a skeptical view, this emerging assemblage of digital mapping might be seen as simply providing a wider and more complete range of information, more easily organized and aggregated. Once the revolutionary transition to scale maps occurred from the seventeenth century onward, everything else can be seen merely as improvements or embellishments.

But this view fails to consider the question of whether or not these new forms of information and representation of physical space, when taken together, constitute an emerging "global information grid" (GIG), and whether such a grid would transform the pursuit of security. A GIG is, essentially, the sum of information—digitally stored and distributed in pictures and text (words and numbers)—about targets, groups, locales, countries, regions, etc. It is produced and accessed by the actors most engaged in the pursuit of security (military and intelligence), who increasingly rely on it to identify, evaluate, and implement security policies and plans. The attempt to organize the global information grid into an integrated, accessible system of information is already under way (the phrase itself is a U.S. military term). And a few years ago the U.S. Defense Intelligence Agency recognized the value of joining security-relevant images, data, and analysis into a single, easily accessible intelligence information system that could facilitate collaboration—called the Joint Intelligence Virtual Architecture or JIVA—among security actors ranging from National Security Agency (NSA) analysts to military forces in the field.[7]

How might the emergence of a GIG as the twenty-first-century map of the world transform how states and societies—in this case the United States—organize for and pursue security? For centuries, the pursuit of security has been focused on threats to territory (and its human and material resources) or to things identified as vital interests in the international realm (such as important allies, oil fields, or communication lines). Two-dimensional scale maps have served well to delineate borders, mark where one's own and one's enemy's forces are located, and where such forces could maneuver vis-à-vis territory and interests. However, such maps are static (distinguishing between one country and another, enemy and foe). And they can impart only a limited amount of information, mostly in the form of geographical representation (terrains, distances, longitude and latitude). The most appropriate perspective for organizing for security on this basis is to focus on lines—at borders, on fronts between enemy forces, and as the best route between two points on land or at sea. Among the famous fronts in recent history was the one between Eastern and Western Europe during the Cold War.

In contrast, the GIG is a dynamic information system that is constantly revising and adding new information based on perceived and recorded changes (whether these are enemy movements or new political conditions). Threats can emerge from anywhere, anytime, within the global grid,[8] which ultimately is composed of various "spaces" that are geographical (e.g., the Middle East or Latin America) and functional (battlespace, economic space, political space, and outer space). In this case, the most appropriate perspective for organizing security is not lines in two dimensions but spaces in five dimensions (length, width, height, time, and data).

What this means in terms of the pursuit of security is that an increasing range of geographic and functional spaces within which people carry out their lives (such as cities, communities, and financial markets) can be subject to surveillance and possible intervention in order to identify, destabilize, or eradicate threats. Whereas total war drew the economic, social, ideological, and political dimensions of a nation into organizing for war, what can be labeled *total security* draws these dimensions, not simply on a national but a global scale, into a digital grid of omnipresent vigilance. The chapters by Landau, Libicki, Rotenberg, and Yould indicate that the division between internal national territory and external international realms is becoming increasingly blurred as total security is pursued across the international/domestic divide.[9] As mentioned above, a concept like "homeland" becomes fuzzy when threats, such as those coming from an organized crime network, can stretch across multiple borders and U.S. trade and investment are anchored in overlapping relations around the world.

No organizational form better expresses the changes associated with the rise of total security than networks (see the chapter by Deibert and Stein). The purview of total security favors a focus on networks as a threat and a mode of pursuing security, because networks are composed of nodes that can operate in a mobile fashion locally and across vast geographical expanses. Such nodes—for example, a terrorist cell in a wider terrorist network organization—can surface and disappear across various spaces, connecting to economic institutions such as banks (to move financial resources) or government organizations, such as intelligence agencies (to utilize expertise). Networks can emerge to fight in cities, jungles, or on mountaintops. As the U.S. military draws closer to this organizational form, U.S. society will have to ask whether there will be space for democratic evaluation of preemptive and reactive military actions in a world where total security actually requires a form of permanent engagement across the grid. Since total security can never actually be achieved but only sought, it will likely remain an ongoing project expanding and deepening its reach into various social spaces across the planet. (See the discussion of this in the chapter by Gray.)

Readers should note that the developments tied to total security—an increasingly global view and an emphasis on networks—were not caused by the emergence of the GIG. If we go back to the example of the scale map, it is obvious that the desire to field and coordinate large armies and colonize lands across large ocean expanses was not produced directly by maps per se. Maps, which developed over decades and centuries, opened up options and suggested the possibility of pursuing war and imperial expansion differently. And the investment in improving maps was sometimes driven by the desire of states to put them to use in war and conquest. Likewise, the GIG evolved as satellites, surveillance systems, intelligence databases, and military-information networks emerged across the post–World War II period. The United States' commitment to a global military system, its role as the ultimate guarantor of international security, and its planetary competition with the USSR were important incentives for putting in place the pieces (such as satellite networks) that ultimately led to the GIG. As the pieces of the GIG fell into place over the decades, it opened up the possibility for pursuing total security.

This back and forth between the means of security (GIG) and the organizational approaches to security (total security) is likely to continue into the future as there emerge new IT applications, new security doctrines, and new understandings of threat. An increasing reliance on a GIG for pursuing security should have two main consequences: One is that global security becomes even more dependent than in the past on assumptions about how security works (such as who and what is a potential threat, what is a relevant piece of intelligence, how elements of the grid connect), which are built into the GIG. To make the grid, hundreds of thousands of big and small choices have to be made about constructing databases and what counts as information, where to place or aim sensors, and which models to employ for analyzing information in real time. Will small choices lead to mistakes, big and small, ranging from a wrong bombing target—such as the Chinese embassy in Belgrade during the Kosovo campaign—to misinterpreted communications that fail to uncover potentially lethal attacks? In the context of large-scale war, will small missteps cause catastrophe?

In her chapter, Landau points to the difficulties intelligence systems have in piecing together data that signal threats. She indicates that this was a large part of the problem with anticipating the Pearl Harbor and 9/11 attacks. This type of difficulty is yet another aspect of the problem of choice in constructing and maintaining the grid: either a computer program has to be in place to anticipate potentially meaningful threat-relevant combinations of data, or intelligence analysts have to know when to rely on their own judgment and analysis to figure out such combinations. In the case of the computer program it is hardly clear that those responsible for creating the program can anticipate all the possible combinations and what they imply. In the case of human intelligence analysis, there is the problem of how to determine when developments and potential combinations warrant close human inspection and analysis. That determination itself requires effective software to signal that attention is required. Considering that there is an incredible amount of communication traffic across the air and wires and millions of square miles to survey and keep track of, this is a great deal to ask of any program.

That is exactly the dilemma total security poses: you dig deeper and deeper to find more data to confront potential threats and perhaps overcome shortfalls in analysis, but that creates even more need for analytical tools that can sift effectively through even more data.

Whether or not such a cycle emerges, a growing reliance on the global information grid has a second consequence: the rise of the GIG as a new realm of vulnerability. That is, the GIG itself is understood to be a resource that needs to be secured against threats to it—cyber intrusion (hacking) and physical disruption such as sabotage of cables or satellites. Recognizing the GIG as the new nervous system of the global military network, the U.S. military has leaked information about secret exercises undertaken to verify the extent of vulnerability and has taken steps to decrease it.[10] Whether or not these exercises were productive, the very attempt to achieve greater security for the GIG has two implications. It further deepens the grid as greater amounts of information about potential cyber-threats around the world are sought after. But the attempt to anticipate attack—and to know potential attackers—assumes that the nature of attacks, as well as the identities of those who might undertake them, can be anticipated. But that is unreasonable, given what was just claimed about how the operation of the grid is only as good as the myriad choices composing it. A second implication is that organizing to secure the grid might produce new vulnerabilities in that efforts to centralize data in protected digital vaults conveniently gather together valuable information for intruders to access.[11] The chapters by Bendrath, Denning, and Yould probe these and other implications of securing grid-related infrastructure.

INFRASTRUCTURE

Infrastructure has been central to security since the beginning of organized war. Transport, communications, and fortification have been among the infrastructures of key concern to military leaderships even before the time of the Roman Empire. The pursuit of total war in the twentieth century carried the mobilization of infrastructure (especially civil infrastructure) to an extreme, as trains, factories, schools, hospitals, and media were dedicated to supporting military mobilization.

Since infrastructures are so valuable to war-making and, more generally, to the well-being of a society, direct attacks on enemy infrastructures became an important aspect of strategy. Such attacks are not a new development. During the U.S. Civil War telegraph lines were cut to sabotage communications. But with the Second World War the waging of war against infrastructure came into its own as extensive aerial bombing campaigns could target bridges, railroads, factories, and government offices.

For forty years after the Second World War, it was taken as a core assumption of U.S. policy makers and the informed public that weapons of mass destruction "not only can nullify any nation's military effort, but can also demolish its economic and social structures and prevent their reestablishment for long periods of time."[12] Yet, just over a decade after the end of the Cold War, most policy makers and the public seemed to be taken by surprise when on September 11 a structure as basic as the aviation system could be not only shut down (temporarily) but also transformed into a destructive weapon itself. The pervasiveness and importance of infrastructures within a social system mean the stakes of their fate are high. (Not only do so many activities depend on such structures but, when weaponized, their prevalence puts large numbers of people at risk.)

Today IT has a privileged place regarding infrastructure. According to the U.S. Critical Infrastructures Assurance Office, developed countries have "become dependent upon computer networks for many essential services" including "water, electricity, gas, voice and data communications, rail and aviation."[13] In this respect, IT is not like other technological developments (such as materials or standards) because it is applied directly as an infrastructure in its own right (i.e., the Internet) and is central to the governance of infrastructure systems (from electric power to finance). In effect, IT becomes the brains and nervous system of the infrastructure overall and thus the "infrastructure of the infrastructure" or what we can call a "core infrastructure."

Infrastructures, and especially core infrastructures, are supposed to be metaphorically invisible. Working beneath (hence, "infra"), smoothly, the quotidian activities of societies. Even so visible an infrastructure as a highway is operational to the extent that it is taken for granted, assumed, unproblematic. On September 11, the aviation infrastructure rose to the surface as visibly problematic. Making the infrastructure operational again is not merely a matter of starting it up again. The problem—insecurity due to terrorism—requires that the infrastructure be redesigned. But what principles, theories, goals, norms, and precedents do we possess to guide such redesign? What knowledge is available, and how have we thought about the relationship between infrastructure and security? The issues of civil liberties discussed by Rotenberg show that we have no clear road map for navigating between rights and security in relation to infrastructure.

What sort of transformation in the way societies are organized for security can we detect in the infrastructure dimension? The range of movement and communications now subject to scrutiny inside and across national boundaries a) bear on an increasing array of infrastructures from roads and airports to media systems; and b) expand the scope of the global information grid discussed above. Moreover, new sorts of infrastructures of surveillance are being put in place for security purposes, relying especially on biometric technologies (from face recognition and iris scanning to hand geometry and brain fingerprinting). These changes will probably reshape the character of social life in the United States and elsewhere around the world, especially as new infrastructures change daily interactions in buildings, on sidewalks, and across the information highway. Outside of what fiction such as *1984* suggests to us, we really have little idea of what that might mean for how security is pursued and the relationship between states and their societies.[14]

The ultimate direction of this transformation will depend on the mix of values attached to infrastructures. Infrastructure has typically been thought of in regard to its economic value, and there is thus a good deal of knowledge in this area. Roads and electricity facilitate national markets and mechanized industry. Even Cold War concern with infrastructure was often treated as a matter—indicated by the quote above—of either protecting "economic and social structures" or attacking those of the enemy. Despite the dominance of economic value in thinking about infrastructure, it has in practice often been double coded—according to both economic and security values. Cities and towns have historically been the most pointed sites for the intersection of infrastructure, security, and economy. Premodern cities and towns were double coded, as castles and city walls did double duty as a means of defense and economic control (policing markets, for example). The way this double coding occurred in modern cities was through the internal organization of cities, especially in transportation systems. Baron Haussmann's redesign of Paris into broad boulevards not only allowed easy access for security forces to suppress popular uprisings (along spokelike roads not easily defended by such populations) but also allowed for smoother economic transactions across the city.

The same sort of duality was also played out in state-formation processes, as railroads, roads, and telegraphs extended military and administrative reach across wide swaths of territory, and at the same time made national economic life a possibility.[15]

In more recent history, the U.S. highway program associated with President Eisenhower ("National System of Interstate and Defense Highways") followed the same dualist strategy (highways to move men and weapons and emergency forces as well as to undergird the trucking and the automotive economy). The highway system furthered the dynamics of this duality, as roadways helped suburbs emerge, which in turn built infrastructures of local security in closed communities (via restricted-access roads and systems of surveillance and the policing of movement). The same suburbs were expected to be the only survivors in the event of nuclear war (unlike the cities).

Sometimes infrastructure is valued differently in different periods. A pointed example is the wartime economy when what had been exclusively economic-directed infrastructures (electricity and railroads) were redesigned for the needs of war-making. During World War I, for example, the U.S. state prompted the interconnection of previously disparate electric utilities, which opened up a postwar option of power sharing (the war also led to the design of the mega–power plant in both the United States and Germany).

The point is that IT-based infrastructures have been deeply double coded. The computer was developed as a crucial tool for security infrastructure (especially air-intrusion detection systems such as the U.S. Air Force's system called the Semi-Automatic Ground Environment or SAGE). The Internet was hatched out of the Department of Defense and often associated with logics of security (the survivability of communication systems).

Nonetheless, the Internet has been commercialized rather rapidly in fundamental ways, from software applications and online commerce to the very provision of the backbone that makes the Internet possible—upon which even the U.S. military relies for its communications. But looking back on the 1990s, we might well detect a whiff of naïveté in our assumptions of an open and exclusively market-driven Internet. While the Internet per se moved out of the Department of Defense's hands into the private and public sectors, this does not mean U.S. security agencies stepped out of the internetworking business. After all, there is the development of the global information grid, which commenced prior to 9/11, and which has only intensified after 9/11 through the infrastructure transformations described above. The question is how the security values of the grid will interact with values associated with other systems in place or being put in place around the world. Will economic and social development agendas be overtaken by security agendas as networks are established or expanded, a process that, according to Rohozinski, is already under way?

Ideas

Whether or not the realm of ideas has been as central as physical space and infrastructure, it has to be counted as a basic dimension of security. Bendrath's chapter shows that at the most fundamental level, perceptions of security and insecurity rest on beliefs among elites, average citizens, and military forces about what a threat is and what one's vulnerabilities to threats are. Perceptions are also shaped by theories about how to respond to threats and vulnerabilities. One such theory held by U.S. policy makers is that the vulnerabilities exposed by 9/11 require in response a War Against Terrorism and a Homeland Defense.

War and conflict have for a long time been tied up with ideas. Citizens are mobilized to fight in the name of ideals such as freedom, the homeland, or the nation. Recognizing the importance of ideals, warring states in the twentieth century have often launched considerable propaganda campaigns to demoralize their enemies. In World War I the Allies concentrated their effort on the German army to create—through media such as pamphlets and flyers—a sense that continued fighting was hopeless. Belligerents in World War II took advantage of mass media (radio and film) to attack the will of citizens on the home front to go on supporting the war. It should also be recalled that global Cold War conflict was not just a competition between two superstates but a contest between those who sought to organize societies along either socialist or capitalist lines. In the 1990s that contest faded as conflicts mobilizing beliefs about ethnic identity as a basis for violence came to the fore.

These examples indicate that the modern state, which is the primary organizational form responsible for security and order, has had a long history of undertaking ideational campaigns. The U.S. state began such a campaign as early as 1802, when it sent agents among the Native Americans to teach "the Arts of husbandry, and domestic manufactures, as a means of producing, and diffusing, the blessings attached to a well regulated civil society."[16] Programs to pacify populations by convincing them of the advantages of American life were applied not just within U.S. territory but also without it, notably in the Philippines around 1900.

With the Cold War, a whole complex of programs was initiated in the "psychological warfare" category, as misinformation and misperception were deliberately sown to confuse enemies and create conditions of disorder. During the very early stages of U.S. intervention in Vietnam, for example, CIA operatives spread leaflets around Hanoi scaring targeted groups into migrating southward in order to foster chaotic conditions that would slow down enemy force movements.

Besides these more clandestine ideational programs, the United States invested heavily in bringing the opinion of foreign publics in Europe and the developing world toward a pro–United States and anti-Soviet stance. Programs relied on publications, films, radio, and, most important, partnerships with and sponsorships of foreign media. Most famous of all is the Voice of America, which broadcast radio programs featuring aspects of American life. In the 1980s the National Endowment for Democracy became very active promoting American-style democracy.

States have targeted their own citizens for various forms of "education" and "public relations." In the name of civil defense and loyalty at home, hundreds of millions of pamphlets, bulletins, posters, films, and training manuals were produced by U.S. security agencies to show how nuclear attack could be a survivable event.[17] In the name of domestic support for foreign policy, the U.S. state has not only produced its own media materials, but much more importantly it has sought to generate backing for its policies through the information disseminated by mass media (especially television and newspapers). Strategies changed across the years. During the Vietnam War, journalists were given relatively free access to the battlefield in order to create sympathy for U.S. GIs. The failure of this approach—as horrific war footage flooded nightly news programs—was not lost on public-affairs strategists planning for the first Gulf War, who sought tight control over information and access, containing journalists in "News Media Pools."

It should not be surprising that the advances in IT of the past decade prompted U.S. policy makers and observers to identify the potential for a new era in diplomatic communication based on "public diplomacy."[18] In such an era, satellites can more easily distribute news-style programs and documentaries explaining UN-sanctioned interventions directly to people's satellite dishes in the developing world, and the NATO website can present a case for NATO expansion. However, against the historical background, the relatively recent surge of U.S. interest in public diplomacy should be seen as only the latest in a long line of commitments to ideational strategies. The application of new technologies in themselves do not constitute a transformation of the ways states and societies are organized to pursue security. Rather, it confirms the longer-term trend in state-sponsored publicity.

To find significant transformation, we have to look beyond the state itself to the realm of nonstate actors and groups, populated by corporations, local communities, ethnic groups, diasporas, militias, grassroots activists, and NGOs. Of course, states never exercised a monopoly over international communications—international wire services such as Reuters have been in operation since the nineteenth century. And rarely have states in the capitalist world controlled all communications inside their own borders (authoritarian states have typically had to face the presses and pamphlets of groups, operating inside and outside national borders, who oppose their rule). What is changing is that the communication activities of civil society groups—from independent community radio programming to website development—are changing the information environment within which states operate. It is simply far more diverse.

In this new environment, states have to compete to get their own messages across. Perhaps the most noted point of competition to U.S. public diplomacy has been the privately owned Al-Jazeera TV satellite–based network operating in the Middle East, which has broadcast anti–United States programming and pictures of Iraqi civilian casualties in the second Gulf War. Even a Western-based global network like CNN can undermine state public relations, as the United States learned when pictures of a U.S. soldier being dragged through the streets in Somalia created a general perception that the UN intervention in that country was a failure. But one need not go to as grand a scale as a regional or global network. On a far more modest scale are the independent, community-based radio stations in the developing world that provide news written from the perspective of people in those communities rather than editors in Washington, New York, London, or Paris.

To grasp the transformation under way, one has to shift the focus of security from states to societies. That is, civil society groups are able to pursue their own security in new ways. Sometimes that means drawing in international support to their cause through global networking on the Internet via websites and e-mail communication.[19] Other times it means influencing world opinion about a situation such as a conflict by providing information about it that would otherwise not be available. Of course, groups have always tried to build international networks of support around causes and to inform world opinion using letters, pamphlets, and posters. What is different about today is the depth and breadth of information a group can provide in real time, including pictures, histories, facts, data, and commentary. Dartnell's chapter looks at one group, the Revolutionary Association of the Women of Afghanistan (RAWA). Their website allowed them to leapfrog the poor communication capabilities of communities in Afghanistan to reach the world with a powerful array of information about the plight of women in that country. Their effectiveness was not just a function of providing more information. Rather, they also were able to quickly communicate their views on new developments and events to counter the positioning of the Taliban.

Another way that security can be pursued by nonstate groups is to use communications to help avoid the further deepening of conflicts and exchange strategies for the resolution of violent conflicts. Kadende-Kaiser's chapter on Burundi shows how well-designed and carefully managed electronic bulletin boards and discussion groups on the Internet can become "coffeehouses" or "meeting places" for individuals to exchange ideas across different sides of a conflict. In such relatively anonymous spaces she finds that individuals are more likely to speak their minds and propose strategies for moving forward positively toward peace. While the Internet may be accessible to only a tiny percentage of

Burundians—especially those living outside the country in the diaspora—Kadende-Kaiser underscores how important it is to have a space to devise strategies for conflict resolution, especially when that space is likely to be populated by young elites and future leaders.

As Rohozinski shows, interaction on the Internet more often than not can deepen divisions between sides of a conflict. It can be used to strengthen support for a belligerent side in a conflict and increase animosity between groups. Even a quick survey of websites of groups involved in violent conflicts, from Palestine (www.hizbollah.org) and Sri Lanka (www.eelam.com) to Colombia (www.farc.org), makes this obvious. Many of these sites are for the benefit of diaspora populations. Diasporas can be critical to the life of a conflict because they can provide financial resources to belligerents, lobby political leaders in the West, and take hard-line positions. This is why it is crucial to pay attention to the developments traced by Kadende-Kaiser that point toward the peace-generating endeavors of diasporas.

Those observers looking for overall trends in the relationship between IT, security, and the realm of ideas are likely to be disappointed. A communication system like the Internet is not a tool for peace or war in itself: it depends on the uses to which it is put by various groups that employ it. The transformation under way in the number and type of groups employing IT directly to disseminate information and facilitate worldwide communication implies that those uses will be diverse and often contradictory.

CONCLUSION

At its broadest, the relationship between IT and security discussed in this volume is shaped by a tension between two worlds. One world is organized as an "order of universal security," where the social life of the planet is made legible in state-sanctioned bodies and flows of information. On the one hand, this order facilitates communication within and across the states and societies participating in the various realms of modern capitalism, from trade and international law to global cultural exchange. On the other hand, it requires the policing of borders, the anticipation of new vulnerabilities, the identification of forces of disruption, and the thwarting of threats.

A second world is composed of innumerable social, economic, and political networks—global in reach—that seek to operate, hidden and illegibly, outside the purview of governments and global surveillance efforts. These networks are hardly homogeneous. They include the illicit business and crime networks discussed below by Nordstrom; the terrorist networks discussed by Deibert and

Stein; the hacker networks discussed by Denning; and the conflict networks discussed by Rohozinski.

The boundaries between these two worlds are murky, and we should not assume that only criminals and the mischievous populate the illegible one. We might easily include clandestine efforts of the U.S. security and intelligence agencies to police borders and threats as part of the second, illegible world. Likewise, we might count the billions of communications between individuals who treasure privacy and assume their interactions are lost in the ether. As Rotenberg implies in his chapter, important political questions about the nature of privacy, open societies, and transparent government lie ahead. The ways that society matters to IT and security will continue to evolve. This volume seeks to show that the relationship between IT and security will be shaped not only by transformations in how societies organize to pursue security, but more fundamentally by how societies try to answer these questions in law and in practice.

PART I

CYBER-WAR AND NATIONAL SECURITY

1. CYBER-SECURITY AS AN EMERGENT INFRASTRUCTURE

DOROTHY E. DENNING

When I began studying computer security in late 1972 as a PhD student at Purdue University, the field was in its infancy. There were few academics working in the area, no research conferences or journals devoted to the field, and no professional societies to join. Security papers were presented at conferences and published in journals that covered more established areas of computer science, such as operating systems, or that treated computing and telecommunications broadly. The number of publications and PhD theses relating to computer security was small enough that it was possible to read the entire literature. If there was any security industry at all, I was not aware of it.

The computing environment at Purdue consisted primarily of two mainframes: one used by the faculty and students for academic work and the other used by the administration. Neither was connected to the emerging Internet. The systems were accessed via punched cards and "dumb terminals" (machines with monitors and keyboards but no computing capability or memory). Security consisted mainly of two mechanisms. First, access to the machines was controlled through accounts and passwords. Second, the administrative system was physically separated from and unconnected to the academic systems so as to protect the more sensitive data handled by the former. We did not use firewalls, antiviral tools, vulnerability scanners, or intrusion-detection systems; such tools had not even been invented.

The field has changed dramatically in the thirty years that have passed. Now there is a multibillion-dollar-a-year security industry offering thousands of products and services to everyone from large corporate enterprises to home computer users. There are more security conferences than I can keep track of, let alone attend, and enough publications to fill a library. Thirty-six universities have been declared Centers of Academic Excellence in Information Assurance Education, and numerous companies offer training in computer and network security and forensics. There are professional societies devoted to security, and certification programs for security technologies, operating environments, and security professionals. Information security has become a topic of conversation at board meetings and social gatherings. It is a priority in business and government. It has led to new laws and regulations, and to new policies and procedures for handling information. It is on the agenda of Congress, the president, and international bodies.

In recent years, governments have become particularly concerned with protecting critical infrastructures from physical and cyber-attacks. In 1996, the Clinton Administration formed the President's Commission on Critical Infrastructure Protection (PCCIP). The PCCIP was tasked to study the critical infrastructures that constitute the life-support systems of the nation, determine their vulnerabilities to a wide range of threats, and propose a strategy for protecting them in the future. Eight infrastructures were identified: telecommunications, banking and finance, electrical power, oil and gas distribution and storage, water supply, transportation, emergency services, and government services. Their recommendations led to several initiatives discussed later in this chapter.

While much of the focus at the national-policy level has been on protecting critical infrastructures, cyber-security is vital to much more. Information technology is woven into practically all business processes and control systems. Cyber-attacks have real-world consequences that impact the economy and our daily lives.

To address today's threats to information-based systems, security has evolved from the simple access controls of thirty years ago to a complete infrastructure in its own right. This infrastructure serves to protect computers and networks, and the information that is generated, acquired, processed, transmitted, and stored by them. Like many of the systems it protects, the security infrastructure is global and interconnected. It is growing and evolving, and will continue to do so as long as information technology itself evolves.

The objective of this chapter is to explore this emergent infrastructure and the factors that are shaping its development. The focus is on cyber-security, which includes computer security and network security, but excludes those aspects of information security that deal with information that is not computerized (e.g., print media).

The factors shaping the development of the security infrastructure are divided into five areas: threats, technology developments, economic factors, psychological factors, and social and political factors. These areas will be discussed after first describing the elements of security infrastructure.

Limitations of space preclude giving more than a broad overview of the topics here. Many issues are ignored or brushed over lightly. Further, more attention is paid to developments in the United States than elsewhere. The aim of this chapter is a conceptual framework for understanding the state of security today rather than complete coverage of all the pieces of the framework.

THE CYBER-SECURITY INFRASTRUCTURE

The cyber-security infrastructure consists of those elements involved in the protection of networked computers and information from cyber-threats. The objective is to deter, prevent, detect, recover from, and respond to threats in cyberspace. The threats take a variety of forms and include unauthorized access to or use of information resources, and computer network attacks that deny, disrupt, degrade, or destroy information and network resources. They include theft of information, computer viruses and worms, defacement of websites, denial-of-service attacks, computer and network penetrations, and sabotage or fabrication of data. The security infrastructure serves to protect against these threats and ensure the confidentiality, authenticity, integrity, and availability of data.

The security infrastructure includes information technology, procedures and practices, laws and regulations, and people and organizations. These areas are interrelated and impact each other. Developments in technology, for example, can lead to new procedures and practices, new laws or regulations, and the formation of new security companies. Each is discussed briefly below.

Information Technology

Information technology consists of the hardware and software used to generate, acquire, process, distribute, and store information. Of interest here are technologies that serve to protect cyberspace from attack through prevention, detection, investigation, and recovery. Prevention technologies include authentication systems (e.g., passwords, biometrics, and smart cards), encryption systems (for scrambling data and network communications), access controls, firewalls, vulnerability scanners, and security-management systems. Detection and investigation technologies include auditing and intrusion/misuse detection systems, antiviral tools, honey pots for trapping and studying intruders, trace-back mechanisms for determining the origin of an attack, and computer and network forensic tools for handling and processing evidence. Technologies for recovery include backup systems.

None of the technologies offers a "silver bullet" for security. They all have their limits. Encryption, for example, can protect e-mail from snoops, but not from viruses or spam attacks. Security is possible only through a combination of controls coupled with good management and operating practices, supporting laws, and effective law enforcement—in short, the security infrastructure. Even then, security is never foolproof.

Further, some security technologies are also employed as attack technologies. Password crackers and software tools that scan networks for vulnerabilities are good examples. While system owners use them to find and fix their own problems, their adversaries use them to find security holes, which are then exploited in an attack.

Technology standards play an important role in security. They establish baseline requirements for security and promote interoperability between devices that need to communicate. A good example is the Secure Socket Layer (SSL) protocol. SSL is implemented in web browsers and servers, and is used to encrypt confidential data such as credit card numbers that are transmitted between a user's browser and a website.

Standards have a downside as well. The TCP/IP protocols, which are the foundation of the Internet, facilitate massive attacks against large numbers of computers. That so many computers are running the same software (e.g., versions of Microsoft Windows, Linux, and Unix) further aggravates the problems.

Procedures and Practices

These relate to the management of security and information technology. They include "best practices" for developing, installing, and operating computers and networks so as to minimize security vulnerabilities and risks. Best practices have been developed in areas such as selecting and managing passwords, deploying firewalls, configuring and upgrading systems, and planning for and responding to security incidents.[1]

Good management practices are at least as crucial to security as deploying security technology. Most outsider attacks—perhaps all but one or two percent—exploit known vulnerabilities that could have been avoided by system administrators and users. Humans are often the weak link. They make mistakes, pick weak passwords, and are vulnerable to social engineering (being conned by attackers into providing passwords or access to systems, for example). They develop software with security flaws and open virus-laden e-mail attachments from strangers.

Laws and Regulations

In the United States and elsewhere, it is illegal to access a computer or information stored on a computer or transmitted over a network without authorization and with intent to defraud, trespass, or cause damage to data or systems. It is also illegal to traffic in passwords or similar access codes. Such activity is covered at the federal level by the Computer Fraud and Abuse Act of 1986 and subsequent amendments, and by various other federal and state laws. However, not all countries criminalize these activities, and those that do may not have consistent laws.

A second set of laws and regulations governs the investigation of cyber-attacks and threats by law-enforcement and intelligence officers. These include laws that govern how such agencies are allowed to go about acquiring data about a subject of investigation from third parties, intercepting a subject's communications, and searching and seizing a subject's computing devices.

A third class of laws and regulations mandates security for certain systems. In the United States, the Office of Management and Budget requires federal agencies to conduct security certifications of systems that process sensitive information or perform critical support systems. Such requirements do not, however, apply to the private sector, which is generally unregulated with respect to security. One exception is the Health Information Portability Accountability Act (HIPAA), which specifies security and privacy requirements for systems that handle patient records. However, many private-sector organizations choose to impose internal security policies on their IT operations.

A fourth set of laws and regulations restricts trade in information security technologies. For example, certain encryption technologies are subject to export controls, although these controls have been substantially lifted in recent years.

People and Organizations

The security infrastructure includes individuals and organizations with an interest in security. Both formal and informal organizations participate, including government agencies, corporations, educational institutions, professional societies, nonprofit organizations, research communities, standards committees, international bodies, and consortia. Some groups come together temporarily for a specific purpose, for example, to participate in a security-related seminar, workshop, or meeting. Groups can operate domestically or internationally, and meet physically, virtually, or both. Many use the Internet, especially e-mail and the web, to facilitate their activities, collaborate with others, and reach a broader audience.

The people and organizations participating in the security infrastructure perform a variety of different functions. These include education and training, research, publication, product development and marketing, network security administration, security support services, policy and standards making, law enforcement, and research funding.

None of these parties "owns" the security infrastructure. However, individuals and organizations are responsible for the security of their own systems. Governments are not responsible for the security of systems in the private sector, but they can influence the security of those systems through laws and regulations (e.g., HIPAA), public/private partnerships, research programs and grants, and other efforts.

Participants in the security infrastructure constitute a loosely structured network. Organizationally, this network resembles an all-channel or full-matrix network[2] where everyone is connected to everyone else through the Internet (and other communications media). There is no central command or headquarters for the network as a whole and decision making takes place across the network. When a major security incident affecting multiple organizations occurs, as with a major virus outbreak, many participants in the security network respond simultaneously to the attack, issuing alerts, releasing software tools and upgrades, reconfiguring systems, and hunting down the attacker. Even though organizations are responsible only for protecting their own systems, they can draw upon the network for products, services, standards, training, and other types of assistance.

We now turn to the factors shaping the security infrastructure.

CYBER THREATS

A major force behind the security infrastructure is the real and perceived threat of cyber-attacks. After briefly reviewing the characteristics of the threat, we will summarize some of the incident data showing the prevalence of the threat.

Threat Characteristics

Cyber-threats are characterized by an attacker, a target system, a set of actions against the target, and the consequences resulting from the attack, including damages to the target, direct and indirect losses to victims, and impact on third parties. A prolonged denial-of-service attack against an Internet service provider (ISP), for example, can result in lost revenue, incident handling costs, and even bankruptcy for the ISP. Customers of the ISP will also suffer, to the extent that they depend on the Internet for their business or home activities.

Threats are often classified by the nature and mission of the attacker. There are six major categories: hackers, insiders, corporate spies, criminals, terrorists, and nation-states. Although the term "hacker" can denote any computer buff, in the context of cyber-threats, it usually means a person who gains access to or breaks into computers and networks in a way that was not intended and is generally not authorized. For example, the objective may be to deface a website, steal passwords to facilitate further attacks, or launch a computer virus or denial-of-service attack. Not all hacking is illegal, as when users hack their own systems or companies use employees or security consultants to test the security of their systems, so the threat pertains only to those who hack without authorization. Many hackers are teenagers who pursue hacking more as a game or hobby than as an attempt to wreak damage. Nevertheless, their actions do harm their victims.

Insiders consist of employees, former employees, temporaries, contractors, and others with inside access to an organization's information systems. They are behind many of the most serious attacks, including theft of trade secrets, financial fraud, and sabotage of data. Insiders are generally considered to be an organization's biggest threat, accounting for perhaps 80% of all security incidents (not all computer-related) in some firms. However, only 35% of cases involving theft of intellectual property were attributed to insiders, according to a survey conducted by the New York–based security firm Michael G. Kessler & Associates.[3]

Corporate spies include both foreign and domestic companies. They steal trade secrets primarily for competitive advantage. The Kessler study attributed 18% of the thefts to other U.S. companies and another 11% to foreign companies.

The category of hackers considered to be criminals generally refers to persons who attack systems for money. They steal credit card numbers, identities, and intellectual property. They siphon money from bank accounts and extort their victims by threatening to expose stolen secrets or cause serious cyber-damage. They operate alone, in concert with insiders, and through organized-crime rings.

So far, terrorists are using the Internet primarily to support their physical operations rather than to launch cyber-attacks. There have been a few incidents of hackers affiliated with or at least sympathetic to terrorist causes engaging in typical hacker-type activity such as web defacements and denial-of-service attacks.[4] For example, after the September 11 attacks, one group of Muslim hackers defaced U.S. government websites with messages proclaiming that they stood by bin Laden and announcing an "Al-Qaeda Alliance Online."[5]

There is a growing concern that terrorists might launch cyber-attacks against critical infrastructures. According to reports, Al Qaeda operatives visited websites that offered software and programming instructions for the digital switches that run power, water, transport, and communications grids. Interrogations of Al Qaeda prisoners revealed general intentions to use those tools. In February 2002, the CIA issued a revised Directorate of Intelligence memorandum, indicating that Al Qaeda had far more interest in cyber-terrorism than previously thought.[6]

Nation-states are often considered the most serious threat, if not the most likely. They have the most resources and may decide to employ cyber-weapons to augment or replace physical ones. According to some analysts, as many as twenty countries have cyber-warfare capabilities, including China, Russia, North Korea, and Iraq. China in particular is said to have an aggressive information-warfare program, motivated in part by the recognition that it could not defeat the United States with conventional warfare.[7]

Security Incidents

Computer network attacks have been rising steadily, in some cases dramatically, in recent years. Figure 1A shows that the number of incidents reported to the Computer Emergency Response Team Coordination Center (CERT/CC) has more than doubled each year since 1998, reaching 52,658 in 2001.[8] Considering that many, perhaps most, incidents are never reported to CERT/CC or indeed to any third party, the numbers become even more significant. Further, each incident that is reported corresponds to an attack that can involve thousands of victims. The Code Red worm, which infected about a million servers in July and August, was a single incident. Web defacements have also more than doubled annually in the past few years, according to the London-based firm mi2g, reaching 30,388 in 2001.[9]

The prevalence of computer viruses and worms has been increasing at a similar rate. Message Labs, which scans its clients' e-mail for viruses, reported that 1 in 1,400 messages had a virus in 1999. The infection rate doubled to 1 in 700 in 2000, and then more than doubled to 1 in 300 in 2001.[10] ICSA.net (now TrueSecure) also has reported an increase in infection rate, from about 1% of computers in 1996 to 11% in 2001.[11]

Denial-of-service (DoS) attacks, which until a few years ago were relatively unheard of, are now commonplace. A study conducted at the Cooperative Association for Internet Data Analysis (CAIDA) at the University of San Diego Supercomputer Center observed about 12,000 attacks against 5,000 different targets during a three-week period in February 2001.[12]

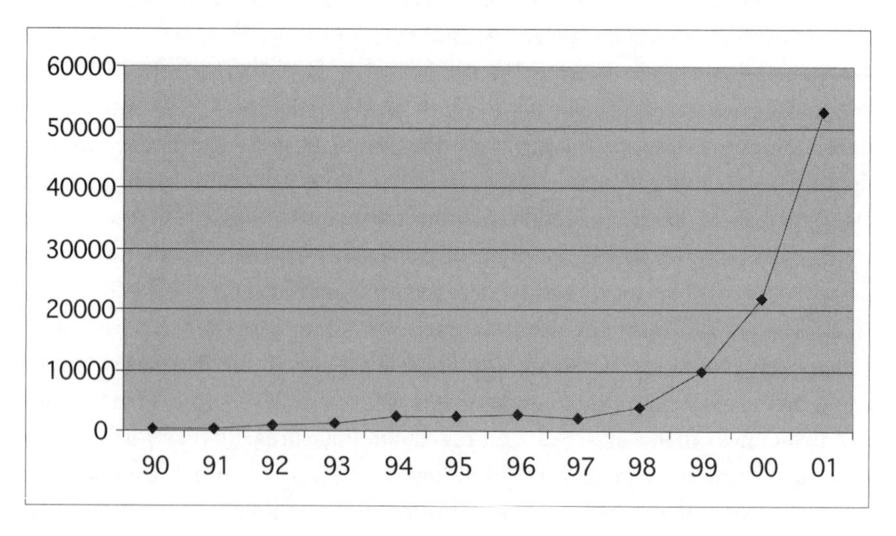

Figure 1A. Security Incidents Reported to CERT/CC.

Riptech, which offers security management and monitoring services, reported a 28% rise in attack activity in the first six months of 2002 as compared with the last six months of 2001. On average, their clients each experienced an increase from twenty-five attacks per week to thirty-two attacks per week. From this data, they projected an annual growth rate of 64% in attack activity.[13] The majority of attacks came from the United States and its allies. Less than 1% of the attacks came from countries on the U.S. cyber-terrorism watch list. There were no attacks from Iraq, Libya, North Korea, or Syria.

INFORMATION TECHNOLOGY TRENDS

Developments in technology shape the security infrastructure both directly and indirectly. The direct impact comes from technologies that enable new or improved security tools and services. The indirect impact results from technologies that aggravate the threat, thereby leading to actions that enhance security. This section briefly reviews three trend areas: ubiquity, power, and vulnerability.

Ubiquity

Information technology is becoming increasingly pervasive and connected. It is spreading throughout our offices, our homes, our automobiles, and elsewhere. It is being integrated into everything from appliances and vehicles to business processes and control systems. It resides in both fixed and mobile devices. Software moves through the networks, carrying computer viruses, worms, Trojan horses, and other forms of malicious code.

This trend toward ubiquitous computing affects information security in two ways. First, there are more targets to attack, and more attackers. Second, attacks can have real-world consequences. The Code Red worm, for example, led to the delay of fifty-five Japan Airlines flights after shutting down a computer used for ticketing and check-in.[14] Another incident that took place in early 2000 led to loss of wildlife and environmental damage when a forty-nine-year-old Brisbane man allegedly penetrated the Maroochy Shire Council's waste-management system and used radio transmissions to alter pump-station operations. A million liters of raw sewage spilled into public parks and creeks on Queensland's Sunshine Coast, killing marine life, turning the water black, and creating an unbearable stench. Evidently, the man was angry about being rejected for a council job. He had formerly worked for the company that had installed the system, which gave him inside knowledge and the software needed to conduct the attack.[15]

Approximately 3,000 Supervisory Control and Data Acquisition (SCADA) systems control critical infrastructures such as the power grid, dams, and pipelines.[16] Many of these systems have very poor security. In the past, this did not matter much, because the systems were arcane and isolated. Increasingly, however, they are controlled through networks based on the Internet protocols, potentially making them more open to attack.

The proliferation of mobile computing devices has extended an organization's network security perimeter from the workplace to homes, airports, automobiles, and hotel rooms. Information once confined to office networks can make its way to home PCs, laptop computers, and handheld devices, which may be less protected physically as well as virtually. Each year, tens of thousands of laptops are reported lost or stolen, many with extremely sensitive information, including government classified information.

Organizations are installing wireless networks with little regard for security. Using a technique called "war driving," hackers drive around cities looking for unprotected networks. When one is found, they can access the network to read corporate communications or simply use the network as they would their own. A seven-month audit sponsored by the International Chamber of Commerce found that 92% of the 5,000 wireless networks in London were vulnerable to casual attacks.[17] Network operators had either not turned on the security features or else used them with default settings that were not secure.

The spread of information technology has also had some positive impact on security—for example, by enabling the development of remote security services. There are now services that check a computer or network for vulnerabilities, scan incoming or outgoing e-mail for viruses, monitor client networks for attacks, provide encryption services, manage public-key certificates, and detect and locate stolen laptops. You can download security products and information from the web, and you can find out about new problems by subscribing to one of several security-alert services.

Power

Information technology is getting smaller, faster, cheaper, and more powerful. Processor speeds are doubling approximately every eighteen months according to Moore's law. This yields a factor of ten improvements every five years and a factor of one hundred improvements every ten. By some accounts, storage capacity is increasing at a somewhat faster rate, doubling about every twelve months, and network capacity is growing even faster, doubling approximately every nine months.

Because of these performance trends, spies can steal megabytes of information in just a few seconds, and computer viruses and worms can spread at record-breaking speeds. During the peak of its infection frenzy, the Code Red worm infected more than 2,000 computers per minute.[18] But this was just a prelude of what is coming. At the University of California, Berkeley, a researcher showed how a "Warhol Worm" could infect all vulnerable servers on the Internet in fifteen minutes to an hour. Researchers at Silicon Defense took the concept further, showing how a "Flash Worm" could do it in thirty seconds.[19]

At the same time, high-bandwidth data pipes and increased network traffic can make it more difficult to monitor networks for intrusions and other forms of abuse and to intercept particular traffic in support of a criminal investigation or foreign intelligence operation. Higher-capacity disks make it more time-consuming to scan disks for malicious code and conduct computer forensics examinations.

The relative lag of processor improvements to those of storage and networks could aggravate the challenges, although multiprocessor supercomputers and distributed computing can be used to compensate. A distributed approach is already used by many network-based intrusion detection systems and to break encryption keys in criminal investigations. Breakthrough processor technologies such as quantum and DNA computing might also counter the lag, but these technologies represent long-term solutions and can also benefit the adversary.

Attack tools have become more powerful as developers build on each other's work and program their own knowledge into the tools.[20] The Nimda Worm combined features from several previous viruses and worms in order to create a powerful worm that spread by four channels: e-mail, web downloads, file sharing, and active scanning for and infection of vulnerable web servers. The advanced distributed denial-of-service tools have sophisticated command-and-control capabilities that allow an attacker to direct the actions of potentially thousands of previously compromised "zombie" computers. The zombies carry out the actual attack, using various techniques to thwart tracing.

Many attack tools are simple to use. "Script kiddies" and others with malicious intent but little skill can download the tools and launch destructive attacks without even understanding how the tools work. E-mail worms can be constructed with windows-based software such as the VBS Worm Generator. All the attacker needs to do is type in a subject line and message body for the e-mail message carrying the worm and check a few boxes.

Improvements in hardware and software have also benefited security. Advances in artificial intelligence, data mining, and distributed processing have furthered the development of intrusion and misuse detection, for example.

Vulnerabilities

One might think that over time, security would get better and systems would be less vulnerable to attack. While this is true for some software, overall the state of security has gotten worse, as witnessed by the increases in attacks and also vulnerabilities.

Vulnerabilities arise in two places: first in the products themselves, and second in the way they are installed and used. With respect to the first, the number of product vulnerabilities reported to CERT/CC has more than doubled annually in the past few years (see Figure 1B). In 1998, CERT/CC received reports of 262 vulnerabilities or fewer than one a day. By 2001, this was up to 2,437 or almost seven a day. These security holes can be attributed to several factors, including growth in the size and number of software products, inadequate attention to security and reliability during the software-development process, and unanticipated side effects and interactions among different products.

With respect to the second source of vulnerabilities, products are frequently installed or used in ways that are not secure. Users pick weak passwords and system administrators fail to install security patches (code fixes) or alter default settings that leave their systems open to attack. In September 2001, the System Administration, Networking, and Security (SANS) Institute and the FBI issued a report identifying the top twenty Internet vulnerabilities.[21] At the top of the list was default installs of operating systems and applications. Functions were enabled that were not needed and had security flaws. Second on the list were accounts with no passwords or weak ones.

This trend in vulnerabilities has been shaping the security infrastructure. It

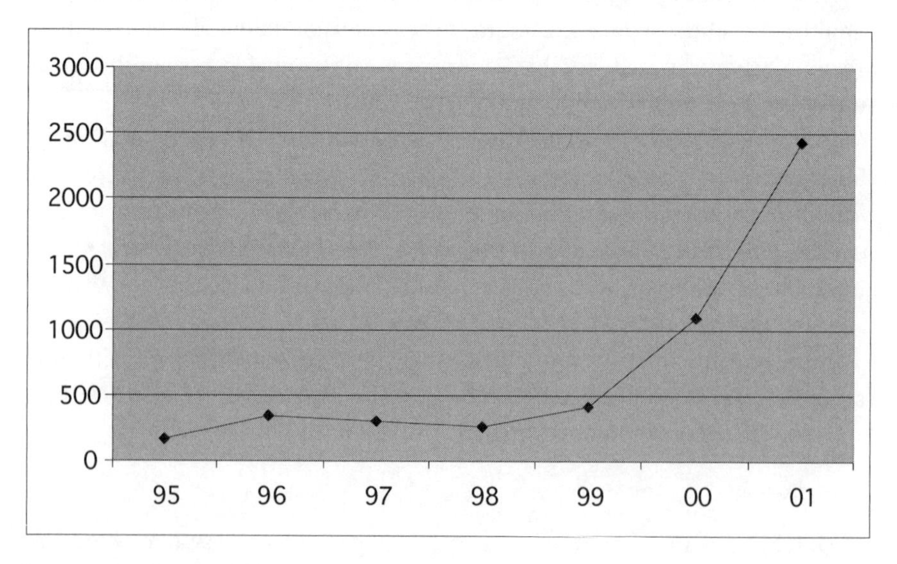

FIGURE 1B. Vulnerabilities Reported to CERT/CC.

has created a market for reports about vulnerabilities and how to correct them. In addition, it is leading software developers to find ways of developing more robust software. In January 2002, for example, Microsoft chairman Bill Gates sent a memo to all employees saying that security would be a top priority for the company. As part of the new Trustworthy Computing Initiative, Microsoft began training their software developers in security and announced a commitment to ship Windows.NET Server 2003 "secure by default."[22]

Building systems that are immune from any attack is a daunting, indeed impossible, task. Whereas the attacker needs to find only one flaw to launch an attack, the defender must find and fix every single one of them. However, considerable improvement is possible, as many common flaws are avoidable. Researchers have shown that introducing secure software-engineering principles into the early stages of software development can yield significant cost savings.[23]

Vulnerability trends are drawing attention to issues of product liability. Software is frequently distributed under shrink-wrap and click-wrap licenses that absolve vendors of any problems. This practice is being questioned, however, as users become increasingly fed up with faulty software. If vendors are held liable for security flaws, or at least flaws resulting from sloppy software-development practices, this would provide a strong incentive to deliver better products.

The growing vulnerability problem has also stimulated a lively debate over "open-source" software, that is, software such as Linux, whose source code is open for public scrutiny, versus closed systems like Windows, whose source code is proprietary and kept secret. On the one hand, open systems have the potential of being more secure than closed ones, because it is easier to find and fix flaws when anyone can examine the source code and anyone can post a fix. With closed systems, users are dependent on vendors to fix, if not find, the flaws. On the other hand, hackers also have an advantage when they can get access to source code, and they may decide to exploit the problems they find rather than report them. Moreover, making the code available to public scrutiny does not mean anyone will in fact study it closely. On balance, whether a system is open or closed might not matter much in terms of security.[24] Security might be affected more by the priority and practices of the vendor.

ECONOMIC FACTORS

The economic factors shaping the security infrastructure can be analyzed in terms of three groups of people: buyers, sellers, and donors. Buyers pursue security primarily to avoid economic losses. Sellers, on the other hand, see security as a business opportunity and way of making money. Finally, donors, who are predominantly government agencies, see security as a national issue worthy of funding.

Economic Losses

Organizations invest in security to avoid or at least contain the damages that result from an attack. These damages can include the cost of investigating and responding to an attack (e.g., clearing out viruses and restoring data), lost revenue and employee productivity from system downtime, lost business due to lost credibility and customer confidence, and litigation costs. Company stocks can also drop following press reports of certain types of incidents. A study of the economic effect of information security incidents conducted at the University of Maryland found a significant negative stock market reaction to security breaches involving unauthorized access to confidential data. Interestingly, there was no significant market reaction for other types of incidents (e.g., website defacements and denial-of-service attacks).[25] Finally, some companies have been put out of business by attacks. In February 2002, CloudNine Communications, one of Britain's oldest Internet service providers, shut its doors following a distributed denial-of-service attack. They concluded that repairing their network would have required too much downtime to remain in business.[26]

A few studies have attempted to quantify losses on a global or organizational basis. *Information Week* and PricewaterhouseCoopers LLP estimated, based on their global survey, that computer-based attacks took a $1.6 trillion toll on the worldwide economy in the year 2000. The cost to the United States alone was an estimated $266 billion, or more than 2.5% of the nation's Gross Domestic Product. Computer Economics of Carlsbad, California, estimated that the ILOVEYOU virus and variants, which crippled computers in May 2000, cost $8.5 billion in damage worldwide, vastly exceeding the damages from any previous or subsequent virus.[27] The Computer Security Institute and the FBI reported that their 2002 survey received reports of incidents costing a total of $456 million.[28] These losses represented 223 companies (out of 503 responding to the survey), for an average loss of more than $2 million. Whether any of these numbers is accurate or not matters less for security than that they are being used to justify the expenditure of more resources to solve security problems.

Ideally, security would be free, fast, and foolproof. In practice, it is never all three, and companies need to make hard choices about how much to spend and what to spend it on. In determining security expenditures, a reasonable goal is a positive return on investment (ROI): spend x dollars on security and save at least x in losses from attacks. The difficulty, however, is that it can be hard to compute ROI for a given approach. Consequently, security purchases and practices are often based on other factors such as industry best practices, fear of attack, product ratings, salesmanship, advice from consultants, budget restrictions, and so forth.

Quantitative measures, however, have proven effective for evaluating certain security options. Virtual private networks (VPNs) that run over the Internet, for example, have been shown to provide a cheaper means of protecting communications than separate leased lines. And research conducted by @stake Labs has shown that by following certain steps to harden network servers from attack, thruput on their sample networks improved by 1.93% to 3.28% on average.[29] As a third example, RTI International assessed the benefits of role-based access controls (RBAC) relative to alternative access-control systems (e.g., lists of specific users authorized to access particular files). From their study, they projected a net present value of RBAC through 2006 of approximately $671 million.[30] The figure takes into account end-users' operational benefits as well as their implementation costs and research-and-development costs.

Economic incentives to invest in security will be influenced by liability and insurance factors. If organizations are held liable for attacks against third-party systems that exploit easily avoidable weaknesses in their own, they will be driven to purchase better products and services from vendors and to follow better security practices internally. Similar effects are likely if insurance premiums are tied to the security posture of an organization. Standards and best practices will play an important role in establishing security baselines for negligence and insurance premiums.

Business Opportunity

The growing rate of cyber-attacks led many entrepreneurs to view the attacks not just as a threat but also as a business opportunity. In 2000, the worldwide Internet security market reached $5.1 billion in revenue, according to market researcher IDC. This was a 33% increase over 1999. IDC projected that revenues would surpass $14 billion in 2005.[31]

Industry is often accused of hyping the threat or overstating the benefits of their products in order to stimulate demand and increase business. However, the threat is real and serious. Moreover, it is aggravated by hackers, who attack systems and publish vulnerability information and hacking tools, in some cases as a way of getting jobs in the security industry and selling themselves as security consultants.

Until recently, security was not a priority for most organizations. Product selections were based more on factors such as cost, functionality, performance, and ease of use than on security. Consequently, vendors could not make a business care for building secure products in an environment where cost and time-to-market were critical. This is changing, as security has become a higher priority.

The adoption of standards by government and industry groups affects the market by helping some products and vendors while hurting others. For example, by selecting the Rijndael encryption algorithm for its Advanced Encryption Standard, the U.S. government pushed the market to favor Rijndael over certain competing methods. De facto standards also matter, as when the industry began using SSL to encrypt web traffic.

Patents also affect the market. They stimulate innovation by offering inventors a means of protecting their work; this is the usual rationale for patents. They do more than that, however—patents also push companies to invent new technologies so as to avoid paying license fees for products protected by existing patents. In this regard, they stimulate innovation, but at a cost of decreased standardization and interoperability.

Another factor affecting the market is government regulation, including trade restrictions. Until a few years ago, export controls on encryption technologies placed U.S. companies at a disadvantage in international markets and generally held back the spread of encryption. Those controls were substantially liberalized in 1999, however, so this is no longer a significant factor.

Government regulation can take the form of product requirements. In March 2002, Senator Fritz Hollings introduced a bill that would prohibit the sale and distribution of "digital media devices" that did not feature copyright-protection standards to be set by the federal government. The Consumer Broadband and Digital Television Promotion Act received considerable support from Hollywood, which seeks technology to protect their intellectual property from distribution on the Internet in violation of copyrights. The IT industry, however, generally opposes any government regulation, as it denies them certain business opportunities.

Governments have influenced the security market by issuing criteria for assessing the security offered by a product. The U.S. Department of Defense Trusted Computer System Evaluation Criteria (the "Orange Book") and more recent international Common Criteria, for example, have led to products that meet specified security objectives and an industry segment concerned with product evaluations. The cost of building to standards and performing product evaluations, however, has limited the market for evaluated products.

Security Funding

Grants issued by the National Science Foundation, Department of Defense, and other public- and private-sector organizations have encouraged security research and the development of security courses and programs in academia. These efforts have led to innovations in security and to a growing cadre of security specialists.

One grant program specifically aimed at increasing the cyber-defense capability of the nation is the Federal Cyber Service Scholarship for Service program. The program offers scholarship and capacity-building grants to universities in the area of security. The objective is to increase the number of qualified students entering the fields of information assurance and computer security, and to increase the capacity of colleges and universities within the United States to produce professionals in these fields. Students receiving scholarships are required to work for a federal agency for two years as their federal cyber-service commitment. The program, which is administered by the National Science Foundation, ties in with another educational initiative operated by the National Security Agency. Their program promotes higher education in information assurance and security by designating qualified institutions as Centers of Academic Excellence in Information Assurance Education.[32] Other programs are focused on research and development in security.

Internal funding within government agencies has also significantly impacted the security infrastructure. The National Institute of Standards and Technology (NIST), for example, has contributed numerous standards and guidelines for security, particularly in the area of cryptography, but in other areas as well.[33] The value of NIST to security developments was measured in the RTI study of role-based access control mentioned earlier. RTI found that NIST's contributions accounted for 44% of the benefits of RBAC.[34]

PSYCHOLOGICAL FACTORS

The security infrastructure is driven in part by psychological factors. These are divided into two categories: intellectual and emotional. Both relate to why people get involved in security as attackers, defenders, and participants in policy debates.

Intellectual Factors

I was drawn to security primarily by intellectual interests. I wanted to find ways of making systems secure, not because I had sensitive information that needed to be protected but because I found the problem to be intellectually challenging. I recognized that security was important for protecting against cyber-threats, but I was not out to save the world from hackers and information thieves.

I expect that many people in the field were similarly motivated. I recall in the mid 1990s, during the heat of the debates over cryptography policy, a prominent government official remarked that it was impossible to control cryptography because of its intellectual appeal. He was right, of course.

The intellectual attraction of security comes not only from designing security mechanisms, but also from breaking them or just attempting to break them. This is fortunate, because it is not possible to build secure systems without understanding how they might be attacked. Security is an interactive process between finding and fixing vulnerabilities that can be exploited by an adversary. The downside is that the intellectual appeal of cracking systems also motivates the hackers. A survey of 164 hackers conducted by Nicholas Chantler of Queensland University of Technology in Brisbane, Australia, found that the top two reasons for hacking were challenge and knowledge.[35]

Emotional Factors

People pursue security for emotional as well as intellectual reasons. They might enter the field because they see cyber-threats as a serious threat to society or are paranoid of being a victim themselves. They might find that working in security gives them a feeling of satisfaction or self-esteem. They might recommend security purchases, funding, or legislation out of fear, uncertainty, and doubt (FUD) over the seriousness of the security threat. FUD is often cited when it appears that it is being used to promote an agenda that does not stand on its own merits.

Hackers also pursue their activities for emotional reasons. Chantler's study found that the number-three reason for hacking was the pursuit of pleasure. After that came an assortment of emotional, social, and financial reasons, including recognition, excitement (of doing something illegal), friendship, self-gratification, addiction, espionage, theft, profit, vengeance, sabotage, and freedom.[36]

If hacking had no intellectual or emotional appeal, it is unlikely we would have the serious problem we have today. Hackers may not be responsible for some of the most serious attacks, but they have contributed substantially to the base of knowledge and tools needed to carry out an attack. Of course, hackers alone cannot be blamed for this, because security professionals also publish information about security vulnerabilities on the grounds that doing so will lead to better security.

SOCIAL AND POLITICAL FACTORS

The security infrastructure is shaped by social and political factors. This section describes four areas of influence: national security and public safety, privacy, information sharing, and international cooperation.

National Security and Public Safety

Governments are responsible for the national security and public safety of their countries. To address the cyber-threats, they have adopted laws that criminalize cyber-crimes and made regulations mandating security in certain sectors; established organizations and programs that help with cyberspace defense; and allocated money for cyber-defense research, education, and other programs.

In the United States, improving the security of critical infrastructures and cyberspace more generally received greater attention within the administration and Congress following the formation of the President's Commission on Critical Infrastructure Protection in 1996. Their recommendations led to Presidential Decision Directive (PDD) 63, which created the Critical Infrastructure Assurance Office (CIAO) within the Department of Commerce and the National Infrastructure Protection Center (NIPC), housed at the FBI but with representatives from several agencies. The CIAO was established to coordinate national planning efforts related to critical infrastructure protection.

The NIPC serves as a national critical infrastructure threat assessment, warning and vulnerability assessment, and law-enforcement investigation and response entity. Its focus is as much on prevention as on investigation and response. Toward that end, it issues security assessments, advisories, and alerts, the latter addressing major threats and imminent or in-progress attacks targeting national networks or critical infrastructures. The NIPC also established InfraGard chapters at all fifty-six FBI field offices. The chapters provide formal and informal channels for the exchange of information about infrastructure threats and vulnerabilities among people in law enforcement and the private sector. As of July 1, 2002, membership had reached 4,609.

PDD 63 also encouraged the private sector to create Information Sharing and Analysis Centers (ISACs) in cooperation with the government. The centers serve as a mechanism for gathering, analyzing, appropriately sanitizing, and disseminating private-sector information related to infrastructure vulnerabilities, threats, and incidents. So far, ISACs have been established for numerous sectors, including banking and finance, telecommunications, electric power (operated by the North American Electric Reliability Council), oil and gas, and information technology. In addition to the ISACs and InfraGard chapters, numerous other groups facilitate information sharing, including the CERT/CC and other computer emergency-response teams, the Partnership for Critical Infrastructure Protection, the High Technology Crime Investigators Association, the United States Secret Service Electronic Crimes Task Forces, the Joint Council on Information Age Crime, and the Center for Internet Security. All of these efforts can help strengthen the cyber-defense and crime-fighting capabilities of their members.

One of the challenges facing all of these groups is that industry has been reluctant to share information out of concern for its confidentiality. In particular, companies are concerned that sensitive information provided voluntarily might not be adequately protected, or that it could be subject to Freedom of Information Act (FOIA) requests or lawsuits. Industry is also concerned that cooperation with industry partners might violate antitrust laws. Bills have been introduced in the House and Senate to provide limited exemption from FOIA.

On October 16, 2001, President Bush issued an Executive Order on Critical Infrastructure Protection in the Information Age. The order established the President's Critical Infrastructure Protection Board (PCIPB), and charged it to recommend policies and coordinate programs for protecting information systems for critical infrastructures. It assigned several areas of activity to the board, including outreach to the private sector and to state and local governments; information sharing; incident coordination and response; recruitment, retention, and training of executive-branch security professionals; research and development; law enforcement coordination with national security components; international information infrastructure protection; legislation; and coordination with the newly formed Office of Homeland Security.

The Department of Justice has launched several initiatives aimed at strengthening the cyber-crime-fighting capability of the criminal justice community. The Electronic Crime Partnership Initiative is tackling a broad range of issues, including technology, technical assistance, legal and policy issues, education and training, outreach and awareness, and standards and certification. The partnership includes representatives from law enforcement, industry, and academia.

Within the Department of Defense, the commander in chief of Space Command has primary responsibility for computer network operations. Space Command's Joint Task Force Computer Network Operations (JTF-CNO) serves as the operational component for all CNO, which includes both computer-network defense and computer-network attack. In conjunction with the unified commands, services, and DOD agencies, the JTF-CNO coordinates and directs the defense of DOD computer systems and networks.

The events of September 11 and the war on terrorism are leading to new initiatives, funding, and legislation aimed at combating all forms of terrorism, including cyber-terrorism. These include establishment of a Department of Homeland Defense, which will bring together programs currently housed in other agencies.

Privacy

Privacy issues have shaped the security infrastructure in two ways. First, they have led to laws and regulations, such as HIPAA, that mandate security for the purpose of privacy protection, and to the development and use of security technologies that protect information and therefore privacy. The popular encryption package Pretty Good Privacy (PGP) was developed primarily to protect the private files and e-mail correspondence of citizens from government eavesdroppers and other spies. Its author, Phil Zimmermann, was especially concerned with helping human-rights activists in countries with repressive governments. There are numerous other examples of technology that offer encryption and anonymity services to enhance privacy.

Second, privacy issues have led to policies, regulations, and technology that constrain government investigations of cyber-crime and cyber-terrorism. Although they have provided strong privacy protections, those protections are being challenged by changes in laws and policies aimed at facilitating the fight against terrorism. The USA PATRIOT Act, for example, raised numerous concerns.[37]

In the United Kingdom, the Regulation of Investigatory Powers (RIP) bill has provisions that facilitate government monitoring of Internet traffic and access to encryption keys.[38] Opposition to the bill led one mathematician to develop a new operating system, called M-o-o-t, that would foil government surveillance by storing all data and keys on servers outside the U.K. government's jurisdiction.[39]

Information Sharing

Information sharing, both publicly and within closed groups, has helped advance the science and practice of security, and increase knowledge and awareness about security. While these effects are all positive, open publication has raised concerns about information getting into the hands of the "bad guys." Today, these concerns generally involve the publication of information about security vulnerabilities and of software tools that exploit those vulnerabilities. At one time they also included the publication of information relating to particular security technologies, most notably cryptography, but these concerns generally gave way to those recognizing the value of publishing such information so as to promote security.

The open publication of vulnerability information raises two issues: first, how much information should be made public, and second, when should publication take place. At one extreme, under a policy of full and immediate disclosure, all information about vulnerability, including any attack software that can be used to exploit it, is posted following its discovery. The rationale is that it forces vendors to fix problems while also keeping users informed. This is supported by numerous cases in which vendors did not fix problems until the vulnerability information was published.

At the other extreme no information about vulnerability is posted, at least until the vendor has released a patch that fixes the problem; even then, only minimal information is disclosed. The argument in this case is that posting vulnerability information, particularly hacking tools, leads to attacks. Indeed, data reported to CERT/CC showed considerably heightened attack activity following the release of exploit tools associated with certain vulnerabilities.[40] The increased activity lasted many months beyond the release of the patches, as system administrators were slow to install the fixes. Publication of exploit software had a much greater impact than publication of vulnerability information alone, because it enabled script kiddies with little skill to launch attacks.

In between the extremes are policies that favor disclosing information about vulnerabilities, but generally not the attack tools, and giving vendors a grace period in which to release a patch before publication. The CERT/CC follows a policy giving vendors forty-five days to fix their problem.[41] However, many security practitioners favor a shorter grace period. An April 2002 industry survey conducted by the Hurwitz Group found that 39% of the more than 300 respondents favored disclosure immediately, with another 28% favoring disclosure within a week. However, only 13% favored posting "proof of concept" exploit software.

Although supporters of full disclosure make their argument on security grounds, they may be motivated as much by self-promotion as a desire to make systems more secure. Being first to publish can increase one's stature in the scientific, security, and hacking communities and lead to new business opportunities.

In general, it is lawful to publish exploit software, even though use of such software to conduct an actual attack is a crime. There are, however, exceptions. The Digital Millennium Copyright Act restricts the production, distribution, and use of software that circumvents copyright protection, on the grounds that such software harms copyright owners.

The DMCA and its application has been challenged on First Amendment grounds. In one highly publicized lawsuit, eight movie companies sued *2600* magazine for posting and linking to the DVD-descrambling program DeCSS.[42] After a federal district court ordered *2600* to remove the software and links from their website, the Electronic Frontier Foundation asked a federal appeals court to overturn the ruling. The EFF, which represents *2600,* claimed that the ruling was an "unconstitutional constraint on free speech," because it blocked legitimate uses of DeCSS, such as for educational purposes. The court rejected EFF's appeal. However, Professor David Touretzky of Carnegie Mellon University has more than two dozen different versions of the DeCSS on his website, including a haiku version and a "dramatic reading" of the code, as well as versions in various programming languages.[43]

International Cooperation

Cyber-attacks frequently cross national borders as attackers hack one system after another, using each to launch an attack against the next. Such behavior severely complicates investigations, as it requires cooperation from every country involved. Further, prosecution may not be possible if the attack is not a criminal offense in the perpetrator's own country.

Governments have come together in several forums, including the G8, Council of Europe (CoE), and European Union to address the problems associated with international attacks and facilitate international cooperation. The CoE's effort led to the adoption of the Convention on Cybercrime in 2001. The Convention aims to harmonize domestic statutes relating to cyber-crime and procedures relating to extradition, mutual assistance, and evidence collection and preservation.[44] However, because the signatories to the convention are limited to the Council of Europe members and official observers (the United States, Canada, Japan, and South Africa), a broader-based international treaty is needed to address cyber-crime on a global scale. A group at Stanford University proposed an International Convention on Cyber-Crime and Terrorism that builds upon the CoE's work.[45]

CONCLUSIONS

This chapter has approached the topic of cyber-security and critical infrastructure protection from a right angle. Instead of focusing on infrastructure defense, the chapter has viewed cyber-security as an infrastructure in its own right, and focused on the factors shaping its development.

This security infrastructure consists of technologies, procedures and practices, laws and regulations, and people and organizations. It is not owned by any party, and is dispersed globally throughout the public and private sectors. It is regulated only to the extent that regulations apply to elements of the infrastructure, for example, the adoption of cyber-crime laws and the formation of corporations and associations that specialize in security. It is a relatively new infrastructure, tied closely to the emergence of information technology as a fundamental component of business practices, control systems, and other processes.

The factors shaping the infrastructure include threats, technology trends, economic factors, psychological factors, and social and political factors. Examining these factors shows why security is a major problem today. Security threats, amplified by technology trends, have outpaced the economic and social case for developing and operating secure systems. However, that case has been building, stimulating rapid growth of the security infrastructure and lending hope that enough progress can be made to avoid a major catastrophe from a cyber-attack against critical infrastructures. Just as the international community responded to the Y2K bug, which also threatened critical infrastructures, it may effectively respond to the security problems that still plague information systems. That security is now a high priority in both the public and private sectors is encouraging.

2. THE AMERICAN CYBER-ANGST AND THE REAL WORLD—ANY LINK?

RALF BENDRATH

"... what has now become known as cyberterrorism."

PETER G. NEUMANN, IN A REVIEW OF *PEARL HARBOR DOT COM* BY WINN SCHWARTAU[1]

WHAT IS THE PROBLEM?

Threats and risks from cyberspace have become a popular meme in the mass media, the security policy community, and the risk-consultant and IT industries. Probably everybody with some interest in computers and politics has already heard of the (purported) possibility of hackers, cyber-terrorists, or foreign intelligence agencies electronically breaking into computers that control dams or air-traffic control systems, wreaking havoc and endangering not only thousands of lives, but national security itself.

A good indicator of the popularity of these scenarios is the fact that the entertainment sector has already capitalized on this, producing movies like the 1995 James Bond *Goldeneye*[2] or novels like Tom Clancy and Steve R. Pieczenik's *Net Force* series.[3] Sometimes it is hard to tell what is science and what is fiction. Winn Schwartau, for example, the rock manager turned preacher of "information warfare" who runs the famous website infowar.com, has testified several times as an IT security expert before Congress, and has written two novels on cyber-terror.[4] Even renowned cyber-war theoreticians like John Arquilla have not hesitated to publish thrilling cyber-terror scenarios for the general audience.[5]

But these works are not made only for entertainment. They produce certain visions of the future and of the threats and risks looming there. In doing so, they can be lined up with the works of serious scientific groups or professional intelligence agencies who produce threat warnings and trend estimates, like the National Academy of Sciences or the National Intelligence Council.

The whole debate started around 1990, when the Soviet Union collapsed and the threat-estimation professionals in the security community began looking for new ideas. The rise of widespread Internet use and the debate on the emerging "information society" sparked several studies on the risks of the highly networked, high-tech-dependent United States. The National Academy of Sciences began a report on computer security as early as 1990, with the words:

> We are at risk. Increasingly, America depends on computers. . . . Tomorrow's terrorist may be able to do more damage with a keyboard than with a bomb.[6]

At the same time, the prototypical term "electronic Pearl Harbor" was coined,[7] which linked the whole debate to a historical trauma of U.S. warfare. It did not take very long until the highly technical problems of IT security—encryption, password protection, and intrusion-detection systems, to name but a few—were framed in terms previously known only from military policy.

> "Password security" became "computer security," then "information-systems security," "information protection," and now "information warfare."[8]

It is still unclear, though, how dangerous the threat from cyberspace really is. Some liken it to weapons of mass destruction. Then–CIA Director John Deutch, testifying before the U.S. Senate in 1996, for example, when asked to compare the magnitude of the cyber-threat with nuclear, chemical, or biological weapons, answered, "it is very, very close to the top."[9] Others, like now–CIA Director George Tenet, used the term "weapons of mass disruption,"[10] suggesting that in the information age an electronic attack might be as dangerous to the fabric of society as an attack with intercontinental missiles would have been in the nuclear age.

Others doubt this perception. George Smith, editor of the "Crypt Newsletter," for example, published a widely read article in *Issues in Science and Technology* under the headline "An Electronic Pearl Harbor? Not likely."[11] Many of the more technically educated political advisors and journalists wrote about the practical difficulties of a serious cyber-attack or the inability of bureaucracies like militaries or intelligence agencies to really acquire the skills needed to become successful hackers. Others saw a hidden agenda behind all the fuss they preferred to call "fearmongering."[12] They suspected it to be a pretext for the security agencies to obtain greater powers for surveillance, oppression, or censorship in cyberspace, which in the early nineties was seen—and praised—by many as the land of total freedom, with little or no government intervention.[13] As we can see, the cyber-threat assessment is far from being agreed upon by different experts, government agencies, or scholars working in this field. As David Gompert wrote in the *Rand Research Review*:

> How grave is the threat from cyberspace? Are those electrons really "10 feet tall," or is information war being oversold? We don't know.[14]

The debate about national security in cyberspace, though, is not only one about predicting the future, but also about how to prepare for it in the present; it is therefore highly political. The divergent views on how the different government agencies and all the other actors—from the technology community to insurance companies—should be involved cannot draw from experience, as there have been no major destructive cyber-attacks so far. When experience is lacking, you cannot make claims or even formulate a policy based on the past. Instead, different scenarios—stories about possible future events—are providing the grounds on which decisions have to be made here. The different actors with their different interests are therefore competing with each other by means of versions of the future. The problem, then, of course, is that there is no clear and proven truth anymore. This reflects a general trend in Western societies:

> The extrapolated or narrative future has replaced the historical past . . . as our most fundamental and decisive reference. But this homecoming of science fiction culture has resulted in the criteria for scientific truth being set adrift.[15]

The so-called "information society" is thus showing significant signs of a "risk society." The new risks, according to Ulrick Beck, who coined the term in the eighties, cannot be perceived immediately anymore, and therefore they are especially open to political interpretation and instrumentation. Beck notes, "It never is clear if the risks have become worse or our look at them has just sharpened."[16]

What makes this especially true and different from past security-threat estimates and vulnerability analyses is the nature of the environment in which any attack would occur. In the physical landscape of the real world, any action has its constraints in the laws of nature. Therefore, the equations for calculating the flight curve of a ballistic missile, for example, are the same, no matter from where the specific missile is fired or where it is targeted. Cyberspace, in contrast, is a landscape where every action is possible only because the technical systems provide an artificial environment that is built to allow it. The means of an attack therefore change from system to system, from network to network. This makes threat estimation and attack recognition much more difficult tasks. Instead of an easy-to-see exploding bomb, you have to look for the values in the registers of the computer and interpret their patterns. To detect a virus on your hard drive, you need a virus scanner as a sensoric tool; to find out if there is a cracker in your network, you need an intrusion-detection system or a good systems administrator with some spare time. For the average user, an intentional hacker attack cannot be distinguished from a technical failure, like a hardware defect, a software malfunction, or a "normal" system crash. In the case of denial-of-service, it is not obvious at all if the computer that is not providing its service anymore has just crashed, if the cable connecting it to the Internet was physically damaged, or if it is the victim of a targeted flood with packets and requests. Considering the dynamics of computer development, the whole threat perception/estimation problem gets even worse when you have to predict the development of these things in the future.

Social scientists, because of the highly technical nature of the new threat, cannot really estimate it, but they can draw some conclusions by looking at how the problem is perceived. The way a problem is framed normally determines or at least limits the possible solutions for it.[17] These policy choices left aside, the change in the perception of a problem can tell a lot about the underlying agendas and mind-sets of the perceiving actors. This is the aim of this contribution.

On the following pages, I will show how the cyber-threat discourse changed dramatically during the first year of the George W. Bush Administration. The first change took place a short time after the Republican government came into office. The main danger in cyberspace was no longer perceived as coming from substate actors like terrorists, freedom fighters, or even teenagers, but from states. China especially, which among many conservatives in Washington is seen as the emerging strategic rival, was seen as a potential cyber-threat.

Then, after September 11, the whole discourse quickly focused on cyber-terrorism. This seems understandable, because everybody then was concerned that more terrorist attacks might happen using other means. But the evidence for this is really thin, and especially the experts who have been working on cyber-security before should know this. Still, the U.S. government and others immediately concentrated on "cyber-terrorism."

After one year, though, with a war against Iraq behind the horizon and Homeland Security trapped in the trenches on Capitol Hill, the debate seems to turn back toward states as possible enemies. If the trend goes on, this will be the third change in the cyber-threat discourse within less than two years.

How are these discourse serpentines linked to the real problem, if at all? A reality check at the end of this chapter will provide some insight on the possible reasons and effects for the change in perception of the cyber-threat. In the end, we will see that "cyber" has more to do with discursive trends and hidden agendas than with electronic terrorism or digital enemies.

THE HERITAGE OF THE CLINTON YEARS: "CYBER-TERRORISM"

The basic question for security policy makers, since the debate over cyber-threats started, has always been: are the most dangerous actors terrorists, enemy states, or just criminals? In other words: will we have to deal with "cyber-terrorism," "cyber-war," or just "cyber-crime"? This debate has, naturally, never really been solved. But the Clinton Administration chose to focus on cyber-*terrorism*. One main reason was the new threat perception after the first World Trade Center attack in 1993 and the Oklahoma City bombing in 1995. The foundations for the National Infrastructure Protection Center (NIPC), located at the FBI, were in fact laid as a reaction to the Oklahoma City bombing in April 1995. The interagency Critical Infrastructure Working Group (CIWG), set up by Bill Clinton and his attorney general, Janet Reno, two months after this event in June 1995,[18] was tasked with studying the infrastructural vulnerabilities of the United States by terrorist attacks. The CIWG issued its report in January 1996, which in turn led to the establishment of the President's Commission on Critical Infrastructure Protection (PCCIP).[19] The PCCIP report of 1997 finally led to Presidential Decision Directive NSC-63 in May 1998[20] and its more elaborated version, the National Plan for Information Systems Protection[21] in January 2000.

The newly established infrastructure security institutions perceived terrorists, sometimes connected with "rogue states," as the main danger. Allan B. Carroll from the National Infrastructure Protection Center, for example, in December 1999 warned of Osama bin Laden possibly planning a computerized version of the Oklahoma bombing.[22] Others even saw juvenile hackers as a serious threat. For example, Jaques Gansler, then–Assistant Secretary of Defense for Aquisition and Technology, in 1998 called teenagers a "real threat environment" for national security.[23] This view was influenced by the idea that information technology is the great equalizer. This fed into the general trend in the security-policy community not to talk about whole threats anymore (which would consist of an actor, his intention, and his capabilities), but to focus just on the technologies needed to start an attack:

> Today, however, malefactors are no longer necessarily nation-states, and expensive weapons of war are joined by means that are easier to acquire, harder to detect, and have legitimate peacetime applications. The tools designed to access, manipulate, and manage the information or communications components that control critical infrastructures can also be used to do harm. They are inexpensive, readily available, and easy to use.[24]

In the context of the debate about the new "international terrorism" and the other new fear in security policy thinking—"asymmetric warfare"—the concept of "homeland security" or "homeland defense" was developed by American think tanks in the late 1990s. The basic idea was the end of the American invulnerability based on its special geographical position. Possible enemies, the security analysts feared, would no longer try to attack the United States by conventional means and tactics of warfare, but by terrorist attacks from the inside—or from borderless cyberspace. Indeed, the idea of "homeland security," including the protection against cyber-terrorism, was taken up by the new government under George W. Bush in May 2001.[25]

The media thankfully took up these debates in the security community. CNN, for example, in April 1999, brought a headline about "guerrilla warfare in cyberspace."[26] This "cyber-terrorism" discourse had gained enough momentum in the Clinton years to even persist for a while after the conservative government under George W. Bush came into office in January 2001. The tabloid *USA Today* is probably the best indicator for the general threat perception in the mass media. In February 2001, the paper published a story about how Osama bin Laden's Al Qaeda may be using a special form of encryption called steganography, where messages are hidden in the least significant bits of electronic pictures, or audio or video files. This case is especially interesting, because the cyber-threat was combined not only with the terrorist threat, but with pornography as well, which for the puritan Christian politicians in America makes it look even worse:

> Hidden in the X-rated pictures on several pormographic Web sites and the posted comments on sports chat rooms may lie the encrypted blueprints of the next terrorist attack against the United States or its allies. It sounds farfetched, but U.S. officials and experts say it's the latest method of communication being used by Osama bin Laden and his associates to outfox law enforcement. Bin Laden, indicted in the bombing in 1998 of two U.S. embassies in East Africa, and others are hiding maps and photographs of terrorist targets and posting instructions for terrorist activities on sports chat rooms, pornographic bulletin boards and other Web sites, U.S. and foreign officials say.[27]

The *USA Today* story is interesting from another point of view as well. One day after this discursive connection between bin Laden, cyber-terror, and pornography had been published (and immediately quoted in many other newspapers), the conservative congressmen Jim Saxton and Saxby Chambliss introduced a bill in the House of Representatives that would make the United States Congress declare cyber-terrorism "an emerging threat to the national security of the United States."[28] Later, we will see more examples of this close connection between headlines in the mass media and a political initiative along the same lines on one of the following days.

If terrorists are able to use encryption, they are not far from planning cyber attacks—this obvious (but false)[29] assumption was repeated a month later by the new director of the National Infrastructure Protection Center, Ronald Dick. Already on his first day in office, he warned of a possible cyber attack by bin Laden and other terrorists:

> Ronald Dick . . . said there was not yet evidence of a cyber attack by organized groups such as Osama bin Laden's Al Qaeda organization. Terrorist groups did use the internet for encrypted communications, but were focusing on ways to use the net for cyber-terrorism. "Most of the terrorist organizations out there have found it cheaper to use

> physical means," said Mr Dick. "But we are picking up signs that these groups are looking at uses of the technology to disrupt" critical networks.[30]

At the end of the Clinton years, to sum up, cyber-terrorism was clearly established as one of the new security policy threats of the twenty-first century. Bill Clinton himself made this very clear in December 2000 in his foreign policy farewell lecture at the University of Nebraska at Kearney. In this speech, he named five principles for future U.S. foreign policy: Strengthen alliances like NATO, pay attention to Russia and China, confront local conflicts in other parts of the world, pursue global trade with a "human face," and, finally, face new security challenges like cyber-terrorism and infectious diseases like AIDS.[31] He went on to say:

> One of the biggest threats to the future is going to be cyberterrorism—people fooling with your computer networks, trying to shut down your phones, erase bank records, mess up airline schedules, do things to interrupt the fabric of life.[32]

The government response to this threat had been twofold. On the one hand, the intelligence community, together with the law-enforcement agencies, tried to build up capacities for cyber-investigations, like computer forensics tools or close surveillance of the hacker community. Of course this debate was used by the FBI and others to ask for more surveillance powers on the Internet (see Marc Rotenberg in this volume). On the other hand, because of the amorphous nature of these nonstate and unknown enemies, a lot of effort was put into hardening the critical infrastructures and making the private companies who run most of them work together with the government.[33]

THE BUSH GOVERNMENT: TURNING ATTENTION TOWARD STATES

Shortly after the start of the Bush Administration in January 2001, the debate about the cyber-threat changed quite radically. "Cyber-terrorists" were still taken into account, but the new government strongly focused on other states as possible attackers. As a result, the National Security Council, the armed forces, and the intelligence community became more relevant and thus more influential in the debate. These institutions were still living very much in the state-centric world of classical security policy. Therefore, their threat assessments were centered on states, which became the dominant sources of fear from cyber-attacks.

A linkage between the "cyber-terrorism" perception of the Clinton years and the "cyber-war" fears of the first Bush year was the concept of "rogue states." This term, which had been abandoned by Clinton[34] but was quickly revived by Bush, implies that some states will use terrorist means to attack the United States. Surprisingly, the first "rogue state" to be accused of planning cyber-attacks against the United States was not Iraq, Iran, or North Korea, but Cuba. During the hearing of the Senate Select Committee on Intelligence on "The Worldwide Threat in 2001" in February 2001, Defense Intelligence Agency Director Thomas R. Wilson identified Fidel Castro's almost-bankrupt regime as a possible cyber-attacker.

> ADMIRAL WILSON: Cuba is, Senator, not a strong conventional military threat. But their ability to ploy asymmetric tactics against our military superiority would be significant. They have strong intelligence apparatus, good security, and the potential to disrupt our military through asymmetric tactics. And I think that is the biggest threat that they present to our military.
> SENATOR WYDEN: What would be an example of an asymmetric tactic that you're speaking of?
> ADMIRAL WILSON: Using information warfare or computer network attack, for example, to be able to disrupt our access or flow of forces to the region.
> SENATOR WYDEN: And you would say that there is a real threat that they might go that route?
> ADMIRAL WILSON: There's certainly the potential for them to employ those kind of tactics against our modern and superior military.[35]

Within a month, though, not only these traditional "enemies," but strategic rivals of the United States were also named as possible cyber-threats. In March 2001, the Defense Science Board issued a report on the United States' vulnerability from cyber-attacks. According to this study, already more than twenty states are supposed to have information-warfare capabilities or have started developing them.[36] Especially interesting is the perception of China. The chairman of the DSB study group explicitly warned of this country:

> China has made clear its intention to use Information Operations (warfare) as an asymmetric response in any conflict with the United States.[37]

This is a clear departure from the "cyber-terror" warning of the Clinton era. China, even by the most hawkish politicians, is not considered a "rogue state" but rather a strategic rival. From this new perception of the possible cyber-enemy as another state, it is only a short way to related strategic thought. Here as well you can find many analogies to the traditional state-against-state military- and security-policy thinking. For example the above-mentioned March 2001 Defense Science Board report called the Pentagon's "Global Information Grid" a weapons system, and concluded that the United States is in an "arms race" over information systems for warfare.[38]

The classical security policy idea of the Cold War—deterrence—is already waiting around the next corner if you think like this. Bush's National Security Adviser, Condoleezza Rice, was the first government official to explicitly name it three weeks later in her speech at the second Internet Security Policy Forum:

> Critical infrastructure protection is a core issue for security for the United States, and one that therefore sits squarely on the radar screen at the National Security Council. . . . One thing that we can learn from the atomic age is that preparation, a clear desire and a clear willingness to confront the problem, and a clear willingness to show that you are prepared to confront the problem, is what keeps it from happening in the first place. . . . In some ways, this is a classic deterrence mission.[39]

The commander of the U.S. Space Command, General Ralph E. Eberhardt, publicly renewed the warnings of China as a possible cyber-attacker at the end of March 2001. This is even more important because SpaceCom is responsible for the coordination of cyber-security and computer network attacks within the whole U.S. military.[40]

This perception was taken up by the media after the spy plane incident in April 2001, when an American spy plane was forced to land in the People's Republic of China. Afterward, Chinese hackers fought against U.S. hackers on the Internet, and the upcoming first anniversary of the U.S. bombing of the Chinese embassy in Belgrade made the public fears worse. Though this was not at all comparable to a real war, the media called this the first United States–Chinese "cyber war."[41] In this case it is especially hard to tell what was reality and what was media invention. Some insiders even warned that the media stories about the "coming cyber-war" between the United States and China had started the whole problem, because they gave the juvenile hackers an excuse for attacking the other side. The hackers' documentation group Attrition.org, for example, issued a press release titled "Cyberwar with China: Self-fulfilling prophecy."[42] Even so, the FBI's National Infrastructure Protection Center issued a threat warning, and the Pentagon raised its cyber-threat level from "alpha" to "bravo" and prepared for "charlie," which would have pulled all government and military computers offline.[4]

Nevertheless, by the end of spring 2001 the new threat perception was established in the media and the security policy community. In early summer it had its first international political impact. Secretary of Defense Donald Rumsfeld, in his speech at the NATO Council in Brussels on June 6, 2001, told the allies that the United States was not the only country threatened by attacks from cyberspace, but that the other NATO countries, and therefore the alliance as a whole, were in danger. As "future challenges" for NATO, Rumsfeld named traditional terrorism, high-tech weapons, and missiles with weapons of mass destruction, but also "cyber attacks."[44] Less than half a year after the new government came into office, the new threat perception had gained enough ground in Washington to be discussed with the NATO allies at ministerial level for the first time.

But Donald Rumsfeld merely laid the groundwork for the president. One day later, on June 7, 2001, George W. Bush in his Iowa speech talked about the "true threats of the twenty-first century," among them "informational warfare":

> Our United States and our allies ought to develop the capacity to address the true threats of the twenty-first century. The true threats are biological and informational warfare.[45]

Again, *USA Today* is a good indicator for this change in threat perception. While the paper had published a story in February 2001 about the possible use of computer technology by Osama bin Laden, only four months later it had a front-page article about the threat by states in cyberspace. Citing anonymous "military analysts," *USA Today,* in its June 19, 2001, edition, reported twenty governments that were preparing for cyber-attacks. Among them were the usual "rogue states" and China, but also Russia, France, Great Britain, and Israel.[46]

In this case, again, a political event on Capitol Hill was prepared by this story. The public opinion was influenced by this tabloid article before the event—the expert hearing in Congress—had taken place. Two days later, CIA technology analyst Lawrence K. Gershwin told Congress that nonstate actors were not really dangerous in cyberspace, that states were dangerous:

> Traditional terrorist adversaries of the United States, despite their intentions to damage U.S. interests, are less developed in their computer network capabilities and propensity to pursue cyber means than are other types of adversaries. They are likely, therefore, to pose only a limited cyber threat. . . . National cyber warfare programs are unique in posing a threat along the entire spectrum of objectives that might harm U.S. interests. . . . Among the array of cyber threats, as we see them today, only government-sponsored programs are developing capabilities with the future prospect of causing widespread, long-duration damage to U.S. critical infrastructures. . . . For the next 5 to 10 years or so, only nation states appear to have the discipline, commitment and resources to fully develop capabilities to attack critical infrastructures.[47]

After the quality of the threat had been changed in public and political perception, the next step was to increase its quantity. In a hearing in the House of Representatives in August 2001, Keith A. Rhodes, chief technology officer of the General Accounting Office, said:

> Over 100 countries already have or are developing computer attack capabilities. . . . NSA has determined that potential adversaries are developing a body of knowledge about U.S. systems and methods to attack them.[48]

Compared with the twenty countries the Defense Science Board had mentioned in its report just five months earlier, this is an increase by 400%. So either the criteria for estimating the cyber-war capabilities of other countries had been changed, or the numbers were deliberately exaggerated to make the threat look more serious.

By early September 2001, the new U.S. government had established a new, state-centric discourse on cyber-threats. These arguments were not completely new—then–NSA Director Kenneth Minihan had already warned, in 1998, of states being the biggest threat in cyberspace[49]—but only under the new government could this view gain support in the highest positions in Washington and in the media.

Terrorism was no longer considered an urgent threat in cyberspace. Leslie G. Wiser, Jr., the NIPC's Training, Outreach, and Strategy Section chief, in his testimony on "Cyber-Security" before the House of Representatives in late August 2001 (less than two weeks before the September 11 attacks), mainly mentioned terrorists' use of IT for communication and organizational purposes:

> Terrorist groups are increasingly using new information technology and the Internet to formulate plans, raise funds, spread propaganda, and to communicate securely.[50]

Though he called cyber-terrorism "a very real threat," he supported this claim by citing estimates made earlier that year by the intelligence community. This shows the importance of specific texts that could be called "canonical." They become standards for threat perception and are repeated again and again. Wiser said:

> The prospect of "information warfare" by foreign militaries against our critical infrastructures is perhaps the greatest potential cyber threat to our national security. We know that many foreign nations are developing information warfare doctrine, programs, and capabilities for use against the United States or other nations. In testimony in June, 2001, National Intelligence Officer Gershwin stated that "for the next 5 to 10 years or so, only nation states appear to have the discipline, commitment, and resources to fully develop the capabilities to attack critical infrastructures."

In late August 2001, states were clearly established as the main cyber-threat. Then, less than two weeks later, something unforeseen happened and made the whole debate change again.

SEPTEMBER 11 AND THE IMPACT ON THE CYBER-THREAT DISCOURSE

The September 11 attacks in New York City and Washington led to a complete change in the threat perception. This is true for the general debate—suddenly everybody was afraid of new terrorist attacks—as well as of its cyber dimension.

How great was the threat of the next terrorist attack being led via the networks? This is what experts had forecast for a while: a hacker attack against the emergency communications systems and a large-scale conventional attack at the same time. IT and security-policy magazines were the first to start articles on cyber-terrorism as soon as September 11. At this time, of course, no leads at all were available in this direction. Nevertheless, *Federal Computer Week* (FCW), as early as the evening after the attacks on September 11, published an article about the U.S. Space Command, whose Joint Task Force on Computer Network Defense (JTF-CND) is responsible for the cyber-defense of the U.S. Armed Forces.

There were no special events to report from the generals, but the usual threat warnings and cyber–war game scenarios from the Pentagon-funded think tank RAND were presented as real possibilities.[51]

On September 12 the National Infrastructure Protection Center (NIPC) issued a threat warning for the members of the InfraGard program,[52] recommending that they shut down all nonessential computer systems or to at least take them offline. All this happened in spite of the fact that any evidence for looming cyber-terrorist acts was still missing, as the vice chairman of InfraGard, Phyllis Schneck, had to admit.[53]

In the next days, many newspapers published articles about the looming cyber-danger, and again *USA Today* was one of the first. Two days after the attacks, on September 13, the paper wrote about coming cyber-attacks in the near future—"another wave of terrorism"—and quoted a former Pentagon official's warning of an "electronic Pearl Harbor."[54] The government agencies, too, helped to fuel this new fear of "cyber-terrorists." For example, the NIPC issued another "Cyber Awareness" warning on September 14, this time for the general public. They warned especially of politically motivated website defacements and some modified computer viruses and worms. For example, the old virus "life_stages.txt.shs" had been renamed "wtc.txt.vbs," alluding to the World Trade Center.[55] This, of course, posed no real danger, especially not comparable to terrorism. But still, to people who are not IT security experts, the context in which this warning was issued made it look like a warning of cyber-terrorism.

Even organizations that before September 11 had mostly dealt with technical and economic aspects of IT security were now talking about foreign and/or Islamic terrorists. For example, the West Virginia Information Assurance and Computer Security Alliance, which, since its establishment in the summer of 2001, had been concerned mainly with insider sabotage and disgruntled IT employees, warned of "outsiders" attacking computer systems on its first meeting after September 11.[56]

By the end of the month, this debate had already created enough pressure to force the government to move. On the eighth of October, President Bush set up an "Office of Cyberdefense" at the White House, as part of the new Homeland Security Office at the National Security Council.[57] The former coordinator for counterterrorism and critical infrastructure protection at the NSC, Richard A. Clarke, was given charge of this office.[58] This was mainly a symbolic act, as this job had been there since Clinton's PDD 63 in 1998, just called by another name.[59] This shows how important it seemed to the government to at least give the impression of doing anything it could to prevent cyber-terrorist attacks.

The first draft of the Justice Department's proposal for a new Anti-Terrorism

Act (ATA), which had been presented on September 23, accordingly treated most cases of computer crime as "terrorism" and proposed lifelong imprisonment as the appropriate punishment. Even harmless teenage activities like defacing websites would have been treated as cyber-terrorism under this act.[60] The USA PATRIOT Act that finally became law on October 26 followed this definition of cyber-terrorism, but reduced the maximum penalty for hacking to ten years in jail for a damage of $5,000 or more. But it now criminalized break-ins into any computer outside the United States "that is used in a manner that affects interstate or foreign commerce or communication of the United States."[61] This is clearly the cyber equivalent of the worldwide "war on terrorism" the U.S. government has been fighting since September 11, 2001, as it systematically expands beyond the American territory.

While the debate had been mostly abstract up to that point, in November it became more focused on Osama bin Laden, who by then had clearly been established as public enemy number one. Frank J. Cilluffo, who had been a member of the "cyber-crime" group in the CSIS's project on Homeland Defense, testified in a hearing before Congress:

> While bin Laden may have his finger on the trigger, his grandson might have his finger on the mouse.[62]

The way these conclusions were drawn is quite telling. Sometimes it seemed like anybody who could book a flight ticket online was suspected of being able to start cyber-attacks. *Newsbytes,* for example, a normally well-informed news service on IT issues, quoted computer security professor and government consultant Dorothy Denning as saying:

> Terrorists use the Internet to send e-mail and book airline tickets, and many groups have Web sites.[63]

This would normally not be worth mentioning, as almost everybody with Internet access has shopped or booked flights online. But mentioning this in an article generates the impression of a particular cyber-terrorism danger, especially when, as in this case, the story has "cyber-terrorism" in the headline.

In December, an alleged member of Al Qaeda who had been caught in India was quoted by *Newsbytes* as saying his organization had infiltrated Microsoft and manipulated the source code for their new operating system, Windows XP.[64] This report quickly made its way around the world, though it relied on just a single and somewhat sketchy source: the Indian IT security businessman Ravi Visvesvaraya Prasad, who among infowar experts was already known for his sensationalist op-eds on the "threat" of Chinese information warfare in Indian newspapers.[65]

The Al Qaeda hysteria led to bizarre ways of handling news, even within the big news networks. In January 2002 the NIPC publicly warned of running websites with "data of potential use to persons with criminal intent." Al Qaeda was not even mentioned.[66] The same day CNN turned this into the headline "Al Qaeda may have probed government sites."[67]

The U.S. government found this threat perception serious enough to try to convince its international allies of it. Defense Secretary Donald Rumsfeld at the NATO council meeting on December 18 warned of cyber-terrorism as one of the new "asymmetric threats":

> We need to prepare, as an Alliance, for the full range of asymmetric threats: new forms of terrorism, to be certain, but also cyber-attacks, attacks on space assets and information networks. . . .[68]

Remember, half a year before the same thing had happened at the NATO Council. The only difference was the complete change in the concept of the potential attacker. While the threat in June 2001 came from foreign countries, in December it came from terrorists. The same could be seen in other parts of the U.S. government.

Dale L. Watson, the FBI's executive assistant director on counterterrorism and counterintelligence, in his Senate testimony on "The Terrorist Threat Confronting the United States" in February 2002, exactly followed these lines:

> Beyond criminal threats, cyber space also faces a variety of significant national security threats, including increasing threats from terrorists. . . . Cyberterrorism—meaning the use of cyber tools to shut down critical national infrastructures (such as energy, transportation, or government operations) for the purpose of coercing or intimidating a government or civilian population—is clearly an emerging threat.[69]

In December 2001, Congress had already approved the establishment of a Cyber Division at FBI Headquarters that was tasked with coordinating, overseeing, and facilitating FBI investigations into computer-related crime and foreign intelligence.[70] In March of 2002, the intelligence community's new "global threat" estimate was presented to Congress. CIA director George J. Tenet, when discussing possible cyber-attacks, mostly talked about terrorists:

> We are also alert to the possibility of cyber warfare attack by terrorists. . . . Attacks of this nature will become an increasingly viable option for terrorists as they and other foreign adversaries become more familiar with these targets and the technologies required to attack them.[71]

Defense Intelligence Agency director Thomas R. Wilson, who one year before had warned of Cuba's potential cyber-war capabilities, now called cyberterrorism the clear and present danger:

> Foreign states have the greatest attack potential (in terms of resources and capabilities), but the most immediate and serious threat today is from insiders, terrorists, criminals,

and other small groups or individuals carrying out well-coordinated strikes against selected critical nodes.[72]

FROM FEAR TO FORECAST: INVENTING THE FUTURE (AND EVEN THE PRESENT)

Though nobody really knew how sophisticated Al Qaeda's computer literacy was, more and more people were afraid of them. This created a kind of vicious circle, with the media dramatizing the intelligence estimates and politicians in turn picking up media quotes. It was only a question of time before the plain fear would turn into bold forecasting. *Information Security* was among the first to do this. As early as November 2001, an article on cyber-terrorism made the slight but important move from "might" to "will certainly":

> Though we have yet to see terrorist groups—such as Hizbollah, HAMAS, Abu Nidal and Al Qaeda—employ hacking or malware to target critical infrastructures, their reliance on information technology and acquisition of computer expertise are clear warning signs. While damage caused by hacktivists—and even cyberterrorists—has been minimal thus far, security experts predict that the nation's IT infrastructure will certainly be a target in the future.[73]

In May 2002, *Newsweek* explicitly made the shift from possibility to certainty, even in a headline: "Islamic Cyberterror. Not a matter of if but of when." The article said:

> Al Qaeda terrorists interested in computer hacking are only a few clicks away from a crash course in digital sabotage.[74]

In June, the Business Software Alliance issued a report that was taken up by the media as a threat estimate. *Internet News,* for example, wrote:

> The U.S. government is due for a "major" cyber attack within the next 12 months and is unprepared to counter the threat, according to report released Tuesday evening by the Business Software Alliance (BSA).[75]

The problem: this was plainly wrong. In fact, the BSA had only surveyed "almost 400 IT professionals" about their thoughts for the future.[76] Even without specifying what an "IT professional" is (this can be anybody from a systems programmer to a consultant to a management-level CIO), it should be clear that these people are not very qualified in terrorism research and forecasting. The survey thus told more about the fears of American IT professionals after September 11 than about the real threat. And still, it was taken by the media as a cyber-terror forecast founded in expert knowledge.

A similar poll conducted by *Computer Economics* showed the differences in threat perception between terrorist and military cyber-attacks. According to this study, 48.4% of IT professionals believed that a "large-scale" cyber-attack would be launched by a military operative in the next two years, while 69.6% thought terrorists would launch such an attack.[77]

Having established a firm belief in a looming cyber-terrorist attack among the public and the security-policy community, the next step up the threat ladder was to claim that it was already happening. Because a large-scale cyber-terrorist act would have been noticed, the discourse had to change slightly. Instead of a single event, in late June 2002 the media invented the idea of an already-ongoing "war" between the U.S. security agencies and Al Qaeda terrorists. The news agency Agence-France Presse (AFP) launched a headline claiming exactly this: "Al Qaeda Wages Cyber War Against U.S."[78]

A closer look into the article, though, revealed that it only discussed the problems that U.S. intelligence and law-enforcement agencies had in attempting to follow the opening and closing of a series of websites supposedly run by Al Qaeda followers or members. Still, it was called a "war":

> Osama bin Laden's al-Qaeda is making full use of the Internet in its all-out war against the United States, forcing Washington to chase "Islamist" websites thought to serve as a platform for the terror network.[79]

Again, it was *USA Today* that brought this French news report to the general public in the United States. In early June the paper again ran the eighteen-month-old story about terrorists hiding encrypted messages in images on public websites like eBay.com or Amazon.com. Though here again the substance of the story (which was later proved wrong by several independent experts)[80] was the use of the Internet as a communications tool for terrorist groups, not as a means of attack itself, *USA Today* wrote about the "cyber battlefield":

> This new cyber-battlefield is allowing al-Qaeda and other groups to stay "several steps ahead" of the U.S.-led war on terrorism, a senior U.S. law enforcement official says.[81]

Just a few weeks later, the general notion of the new cyber-threat discourse was again pushed forward. This time it was an article in the *Washington Times* by retired Air Force general and Kosovo veteran Wesley Clark, with IT entrepreneur Bill Conner—a remarkable combination. Clark had led the campaign against Serbia and is still an influential man in Washington security-policy circles. Conner in turn is president and CEO of the IT-security company Entrust Inc. This together—an experienced general who knows how to win a war and a trustworthy IT-security expert—was enough for the *Washington Times* to print their op-ed, though it contained no substantially new information or analysis. One of their key sentences, of course, was: "The next battle in the war on terrorism may be on the cyber front."[82] This op-ed provides an interesting detail on the interconnection of speakers, discourse strings, and canonical texts. Bill Conner's company is a member of the Business Software Alliance, which had conducted the above-mentioned survey on the fears of IT professionals just two months earlier. Conner had been actively involved in this and had presented the survey to the public on behalf of the BSA. "We are at war, but the U.S. government has yet to move at war speed to protect against cyber attacks," Conner had said at that time.[83] He again used this study's results in his op-ed to warn of cyber-terrorism.

As the anniversary of the terrorist attacks on September 11 came closer, the fear of cyber-attacks rose again in the media. The discursive connection to the attacks of September 11, 2001, was made more clearly as well. An article on *IT-Director.com* on September 12 even quoted a pro-Arab hacker who predicted "suicide cyber-attacks" if the United States started a war against Iraq.[84] This was a clear link to the physical suicide attacks in New York City and Washington, D.C., and the practice of suicide bombings in the Israel/Palestine conflict. Though the article explained that a "suicide hacker attack" would be nothing more than a hacker trying to break into computer systems and disturbing them without taking care of hiding his traces, the discursive connection to the real-world suicide attacks makes this sound more dangerous to the public that does not know how hacker attacks really work. It was the closest one could get in discursively equating hacking with terrorist attacks.

SUMMER 2002: FROM TERRORISTS TO STATES?

While "terrorism" kept being the dominant subject in the United States security discourse, during the debate took another spin during the summer of 2002. In August, the Naval War College conducted an exercise called "Digital Pearl Harbor." The simulation brought together a team of experts from the Department of Defense and the Gartner group to assess the vulnerabilities and threats related to critical infrastructures. The outcome was in stark contrast to the fears discussed since September 2001. While local attacks were taken seriously, the experts agreed it would be virtually impossible to bring off any lasting, nationwide damage. Even more, the threat from cyber-terrorists was not considered high at all. If anybody should be considered as dangerous at all, only nation-states would have the capability to even attempt large-scale attacks. But even governments, with all the resources at their disposal, would not be able to inflict serious damage.[85]

Two weeks later, in late August 2001, the government pushed this new threat perception to the media. Richard Clarke, head of the White House Office for Cyber Security, told the press that the government had begun to regard nation-states rather than terrorist groups as the most dangerous threat. He mentioned more reasons for this latest change in the cyber-security discourse. Not only simulations, but also real-world observations and experiences now seemed to be behind it as well, because the government, according to Clarke, had changed its threat assessment after several suspicious break-ins into federal networks. He said:

> There are terrorist groups that are interested [in conducting cyber attacks]. We now know that al Qaeda was interested. But the real major threat is from the information-warfare brigade or squadron of five or six countries.[86]

Clarke did not make clear which countries were now considered "real threats." But the number he mentioned—five or six countries—is remarkably lower than the twenty to 100 states the government had considered as cyber-threats one year before.

It is too early to seriously assess whether this already constitutes a new trend. But the U.S. government again seems to focus more on the real capabilities needed to inflict heavy and lasting damage. Cyber-security czar Clarke repeated this observation some weeks later:

> There's a spectrum of threats out there, some of which we experience every day. That spectrum runs from [individuals] who simply vandalize Web pages to those who conduct nuisance denial-of-service attacks. That's on the low end, which is usually conducted by young hackers—so-called script kiddies.
>
> In the middle, you have criminals who conduct fraud and industrial espionage online. The middle range of threats is usually carried out by organized crime, companies and also nation-states.
>
> On the high end, however, you face people who potentially could conduct attacks to destroy or stop things from working. At the high end, it's potentially nation-states or terrorist groups. These attacks could be conducted in isolation or in conjunction with a physical attack.[87]

Interestingly, here terrorists were mentioned again at the high-threat end of the spectrum. But a closer reading reveals the ongoing virtuality of this threat. Clarke explicitly says "potentially" when talking about terrorist groups. So far, the real-world experience in the government's view is based on attackers ranging from script kiddies to organized crime, companies, and nation-states but not on cyber terrorism. This became even more clear a year after the attacks of September 11.

SEPTEMBER 2002: NO CYBER-TERROR, NO STRATEGY

Despite widespread fears of cyber-terrorism and computer virus attacks, September 11, 2002, passed almost without any incident in the online world. Immediately before the first anniversary, the security intelligence group mi2g was predicting digital attacks. In fact, a pro-Islamic hacking group, the "Unix Security

Guards," hacked into three AOL Time Warner computers on September 8 and kept them down until September 11. Though the analysts at mi2g had predicted even more attacks, nothing else happened. According to the website defacement archive Zone-H, only a few dozen websites were hacked, but with practically no references to September 11. The only things that made the cyber-threat news on September 11 were two poorly written computer viruses that did not spread very far. One of them was even broken, so it crashed regularly.[88]

So what is the real cyber-threat in the eyes of the U.S. government, and how will it be dealt with? Some light was shed a week later. On September 18, one week after the first anniversary of the terrorist attacks, Richard Clarke, together with representatives from the private sector, presented the Bush Administration's first "National Strategy to Secure Cyberspace."[89] The single infrastructure-sector groups had prepared their own "strategy inputs," which had been developed completely without government involvement.[90] The threat perception in this strategy document is ambivalent. It clearly makes references to the September 11 events, and it quotes at length from a letter to the president from fifty scientists, computer experts, and former intelligence officials who try to illustrate the danger of cyber terrorism:

> Consider the Following Scenario. . . . A terrorist organization announces one morning that they will shut down the Pacific Northwest electrical grid for six hours starting at 4:00PM; they then do so. . . . Other threats follow, and are successfully executed, demonstrating the adversary's capability to attack our critical infrastructure. . . . Imagine the ensuing public panic and chaos.[91]

On the other hand, however, the chapter on "Cyberspace Threats and Vulnerabilities" makes perfectly clear that the September 11 attacks—by now the prototypical massive terrorist event against the United States—were *not* as influential in shaping the strategy and the risk perception as one would assume. Instead, the release and within hours worldwide spread of the Nimda computer virus/worm a week later, on September 18, 2001, "was a wake-up call."[92] This is a notable departure from traditional threat warnings, because it focused on the capabilities (the "weapons") of cyber-attacks instead of the attackers. And it is the first official cyber–risk assessment that follows the model set forth for the U.S. military by Donald Rumsfeld in October 2001, in the Quadrennial Defense Review (QDR). The QDR 2001 says:

> A central objective of the review was to shift the basis of defense planning from a "threat-based" model that has dominated thinking in the past to a "capabilities-based" model for the future. This capabilities-based model focuses more on how an adversary might fight rather than specifically whom the adversary might be or where a war might occur.[93]

This is exactly the message of the new National Strategy to Secure Cyberspace. A headline in the "Threats and Vulnerabilities" chapter explicitly reads: "Reduce Vulnerabilities in the Absence of Known Threats."[94]

The bottom line, after all the fears of cyber-terror and cyber-war, is a still-unknown threat. The consequence of this is a policy that mainly focuses on hardening the United States' own systems. Because these are mainly run by the private sector, the new strategy document follows more or less the self-regulation path already laid out by President Clinton in 1998, with even more emphasis on a hands-off approach for the government.

The document, in turn, is not even a real strategy. It is clearly marked as a "draft," and the government gives interested parties—mostly the private sector running the infrastructures—two more months for feedback.[95] "We've said all along that this is a living document," explained Tiffany Olsen, an aide to Clarke.[96] Clarke emphasized, "We're not creating regulation, not creating mandates."

The strategy, and especially this hands-off approach, drew a lot of criticism from the computer-security sector. The former Justice Department's top computer-crimes prosecutor, Mark Rasch, for example, said, "All of these are good recommendations, but none have the force of law. There is no carrot and there is no stick. You need to put some teeth into some of the proposals."[97]

The government implicitly admitted that the strategy mainly consists of recommendations for others. This is not what one would normally call a strategy for one's own—in this case the government's—actions. An updated version of the strategy is therefore already planned for January 2003. Howard Schmidt, the vice chairman of the Critical Infrastructure Protection Board, said the revision would include details on "definitive programs."[98] But still, these programs—if they emerge—will attempt to force the private sector to protect its own systems, not to reducing the cyber-threat in the first place.

REALITY CHECK—DISCOURSE DYNAMICS AND THE "CYBER" WILD CARD

In less than two years since George W. Bush became president, we have observed three sharp bends in the threat perception. The first change took place after the new government came into power. The "cyber-terrorists" of the Clinton era were replaced by "strategic rivals and other countries preparing for cyber-war." Then, after the attacks of September 11, this state-centered threat perception was quickly replaced by the fear of "cyber-terrorism" by nonstate entities. The last turn came late in the summer of 2002, when more attention was paid again to nation-states but with a significantly lower threat estimate than a year before.

Such a zigzag course, viewed from a distance, is disturbing. Has the threat in the real world really changed that much? And has it changed that quickly? Or is the cyber-threat perception not linked to the real threat at all? What other explanations are possible? There are four possible explanations for this development: first, a change in the real world and the cyber-threats out there; second, a change in measuring standards for the threat assessments; third, hidden agendas of the actors pushing these different types of discourses; and fourth, "cyber" as a wild card that is just added to the general threat estimates and security policy debates, regardless of the real connection.

A CHANGE IN THE REALITY OF THE CYBER-THREAT?

Hard evidence on the cyber-attack capabilities of other states or even terrorist groups is extremely hard to gather, because it cannot be observed by traditional means of intelligence, such as satellite imagery. But one can draw some conclusions by comparing the quantitative development of cyber-incidents with the prognoses of the government. Here, we can clearly see that the link is less than thin and some evidence even points to the contrary. While the National Infrastructure Protection Center (NIPC) had warned of a rise in hacking and cyber-attack activities after the September 11 events, in fact there were fewer incidents than before. As a study of the security intelligence company mi2g showed:

> The number of web sites defaced globally has risen four-fold from 7,629 in 2000 to 30,388 in 2001. However, the number of defacements in September fell sharply according to the global monitoring conducted by mi2g. In May 2001, there were 3,853 Internet defacements worldwide whilst in September 2001 there were only 815.[99]

Another quantitative study released in 2002 focused more on the origin of hacking incidents. Riptech's "Internet Security Threat Report" of July 2002 had a newly added section called the "Cyber-Terrorism Watch List." The analysts specifically analyzed the data on countries on the State Department's list of "State Sponsors of Terrorism" and some other countries known for terrorist activities. But the results were not showing any link between so-called "rogue states" or terrorism and cyber incidents. Ninety percent of the activities from countries on the watch emanated from Iran, while the remaining 10% was split evenly between Cuba and Sudan. But more importantly, "countries on the Watch List generated less than 1% of all attacks detected during the past six-month period." More than two-thirds of all incidents originated in Europe or North America. More interestingly, our question on the change of the threat over time is directly answered by Riptech:

> The monthly rate of attack activity from countries on the Watch List remained relatively constant over the past six months. At a high level, the variations in attack activity roughly match the patterns observed from all countries throughout the world.[100]

These studies have to be read very carefully, because some of the rogue states use the Internet address space of neighboring countries. And even cyber-terrorists from countries on the "Watch List" could operate from Europe or even within the United States, like the attackers of September 11 did. But this all leads to one conclusion: the cyber-threat has probably not really changed in the last two years, and if it has, it would be terribly hard to tell. It definitely does not justify the claims of Al Qaeda already waging a cyber-war against the United States.

DIFFERENT MEASURING STANDARDS?

The threat perception can change when the criteria for a threat are changed. The problem here is that there are still no clear criteria, even within government organizations, for deciding what is an attack and what is not, and some security agencies tend to overstate the real incidents. Until 1998, the Pentagon counted every attempt to establish a telnet connection (which can be compared with a knock on a closed door) as an electronic attack.[101]

Another example shows even better how arbitrary some estimates are. When asked by the Department of Justice about the number of computer-security cases it encountered in 2000, the Air Force Office of Special Investigations (AFOSI) staff counted fourteen for the whole air force. The Department of Defense's overall count for all services, to the surprise of the AFOSI staff, later added up to some 30,000. The explanation: The other services had counted nondangerous events, like unidentified pings, as hacker attacks, while the AFOSI had considered only serious cases.[102] On the vulnerability side of the problem, there are also no standard procedures. Standards for identifying and estimating the vulnerability of critical infrastructures have been continuously developed since June 2000 in the Critical Infrastructure Protection Office's project "Matrix."[103] Slowly, a discussion seems to emerge on the validity of statistics about the numbers, dangers, and damages of computer insecurities. Even Richard Power of the Computer Security Institute that conducts the annual Computer Crime Survey for the FBI has already been somewhat self-critical on this problem.[104]

The different measuring standards could explain changes and differences in *quantitative* measures (like the number of countries actually preparing for cyberwarfare), but there is no evidence of specific changes in the criteria before the threat perception changed. More important, this does not explain the *qualitative* changes in the discourse that two times in the last two years has moved from "terrorists" to "states."

HIDDEN AGENDAS?

Some of the arguments in the cyber-threat debate can be explained by looking at the obvious interests of the speakers. First of all, security consultants and companies have to earn money by selling their services and products. This was one of the reasons the private industry was arguing for more government spending on IT security. Harris N. Miller of the Information Technology Association of America (ITAA), a lobby group that was very active in the preparation of the National Strategy to Secure Cyberspace, made this clear in an interview in September 2002. "While there's been much more attention in the private sector, there's a long way to go," he said. "But I don't feel the exercise is as futile as it was a year ago. Now the need is to get the money spent."[105] The attacks of September 11 seem to have been helpful for this purpose. But if these companies earn their revenues with hardening the systems, then it does not matter for them who the attackers might be—terrorists or unfriendly nation-states are both welcome in the debate if they just help to get attention paid to the vulnerabilities.

On the other end of the self-interest spectrum we find actors that use the cyber-threat discourse indirectly to achieve different goals. Microsoft's top antipiracy manager, Diana Piquette, for example, claimed in January 2002 that several international terrorist groups would be funded by money made with illegal software copying. According to Piquette, this was an outcome of the study "An Overview of the Manufacture and Distribution of Counterfeit Microsoft Software," which the software giant had commissioned in 2001. Not surprisingly, this study was never released to the public.[106] Considering Microsoft's obvious economic interests this can be regarded as free-riding on the terrorism fear.

In December 2001 Yonah Alexander, a terrorism researcher at the Potomac Institute, a think tank with close links to the Pentagon, claimed the existence of an "Iraq Net." It supposedly consisted of more than 100 websites set up by Iraq all over the world since the mid-nineties to start denial-of-service attacks. "Saddam Hussein would not hesitate to use the cyber tool he has. . . . It is not a question of if but when. The entire United States is the front line," Alexander said. The reason for this statement was obviously an attempt to make the case for an aggressive policy in the Washington struggle over intervening or not intervening in Iraq.[107] Even the Church of Scientology used "cyber-terrorism" in their argument against the Internet search engine Google and its practice of caching (copying) websites. The Church wrote in a press statement:

> Unless certain rules are applied on the Internet, our desired global freedom to communicate and exchange information will be corrupted by cyber-terrorism that often masquerades as free-speech activism.[108]

These cases of hidden agendas behind the cyber-threat discourse are all important to notice, but they had no real impact on the main changes in the discourse. One possible exception might be the government's own agencies. The FBI and others were able to use the cyber-threat debate to argue for more surveillance powers or the prohibition of anonymous Internet access.[109] But even this does not explain the sharp changes in the threat perception. For this objective, the security agencies had been utilizing any kind of threat, be it terrorists, spies, or unfriendly nations, before and after September 11.

"CYBER" AS A WILD CARD

The last possible explanation for the bends and turns of the discourse seems to me the most likely: there is no link at all between the cyber-threat perception and the real world. Not directly as a 1:1 connection, and not even indirectly through the real interests of actors who try to use the discourse for their own purposes. Rather, the prefix "cyber" gets attached to the mainstream security-policy discourse and works as an amplifier for any threat perception. Then we have to explain the change in the general security-policy discourse.

The turn toward a state-centered discourse at the start of the Bush Administration can be explained as a return to old perception patterns from the Cold War. The Bush Administration contains several people in important offices who had already served in former administrations prior to 1989. The clearest example is Secretary of Defense Donald Rumsfeld, who already had held this job in the eighties. National Security Adviser Condoleezza Rice, who nowadays compares "cyber-war" with nuclear deterrence, worked on nuclear strategy planning for the Joint Chiefs of Staff in the mid-eighties. This turn toward a worldview in which states are the most important and most dangerous actors first took place in the "normal" security-policy discourse. The "cyber" discourse followed later.

The second turn toward "cyber-terrorism" accordingly took place due to the general political climate after the attacks of September 11, not because of a change in real cyber-threats. When the whole security policy debate is focused on terrorism, it is no wonder that "cyber-terrorists" were considered the main threat for cyberspace. The rising emphasis again on possible cyber-attacks by nation-states can be connected to the general security policy the Bush Administration developed during 2002. Though Osama bin Laden and Al Qaeda are still at the top of the "most wanted" list, the president's "axis of evil" speech in January 2002 clearly marked a return to states as the perceived main threats. When the debate moved from this pure concept toward concrete plans for a new war against Iraq, the terrorism part of the general threat perception faded into the background. This has clearly influenced the government's cyber-security czar Richard Clarke, when he said in August 2002 that states were once again the biggest source of concern for U.S. cyber-security.

One question remains: How can anybody still believe that cyber-attacks—conducted by whomever—are a serious danger at all? After more than ten years of cyber-angst, the initial hype and fear might have hit its peak after the September 11 attacks in 2001. But one year later, without any serious acts of cyber-terrorism or cyber-war having happened, and with a growing understanding within the administration of the practical difficulties of really waging a full-scale war through the networks, the idea of large-scale cyber-attacks is still getting a lot of attention in the media and the expert communities. Maybe it is like Roland Emmerich's movie *Independence Day*: a bad and completely fictional story, but full of horror and thrill—and therefore extremely successful. Luckily, the American public seems to love these kinds of stories more than the real terrorists. As John Pike from Globalsecurity.org said:

> If you pitch a bad script in Hollywood, the worst that can happen is you get thrown out of the office. If I were some guy from al-Qaida pitching a (complicated and risky) cyberterrorism plot to Osama bin Laden, I would be a little nervous about making it out of his office alive.[110]

3. BEYOND THE AMERICAN FORTRESS: UNDERSTANDING HOMELAND SECURITY IN THE INFORMATION AGE

RACHEL E. D. YOULD

On June 24, 2002, United States Representative Richard Armey introduced H.R. 5005 at the request of the Bush Administration and the White House Office of Homeland Security. This bill, known informally as the Homeland Security Act of 2002, represented one of many legislative attempts in recent years to consolidate existing agencies with homeland defense responsibilities into a single federal department charged with centralized oversight and administration of homeland security efforts. Though this bill incorporated elements of previously released reports, such as the president's *National Strategy for Homeland Security,* its fundamental objectives did not differ substantially from formerly debated proposals, such as Representative William Thornberry's *Homeland Defense Bill,* introduced on March 21, 2001, as H.R. 1158. In fact, the contours of the Department of Homeland Security (DHS) as currently conceived have changed very little from Thornberry's early proposal of a National Homeland Security Agency that would "plan, coordinate, and integrate those U.S. Government activities relating to homeland security, including border security and emergency preparedness, and act as a focal point regarding natural and manmade crises and emergency planning."[1]

From their inception, recommendations to create a federal homeland defense department heralded an important departure in discussions of national security. Armey's bill proposed that most of the FBI's National Infrastructure Protection Center, the Department of Defense's National Communications System, and the Critical Infrastructure Assurance Office (then operated under the auspices of the Department of Commerce) be transferred to the new Department of Homeland Security and be administered in conjunction with long-standing security and emergency-response agencies. Asserting that "[t]he security of the United States homeland from nontraditional and emerging threats must be a primary national security mission of the United States Government,"[2] Thornberry's legislation, like the Bush Administration's recently enacted proposals, suggests that information technology has evolved into a core pillar of national security, ranking alongside issues of immigration, terrorism, and national-disaster preparedness.

The conception of IT as a primary security concern has been explicitly articulated in ongoing homeland defense studies and debates. Reports on the topic of homeland defense from as early as 1999 regularly divide the most urgent security threats confronting the United States into three categories: missile attacks, CBRN attacks (i.e., attacks utilizing certain weapons of mass destruction),[3] and cyber-attacks. In October 2001, a White House Cyberspace Security Adviser position was established. *The National Strategy for Homeland Security,* issued by the Bush Administration on July 16, 2002, identified the protection of critical infrastructure as one of six critical mission areas. The subsequent "Homeland Security Act of 2002" legislation transmitted to—and later ratified by—Congress recommended that Information Analysis and Infrastructure Protection be designated an under secretary and comprise one of four main divisions of the Department of Homeland Security. That threats to the integrity of the nation's information infrastructure and the potential role of information technologies in attack and retaliation scenarios have been ascribed a level of urgency analogous to nuclear and biological threats has galvanized the relationship between IT and security as a primary policy consideration for the foreseeable future.

Prior to the homeland defense discussions that emerged in the late 1990s, public sector debates pertaining to information technology tended to focus upon commercial opportunities, questions of government regulation, and issues of privacy. "IT security" regularly referred to the protection of systems and networks from viruses and unauthorized penetration ("hacking"), both of which were typically associated with the exploits of mischievous adolescents. Discussions of IT in conventional security circles focused almost exclusively upon information warfare, or the incorporation of emerging information technology capabilities into conventional military action and response tactics. Framing information technology, broadly defined, as a primary basis of national security marks a significant departure in the rhetoric of the United States defense community. It heralds far-reaching implications, both for the security community, as traditionally delineated (introducing a new competitor for limited security funding), and among information infrastructure specialists, who fear being deprioritized if forced to compete for funding and recognition in an unfamiliar government sector crowded with long-established and well-connected security agencies.

This shift in security rhetoric has not gone unnoticed. On September 21, 2001, *Washington Post* Technology Editor Nick Wakeman published an article titled "IT Infrastructure Is Key to Homeland Defense." In this article, Wakeman highlights the increasingly explicit acknowledgment of information technology's importance to national security. Writes Wakeman:

> Amid the death and destruction of the terrorist attacks on Sept. 11 in New York and Washington, the United States received a brutal wake-up call about the vulnerability of

> the nation's critical infrastructures—both physical and electronic. Talk of threats to important infrastructures, such as buildings and transportation, communications, power and information technology systems, will no longer be seen as hype.
>
> "These threats are very real," said Harris Miller, president of the Information Technology Association of America, Arlington, Va. "The people that have been talking about threats, cyber and physical, weren't just trying to get more government spending."
>
> Critical infrastructure protection will be a key component of a policy known as "homeland defense" that is emerging in the wake of the attacks, industry officials said.

The prospect of managing information infrastructure from a newly established Department of Homeland Security raises provocative questions. Is information technology a core national security concern in its own right? What specifically renders IT a primary security issue? Should national information infrastructure policy be planned and administered alongside other security agencies? What are the commercial implications of this shift in conceptualizing IT development? Will it spark new business opportunities in the form of joint government-corporate research and development initiatives? Or does it suggest the introduction of stricter regulatory statutes that could compromise the competitiveness of United States IT firms in the global marketplace? If the control and flow of information itself becomes a topic of security debates, are there also potential implications relating to privacy and information access?

Also of interest are questions relating to the operating context that has been so crucial to the development of information technologies, such as the Internet, thus far. Bolt, Beranek & Newman, the firm contracted by the United States government to design and implement the Internet's predecessor, the ARPAnet, had hoped to gain commercial advantage by refusing to release the operating code for the system into the public domain. The government intervened, noting that because the system had been developed using federal funds, all interested parties must be allowed access to its operating code.[4] This was a landmark event that shaped indelibly the interactive dynamics of an online community. Once the operating code of the nation's information infrastructure and systems is framed as a sensitive security concern, it is doubtful that unfettered transparency and distributed participation among small firms and unaffiliated individuals will be maintained at current levels.

Despite the extensive array of research and analysis pertaining to emerging cyber-threats and the questions these findings raise, the precise nature of IT's relationship with security concerns has not been adequately articulated. Projections, whether apocalyptic or conservative, are rarely founded upon sound evidence, and policy proposals are persistently vague. The purpose of this chapter is to demystify the interaction of IT and security by clarifying terms of reference and suggesting a conceptual framework through which to interpret the permeation of security considerations by information technology. The treatment of information infrastructure policy and administration manifest in the Bush Administration's Department of Homeland Security proposals and implementation plan is then assessed using this framework in order to determine both the organizational requirements dictated by IT's influence upon security issues and the degree to which current initiatives fulfill those requirements.

IT AND INTERNATIONAL SECURITY: A CONSTRUCT OF CONTINUUMS

There is nothing inherently new in associating elements of information and technology with security. Both information (under the rubric of intelligence) and technology (typically in the form of military equipment) have long constituted core components of security strategy. The ancient Chinese military theorist Sun Tzu described the primacy of these interrelationships to sound strategic endeavors 2,400 years ago in his renowned text widely known as *The Art of War* and was unlikely the first to do so.[5] Likewise, the relationship between information technology and security can be traced to the earliest appearance of technological devices that mediated information exchange. A frequently cited example is the Confederate Army's decision to undertake sustained raids on the telegraph lines operated by Union forces during the American Civil War. The efficacy of this initiative in thwarting communications among Union commanders was so great that, by the end the war, some historians estimate that as much as 40% of deployed Union forces were delegated to protect telegraph lines critical to strategic transmissions.[6]

It is the evolution of IT into the central and defining core around which disparate security elements are coalescing that renders contemporary discussions of IT and security unprecedented. Whereas IT might at one time have been considered one of many autonomous factors relevant to security assessments, it is now the ubiquitous force with which all aspects of security are imbued. This transformation began with the diffusion of silicon and network technologies that respectively enhanced the speed and functionality of technological mechanisms and rendered them globally interactive. It has culminated in what I term "differentiated dependence" upon IT. That is, the nature and intensity of the influence exerted by information technology upon discrete events varies from one instance to the next. However, there is no security-related sector that is not operationally dependent upon IT for some aspect of its activities and/or protection.[7]

The recent preoccupation of security specialists with asymmetric warfare has hindered attempts to conceptualize effectively the security implications of information technology. Colin Gray notes that "[i]n American common usage today, asymmetric threats are those that our political, strategic, and military cultures regard as unusual."[8] Broadly speaking, asymmetric warfare is founded upon the principle that methods for achieving military and political ends are increasingly diversified. While conventional military means remain a salient factor in any tactical assessment, unconventional forms of power projection are increasingly prevalent, as are trends favoring the deployment of several methods in tandem. "Asymmetric warfare" is a popular buzzword in security circles and is one of the fundamental philosophical underpinnings of recent military reforms, such as the Revolution in Military Affairs (RMA).

The acknowledgment of a diverse array of power projection mechanisms heralded by asymmetric warfare discourse is, in sum, a positive development. It is a more sophisticated and, I think, more accurate conception of modern conflict and enables a more nuanced view of potential adversarial encounters. However, one consequence of this trend has been a tendency toward hyper-classification. Whereas previous security rhetoric assumed unrealistic levels of homogeneity in power projection methods by expecting that all adversaries would limit themselves to conventional military means, the emerging propensity to divide varied methods into discrete categories inhibits consideration of continuums, overlap, and interaction.

From the prevalence of the asymmetric framework in the American security community followed the characterization of emerging cyber-threats as a new and distinct category in the diversified arsenal of asymmetric means. This tendency to construe cyber-threats as a discrete classification provides an adequate lens for assessing vulnerabilities, defensive postures, and power projection capabilities that are founded exclusively upon and exercised exclusively by means of information technology. However, sacrificed in this impermeable demarcation of IT is treatment of the increasingly influential role information technologies are assuming relative to all elements of security. Indeed, it appears that IT may be the common underlying factor upon which all security sectors are destined to converge.

In order to appreciate the gamut and complexity of IT's influence upon security, one must shed the didactic characterizations that have dominated asymmetric rhetoric thus far. I believe that the best means of embarking upon this exercise is to adopt a construct of continuums, thus displacing the designation of binary attributes with the recognition that every factor represents only one position along a wide spectrum of possibilities. Rather than describing the relationship between IT and security in terms of "this" or "that," it is crucial that we initiate a dialogue that allows us to speak in terms of an infinite range of subtle variations, dictated by (and sometimes unique to) the characteristics and objectives associated with a given encounter.

There are many binary classifications regularly invoked in discussions of IT and security. I have chosen to focus my attention upon the four that I believe represent the most pervasive and egregious contributors to oversimplified conceptions of the relationships between information technologies and security considerations. By reframing these binary opposites as endpoints of shared continuums, I seek to draw attention to the common traits that bind these seemingly discrete factors together, and to suggest that events are increasingly manifest as conditional spaces between these extreme poles. I do not propose that these continuums are themselves distinct, but suggest, rather, that they overlap and interact in an ongoing and reciprocally influential dynamic. This analysis is then overlaid upon the contours of the recently established Department of Homeland Security in order to assess the degree to which current operational recommendations acknowledge and respond to these complexities.

National *versus* International

Discussions of information technology are replete with references to its consequences for geographically defined borders. Indeed, the boundariless nature of the Information Age has emerged as one of the great commonplaces of this era. Of course, national boundaries do continue to exert influence. Market regulations and legal codes continue to be promulgated and enforced in accordance with geographically bound spaces. So, while consumers may order merchandise from anywhere on the globe via the Internet, it remains illegal to deliver certain purchases across national lines, while many legal international deliveries are subject to hefty import taxes. Likewise, while individuals may now use network technologies to commit crimes against Americans from locations far removed from the United States, foreign statutes may inhibit the ability of American law-enforcement agencies to identify, extradite, and prosecute guilty parties.

Despite the persistence of geographically defined jurisdictions, information technology unmistakably mitigates the primacy and impermeability of national borders. Many discussions of IT's influence upon borders as traditionally conceived focus upon the destabilizing role of transborder information flows. The widely accepted conclusion among proponents of this view is that, because data flows are not circumscribed by geographical boundaries, information technology is contributing to economic, political, and social developments that undermine—or, at the very least, render contingent—the sovereignty and significance of the nation-state. According to such perspectives, IT is galvanizing the global marketplace by facilitating the increased interconnectedness of economic systems and transactions. It is destabilizing political regimes that depend upon the ability to insulate domestic discourse from foreign information sources for their survival. And it is fostering the development of transnational communities the solidarity of which may eventually supersede that of national populations.

While elusive phenomena such as transborder data flows may prove to be harbingers of substantial economic, political, and social transformations, the nature of the physical infrastructure and technological apparatus that comprise information networks must also be assessed. Both those who assert and those who reject the unswerving primacy of the Westphalian nation-state have failed to address adequately the border implications introduced by the physical infrastructure associated with IT networks. The Homeland Security Act of 2002 notes explicitly that, for the purposes of the Department of Homeland Security, "the homeland" is conceptualized in purely geographic terms as delineated by the land borders of American territories.[9] Some analysts have attempted to extend this idea of the geographically defined homeland to IT security concerns by suggesting that the physical boundaries of American IT infrastructure be mapped. While the contours of this physical infrastructure might not correspond perfectly with the land boundaries of the United States, the exercise would, according to advocates of the idea, at least afford a geographic shape to the country's cyber vulnerabilities, thus allowing them to be conceptualized in a tangible, physical manner consistent with the legislation's terms of reference.

However, the prospect of mapping America's IT infrastructure is precluded by the fact that this network does not occupy a contiguous physical or regulatory space. In oversimplified terms, physical IT infrastructure can be thought of as being comprised of "nodes" and "links." A "node," broadly defined, is any mechanism connected to a network. In the context of a global information network, a node may be a single computer, several computers linked together (such as a corporation's Intranet), or a server. While a node is a site at which information is generated and stored, and from which it is transmitted, "links" are the interfaces that connect nodes to one another through a distributed communications network. "Links" may be telephone lines, fiber-optic wires, cable lines, or wireless mechanisms by means of which data is transmitted.

Many American-owned and operated IT nodes are located in the midst of foreign-owned and operated links. As a result, American nodes are often subject to the regulatory parameters and technological strengths and weaknesses associated with the data lines and telecommunications infrastructure of foreign networks. Just as many American nodes are located within networks abroad, numerous foreign nodes are situated within networks administered under

United States jurisdiction. Thus, the physical components that comprise information infrastructure cannot be meaningfully designated "domestic" or "foreign." Regardless of domestic regulations, security-enhancing technologies, and nationally accepted best-practice protocols, nodes administered according to foreign norms will continue to operate within American communications infrastructure, while American nodes situated within foreign networks will be exposed to a constant influx of data streams that may not be in accord with American standards. American IT infrastructure cannot be insulated from foreign IT infrastructure in either physical or operational terms.

The fact that domestic and foreign IT components are physically interspersed can in no way be likened to the discontiguous geography of the United States. Whereas certain territories, such as the states of Alaska and Hawaii, are physically disconnected from the continental United States, they are discrete regulatory extensions of the American homeland totally insulated from the legal jurisdictions of adjacent geographic entities. Thus, Alaska's physical proximity to Canada and Russia in no way affects its administration of American laws within its borders. Conversely, all data that flows to and from any IT node is transmitted in accordance with the operational characteristics and technological parameters that characterize the links to which it is connected. Thus, American nodes situated amidst foreign links become incorporated into foreign networks, subject to the foreign regulatory and operational regimes by which adjacent links are administered.

Profound security implications proceed from the fact that American IT infrastructure is inextricably intertwined with foreign nodes and networks. Regardless of the effectiveness of protective measures instituted in the United States, there is no way to ensure that all nodes operating in U.S. jurisdiction subscribe to these standards or that American nodes operating in foreign networks will benefit from them. In effect, any instance of cyber-aggression enacted anywhere in the world is rendered an act of potentially direct global repercussion. This differs from the indirect consequences experienced as a result of most socio-economic network dynamics. For example, a recession in a market either geographically or functionally far removed from that of the United States will typically have some influence upon the domestic economic situation as a function of the increasingly global interconnectedness of financial markets. However, such effects are secondary, as American finance is at least marginally insulated through the autonomous regulation of its own national currency. The United States is afforded no such buffer from cyber-aggression enacted in foreign networks, as American IT infrastructure cannot be operationally differentiated from the foreign infrastructures with which it interacts and is often seamlessly integrated.

In this context, what is "the homeland" and how can it be conceived as something distinct from network dynamics on a global scale? Proposals for the operation of the Department of Homeland Security state explicitly that ensuring the security of the nation's information infrastructure is one of its primary strategic missions. Furthermore, if adversaries are opportunistic, as *The National Strategy for Homeland Security* asserts, targeting those assets deemed most susceptible, then emerging and constantly evolving cyber vulnerabilities can be assumed to be attractive and likely objects of future aggression. Given the high priority assigned to cyber-security and low American preparedness relative to longer-standing and comparatively static vulnerabilities, devising a security construct well aligned with the characteristics unique to information technology is of considerable importance.

Though *The National Strategy* acknowledges the importance of international collaboration, such efforts assume the existence of a discrete homeland for the benefit of which international efforts are merely a secondary and supplementary line of defense. Information technology, whether considered in terms of data flows or physical infrastructure, defies distinctions between "national" and "international." While IT considerations are undoubtedly crucial to homeland security, they cannot be managed effectively from a department for which international interfaces and coordination are merely tangential operational imperatives. From this perspective, the prospect of thinking in terms of a "homeland" sequestered from the international community is highly idiosyncratic.

Cyber-Aggression *versus* Noncyber-Aggression

Cyber-threats are regularly construed as a separate kind of hazard, distinct from other forms of security instruments. Consistent with the division of diversified threats into discrete categories typical of asymmetric models, methods of cyber-aggression have been classified as a new kind of security concern and tend to be analyzed in relative isolation from preexisting security mechanisms. Certainly, there is widespread acknowledgment that any given offensive may be rendered more effective through the combined utilization of several different forms of attack. Thus, there are ample references to the potential application of cyber-aggression in attacks that also incorporate more conventional tactics. For instance, the ability of an adversary to recover from a missile attack could be impeded if that attack were coupled with an IT offensive that compromised communications systems crucial to the coordination of recovery efforts. Similarly, the release of a biological agent could be rendered more deadly if the online resources and communication networks that support the coordination of emergency medical responses were impaired.

However, rarely do homeland security discussions of diversified attacks consider the possibility or implications of hybridized means derived from the amalgamation of multiple classes of offensive instruments. As most forms of offensive apparatus are now either comprised of sophisticated IT components or heavily dependent upon information technology for their deployment, cyber-capabilities can no longer be considered mechanisms distinct from more conventional means. Nuclear weapons facilities are monitored and administered using information technology, as are power grids and telecommunications networks. Guidance systems also rely heavily on IT, and the international financial markets are virtually inextricable from the data networks through which transactions are executed.

This is not to imply that information technology plays a role in every incident of aggression, or to question the existence of autonomous cyber-attacks. Polar extremes constitute the endpoints of every continuum. A strategy that involves the manual detonation of a conventional explosive device may not incorporate IT mechanisms in any form. By the same token, the use of IT to compromise the integrity of an adversary's communications network can rightly be considered a cyber-attack lacking any substantive relationship to conventional means. Nor is it my intent to propose that the classification of offensive methods is without relevance, as an awareness of the nature and function of discrete mechanisms in their purest forms is an invaluable conceptual tool.

However, it is increasingly the case that IT contributes to the development and deployment of most offensive and defensive mechanisms at the same time that autonomous cyber-threats are emerging. The appropriateness of relying upon categorical models for the assessment of security threats and potential strategic responses is undermined by the fact that information technology is a pervasive force influential in all security sectors. While cyber-attacks may, indeed, be undertaken in combination with other distinct offensive methods, the integration of information technology into conventional tactics may also fundamentally alter the nature, reliability, and deployment of more traditional means.

Unfortunately, heightened awareness of the widespread integration of IT among tactical communities has not been translated into a national strategy that incorporates and responds to this dynamic. Materials describing the Revolution in Military Affairs (RMA) assign consistently high priority to the application of IT to the enhancement of existing equipment and operations. The private sector continues to render corporate services and operations more efficient and secure through the creative application of information technology. However, an awareness among administrators of security sectors of IT's increasingly influential integration is only of marginal significance as long as each sector pursues independent and uncoordinated IT strategies.

It is important that disjointed IT efforts across sectors be coordinated in conjunction with a coherent national IT security strategy in order to minimize duplicative efforts and ensure the interoperability of strategic mechanisms. *The National Strategy for Homeland Security* and legislation outlining the organizational contours of the Department of Homeland Security have failed to introduce either a cohesive strategic approach for the consideration of IT-related security issues or organizational mechanisms that might facilitate coordination of such matters across security sectors. Current homeland security proposals frame cyber-threats as strategically and organizationally distinct from other security concerns. It is proposed that IT initiatives be organized and administered under the auspices of a separate division in the DHS that shares few operational objectives with the division charged with oversight of "catastrophic threats." By institutionalizing arbitrary distinctions between cyber-threats and noncyber-threats, current DHS operating proposals ensure that IT initiatives will continue to lack a common strategic vision. This reinforcement of the distinction between "cyber" *versus* "noncyber" also deprives new efforts that target emerging cyber issues of formal organizational channels through which to capitalize upon the IT initiatives already devised and implemented by other security sectors.

Disruption *versus* Destruction

From the tendency to construe cyber-threats and noncyber-threats as mutually exclusive phenomena has emerged a range of terminological distinctions that reinforce such didactic classifications. Discussions of virtually any topic regularly foster the formulation of buzzwords and catchy phrases. Among the most prevalent relating to the issue of IT and security is the designation of cyber-threats as weapons of mass *disruption* in direct contrast to (noncyber) weapons of mass *destruction*. While a clever diminutive, and certainly one that has attained widespread popularity, this specification is wholly unhelpful in advancing accurate ideas about the security implications associated with information technology.

Framing outcomes of cyber-aggression as "disruptive" underestimates the devastation potentially wrought using technological means. In the first instance, IT is increasingly enhancing the destructive capacity of weapons of mass destruction as traditionally conceived. Furthermore, the administration of nuclear plants, power grids, air traffic control centers, and other critical systems using network technologies introduces the possibility that attacks on these and other facilities could be enacted through a breach of IT systems. Such efforts could also delay response to the offensive by compromising technologically supported detection and recovery mechanisms, thus intensifying further the destructive potential of cyber-enacted attacks.

Even those cyber-offensives perpetrated against technological mechanisms unrelated to life-critical systems may culminate in decidedly destructive events. "Destruction" does not necessarily connote human casualties. Inanimate assets and infrastructure are equally predisposed to being rendered nonexistent and with profoundly destabilizing effects. Information is itself an asset, generated and protected at great expense to individuals and organizations alike.

It is not only the corruption of information that poses a security risk. The unauthorized acquisition and dissemination of sensitive data effectively destroys its utility, as exclusive access to such information often constitutes its primary value. The integrity of proprietary information informs fundamentally the competitiveness of private-sector organizations in global markets and, by extension, influences the economic security of their home nations. The insulation of governmental and military intelligence from the consciousness of adversarial institutions is also critical to security efforts.

It should also be noted that cyber-tactics threaten not only information, but also the infrastructure by which it is stored and transmitted. While corrupted data can often be reconstituted quickly and at low expense if duplicate copies are maintained vigilantly, the restoration of a compromised IT network may require the investment of considerable time and financial resources. A "destroyed" IT infrastructure is one that has been rendered unusable. This may follow from the physical destruction of the hardware that comprises a network using conventional military means. It could derive from functional obstructions perpetrated by the introduction of a virus into the system that disables operating software. Finally, if the encryption that renders a system secure is appropriated or deciphered, the network's utility is undermined, thus negating its value despite the persistence of its physical form and operational functionality.

The rhetorical juxtaposition of "disruptive" cyber-threats relative to "destructive" (and, thus, presumably more serious) counterparts has been widely incorporated into American discussions of homeland defense. In addition to adopting terminological references to "mass disruption" in descriptions of IT's security implications, homeland defense proposals have translated this concept of the inherently nondestructive nature of cyber-threats into IT strategies that address potentially disruptive outcomes to the near exclusion of destructive capabilities.

In the report titled *Securing the Homeland, Strengthening the Nation,* the Bush Administration outlines in detail its FY2003 funding requests for the implementation of homeland security measures. The requested expenditures are distributed among four initiatives and three "additional budget priorities." The four primary strategic initiatives around which the Bush Administration's FY2003 budget proposal revolves are 1) supporting first responders; 2) defending against bioterrorism; 3) securing America's borders; and 4) using twenty-first-century technology to secure the homeland. These priorities command 55% of the homeland security expenditures requested for FY2003 and correspond roughly to those portions of the budget proposal destined to be administered or overseen by the new Department of Homeland Security.[10]

The fourth strategic initiative deemed a top priority for FY2003 funding, that designated "Using Twenty-First-Century Technology to Secure the Homeland," is divided into five programmatic areas. The first program is intended to "[a]ssure broad access and horizontal [information] sharing across selected government databases." Its sole line item is the establishment of a program office to "identify and commence information sharing," which is allocated 2.8% of the total sum requested for the IT strategic initiative. The remit of the second program is to "[e]nsure procedures for and handling of sensitive homeland security information" in order to "facilitate information sharing while protecting sources." In support of this second program, 1% of the total IT initiative budget is assigned to the coordination of "[s]ecure videoconferencing with States."

The third program listed under the IT strategic initiative is actually a program in support of the initiative to secure America's borders. The funding for this program, the entry-exit system intended to bolster the development of "smart borders" for America, is requested under the auspices of the IT initiative despite the fact that it is actually considered one of the primary programmatic components of border protection. The purpose of this proposed entry-exit program is as much to streamline "the entry of routine, legitimate traffic" as it is to enhance the ability of American border-patrol agents to "deny access to those individuals who should not enter the United States." The entry-exit program represents almost 53% of the total budget request for the homeland security IT initiative.

The fourth program of which the homeland security IT initiative is comprised is intended to ensure that relevant threat information "is conveyed to State and local officials in a timely manner." It is proposed that this be accomplished through the institution of "threat dissemination systems" and educational programs for state and local officials, which command a combined 2% of the IT initiative budget request.

The fifth and final program included in the homeland security IT initiative is titled, "Cyberspace Security: Protecting our Information Infrastructure." Forty-one percent of the initiative budget—a smaller proportion than that designated for the entry-exit program that supports the border security initiative—is requested for the administration of the ten line items incorporated under this program heading. A full 25% of the funding requested in support of cyberspace security is divided between a priority wireless access network that would ensure effective lines of communication among first responders in emergencies and a catchall line item designated "Other IT/Information Sharing."

The nature of these budgetary requests belies a disproportionate emphasis upon applying IT capabilities in support of homeland defense to the detriment of redressing IT vulnerabilities, insulating information infrastructure from potential threats, and developing capabilities to identify and retaliate against perpetrators of cyber-aggression. Four of the five programs proposed in support of the IT homeland security initiative are dedicated solely to increasing information sharing and the efficient administration of border security efforts. A full 69% of the funding requested for the administration of IT-related homeland security measures is intended to enhance communications and operational efficiency.

The importance of seamlessly integrated and effectively mobilized information was made exceedingly clear by the terrorist attacks successfully executed on September 11, 2001. It has been demonstrated that American intelligence agencies lacked not the data to preempt these attacks, but rather, mechanisms that would have allowed this information to be synthesized and applied more effectively. Information technology has much to contribute to enhancing homeland security. IT can, indeed, be utilized to render operations more efficient and information more widely available in better-synthesized form. While such initiatives should be highly prioritized components of any homeland security agenda, the application of IT to better accomplish operational goals is an objective quite different from securing cyberspace. Current homeland security proposals suggest that the United States focus its attention and resources upon efforts that will heighten dependence upon information technology without instituting sufficient measures to ensure that the nation's information infrastructure is secure.

The tendency to frame cyber-threats as nondestructive has culminated in the deprioritization of cyber-security in current homeland defense proposals. The central importance assigned to information technology in philosophical terms is not translated into commensurate financial commitments. Though the application of twenty-first-century technologies to the enhancement of homeland security is cited as one of four primary strategic initiatives in the Bush Administration's FY2003 funding request, only 2% of this proposal—$722 million of the total $37.7 billion solicited—is allocated in support of this initiative's administration. Of this suggested $722 million, $499 million is allocated toward enhanced information sharing and operational efficiency.

The widely held belief that the greatest security threats posed by the exploitation of cyber-vulnerabilities are transitory, albeit potentially serious, disturbances has led many to underestimate or completely misunderstand the destructive potential of cyber-terrorism. The cyber-security measures recommended by current homeland security budget proposals seem to suggest that managing the interface between information technology and international security is adequately achieved by enhancing operational efficiency and avoiding potentially costly annoyances. In effect, current homeland security strategy suggests that the United States increase substantially its dependence upon information technology for the nation's security without assigning equal emphasis to the protection of the infrastructure upon which these initiatives depend.

"Hacking" *versus* "Information Warfare"

Just as the proclivity for overclassification has contributed to conceptions of cyber-threats as a category distinct from other security concerns, the various manifestations of cyber-aggression have been vigorously subdivided. From this process of fracturing cyber-security into constituent elements has arisen a complex array of related terminology. Though these designations are not applied with any great degree of consistency, some core characteristics of each have gained wide acceptance.[11]

"Hacking" is sometimes used to denote any unauthorized access of a communications system using technological means. However, it is most often associated with the "thrill-seeking" behavior of (typically young) computer enthusiasts whose primary objective is to outsmart a system's security measures. The incentive motivating the actions of these "hackers" is usually the challenge presented by the activity and its entertainment value.

"Cracking" is a more recent addition to the rhetorical landscape. It derives from the more formal designation "*cr*iminal h*acker*" and refers to criminal activity undertaken using information technology. Identity theft and the interception of credit card numbers for fraudulent use are included in this category. Perpetrators may be individuals or formal crime rings acting in concert, seeking personal gains from criminal activity executed online.

"Hacktivism" is also a relatively new term, coined to describe politically inspired campaigns that involve the unauthorized use of technological means. This label usually conjures images of grassroots political activists altering or defacing the content of websites administered by groups who espouse conflicting ideals. "Hacktivism" has become a mainstay in the confrontation between Israeli and Palestinian supporters, with several websites administered by both sides disabled or altered to include derogatory comments. "Hacktivism" may be undertaken by unaffiliated individuals, members of informal political networks, or representatives of coherent activist organizations. In some cases, content manipulation is augmented by more conventional criminal activity. One commonly cited example of this integration of hacktivism with online theft is an incident perpetrated by the Pakistani Hackerz Club in the course of which the security mechanisms protecting the American Israel Public Affairs Committee's website was breached. In this case, hacktivists replaced existing web content with anti-Israeli slurs and then proceeded to record the credit card numbers stored in the site's database of financial supporters.

The criteria by which an activity is deemed to be "cyber-terrorism" have evolved over time. It was previously the case that "cyber-terrorism" referred to any IT-enabled act perpetrated with the intent to inflict damage. By this definition, computer viruses designed and disseminated by individual hackers were subsumed under this term alongside other, more formally coordinated destructive cyber-activity. Since the September 11 terrorist attacks, however, this term has become more narrowly applied, typically referring only to the use of networked media for the execution of destructive acts coordinated by terrorists and terrorist groups.

"Information warfare"[12] and "cyber-war" are applied fairly interchangeably to describe technologically enabled or enhanced destructive acts implemented by nation-states as part of an overall military strategy. These terms often refer to the efforts of military agents to sever communications between an adversary's commanders and their field units. It may also refer to efforts to damage or render nonfunctional an opponent's civilian or governmental information infrastructure. In essence, any activity undertaken by an agency or organization that represents formally the interests of a national government and damages IT components, obstructs IT operability, or uses information technology as a means to conduct a tactical offensive may rightly be considered an act of "information war."

Though these terms provide a useful lens onto the diverse array of activities that constitute cyber-aggression, their inconsistent application and emphasis on agency render them vague and imprecise. The summary definitions catalogued here provide a fair representation of the meaning typically assigned to these terms. However, it is not uncommon for these labels to be applied in descriptions of incidents that diverge markedly from these approximated norms. The terminological landscape is further complicated by the fact that the conferral of these namesakes tends to be determined primarily by the perpetrator of an incident, rather than by an act's outcomes, either intended or realized. Thus, a network breach executed by a mischievous teen will likely be considered "hacking," while an identical act perpetrated by a politically motivated group lacking violent intent may be construed as "hacktivism." Comparable events may be designated "cyber-terrorism" or "cyber-war" depending upon the relative involvement of terrorist groups or a nation-state. Occurrences of cyber-aggression are typically described according to the characteristics of the agents who enact them, rather than according to the objectives or efficacy associated with specific incidents.

These labels are also problematic because of the tendency to treat them as clearly delineated and mutually exclusive classifications. Hackers can easily be mistaken for cyber-terrorists if they roam the virtual domain of military endeavor. Likewise, crime and terrorist organizations often engage in nondestructive (and, indeed, often undetected) hacking in order to troll corporate or governmental networks for useful information that may or may not be applied to the design and implementation of destructive attacks.[13] Hackers lacking any affiliation to formal organizations can impart significant damage through the formulation and distribution of computer viruses. There is some indication that disaffected hackers might be predisposed to terrorist groups' online recruitment efforts, thus suggesting that some proportion of today's troublesome pranksters could constitute the next generation of cyber-terrorist rogues. Furthermore, the aggregate effects of hacking and cracking activities can be profoundly destabilizing on a systemic level. Though hackers and online criminals acting individually are unlikely to cause catastrophic damage, the proliferation of such recreants in large numbers can lead the general public to question the security of an entire network, thus undermining its value and usability. The explicitly political agendas of hacktivists could easily attract financial support from terrorist groups or sympathetic nations, while many postulate that the sizable coffers of terrorist organizations benefit from unacknowledged state support. Cyber-aggression is characterized by a complex interplay of actors and objectives and cannot accurately be described in terms of discrete subcategories.

The considerable overlap and interaction among various forms of cyber-aggression complicates the inherently difficult problem of identifying responsible parties, while the increasing sophistication of cyber-offenders compounds the complexity introduced by a perpetually evolving technological environment. In 1995, the Department of Defense conducted a self-test of its computer security infrastructure by generating 38,000 cyber-attacks on internal systems, of which 65% were successful. Only 63% of these attempts were detected by the users or administrators of equipment targeted by the test.[14] More recent studies suggest that as many as 90% of all cyber-security breaches go completely unnoticed.[15]

Current homeland defense proposals suggest that cyber-security responsibilities be delegated according to widely accepted subclasses of cyber-aggression. The prevention of "hacking" is considered the purview of the private sector, which owns over 90% of America's information infrastructure. The White House

Office of Homeland Security's *National Strategy* associates the management of these cyber-security concerns with corporate stewardship, asserting that private organizations must accept direct responsibility for the security of the networks they administer. Incidents of "cracking," particularly when executed as part of larger coordinated efforts, are assigned to the law-enforcement agencies responsible for prosecuting offenders of non-cyber-crimes. Information warfare has traditionally fallen under the scope of military operations and appears destined to remain a responsibility of the American services. Consistent with the concept that the primary *raison d'être* of the Department of Homeland Security is prevention of, preparation for, and response to terrorist attacks, incidents of cyberterrorism constitute the primary cyber-security role of the new department. Though proposals do delegate the administration of cyber warning systems and the coordination and dissemination of information gathered from the private sector by the DHS, most aspects of the nation's cyber-security are devolved to corporate IT administrators and law-enforcement organizations.

The segregation of cyber-security responsibilities among disparate sectors and agencies is predicated upon the assumptions that cyber-aggression can be subdivided into discrete categories and that any given cyber-incident can be accurately catalogued according to these subclassifications. At the same time, the perspective that the private sector should assume primary responsibility for the security of the infrastructure it owns and operates is founded upon the belief that organizations must accept direct responsibility for the integrity of the equipment and mechanisms that support their activities. While corporate America should likely play a significant role in securing the nation's information infrastructure as its primary administrator, the fact that 95% of all governmental communications are transmitted via these privately owned networks suggests the importance of an equally vigilant public-sector role. If the private sector is to be held accountable for the security of the networks it administers, so too must the United States government assume responsibility for the security and efficacy of the mechanisms it opts to employ for the conduct of its daily activities.

The tendency to discuss IT–related security issues in terms of starkly defined binary opposites is widespread. Certainly the four examples discussed here do not represent an exhaustive list of those characteristics regularly oversimplified. While certain analytical exercises may benefit from this propensity to compartmentalize contributing factors, information technology as it pertains to security issues cannot be discussed constructively in such didactic terms. The predisposition of IT for application in both civilian and governmental endeavors, its rapid and constant evolution, and its complex contributions to all security sectors render problematic the designation of static and diametrically opposed classifiers in its examination. The fact that data flows and IT infrastructure are not circumscribed by territorial boundaries further complicates the application of traditional nation-based security models to IT analysis.

The failure to think in terms of multiple overlapping and reciprocally informative continuums does not constitute the only shortfall in current discussions of information technology and security. The discourse also suffers from a tendency to conflate information technologies and network technologies, characterizing "IT" and "the Internet" as one and the same. Overemphasis upon the importance of the Internet has detracted attention from cable networks, wireless technologies, and pervasive computing, each of which introduces security considerations of considerable import. Finally, the widely held assumption that cyberspace is a seamless dimension free from technical barriers to interoperability is a fallacy in its own right, as illustrated by the proliferation of numerous data networks around the world designed for mobile devices. Many of these networks remain only imperfectly compatible with PC-accessed systems and, indeed, with one another.

The examples noted above are intended to give some indication of the degree to which inappropriate conceptual models are being used to design and administer IT security measures. The extrapolation of existing security constructs for the analysis of information technology is an ill-conceived and unproductive exercise, as are likely to be attempts to cleave an arbitrarily defined "homeland" from a more holistic vision of global security spheres.

THE AMERICAN FORTRESS

Assessments of information technology's relationship with international security have been founded upon a core internal inconsistency. Discussions of the unprecedented nature of both recent technological developments and their ramifications for national and global security interests have proceeded alongside attempts to conceptualize and respond to these supposedly singular factors using generic models and long-standing didactic tendencies. It seems ironic that recent events have not prompted the formulation of new analytical lenses better suited to discern the complex nature of phenomena widely construed as historically inimitable.

Widespread emphasis upon the singularity of information technology's potential security applications has also culminated in a reticence to invoke historical parallels. To be sure, the silicon and network technologies advanced in recent decades embody fundamentally new capabilities that are reshaping the nature, speed, and vulnerabilities associated with information interchanges of all kinds. However, while the specific characteristics and applications of contemporary IT mechanisms may be unique, the sociopolitical shifts they herald, the debates they inspire, and the responses they prompt are not entirely without historical analogy.

The emergence of IT as a decisive factor in the security landscape does not constitute the first time a dominant strategic paradigm has been undermined by technological advancements. It is not the only occasion in which low barriers to acquisition and widespread diffusion of new instruments have empowered previously inconsequential foes to challenge directly the hegemony of regional superpowers. Likewise, the creation of a United States Department of Homeland Security does not represent the first time an established superpower, confronted with a new and uncertain security dilemma, has resorted to an aggrandized version of long-standing and familiar security mechanisms in an attempt to ameliorate threats that fail to adhere to the parameters of prevailing tactical sensibilities.

Though the particular contours of any dynamic and the context in which it transpires preclude unconditional comparison of distinct events, the common themes discernible through tempered comparative exercises can be instructive. In this case, the consequences wrought by attempts of dominant regimes from past eras to counter newly emergent threats by defaulting to the strategic exemplar that formed the traditional basis of the regime's operational superiority resonate with the logical premises that underlie present-day American homeland security initiatives and the outcomes they are likely to generate. Of particular relevance are the historical events and strategic considerations that culminated in the erection of China's Great Wall.

Around 900 BC there emerged a development in military affairs of revolutionary proportion. After centuries of dependence upon chariots for tactical superiority, warriors mastered the ability to fight from horseback without the need for a cumbersome horse-drawn conveyance. Prior to advances that enabled soldiers to engage opponents while mounted on horseback, the military advantages afforded by the use of horses in combat could only be realized in conjunction with carriages such as the chariot. The construction of chariots was a costly endeavor that demanded highly advanced technical skill. The resources and craftsmanship required for the production of horse-drawn equipment represented significant impediments that served to limit the number of politico-military entities capable of undertaking top-tier military campaigns. When the production of chariots was no longer a prerequisite for challenging dominant regimes, nomadic tribes previously excluded from offensives of consequence to entire regions and empires began to pose serious destabilizing threats.

The introduction of mounted warriors shifted regional power dynamics both by diversifying the range of possible participants and by favoring the organizational predisposition of previously marginalized groups. Whereas chariot warfare privileged sedentary communities that fostered the concentration of resources, skilled craftspeople, and sites of production, cavalry techniques favored nomadic tribes. The quantity of food required to sustain large numbers of horses was prohibitive for land-bound societies. The grasses of adjacent plains were limited and the allocation of grain reserves for the maintenance of steeds depleted that available for human consumption. Nomadic tribes were unconcerned with such considerations as they could easily migrate from one fertile area to the next.

Chariot warfare was no match for the speed and agility of a mounted offensive, thus necessitating the development of cavalry capabilities by all major regimes. The presence of defensive cavalry forces did not, however, guarantee the protection of communities from mounted invasions. The capacity to fight from horseback afforded nomadic tribes the ability to lay siege quickly and unexpectedly, and to retreat long before countervailing forces could be dispatched. Contemporaries of the period had not expected that tribal collectives lacking significant technical skill and resources would come to pose a serious threat difficult for established regimes to counter. Certainly it was not anticipated that the very characteristics that had contributed to nomadic tribes' technological inferiority would render them particularly well suited for new and superior forms of combat.[16]

The mounted raids that emerged in the northern steppe as early as 900 BC did not manifest in the Mongolian region until centuries later, as the barren landscape and frigid climate posed obstacles to its diffusion. Though the territories of modern-day China had long been plagued by frequent "barbarian" invasions, contemporary historical records indicate that nomadic cavalry skills did not constitute a chronic problem for the region until the fourth century BC.[17] Even then, these mounted invasions did not assume serious consequence until several regional nomadic groups coalesced into a loosely organized collective that came to be known as the Hsiung-nu around 210 BC.

The "barbarian" invasions that had posed a threat to China from its earliest history assumed new significance under the Hsiung-nu regime and prompted the introduction of heightened security measures by the region's newly centralized administration. The territories of modern-day China had long depended upon elaborate fortresses for their defense. In response to the cavalry incursions of the Hsiung-nu, Shih huang-ti, the first Ch'in emperor, resorted to the age-old exemplar of walled fortification writ large by ordering the construction of a protective wall 5,000 kilometers in length. The wall itself was not produced as an entirely new structure. Rather, it was the product of connecting the fortifications erected over time by the various regional regimes. The autonomous strongholds subsumed by the Great Wall were structurally diverse, as were the perceived threats that originally prompted their construction. This extensive barrier dividing Chinese civilization from the northern "barbarians" was, in effect, an attempt to consolidate the entire region into one vast fortress as traditionally construed.

The construction and administration of the Great Wall contributed to a comprehensive regional strategy. In addition to protecting territories from invasion by the mounted forces of the Hsiung-nu and other tribes, the structure was intended to enhance centralized oversight of travel and commerce. In conjunction with the construction enterprise, Emperor Shih huang-ti also ordered the elimination of walled fortifications that divided the territory's states, on the premise that they impeded internal travel and central administration. These efforts required the commitment of enormous resources and the institution of repressive measures.

Despite sustained efforts to maintain and reinforce the Great Wall over several centuries, it failed to provide ample defense against the mounted raids of northern tribes. Hsiung-nu invasions continued and intensified. The onset of the period referred to as the era of "barbarian" invasions (c. 304–589) is often attributed to the leadership of a Hsiung-nu invader named Liu Yuan. Liu Yuan eventually conquered the Chinese region and proclaimed himself emperor of a new Han dynasty. Ultimately, the traditional Chinese system of defense that was characterized by erecting ever-grander walled fortifications proved an inadequate countermeasure to the new form of security threat embodied by mounted invasions.

Though the more tempting comparison might be that of the nomadic tribes with present-day terrorist organizations, the more substantive is likely the correlation between information technology and the horses the ancient invaders rode in on. Both IT and mounted warfare have, in different eras, introduced new security concerns that enabled parties with relatively low access to resources and technical expertise to exert unprecedented levels of influence and engage directly with dominant military powers. Both have undermined the effectiveness of long-standing approaches to defense. Both have represented new forms of warfare difficult to comprehend using the lexicon and conceptual frameworks of contemporary security constructs.

CONCLUSION

The consequences and potential manifestations of cyber-aggression remain vaguely articulated and poorly understood. They tend to be described and analyzed according to terms of reference associated with asymmetric warfare. While this tendency to classify and subclassify security threats into discrete categories may be appropriate when assessing certain diversified security environments, it masks the complexity and overlap that characterize IT's security implications. If we continue to discuss information technology's involvement with security issues in binary terms, we cannot hope to design and implement an administrative structure capable of monitoring, preempting, and responding to acts of cyber-aggression.

The contours of the Department of Homeland Security as currently envisioned provide a perfect example of the ways in which misunderstanding the nature of a problem can result in a poorly conceived countermeasure. The DHS as currently conceived fails in two fundamental respects. Suggested cyber-security measures reveal inadequate analysis of the threats associated with information technology, while proposals to "apply twenty-first-century technology" to the realization of security objectives belie a limited awareness of the scope and potential organizational relevance of current IT capabilities.

The failure of attempts to apply existing conceptual frameworks to the assessment of cyber-aggression is readily apparent. Though DHS proposals claim that the security implications of information technology are a primary concern, IT initiatives represent only 2% of the total expenditure requested for the implementation of FY 2003 homeland defense measures. The cyber-security strategy is characterized largely by the devolution of critical infrastructure protection to private-sector owners and administrators and focuses almost exclusively on protective measures in the form of enhanced security software, incident reporting, and information sharing. The government proposes to assume only a limited role in facilitating these defensive efforts. There is no articulation of proactive measures to detect, interrupt, or retaliate against cyber-aggression. In effect, the inability to discern the subtle nuances of cyber-threats has prevented the development of detailed and proactive strategic imperatives.

Claims that the DHS will enhance the application of advanced technologies to homeland defense are equally hollow. In the age of distributed computing, it is not necessary to consolidate or centrally administer agencies in order to coordinate activities among them. Nor does situating agencies in a common bureaucracy guarantee increased collaboration between them. In fact, the consolidation of existing agencies with homeland security roles poses significant risks. Subsuming all homeland security efforts into a single and seamless operating environment eliminates natural diversity from America's homeland security infrastructure, thus rendering it more vulnerable to cyber-aggression. If all primary homeland defense efforts are administered under the auspices of a single organization, one successful attack—cyber or otherwise—could compromise the entire infrastructure. Centralization also implies conformity to commonly held procedures and priorities, which may inhibit optimal operating efficiency. For example, the Federal Emergency Management Agency's (FEMA) responsibilities are associated with intense surge requirements that may not be suited for implementation alongside more administratively oriented divisions the activities of which are not dictated by the unpredictable necessities of crisis management.

Furthermore, and perhaps most ironically, is the proposed creation of a bureaucratic institution that galvanizes the collective administration of disparate organizations when all parties acknowledge the inherently evolutionary nature of present-day homeland security threats. As terrorists shift their targets to capitalize upon perceived vulnerabilities, and as information technology continues to reshape the nature of society, organizations, and security threats, those institutions consolidated into the DHS today may be only tangentially associated with homeland defense efforts tomorrow. While the United States may, indeed, require a permanent agency to centrally coordinate homeland defense initiatives, its ability to establish and dissolve interactive and collaborative networks at will is fundamental to its ability to evolve alongside perpetually changing security threats. Unfortunately, the true potential of network technology to facilitate cooperative efforts among diverse organizations is not exploited by DHS proposals. The primary technological initiative advanced involves the enhancement of information sharing as a function of reconfigured database designs. Hardly a recently emergent twenty-first-century technique, database technology is situated squarely within the parameters of long-standing twentieth-century computer capabilities.

The unification of China's Great Wall shares many strategic characteristics with current DHS proposals. On a superficial level, both initiatives sought to consolidate disparate structures into a centrally administered superstructure and to eliminate barriers to internal activities, while enhancing oversight of travel and trade. More fundamentally, both represent efforts to respond to new and uncertain threats through the application of traditional, and largely ill-aligned, means. Rather than modifying existing strategic norms to accommodate emerging threats, the United States is resorting to long-standing bureaucratic principles in the hopes that establishing a department of sweeping scope and magnitude will compensate for its failure to address threats in a specific and targeted manner.

In her article titled "Applying 21st-Century Government to the Challenge of Homeland Security," Elaine Kamarck denounces the formulaic response characteristic of twentieth-century United States government—that is, the tendency to "identify a problem and create a bureaucracy with the same name"[18]—as contemporary security dilemmas are "immune to bureaucratic routines."[19] Like the Great Wall, the DHS represents a reversion to outdated security models ill-suited to the contemporary security landscape and unlikely to actualize articulated objectives. From this perspective, President Bush's comparison of the new department's establishment with President Truman's reorganization of the defense complex following World War II[20] assumes an unintended resonance. Indeed, current NHSA recommendations do seem more appropriately aligned with the security concerns that characterized the 1940s than with contemporary factors.

Perhaps as disappointing as the failure of DHS proposals to articulate and respond adequately to the security implications of cyber-aggression and to capitalize upon the organizational potential of advanced information technologies was the near absence of serious opposition to the department's creation. As the American Congress initiated debate on DHS legislation in late 2002, the most contentious factor pertained to the union rights and civil-service protections destined to be afforded to personnel employed by the new department. The creation of the organization itself was treated as a *fait accompli* in the absence of any substantive Congressional effort to question the appropriateness of a centralized superstructure for the administration of homeland security. It is ironic that, in a debate rife with examples of overclassification and the perpetuation of didactic conceptual models, the most important distinction was overlooked—namely, the difference between advocating the enhancement of homeland security and endorsing a bureaucratic institution bearing the same name.

PART II

SURVEILLANCE AND SECURITY

4. TOWARD A THEORY OF BORDER CONTROL

MARTIN C. LIBICKI

As of September 10, 2001, the worst terrorist incident on American soil was the one perpetrated in Oklahoma City by a native son. The next day, three thousand people were killed in the United States by nineteen foreigners. Although no one can guarantee that the next large-scale attack on America will originate overseas, many policy responses to the tragedy presume that improvements in the ability to stop bad people and dangerous things at the border will improve U.S. safety.

Exactly how the borders are to be secured is another question. Can bad people be kept out of the country? In theory, if we (1) knew who the bad people were before they came over the border, and (2) detected them attempting to cross the border, and (3) could distinguish them (e.g., by name) for who they are, then they could be apprehended. In practice, (1) we often do not know who such people are until after they are inside the country (or worse, have committed their crimes), (2) hundreds of thousands of people cross surreptitiously into the United States every year, and (3) the identities that people present are not always the same as the identities by which they are known. The first is a problem of intelligence; the second, a problem of surveillance; and the third a problem of identity.

Of the three, it may be possible to make the greatest progress on identity. The U.S. government may not know who people truly are; many terrorists hail from regions with inadequate or indifferent record-keeping. Yet, with modern biometrics (e.g., fingerprints, iris scans, DNA), it is possible to at least freeze someone's identity from a specific point (e.g., someone's first official interaction with the U.S. government) forward. Thereafter all interactions that call for people to present identity documents can be correlated with a single specific individual. However, once potential national security threats are in the United States, they become, in many important respects, indistinguishable from U.S. citizens, from whom hard proof of identity is rarely required.

A phrase that might describe the coupling of strict border controls with few if any internal controls—a crunchy outside over a chewy inside—is used frequently in dealing with information-systems security. People often put a great deal of time and attention into devising ways to keep bad packets out of their system—elaborate passwords, virus detectors, and firewalls. They typically pay far less attention to such internal measures as ensuring that users cannot accord themselves the same right to alter or erase files that administrators assume. Such systems are vulnerable to intruders who can think past or luck past a border control system and, once inside the system, cause all sorts of mischief simply by exploiting all the privileges that every normal user possesses or could easily acquire.

There are other fields that present the problems of allocating resources between border control and internal surveillance and not all of them necessarily point to excessive attention paid to the former at the expense of the latter. During the Vietnam War, for instance, U.S. forces were allocated between efforts to "search and destroy" enemy forces in the country, and those busy interdicting supplies coming down the Ho Chi Minh trail. Many hawkish critics of the war's prosecution maintained that the United States should have cut the trail by, in effect, extending the border between North and South Vietnam (i.e., Demilitarized Zone) a few hundred kilometers west to the Mekong River. The fear of compromising a technically uninvolved Laos prevented executing what, to many, would have been the superior strategy. In their minds greater efforts at border control should have substituted for internal control.

A similar phenomenon—a mismatch between border control and internal surveillance—may also characterize disease surveillance. Once a disease gets into the United States, high levels of health care coupled with a vigorous (if somewhat haphazard) medical informatics system raises the likelihood that it will be detected as such and doctors will be on the lookout for its recurrence. But compared to the trillion dollars plus that the United States spends internally, it expends comparatively little on monitoring the evolution of diseases where they come from—especially those that come from the tropics,[1] where health-care systems are deficient. There is also much less surveillance for infectious diseases at the ports of entry compared to one hundred years ago (although HIV-positive travelers can, legally, be turned back if detected).

The recurrence of the patterns in fields as diverse as immigration, cybersecurity, military conflict, and disease control suggests a role for analogy between and generalization across such domains. Analogy is often a way to start thinking about entirely new topics. After the eleventh of September, the problem of homeland defense suddenly loomed large. U.S. policy makers lacked a good theoretical foundation for how to think about it. If there are valuable lessons to be learned from more long-pondered domains such as computer security, defense, or public health, they ought to be brought forward. Furthermore, phenomena that repeat themselves throughout many separate domains may very well reflect what they have in common—the complex interaction between border control and internal surveillance. That might help explain why certain characteristics appear;

one would look at systemic characteristics of war, disease, etc., rather than other characteristics (e.g., that war is violent and is policy by other means, or that diseases have a specific etiology). Furthermore, should another such topic arise in the future, one would have an initial kit bag of potential characteristics and rules from which to draw.

The remainder of this chapter will attempt to tease out some systemic generalizations about the relationship between border control and internal surveillance through a several-part discussion:

- A generalized model of border control and some issues that ought to be asked across domains.
- A quick sketch of the human immune system as an example of how Mother Nature deals with such issues.
- Brief surveys of the four fields—immigration, cyber-security, warfare, and disease—in which concepts of border control play a role.

GENERAL CHARACTERISTICS OF BORDER CONTROL

Border-control issues can be considered both normatively and positively. Normatively, the basic issues for those who would control borders come down to (1) how much and (2) how to. Positively, they also entail consideration of why nations, enterprises, and other entities choose to defend borders with the degree of effort and the processes they choose to exert. The two perspectives are related. Seen from the outside, an entity is free to select an optimal border-control policy. Those charged with border controls, however, are not free to focus on policy performance alone. They must weigh how well their strategy works against the constraints put on it by policy-making; both the former and the latter are measured in political terms.

Start with some basic tenets.

One, border control can be modeled as a contest between attackers and a defender.

The attackers seek to get inside the defender's terrain, howsoever defined. Once they get there, they are better able to do mischief (e.g., terrorism, erasing files, destroying friendly military assets, making people sick). Mischief, however (or at least serious mischief), is not necessarily inevitable at that point—otherwise there would be no point to internal defense. Conversely, were there high enough confidence in the ability to stop mischief through internal methods (preferably costless ones), there would be little or no incentive for border control. Because an optimal strategy is likely to include elements of each, trade-offs, synergies, and tensions among the two are potentially important.

A good going-in assumption is to posit defenders as constrained by institutional factors while attackers are free to develop optimal strategies. Why? First, as just noted, defenders are generally not free to pursue an optimal strategy, for reasons discussed below; they must work within constraints, although these constraints need not be absolute. Second, while the attackers can afford to be single-minded about their conflict (after all, attackers in many domains are self-selected), defenders have no such luxury. They must not only fend off attacks but keep themselves functioning as best they can in all other respects. It may appear to be a cliché to aver that if terrorists disrupt our way of life, they win, but the idea has a certain validity nonetheless. Defense must not only be achieved but be achieved at reasonable cost. Third, as an empirical matter, defenders tend to be larger and more established; attackers smaller and more opportunistic. This is certainly true when the arena is terrorism and computer hacking. It also holds—at least in some respects—for conventional conflict when the United States is one side. Fourth, as a related matter, since the presumptive advantage is with the defender, evolution may favor the emergence of attackers with more optimal strategies. Defenders will go on and on until overwhelmed. They will or will not learn to improve depending on who they are and how they work. Attackers that fail may well be eliminated (or fail to recruit new partisans) and others, putatively more likely to succeed, often take their place. Attackers are expected to seek out an optimal strategy from the vantage point of getting in and wreaking mischief. The defender is looking for a tenable strategy that balances various considerations and works within bureaucratic constraints while maximizing defense at some minimum cost.

Two, border control is largely about information, specifically what helps distinguish the anodyne from the unwanted.

Information—its acquisition, evaluation, and control—matters because the defender usually has the overwhelming preponderance of force in most circumstances (and where this assumption is not true, notably in conventional defense, information about the nature, timing, and location of attack can be decisive). Thus, in theory, once the threat has been identified as such, its disposition is often a matter of time, and not much time at that. In practice, outcomes vary. Terrorists, once detected, can be apprehended and brought to justice (whether justice is done, depends, of course, on the quality of the information behind the apprehension). National security threats, or alternatively those ill with communicable diseases, can be turned away at the borders. Computer hackers, once detected, can be locked out, but cleanup of their effects (e.g., leave-behind programs that can cause later mischief) may not be so easy. Similarly, the ability to detect the outbreak of a disease should sensitize medical professionals to scrutinize in a new light others who present similar symptoms; but this is no guarantee that a contagion can be contained. With modern military weapons, a target detected is one destroyed; however, many of the strategies employed on front lines count on attackers being able to overwhelm defenders in a specific zone. Still, as a general rule, information superiority, so to speak, puts one more than halfway on the road to an effective defense.

The very notion of border control presupposes some ability to distinguish what can pass the border from what cannot. As already suggested, this requires the ability to (1) detect attempted passage, (2) determine criteria that best distinguish what is bad from what is normal, and (3) identify entries so characterized as opposed to innocent ones. The latter two are redolent of the self/nonself distinction. Detection has modalities: good from bad; bad from background; and normal from abnormal. Not every modality can be applied universally.

Three, border control has a very important relationship to wide-area surveillance.

The former requires the inspection and evaluation of people, things, packets, etc., that cross a particular boundary line.[2] The latter is the continuous or at least episodic inspection of people, things, packets—or states—on either side of the boundary line.

In some cases, such as immigration control or protection in cyberspace, the primary competitor to border control is *internal* wide-area surveillance. In other cases, such as conventional defense, the primary competitor is *external* wide-area surveillance. In yet other cases, such as guerrilla warfare, the hunt for weapons of mass destruction (WMD) or disease surveillance, both internal and external wide-area surveillance may be called for. Including external actions puts the usefulness of the self/nonself distinction in doubt and replaces it with something more like a good/bad notion. That which is actionably bad should be eliminated, regardless of where it is.

There are several reasons to concentrate more on internal rather than external wide-area surveillance. Some forms of bad are bad only in context—the right stuff in the wrong place. Take immigration policy. Those who apply for tourist visas to come to the United States are often rejected on the grounds that such so-called tourists are coming to disappear into the economy and find work: understandable, and even laudable on a personal basis, but not necessarily always in the best interest of the United States. Visa processes are meant to screen these people out, and the INS can later apprehend people who overstay their welcome.

But the United States has neither reason nor right to take action against them overseas. Similarly, someone attempting to log into a computer system in which they have no privileges may enjoy privileges on other systems that one has little right to enjoin them from. The other reason to focus on internal surveillance is scope. The rest of the world is large, and the resources that one can bring to bear externally are not always proportionate. It is difficult (but not impossible) to imagine a computer system launching search-and-destroy missions on the Internet in search of computer viruses. A human body cannot do active external surveillance against any pathogens outside it. In the classic World War II movies, the enemy within was distinguished by having a deficient knowledge of baseball; that rendered them dubious, and, if found inside an army facility, suspicious as well. But, outside the typical World War II army base, the world is full of such foreigners, and it is not their fault if they are ignorant of America's erstwhile national pastime.

As a policy, vigorous border control has pluses and minuses when compared to internal surveillance. Broadly put, most objects spend far more time subject to wide-area surveillance than to border surveillance. To use a simple geometry metaphor: borders are lines and thus one-dimensional (or zero-dimensional, if reduced to a finite number of legal entry points); everything else is an area and thus two-dimensional and therefore far larger. Empirically, the number of border crossings is generally fewer than the total number of interactions. As long as everything that would get inside a system must present itself at the border, success at border control eliminates at least one class of threat. Another big plus, albeit a political plus rather than an operational one, is that the percentage of those people (things, messages) appearing at the border that belong to one's constituency is almost always lower than the percentage of those people (things, messages) that circulate internally. The big minuses are that border control is a one-shot (or at least a few-shot) deal, while internal surveillance can be repeated continuously. Finally, in many cases the actual threat is to internal targets. An unfolding operation (e.g., someone approaching a building in an overloaded van, files undergoing unexpected alternations), if spotted as an imminent threat, is a matter of internal rather than border operations. From another perspective, this is an *attraction* of border control—people are caught at a point when they are farther from being in a position to do mischief.

The competition between border control and internal wide-area surveillance should not imply an either/or choice. Resources for the two need not compete for the same pot. To put this in economic terms, it is not obvious that the marginal utility of additional border control declines as more resources are put into wide-area surveillance, and vice versa. They may be synergistic. Systems that are established to help wide-area surveillance (e.g., digital signatures to authenticate internal messages in an enterprise's system) may contribute to border control (i.e., meting out access). Hazards or faults detected thanks to an energetic border-control process, may, in turn, energize wide-area surveillance. That said, a *perfect and costless* border-control system may remove all motivation for wide-area surveillance.

As a final link between the two, certain methods of wide-area surveillance, especially for internal uses, may look like nothing so much as the elaboration of border-control techniques. Simply put, internal compartmentalization—the division of a space into zones through which passage is monitored—can be an effective means of wide-area surveillance. Thus, internal firewalls (or, alternatively, need-to-know restrictions) can and do bolster external firewalls (or personnel vetting) in protecting information. Many third-world countries monitor travel between regional zones almost as intensively as travel over the border. Techniques that record who is taking international flights can be, with little elaboration, applied to domestic flights. The division of a war zone into separately guarded districts was one of the methods used by the British to combat opponents in the Boer wars.

Four, border-control decisions are ineluctably political—almost psychopolitical—ones.

The attractions of border control are nestled deep within the human psyche; its exercise can emphasize the role that maintaining distinctions plays in the life of the nation or institution. They separate "us" from "them." We are treated benignly as members of the community in whose fate we care collectively. What happens to "them" is much less our concern; if they approach our borders, we are under no obligations to treat them well. Statistically speaking, most of those inside the borders at any one time are "us"; those on the border are, on broad average, "us" only half the time. Any policy option that burdens those who cross borders is far less likely to irritate one of "us" than a policy option that places its burdens internally. Border control can be used to put distance between us and problems sited abroad and thereby weaken any broader responsibility to deal with them or their root causes. It cannot happen here; if they do, it is because we have failed to guard the border well enough. That such claims are largely illusory does not keep them from being comfortable or even occasionally validated by evidence.

Those responsible for protecting the borders are not always the same as those charged with wide-area surveillance. Officials of the Immigration and Naturalization Service and the U.S. Customs Service protect the U.S. border. The INS has but a modest, and oft-contested, role inside the United States; the Customs Service has even less. Law enforcement (e.g., internal surveillance) is the province of state and local police. The FBI handles internal and external surveillance at the federal level. Although armies can do wide-area surveillance, and strike and air forces can protect borders through close-air support, in practice, the very concept of a "front line" is a very army-oriented one while air forces (or at least the U.S. Air Force) are free to range wherever they are needed. In disease monitoring, border control is almost always a function of the public health service; here, private doctors see and evaluate patients. Even if the collection of health statistics (a form of wide-area surveillance) is largely a public function, it relies on public-private cooperation for the most part.

By contrast, differentiations between internal and border roles are largely absent in cyber-defense; both are the province of systems administrators, and the major security-products companies tend to offer a full suite of solutions from intrusion detection to virus detection and firewalls. Where border control and wide-area surveillance are products of competing bureaucracies, one can guarantee that arguments on which to employ when will be colored by bureaucratic considerations.

SKETCHES OF SPECIFIC BORDER-CONTROL ARENAS

What follows is a sketch of the main issues in each of four primary domains—border control (with a brief addendum on some aspects of keeping WMD out of the United States and terrorists out of Israel), cyberspace, war, and disease. A brief portrayal of the human immune system is used as a prologue to illustrate some of the ways Mother Nature has approached the problem of balancing border control and internal surveillance.

The Human Immune System

The self/nonself distinction noted above comes from the world of human (more accurately, mammalian) immunology. Humans actually have two immune systems: innate and acquired. The innate immune system, combined with a variety of barrier systems (e.g., skin), constitutes the equivalent of border control. The acquired immune system, for its part, is more analogous to internal surveillance.

The body's three primary barriers to the entry of pathogens are the skin, the lungs, and the stomach. The skin, if unbroken, can stop proteins large enough to be capable of carrying DNA. The lungs—which must take in air to function correctly—protect the body from the ingestion of harmful particles through a combination of cilias, mucus membranes, and coughing reactions. The stomach—which must also take in material—protects the body by subjecting all inputs to an acid bath, which reduces complex proteins to those too small to carry disease. Should something break the skin, local platelets in the bloodstream rupture and excite the immune system to create a chemical gradient that, in turn, attracts polymorphonuclear cells to the area. Such cells release hydrolytic enzymes, peroxides, and superoxide radicals to the affected area, increasing its toxicity to all life-forms (that is, all complex proteins outside existing cells). The innate immune system, broadly speaking, responds to events and does not specifically differentiate between self and nonself.

The acquired immune system runs on entirely different principles. It is a continuous surveillance system that, in effect, examines every protein presented to it (either by their being presented by dendritic cells or by major histocompatibility cells). So presented, random proteins interact with immune cells, each of which is created to recognize a specific protein (think of this protein as a surficial feature of a virus or bacteria). The act of recognition by an immune cell, to oversimplify, leads to its replication, thereby creating a larger population of immune cells specific to and capable of attacking that protein. This also increases the rate of specific surveillance. The method by which the acquired immune system keeps itself from attacking the body's own proteins is one of Mother Nature's neatest tricks. Embryos make immune cells designed to attack almost every conceivable protein shape. Successful matching encounters between immune cells and proteins *in the fetus* tend to be fatal to the immune cell. After enough such encounters, the only immune cells that remain are those which would attack proteins that are *not* present in the fetus and therefore unlikely to be present in humans once born.

How should the human immune system be assessed? True, humans have survived until now in the face of every conceivable manner of vermin; as such, the system has prevented cataclysmic failure to the human race. Yet, prior to modern medicine, half of all babies commonly died of one or another disease before reaching adulthood.

The innate and the acquired immune systems appear to be loosely coupled. There is little evidence that they compete with each other for resources. What keeps either from having evolved to more powerful states is that overstimulating an immune system is often worse for human health. Allergic reactions, anaphylactic shock, and fever are a few of the ways that immune systems may put lives at risk. The cooperation between the innate and acquired immune subsystems is indirect. The closest known mechanism is that the death of cells releases chemicals into the bloodstream that prompt dendrites to present more proteins to the immune system. One might say, therefore, that signs of border conflict (although it can be conflict anywhere) play a role in revving up the acquired immune system.

In fairness, there is no mechanism within the immune system for transmitting anything but small volumes of information from one cell to the next. Immune responses must rely on a robust but largely preconstructed set of responses called up as needed. This stands in contrast to human defense systems in which many more orders of magnitude of detailed information can be sent (but which leaves the problems of deception, doubt, and deluge of information).

National Borders and Terrorism

Before September 11, the primary problem of U.S. border control was to limit the number of illegal immigrants by requiring that foreign nationals (Canadians largely excepted) be properly documented and enter through regular borders. Technically, the goal was that there be no illegal immigrants. In practice, with the southwestern border being porous, illegal immigration being a crime without a specific victim, and immigration having many benefits, the real goal of enforcement was to keep illegal immigration from getting out of hand. As of September 11, the focus has shifted toward keeping a small number of very bad (but not necessarily obviously identifiable) people out of the country. As argued below, the two goals are synergistic in the sense that tighter controls and more reliable documentation contribute to both of them. But they are not identical.

Keeping bad guys out entails a three-point match: X is a bad guy, Y is at the border (that is, in a position to be inspected), and X = Y.[3] Border control rests on the premise that it is expected and desired for foreigners to come to the country—but not just any foreigner. In preventing the influx of terrorists, the primary distinction is between good and bad. A secondary distinction, at least in theory, is between normal and abnormal. One could imagine a data-mining system that can take the names of everyone coming across the border, look for who might know whom, and detect any abnormal activity (e.g., the simultaneous influx of people in the same line of business crossing at multiple points). This is far easier said than done; statistically speaking, there is always abnormal activity, only a very small fraction of which is harmful. Characterizing harmful abnormality is difficult; detecting it thereafter may be less so. Once people are inside the country, however, the mechanisms that force them to establish a valid identity are only as strong as the nation's citizens will put up with. In the United States, where the activities of honest people are tracked closely, at least by private companies (e.g., through credit card transactions), there are many ways of hiding identity provided one can avoid being arrested and fingerprinted.

Immigration control is helped by the fact that all but a few percentage points of visitors present themselves to inspectors at ports of entry. Although an even higher percentage of cargo (drugs aside) is available for inspection, it is difficult to know what is in a cargo container without opening it up. Only three percent of all containers coming into the United States are so examined. Raising that percentage significantly would not only require hiring more customs inspectors but it would also constitute an implicit tax on all foreign trade. The current approach to keeping really dangerous objects, such as nuclear weapons, outside the country relies on a combination of better intelligence, the development of indicators that suggest that a particular container warrants inspection, and, conversely, a list of trusted shippers whose containers are assumed benign. Detecting a nuclear weapon, once it is inside the country, requires alternative methods such as detecting particular levels or types of radiation. The latter search is helped a little bit by the assumption that those fortunate enough to possess a nuclear weapon are likely to use it in some internationally recognizable downtown area rather than in some cornfield. Unfortunately there are little grounds for hope that either border control or wide-area surveillance will detect a loose nuclear weapon.

Israel's method of protecting itself against suicide bombers combines (of late) aggressive military action against suspected radical ringleaders, attempts to prevent illegal entry from the West Bank into Israel proper (similar to what the U.S. Border Patrol is charged with), the scrutiny of those who have to go through checkpoints, and a citizenry that is highly vigilant against suspicious behavior. Success, though, has been elusive. Although Israeli officials do not have the qualms about profiling that U.S. officials have, very few of the suicide bombers have histories that would have raised warning flags (many were sent into action within a few days of having volunteered). What Israel has only just started to develop is a physical barrier between Israel proper and the West Bank. Such a barrier could cut down on surreptitious entry, but it would also be an admission in concrete that there are borders between Israel and non-Israel in the West Bank, and thus it would abandon even a notional claim to the whole area between the Jordan River and the Mediterranean Sea. It would also denote the land claims that Israel would be willing to make in a peace settlement, and, by contrast, those it would concede up front. For these political reasons, it arrived late on the scene.

Borders of Cyberspace

The challenge in cyberspace is to prevent three basic bad events: damage to the proper functioning of the computer system, corruption or destruction of contained information, and leakage of sensitive information. Mischief in cyberspace can be divided into those perpetrated directly (i.e., by hackers) and indirectly (e.g., worms—although distributing bad code in general may, in theory, be a tool that softens sites to be hit).

The standard rule of thumb is that over two-thirds of all hacker attacks come from insiders—a good statistic to keep in mind when devising border controls in cyberspace. Nevertheless, the popular attention is focused on the outsider hacker, and not without cause. The very size of the Internet has multiplied the number of potential attackers as well as the potential reach of any of them. Oft-posited cyber-attacks by nations or well-organized terrorist groups are, by definition, from outsiders. The statistics that say that outside attacks are overstressed (at least compared to insider attacks) do not assuage those who believe that mere lack of precedent is proof against worry. The upper range of what an outside attack can do to the national information infrastructure is likely to exceed the upper range of what an insider attack can do to it. Besides, protection against outsiders that lack authorized privileges or many entry points is more straightforward than protection against insiders, who, collectively, have a bewilderingly large array of authorized privileges and entry points. Insider defense inevitably means discomfiting those one might have to face the next day.

By contrast, almost all malevolent code is an outside attack (albeit perpetrated because insiders are often feckless about these matters).

In protecting cyberspace, all four modalities come into play in the form of firewalls, virus detectors, and intrusion detectors. The classic border-control problem is to distinguish legitimate users (and user-initiated processes) from the rest. Internally, this problem is echoed by the often greater difficulty of distinguishing among various classes of users (e.g., those who may access certain files but not other files) from each other, and differentiating everyday users from superusers such as system administrators. The good/bad distinction is often used to distinguish viruses and worms from (rarely) legitimately exchanged executable files and (more often) code that masquerades as nonexecutables (e.g., data files, pictures). Most antivirus software works by distinguishing specific features of files (programs that call certain low-level routines are suspicious; files with certain extensions are stripped from e-mails), and looking for files that have the signatures of known troublemakers. The last two distinctions, bad-versus-background and normal-versus-abnormal, are applied largely internally and depend on being able to distinguish activity that in small doses should not cause alarm and activity whose volume, timing, or other characteristics suggest mischief is going on. To do so, intrusion-detection systems, still in their infancy, rely on comparing activity patterns to a repertoire of known patterns of harmful activity.

Front Lines

The military equivalent of the controlled border is the front line. Behind it is everything that one wants to and has a reasonable hope of defending. In front of it is the rest of the world, including enemies. An important issue in defense and operations planning is whether one should allocate resources to combat units and systems that can kill a daunting percentage of enemy units as they attempt to breach front lines (be they stationary or moving forward) as opposed to units and systems capable of reducing enemy units and systems back from the front lines (or, in the case of guerrilla warfare, inside the front lines).

Until the late nineteenth century, it was generally infeasible to protect countries by putting them behind front lines. The size of any fighter's near-certain killing radius multiplied by the number of fighters (plus adequate backup) was too small in comparison to what had to be protected (city walls being the primary exception to this rule). The best one could do was erect barriers and hope that attempting to surmount them would put attackers at a great disadvantage. Accurate rifles coupled with trenches created the possibility of extended defense lines; they appeared in the late years of the American Civil War. Fifty years later, both France and Germany had sufficient manpower and weaponry to make long trench lines mutually impenetrable, and so true border defense was possible. Not so coincidentally, airpower was invented to get around the problem.

This dichotomy between border defense and wide-area surveillance (and strike) echoes in today's army–versus–air force debates. Air forces cannot defend (except from other air forces), at least not directly; they can reduce enemy assets, and the U.S. Air Force can do so over long periods of time against most potential enemies without great losses to themselves. Armies can defend, but they do so at higher cost, and they can be, at least in theory, overwhelmed at specific points if the enemy is willing to pay a sufficiently high price.

Conventional warfare also uses a mix of modalities in making distinctions necessary for border control and surveillance alike. The quest for a perfect self/nonself distinction is reified in IFF (identify-friend-or-foe) systems of increasing sophistication, accuracy, and responsiveness. Spies and saboteurs in one's midst present a more subtle and difficult problem, especially when dealing with allies (a proxy version of self). Many a South Vietnamese officer during the war was, in fact, a Viet Cong. The good/bad distinction is another important one, whether the conflict is within the borders (e.g., which are the peasants and which are the part-time guerrillas) or beyond them (e.g., which trucks constitute the peasant convoys and which constitute troop supply movements). Similarly, the bad/background distinction is part and parcel of all high-intensity combat; a good example was the ability of U.S. combat pilots to distinguish Iraqi tanks from the sandy background at dusk by virtue of the former's heat retention and the latter's rapid cooling. By contrast, tank plinking in Kosovo was complicated by the fact that tanks hunkered down in villages or woods are not easy to distinguish from the background from 18,000 feet up. Finally, the normal/abnormal distinction is a difficult one to make without a fairly deep knowledge of the local norms and customs, the learning of which is not a high priority within the U.S. military, at least in peacetime.

Many of these distinctions become easier for those who can mandate that no movement take place in a certain zone (e.g., no-fly zones, no-man's-land). More to the point, borders of any sort and the démarches to movement they permit eliminate many of the ambiguities of combat. They thereby reduce the need for information superiority compared to more traditional metrics of military power such as firepower and range.

Disease Surveillance

Today's challenge to disease surveillance as border control comes from the threats of communicable diseases and bioterrorism (some but not all forms of which involve communicable diseases). Far less relevant are diseases of genetic origin, environmental origin, waterborne diseases (at least for the United States, thanks to sanitation levels here), and diseases borne by creatures not prevalent in temperate climates (although global warming may change some particulars). The techniques for suppressing bioterrorism that employs noncommunicable diseases (e.g., anthrax) are akin to those applicable to chemical, radiological, or, in some cases, nuclear terrorism. So the focus, here, is on communicable diseases.

A generation ago such diseases were a nonissue. Some doctors confidently predicted the end of *all* communicable disease. Since then, the rise of drug-resistant disease strains, the discovery of retroviruses (notably HIV), the acceleration of contact between the United States and the tropics, global warming, and the threat of bioterrorism have reintroduced the threat of communicable diseases.

The general approach to reducing communicable diseases entails the detection, treatment, and/or quarantine of those who have them. A hundred years ago, carriers of tuberculosis were barred from immigration (until their disease was no longer communicable). In theory, procedures exist to quarantine localities or regions where serious communicable diseases (e.g., smallpox) are detected—but once polio was eradicated, quarantines became an increasingly notional topic. In the meantime, the rate and speed of travel have increased tremendously, forcing attention away from movement-based control strategies and toward those that rely more heavily on treatment. Politics are also involved in disease-motivated border control. An active Western-funded program to scour the third world for communicable diseases may be rejected by countries who fear that at best such efforts will lead to their countries being placed in isolation (e.g., China's late response to SARS); treatment and amelioration have to be part of the package to elicit cooperation.

The ability to discern disease outbreaks must make do with a mix of good/bad and normal/abnormal distinctions. People are discernibly sick or not; their symptoms present clearly or they do not. Unfortunately for public health, people's disease states are hard to monitor casually; people must either present themselves to health officials or, collectively, exhibit out-of-norm behavior (e.g., while no one purchase of over-the-counter antidiarrhea medicines is remarkable, unusually high demand can indicate an attack of cryptosporidium). In theory, everyone coming across the border could be a candidate for presentation; in practice, this is confounded by the expectations of travelers to get through immigration and customs swiftly and without hassle.

SUMMARY

The following chart is a quick sketch of which distinctions matter to which forms of border control. The chart is necessarily suggestive, illustrating, as it does, both the parallels among these forms as well as some of their different features.

Border control remains beset with questions. More emphasis may be put on it than is cost effective, if only because the we-versus-they model is so psychologically and thus politically compelling. Border control is rarely sufficient by itself, but it cannot be ignored altogether either, and while a policy that leans on border control may be unsatisfactory, the politics that support it suggest that it cannot be dispensed with as long as people are people.

	Self v. Nonself	Good v. Bad	Background v. Bad	Normal v. Abnormal
Terrorists (U.S. perspective)	N/A	Exercised at border; not well exercised internally	N/A	Nascent data-mining attempts
Keeping WMD Out	N/A	Through border inspection, potentially through sensors internally	N/A	Nascent data-mining attempts
Suicide Bombers (Israeli perspective)	Palestinians are considered nonself.	Attempts to catch known terrorists at checkpoints	N/A	N/A
Cyberspace	Relevant to log-in and access privileges; assumes few outsiders have privileges	Hard to do by characteristic; firewalls more likely apply to categories of inputs	Hard to do; cyberspace is a noisy environment	Intrusion-detection systems are internal
Defense	Aspect of internal security	Discrimination required for external operations	Similar to good/bad; logic applies to no-go zones	Requires understanding of local environment
Disease Surveillance	N/A	Requires presentation of patient; hard to do at border	N/A	Better theory to support data mining

5. THE TRANSFORMATION OF GLOBAL SURVEILLANCE

SUSAN LANDAU

INTRODUCTION

On December 7, 1941, the information was present before the event—the meaning of the transmission from Tokyo to the Japanese embassy in Washington saying "Will the Ambassador please submit to the United States government (if possible to the Secretary of State) our reply to the United States at 1:00 pm on the 7th, your time"[1,2]—but this information was not conveyed quickly enough to prevent Pearl Harbor. On September 11, 2001, the disparate bits of information were also all present before the event, but in separate places, and were not put together until afterward.[3] In both cases, electronic surveillance picked up crucial data; in both cases, this data was not acted upon early enough to prevent the attack. But the similarities end there. In Pearl Harbor, U.S. intelligence was targeting a known quantity—the Japanese government—using a known communications system—telex—with an already-broken encryption system. Although on September 11, the United States was targeting a known quantity—Osama bin Laden—his location, methods of communication, and encryption techniques were undeciphered.

In the half-century since Pearl Harbor, global surveillance has undergone several major transformations. During the first thirty years after the Second World War, the decryption agencies were largely hidden from public view; now information on surveillance is considerably more subject to public scrutiny. New forms of communication media mean there are vastly more communications intelligence available for surveillance. The technological changes of the last several decades—exponential increases in speed and similar decreases in the cost of storage, and vastly improved search engines—have greatly increased the government's ability to conduct surveillance even while tools for preserving confidentiality of communications and even preventing traffic analysis (these include Mixmaster,[4] Anonymizer,[5] and Onion Routing[6]) have entered the public domain. The end of the Cold War has changed the global equation, with the current threat to the United States, Western Europe, and industrialized Asia being a stateless entity. This poses a more complex challenge than the Axis states did during World War II.

In this chapter we survey the development of U.S. global surveillance post the Second World War, concentrating on developments over the last twenty years. We briefly discuss legal restraints on surveillance, and consider the U.S. perspective in a global context. We will touch on the "crypto wars," and how they have been affected by ECHELON, the United Kingdom–United States global surveillance effort. Finally we discuss how global surveillance plays out in a post–September 11 world. We begin with a brief discussion of the technologies involved.

THE TECHNOLOGY OF SURVEILLANCE

Surveillance takes many forms. The most straightforward to conduct, and the one practiced by many not usually viewed as being in the intelligence business, is "open-source intelligence," gathering data from public sources—newspapers, radio, television, the Internet, government documents archived in so-called "government depository" libraries (typically university libraries), even public phone books (public white pages were not generally available in the Soviet Union). The World Wide Web has vastly increased the availability of such open-source material. Post September 11, the U.S. government has adopted a policy of restricting availability of what it terms "sensitive but unclassified" information, most particularly technical material, including some that was declassified as much as forty years ago.[7]

"Operations intelligence" is intelligence gathered through observation of the opponent's actions, and through deduction. September 11 would have to be viewed as a major failure of the FBI and the CIA in their operations intelligence effort. "Human intelligence," which ranges from planting spies deep within a network to interviewing travelers, is probably the oldest form of intelligence. It has the ability to glean information unobtainable in other ways. For example, for twenty years a CIA operative, Chang Hsein-yi, worked in Taiwan's secret nuclear program and was a CIA spy. In the 1970s Chang worked in Taiwan's secret weapons program. At a crucial point in the eighties, Chang stole information on Taiwan's nuclear bomb efforts and gave the data to the United States, which then pressured Taiwan to abandon the nuclear work.[8] As the Taiwanese nuclear-weapons information was tightly held within a single agency, it is highly unlikely that the information could have been obtained by the United States through techniques other than human intelligence.

Human intelligence is expensive, and it is a resource that can quickly become outdated as the world situation changes. For example, when the Cold War ended, operatives working in the USSR found that their expertise did not easily translate to the next hot spot, the Middle East. "Photographic intelligence," the collection of intelligence typically gathered by high-flying planes or satellites, has resulted in some of the most important intelligence successes of the last half-century, including the discovery of Cuban missile sites and the mapping out of targets during the Gulf War. Often the photograph is not so important as the difference between it and a picture of the same site at a different time. Then one can see where bunkers may have been built or where mass graves might be (such information was uncovered by camera-equipped drones during the Bosnian war). "Signals intelligence" is the analysis of the target's communications signals. It is this type of surveillance that is typically meant by the term "global surveillance." Signals intelligence includes "communications intelligence," which is the extraction of information from the target's communications and electronic intelligence, and the analysis on noncommunications electronic transmissions, including radar intelligence, telemetry intelligence, and emissions intelligence. Signals intelligence has four distinct parts: collection, processing, analysis, and dissemination.

Collection consists of finding, acquiring, and intercepting signals. As the type of communication has changed, so has the technique for interception. Early electronic communications—telegraphy, telephone, and telex—traveled by wire and were intercepted through wiretaps. (During the Civil War, General Jeb Stuart traveled with his own wiretapper.) The invention of radio gave military commanders an unparalleled opportunity to communicate at a distance, but this opportunity came at a cost: radio transmissions are easily intercepted. Hence the importance of cryptography (and cryptanalysis) during the Second World War, where high-frequency radio, whose signals travel thousands of miles—and onto opponents' territory—was the communication medium of choice.

By contrast, although microwave transmissions, which became common in the United States in the 1970s and 1980s, also travel through the air, they do not travel far—only tens of miles. Thus, unless the opponent can place receivers close to the towers, microwave transmissions are less subject to interception. The Soviets succeeded in doing so at their country "dacha" at Glen Cove, Long Island, within eavesdropping distance of microwave towers in Connecticut.[9]

Airborne interception through the use of specially equipped planes,[10] satellites, and strategically placed intercept facilities are all important collection mechanisms in modern communications intelligence. Satellites are the most interesting and ambitious forms of communications intercept. Long-distance microwave radio relays may use many intermediate stations to pass the signal along. Each station receives only a small part of the signal, the rest of which passes off into space and can be collected by an intercept satellite. This technology has been used since the 1960s. In 1965 the first Intelsat communications satellite was launched; the current generation can handle 22,000 simultaneous phone calls.

All this makes satellite communications interception most attractive. Low-altitude satellites move too quickly relative to the earth to be useful for interception. But high-altitude intercept satellites must carry huge antennas, as many as hundreds of feet across.[11] The problems are complex, but solvable. According to Duncan Campbell, the United States has significantly more advanced satellite interception capabilities than any other nation.[12] These forms of radio collection are all threatened by a new technical development—fiber optics. Optical fiber is the most efficient way of transmitting data, able to carry up to forty gigabits of data per second. This also makes it far cheaper than competing data-transmission schemes, so there is a worldwide shift to fiber. But fiber complicates surveillance; signals cannot easily be detected without damage to the cable, and physical taps into fiber-optic cables are easily detected. "It's over. Everywhere I went in the Third World, I wanted to have someone named Ahmed, a backhoe driver, on the payroll. And I wanted to know where the fiber-optic cable was hidden. In a crisis, I wanted Ahmed to go and break up the cable, and force them up in the air," said a retired senior CIA officer from the Directorate of Operations.[13] This effervescent hope is reminiscent of a statement made about the first military action of World War I. This claimed to be the cutting of an undersea cable, which forced the Germans to use radio for messages to North America, thus making their communications vulnerable to interception.[14]

One of the problems of interception, however, is not only lack of information, but excess. Targeting correct data is difficult and requires not only knowledge of where to search but also the ability to collect the correct data. In a fraction of a second, communications intercept equipment must determine whether a detected message is worth saving. Often the decision must be made on the basis of fragments of information, including perhaps just one side of a conversation.[15] But there has been one recent technical change that has benefited signals intelligence: the inclusion in the 1980s of an "origination number" in the call-signaling information in international phone standards.

Analysis of the communication's overall characteristics—its timing, length, addressing, etc., which is called "traffic analysis"—may leak a great deal of information about an opponent's activities. One successful occurrence of this was in the 1950s, when British counterintelligence employed "watchers" to follow the Russian diplomats in Britain. The watchers communicated in code, but their communications traffic was sufficient to enable the Soviets to determine where the watchers were operating.[16] By contrast, the increased encrypted communications within the Egyptian army in September 1973 should have alerted the Israeli army to the fact that something was happening.[17] Similarly, the U.S. intelligence agencies noted "a great deal of chatter" in the system in the weeks prior to September 11, and that was a clue that some form of Al Qaeda action was in the works. Understanding the traffic pattern is fundamental to being able to decipher the communications. Processing the data means transforming the intercepted communications into human-readable form. This may be as simple as what a fax machine standardly does, or it may involve a number of complex steps including decryption (of course, not all intercepted communications can be decrypted). As communication systems have evolved into more complex systems, processing has become less straightforward.

Communications intelligence is a resource whose existence is threatened by revelations that an opponent's traffic is being read; any hint of this and the encryption method is likely to change. For this reason national-security agencies doctor the product of communications intelligence before it is released. "Raw" intelligence is rarely disseminated outside actual intelligence agencies; instead, the agencies issue reports containing summaries and analyses of the intercepted communications.

GLOBAL SURVEILLANCE IN THE POSTWAR PERIOD

Communications intelligence was crucial to the Allies' success during World War II. Lessons learned included the importance of coordination of intelligence between the various military services (signals intelligence responsibility split between the Army and the Navy had contributed to the Pearl Harbor intelligence failure) and the value of international cooperation. During the war, the British had concentrated on breaking the German codes, while the Americans worked on the Japanese. Immediately after the war, communications intelligence responsibilities continued to be split between the various services, which were required to coordinate with one another. It was clear that a single department would be much more effective. On November 4, 1952, in a secret directive, President Truman established the National Security Agency (NSA), with the dual responsibilities of providing information security for the U.S. government as well as organizing and obtaining intelligence information.

The agency's existence was not made public until 1957. For many years the agency's acronym was said to stand for "No Such Agency." Information about NSA activities was quite scarce until the 1982 publication of James Barnford's *The Puzzle Palace.* NSA operates out of facilities sometimes known as SIGINT City at Fort George Meade, Maryland. During the Cold War, the NSA had 95,000 employees, more than half of whom were military personnel.

The NSA was particularly effective during the Cold War. The NSA provided more information on the Soviet Union than the CIA did.[18] They listened in through specially configured Boeing 707s equipped with antennas and signal-processing equipment, satellites, and listening posts all over the world. There was also a brief period of experimenting with ship-borne signals-intelligence collection as well, but the experiences of the USS *Liberty* and USS *Pueblo* ended the effort.[19] Another weapon during the Cold War was the denial of the fruits of Western technology to Communist nations. High-performance computers (HPC), first developed by engineer-entrepreneur Seymour Cray in the 1970s, was one such technology whose export to Soviet-bloc states was not permitted. (In the Cray Computer Corporation's early years, it was said that the NSA owned half the Crays manufactured.)

When, in the 1980s, Japanese companies also began building HPCs, the United States negotiated an arrangement with the Japanese government to control their export. The United States also used the Coordinating Committee on Multilateral Export Controls, or COCOM, whose membership included the major industrialized democracies,[20] as a way to prevent advanced technology from being exported to Communist countries. Cryptography, a "dual-use" technology that was important for Internet economic activity as well as for communications security, was among the items whose export COCOM restricted.

U.S. signals-intelligence surveillance was limited neither to enemy states nor to military and diplomatic traffic. During the Second World War, the United States and United Kingdom closely collaborated on intelligence issues. In 1947 the two nations signed the U.K.–U.S. agreement—which has never been made public[21]—to continue a secret collaboration on signals intelligence. Canada, Australia, and New Zealand, the three other major English-speaking democracies, agreed to participate as secondary partners. There are also third-tier parties—the signals-intelligence agencies of the NATO countries and some other nations, including Japan and South Korea.

Intercept stations at these geographically dispersed nations enable global coverage of the world's communications. According to the U.K.–U.S. agreement, Britain was responsible for covering Africa and the domain of Europe east of the Urals; Australia, coverage between the eastern Indian Ocean and portions of southeast Asia and the southwest Pacific; New Zealand, the southwest Pacific; Canada, the northern part of the former Soviet Union and parts of northern Europe. The United States was responsible for all other coverage.[22] There was an agreement to standardize terminology and procedures.

ECHELON and Other Global-Surveillance Efforts

Because of the vulnerability of communications intelligence, information about it is tightly held. Information about international cooperation on communications intelligence is even more secretive. For many years, nothing was known about ECHELON, the global communications-interception system run by the U.K.–U.S. alliance (consisting of the United States, United Kingdom, Canada, Australia, and New Zealand).

Then, in 1996, journalist Nicky Hager produced a rather detailed discussion of New Zealand's participation in ECHELON.[23] The Scientific and Technical Options Assessment Program of the European Parliament chartered a report that discussed ECHELON. Duncan Campbell, an investigative journalist, conducted a more extensive study.[24] Concerned that the United States was conducting industrial espionage against its allies, including those in Europe, the European Parliament formed a temporary Committee of Enquiry, which visited the United States in May 2001. At the last moment, the U.S. intelligence agencies canceled meetings with the committee, which nonetheless issued a report that ECHELON does exist and recommended that individuals encrypt their e-mails.[25]

ECHELON is a dual-purpose communications-interception system. It is known that ECHELON collects national security intelligence, some of which it shares with other nations that are not members of this group. For example, ECHELON intercepts on the Basque separatist movement, ETA, were shared with Spain.[26] But Campbell uncovered evidence that ECHELON was also conducting commercial espionage. Commercial transactions play a large and growing role in government communications (both military and nonmilitary) and are thus a "legitimate" target of traditional national intelligence collection.[27] For example, an NSA interception revealed that the Iranians were seeking to buy anticruise missiles from the China National Precision Machinery Import and Export Corporation in Beijing.[28] A summit meeting between President Clinton and Chinese president Jiang Zemin ended that. ECHELON intercepts revealed that the Iranians sought to purchase what appeared to be a turbojet engine from Microturbo SA in Toulouse, France.[29] A more thorough investigation, including French export inspectors traveling to Antwerp to view the "special items" being purchased, revealed they really were generators, as Microturbo had claimed, and not, as the United States had feared, engines that could easily be converted into engines for an Iranian-built cruise missile.[30]

The United States maintains that it does not provide covert intelligence information to U.S. companies. Former CIA director James Woolsey acknowledged that the intelligence agency does listen in on commercial communications, but he said the information is not passed on to U.S. companies. He acknowledged that the U.S. government does use intelligence information obtained through ECHELON (or otherwise) to assist U.S. business in countering corrupt foreign practices.[31] ECHELON uses a variety of mechanisms for its global ear. Primary among these are its listening posts stretched across the globe: Alice Springs, Australia; Missawa Air Base, Japan; Camp Humphreys, South Korea; Karamursel, Turkey; Bad Aibling, Germany; Menwith Hill, England; Sugar Grove, Virginia; Yakima, Washington; Shemaya, Alaska; and Kunia, Hawaii.[32] The British listen to Europe and the Middle East, the Australians and New Zealanders to Asia, the Canadians to Russia, and the Americans to . . . all. Although there are five partners in the U.K.–U.S. agreement, the United States is primary. Interception satellites are an important collection mechanism; the main ground stations for interception are in Denver, Colorado; Pine Gap, Australia; Menwith Hill, England; and Bad Aibling, Germany.[33]

The Internet is also the subject of ECHELON surveillance; its digital content makes searching particularly easy for the NSA's computers.[34] The FBI had spent much of the 1990s pressing for standardization of modern telephone systems. Meanwhile, the breakup of the Bell System had encouraged a proliferation of competitors and a plethora of new technologies; both changes complicated wiretapping. The FBI urged Congress to mandate the building in of sufficient capacity and appropriate technology for wiretapping in new systems. The Bureau was rebuffed on its first attempt, but in the fall of 1994, in the waning days of the second session of the One Hundred and Third Congress, the FBI was successful in getting the Communications Assistance for Law Enforcement Act, or CALEA, passed. The FBI intensified its resolve; within a year the FBI held meetings to brief law-enforcement agencies in other nations on interception and CALEA-like laws; shortly afterward the European Union opened discussion on its requirements for real-time interception.[35] The United States and its partners in the U.K.–U.S. agreement are not the only nations conducting global surveillance. The USSR and its satellites conducted extensive surveillance, including in the United States, and the Soviet Union had many of the same capabilities as the United States.[36]

With the fall of the Soviet Union, Russia's capabilities are no longer in the same league, but the nation continues to conduct communications surveillance, including surveillance of the Internet. China has a substantial signals-intelligence system. The Europeans, despite strong connections with the United States, strongly dislike the military domination of their NATO ally. France, in particular, has led the way in launching a series of surveillance satellites; at times it has been joined by Italy and Spain. Another nation that conducts substantial surveillance is Israel. Its survival is undoubtedly due to its ability to keep aware of its neighbors' activities. In May 2002, Israel launched a spy satellite to provide military information. India and Pakistan have also invested substantially in signals intelligence.[37] But none of these systems, even in combination, approach the depth and breadth of ECHELON.

RESTRICTIONS ON SURVEILLANCE

In general, global surveillance is a matter of spying on the communications of residents elsewhere. Thus the laws that apply are typically the laws in the nation in which the surveillance is occurring, and frequently such surveillance by a foreign power is illegal. However, since such spying is typically done without the knowledge of the host government, there is little that is done about it. ECHELON is different, since it involves the signals-intelligence organizations of five nations. What are the protections for the nationals of the United States, United Kingdom, Canada, Australia, and New Zealand? The United States restricts aspects of extraterritorial surveillance; the U.S. Foreign Intelligence Surveillance Act (FISA), passed in 1978, strictly limits the wiretapping of "U.S. persons" for national-security purposes. It defines a U.S. person as a citizen, a permanent resident alien, a group of such people, or a U.S. corporation. (U.S. persons in the United States may be subject to FISA surveillance if they are suspected of participating in international terrorism.) This restriction grew out of concerns raised during Senator Frank Church's hearings on intelligence abuses in the 1970s. Under Church's leadership, the Senate conducted a lengthy investigation of government wiretapping and surveillance abuses of the previous five administrations. The committee discovered that the government had tapped congressional staffers, Supreme Court justices, and many political figures under the guise of "national-security" investigations. The committee observed that "[t]he surveillance which we investigated was not only vastly excessive in breadth . . . but was also often conducted by illegal or improper means."[38]

Title III of the section of FISA that applies to criminal investigations has stringent requirements for when a wiretap can be used. For example, the crime must be one of a specified list of serious crimes, the targeted communications device must be being used in the commission of the crime, and other forms of surveillance must be unlikely to succeed. FISA allows wiretap investigations for "probable cause" that the target is a foreign power or agent of a foreign power. In contrast to Title III, FISA wiretaps may also be used for "intelligence gathering," which is a much looser criterion. In 1995, the U.S. Attorney General proposed "intelligence-sharing procedures" between law-enforcement and intelligence investigations with the same target. The proposal was that information gathered under a FISA warrant could be shared with a law-enforcement investigation, provided a proper wall was kept between the two investigations. The guidelines for these procedures required that any FISA investigations that turned up "significant" federal crimes were to be reported to the Criminal Division of the Department of Justice, which may then consult with the FBI, but which *may not direct or control* the FISA investigation toward law-enforcement objectives.[39] The proposal was accepted by the Foreign Intelligence Surveillance Court, which decides upon all FISA applications; they were formally adopted by the court in November 2001.

Despite controversy in the United States over whether the FISA protections are sufficient, other member countries of ECHELON do not seem to have such explicit laws for protecting their citizenry against intelligence gathering. Britain, for example, is far more of a surveillance society than the United States. There are 1.5 million closed-circuit television cameras in the U.K., for example, making the nation "one of the most closely monitored nations on the planet."[40] The U.K. did not have a wiretapping law until 1985, and then only in response to a European Court ruling that the current regime was too much within the discretion of the executive.[41] Current British law is looser than its American equivalent, and it permits wiretapping "to safeguard the economic well-being of the country."[42]

Canada began its oversight of its signals-intelligence community in 1986, with the appointment of lawyers to oversee the signals-intelligence organization; in 1997, a commissioner was appointed to oversee its Communications Security Division.[43] Australia has an Inspector General of Security and Intelligence, who is empowered to examine the workings of the intelligence agencies. The intelligence agencies work under a directive approved by the Australian cabinet, which claims "to prohibit the deliberate domestic interception of Australians, the dissemination of information on Australians accidentally gained during the routine collection of foreign communications, and the reporting or recording of Australian names mentioned in foreign communications."[44] But unlike FISA, whose wiretaps are decided upon by a special court of judges, the Australian procedures do not have the rule of law behind them.

New Zealand does not even have such a provision.[45] Until Nicky Hager's book, little was public about New Zealand's participation in global surveillance. In a rather startling statement, former Prime Minister David Lange wrote that during his tenure as prime minister he was unfamiliar with New Zealand's participation in an "international integrated electronic network."[46] Such a statement makes one doubt what privacy protections are afforded New Zealand citizenry. Campbell, however, reports that oversight protections do exist within the ECHELON framework. He reports that the signal-intelligence organizations of each nation "may not normally collect or (if inadvertently collected) record or disseminate information about citizens of, or companies registered in, any other UK-USA nation."[47] If a citizen, however, has been targeted by his own country, then intelligence collection on that person (or company) is allowed.[48] There are no protections at all for citizens of non–U.K.–U.S. countries.

THE CRYPTO WARS

Cryptography is central to communications security, the counterforce to communications intelligence. But although cryptography is what is known as a "dual-use" technology, having both civilian and military applications, for a long time cryptography was subject to various government controls. During the Second World War, cryptography was a military tool, and in the immediate aftermath of the war, there was little incentive to change that. During the mid 1970s, the National Bureau of Standards (NBS, later renamed the National Institute of Standards and Technology, or NIST) and the NSA realized the importance of protecting unclassified but sensitive data and put out a request for proposals; eventually the fifty-six-bit Data Encryption Standard, or DES,[49] was chosen, and became widely implemented in both hardware and software. With the exception of RC4 in web browsers and relatively insecure cable-TV signal encryption, DES is the most widely used public cryptosystem in the world.[50] Another major development, almost simultaneous with DES, was the invention of *public-key cryptography,* the technology that enables Internet commerce. The NSA, which had had a lock on cryptography, made several unsuccessful attempts to rein back this public activity. The agency hoped for "born classified" status on cryptography research, but there was not public support. So the NSA settled for a regime of voluntary prepublication review of cryptographic research and de facto industrial controls in the form of cryptographic export controls.

This control held through the 1980s, but by the 1990s, with the end of the Cold War, the export regime was growing increasingly untenable. Through a variety of venues, including the Organization for Economic Cooperation and Development (OECD) and the European Union (EU), the U.S. government tried to create a worldwide mandate for international controls on encryption. But the tide of technology was turning against cryptography controls. Then ECHELON added a new complication.

Duncan Campbell's ECHELON study brought to light the extent of U.S. eavesdropping on European communications.[51] Europeans were outraged that the United States was conducting commercial espionage against them. Their willingness to go along with U.S. cryptographic controls evaporated. In short order, they removed cryptographic export controls on trade within the "EU plus ten."[52] The United States did likewise a short time later.[53]

THE CHANGING ENVIRONMENT

The Internet, a university artifact since the 1980s, took law enforcement and national security by surprise with its rapid emergence as a mainstream communications medium in the 1990s. Both organizations were ill-equipped to handle the challenges, though the problems surfaced in different ways. The Internet was no exception to new human activities being followed by criminal versions of the same. Internet porn, hacking attacks, and numerous debilitating computer viruses became the subject of newspaper headlines. But the fact that the Internet is international and respects no borders made tracking Internet criminals—and prosecuting them—difficult. The Council of Europe, an intergovernmental organization whose decision-making body consists of the foreign ministers of its member states, proposed a treaty on cyber-crime.[54] Harmonizing a continent's worth of wiretapping law was not easy. This is probably an understatement; the draft treaty was quite controversial. There is widespread agreement that disrupting the communications of an air-traffic control tower is a criminal activity (though the fact one can do so remotely with simple hacking tools may involve criminal negligence on the part of the designers of the system). There is less widespread agreement on what constitutes pornography. There is little agreement on speech. In the United States, political speech is protected by the Constitution, but in Germany, for example, speeches extolling the Nazi doctrine are illegal. Thus the extraterritoriality and inhomogeniety of the different nations' laws posed many problems for the proposed Cybercrime Convention. If an activity was legal in the United States and illegal in Germany, could the United States be a signatory to a treaty that would allow a U.S. resident to be extradited to Germany for an activity committed on U.S. soil (e.g., putting up a web page selling Nazi paraphernalia)? After September 11, the treaty quickly moved closer to adoption.

The NSA was an information agency before there was an Information Age, but in the 1990s the world caught up with the agency. Even before September 11, it had become clear that the NSA's successes of the Cold War were not continuing in a post–Cold War world. The United States was taken by surprise by India's atomic weapon test in May 1998. Despite its listening posts around the world, the NSA had been blind to India's efforts. This was far from the only failure of the 1990s.[55]

The agency faces a myriad of challenges. Fiber optics is burying the agency's ability to eavesdrop; one cannot wiretap that technology. High-quality cryptography is available internationally, and many tapped messages remain undecipherable. (The change of focus from Eastern Europe and the Soviet Union to the Middle East and central Asia did not help matters either. U.S. intelligence agencies lacked sufficient language specialists for those regions.) And then there is the problem of the Internet. Like the rest of the world, the NSA is being buried by the deluge of data on the Internet. The NSA, with its government salaries, has not kept pace with Silicon Valley. While the brightest mathematicians may continue to be intrigued by the complex code problems of the NSA and attracted to what is said to be the largest employer of mathematicians in the world, the brightest engineers head to California instead. NSA no longer necessarily leads the world in the fastest search engines and the fastest computers. This torrent of information makes it quite possible for those who wish to communicate in secret to use publicly available communication channels, including Internet cafés. On the other hand, Internet-mediated communication is in machine-readable form, making it much more accessible to the NSA. Speaking to a Senate committee in 2000, NSA Director Michael Hayden testified, "E-mail is a bit going back to the future, looking a lot more like telex . . . reading the printed word, rather than . . . dealing with the spoken word. . . . The telecommunications [revolution] not only makes our job more difficult. It . . . makes our job easier."[56]

GLOBAL SURVEILLANCE IN A POST-SEPTEMBER 11 WORLD

At the beginning of the Cold War, the U.K.–U.S. alliance was secret, the NSA was known (or unknown) as "No Such Agency," and wiretapping had no legal foundation in U.S. law but was rather routinely done by the FBI (and some state police forces). Information about the intelligence agencies was hard to come by. The methods for ensuring privacy of communications was little better than the decoder rings found in cereal boxes. The government held most of the cards.

A half-century later, the public is much better informed about surveillance, and the tools for confidential communications—most notably cryptography, but also various forms of anonymizers—are in public hands. But it is not clear that the public is that much better off. While the tools for confidentiality are in public hands, they appear to be used more in the breach. We now leave electronic records everywhere, from the ubiquitous credit card receipts to the ever more common closed-circuit recording camera. The extremely rapid reconstruction of Mohammed Atta's travels over the several years prior to September 11 is proof of the value of these records to law enforcement and national security.[57] There is simply so much more data, and the government has much better tools for conducting surveillance. However, it appears true that the intelligence agencies have not kept up with the times. Some claim ECHELON is just one big black hole, burying the National Security Agency in a torrent of information that they lack resources to evaluate.[58] It is certainly true that in the 1980s and 1990s, as the world was relying more and more on the Internet for communications, the NSA was not a destination of choice for the computer scientists who, to a large extent, are this generation's information analysts. The events of September 11, however, appear to have changed the career interests of college graduates, and many are flocking to the intelligence agencies, including, presumably, the NSA.

The laws have worked in favor of the government. The USA PATRIOT Act and an appropriations act passed a few months later include provisions for "roving" wiretaps (wiretaps that do not necessarily name the person or number to be tapped); the USA PATRIOT Act also changes FISA requirements that "foreign intelligence" only be a "significant purpose" of the wiretap rather than "the purpose." The latter is a significant shift, as it breaks down barriers between law enforcement and national security. Other changes in the USA PATRIOT Act include that stored e-mail messages now require only a search warrant, rather than the more-difficult-to-obtain and more restrictive wiretap search warrant.

However, an attempt by U.S. Attorney General John Ashcroft to change the 1995 guidelines on FISA investigations to permit law-enforcement investigators to determine the course of FISA procedure for criminal prosecutions was emphatically turned down by the FISA court.[59] Observing that FISA procedures already give "the government a powerful engine for the collection of foreign intelligence information targeting U.S. persons,"[60] the court noted that post–September 11, there were numerous cases where there were simultaneous intelligence and criminal investigations or interests.[61] "In order to preserve both the appearance and the fact that FISA surveillances and searches were not being used sub rosa for criminal investigations, the Court routinely approved the use of information screening 'walls' proposed by the government in its applications."[62]

For the first time in the quarter-century history of the Foreign Intelligence Surveillance Act, the FISA Court's decision was appealed. In an unanimous ruling, the three judges who constituted the Foreign Intelligence Surveillance Court of Review agreed with the Justice Department's interpretation that FISA does not require a "wall" between investigative and intelligence sides.[63] Other ECHELON nations also proposed and, in some cases, adopted invasive electronic surveillance procedures. In Australia, a proposal to allow warrantless law-enforcement interception of electronic communications did not make it into the final bill passed as part of the 2002 antiterrorism measure, but this proposal may resurface.[64] In New Zealand there is a pending bill granting major new powers to surveillance agencies, as well as proposals requiring telecommunications operators to ensure that their systems are "wiretap-ready."[65] And in Europe, law-enforcement agencies obtained wider powers to monitor telecommunication through a 2002 European Parliament act on data retention that requires all ISPs and phone companies to retain detailed logs of their customers' communications for an unspecified period. Presently such records are kept only as long as they are needed for billing. The act must be approved by all fifteen European Union states before it becomes law.[66]

The pendulum swings. In the seventies, it swung toward providing greater oversight of the watchers; in the nineties, it moved in both directions, but in the first year of the new millennium its movement has been in the direction of bringing more power to the government and not to the governed.

Selected Bibliography

Peter Schweitzer, *Friendly Spies*, Atlantic Monthly Press, 1993.

6. PRIVACY AND SECRECY AFTER SEPTEMBER 11

MARC ROTENBERG[1]

It is difficult to speak about privacy in the United States today without considering the significance of September 11. That day has had a profound impact on the public perception of privacy, the actions of Congress, the development of new technologies, and most likely even the decisions of courts. Polls indicate increased public support for new forms of surveillance.[2] Congress has moved swiftly to expand the surveillance authority of the state.[3] New technologically advanced means of surveillance, such as biometric identifiers and a national ID card, are now under serious consideration.[4] Even the courts have shown a new deference to claims of national security.[5]

During such periods in history it is appropriate to reexamine core values and consider the structure and purpose of principles in law that today are constantly under attack. This is only partly to reaffirm critical political goals; it is also to explore and clarify the relationship and significance of critical concepts that are too easily misunderstood.

In this article, I will examine two critical concepts in the world of privacy—privacy and secrecy—and discuss what the developments since September 11 tell us about the relationship between these two key legal categories. I will argue that they are very different ideas, reflecting very different political values, and that they are fundamentally at odds in the structure of privacy law in the United States. But it is fair to note at the outset that the terms are often used interchangeably. We speak of meeting "in secret" and meeting "in private." We communicate secretly and we communicate privately. There are aspects of our lives that we wish to keep secret, or private. These terms require more careful examination, particularly after the events of September 11.

I. DIMINISHMENT OF PRIVACY BY LEGAL MEANS

One clear impact of September 11 has been the reduction in privacy protection under U.S. law. The USA PATRIOT Act is the most sweeping expansion of government surveillance authority since the passage of the Communications Assistance for Law Enforcement Act (CALEA) of 1994.[6] Where CALEA established for the first time the premise that the government had the authority to require by law that new communication services be designed to enable surveillance by the state, the USA PATRIOT Act limited in multiple ways the scope, impact, and effect of many privacy laws previously in force in the United States.

To understand the impact of the USA PATRIOT Act on privacy law in the United States, you must understand that the protection of privacy by statutory means typically incorporates a wide range of Fourth Amendment values, such as an articulated probable-cause standard, a notification requirement, a nexus between the authority granted and the area searched, and means of judicial oversight.[7] Taken separately and as a whole, these provisions limit the state's ability to conduct searches, thereby seeking to safeguard certain aspects of private life that may be recorded in paper or electronic records.

Broadly stated, these provisions develop from two lines of cases that provide the twin cornerstones for information-privacy law in the United States. The first is the *Olmstead* v. *United States* and *Katz* v. *United States* line, which gave way to enactment of the federal wiretap act in 1968.[8] The second is the *United States* v. *Miller*[9] and *California Bankers Ass'n* v. *Schultz*[10] line, which led Congress to recognize that if there were to be constitutional safeguards for the disclosure to police of personal information held by third parties, congressional action would be required.[11]

Since the mid 1970s a range of privacy laws in the United States has been enacted to limit government access to a wide range of record systems, including government records, financial records, medical records, cable subscriber records, electronic mail records, video rental records, and more.[12] In just the last few years, Congress extended new safeguards to medical information,[13] financial information,[14] and records on students.[15]

The USA PATRIOT Act did not destroy the edifice of U.S. privacy law, but it did significantly weaken the structure and limit the coverage of many key statutes. The act limits safeguards created by fifteen statutes.[16] It reduces probable-cause standards in key laws.[17] It significantly expands the authority of the Foreign Intelligence Surveillance Act. It limits judicial review.[18] It creates a new "sneak and peak provision" for police to undertake searches without the customary notification requirement.[19]

Still, the USA PATRIOT Act is not the only means by which privacy provisions in the United States have been diminished since September 11. The Attorney General has also indicated that attorney-client privilege, one of the oldest privileges in common law, may be violated by police.[20] And proposals currently pending in Congress would enable state police to access records previously restricted under the Foreign Intelligence Surveillance Act.[21]

Apparently the only area that the Attorney General believes should not be subject to reduced protection following September 11 are the records provided by individuals seeking the right to carry personal firearms. There the Attorney General has said that, because there is no current legal authority, investigators seeking access to this information should be restricted.[22] The Attorney General had not made a similar argument during the debate over the USA PATRIOT Act with regard to the information that might be sought in telephone records, banking records, voicemail records, educational records, library records, or business records.

II. LOSS OF PRIVACY BY TECHNOLOGICAL MEANS

The expansion of state surveillance authority under the USA PATRIOT Act is only one way that personal privacy has been diminished after September 11. The government has also sought to expand monitoring and profiling of individuals by technical means. At the moment, the three proposals that have received the most attention are a national ID card, new face-recognition technology, and systems for border control.[23]

A. National ID Card

The proposal for the national ID card reflects, perhaps more than any other example, the great ambivalence of the American people about the appropriate response to the events of September 11. In the days following that event, public opinion polls showed sharp increases for support of a national ID.[24] Prominent American businessmen, law professors, and political leaders also expressed support for the idea.[25] A congressional hearing in the late fall suggested that a national ID card, defined as one issued by the federal government that individuals in the United States would be required to carry, would still face strong political opposition.[26] Technical experts also noted the significant privacy and security risks in the development of a true national ID.[27] And subsequent polls indicated that the initial wave of support for a national ID card had diminished.[28]

Thereafter, the focus shifted to a proposal put forward by the American Association of Motor Vehicle Administrators (AAMVA) to build upon the current state-issued driver's license and to create a document that was both more secure, by means of a biometric identifier, and more easily integrated with a variety of record systems.[29] At present, it remains unclear whether the AAMVA proposal to create a de facto national ID card will go forward. There are both legislative and budgetary obstacles, and Americans still appear deeply divided.[30]

B. Face Recognition

A second proposal to significantly expand surveillance is the idea of putting in place new "smart cameras" that have the ability to match in real time the images of individuals viewed in public and private places against a stored database of facial images, which could be those of either suspected terrorists, licensed drivers, gamblers in Las Vegas casinos, or children in the Washington, D.C., public school system.[31] Joseph Attick, CEO of the company Visionics, has argued that his system for face recognition would reduce the risk of terrorist threat, and several pilot projects are under way.[32] However, independent studies have also raised questions about the reliability of face-recognition systems, and at least one airport has decided not to go forward with the system after the chief of security determined that it might actually diminish the effectiveness of current security procedures.[33]

C. Border Control

A third area of significant focus is the effort to improve the tracking of non–U.S. citizens in the United States. It is clear that many people in the United States who receive visas often do not comply with the reporting requirements.[34] It is also clear that current means to track those individuals are not particularly effective.[35] But it is less clear what role technology would play in solving this problem. While it may be possible to integrate databases to enable more detailed monitoring of individuals in the United States on visas, the idea of real-time tracking, as has been proposed by some political leaders, would require extraordinarily intrusive surveillance techniques and also be extraordinarily expensive. It might also be fair to ask whether U.S. citizens traveling abroad would accept a system that would track their activities and their meetings with others.

Some systems for real-time tracking of individuals are currently being pursued for parolees and those serving in-home detention.[36] These systems enable remote tracking of a person's location and are designed to ensure that an individual stays within a circumscribed geographic region.[37] Similar technologies widely available for pets administer a small shock to the animal if the animal strays beyond the prescribed region.

We can briefly summarize this part by noting that since September 11 there has been a dramatic reduction in privacy in the United States and that further proposals are under consideration. Some of this may be ascribed to specific changes in federal statutes; some to new technologies that enable greater surveillance and tracking. The interesting question now is whether we can say that there has been a similar decrease in secrecy.

III. EXPANSION IN GOVERNMENT SECRECY

There are two ways to understand the expansion of government authority resulting from passage of the USA PATRIOT Act on October 26, 2001. One way is to assess the variety of ways in which personal information may be made more readily available to police in the course of a criminal or national-security investigation. This is apparent in the diminished probable-cause standard in several key statutes.[38] We can reasonably say that these changes result in diminished privacy protection for the person whose information is now more readily available to government agents.

The second way to assess the means of expansion of government authority is the various ways in which the conduct of government is more difficult to detect, is more readily concealed, or fails to follow the requirements that might otherwise apply. It is to this change—the increase in secrecy—that we now turn.

Central to this analysis is the expanded role of the Foreign Intelligence Surveillance Act (FISA) in the post–USA PATRIOT Act world. The FISA was originally enacted in 1978 to address a problem raised in the *Katz* decision and left open by the enactment of the federal wiretap statute in 1968.[39] That is what would be the statutory standard for a search undertaken in matters of national security. The *Katz* court suggested that all forms of electronic surveillance that violated a reasonable expectation of privacy would be subject to a Fourth Amendment standard.[40] But clearly there was concern that the standard appropriate for the investigation of a person engaged in an illegal gambling operation may not be the same as an agent of a foreign power, not a U.S. citizen, who intended harm against the United States.[41]

In 1978 Congress adopted the FISA with the narrow goal of enabling electronic surveillance of foreign agents in the United States pursuant to federal statutory authority.[42] The act also established the Foreign Intelligence Court, which, unlike a traditional Title III court, issued orders authorizing wiretaps without indicating the jurisdiction, purpose, or duration of the order.[43] The FISA court met within the Department of Justice office building in Washington, D.C., and was in physical orientation as well as statutory structure more closely aligned with the interests of the executive branch of government than other courts.[44]

A. Diminished Access to Public Records

Not only has the prosecution of crime been made more secretive since September 11, but so too have the routine activities of government. The Attorney General indicated in a memo published on October 11, 2002, that federal agencies would be encouraged to withhold public records that are subject to the Freedom of Information Act if there was a "reasonable basis" for the application of a statutory exemption.[45] This standard is in contrast to the one under which the federal agencies operated when Janet Reno served as Attorney General. As President Clinton's Attorney General, Reno had required that agencies adopt a "foreseeable harm" test, similar to the standard that Attorney General Levy had adopted in the 1970s.[46]

The new standard for litigating FOIA cases is a clear indication that the Department of Justice is less committed to open government since September 11, 2001.[47] On several occasions the Attorney General has expressed his opinion that the U.S. federal government cannot make information publicly available that may be a threat to the country.[48] This policy has extended to decisions to severely limit the availably of public information that was previously available over the Internet prior to September 11.

B. Closed Hearings

Government secrecy has also become apparent in the reluctance of the president and the Congress to pursue public hearings in what many have described as a "massive intelligence failure."[49] While CIA Director George Tenant appeared in an open hearing to discuss the annual CIA budget request, subsequent hearings on the adequacy of intelligence gathering prior to September 11, the current status of the anthrax investigation, the justification for significantly expanding certain CIA programs, as well as a range of questions related to the effectiveness of the CIA have been kept from public review.

C. Consequences of Government Secrecy

One of the consequences of the expanded secrecy is clearly that public accountability is diminished. This has consequences both large and small. In the context of electronic surveillance undertaken pursuant to the new powers created by the USA PATRIOT Act, it means that targets of government searches who might previously have been notified that they were subject to government surveillance will not be so told.[50] It means that public reporting of the use of surveillance authority by federal investigators will be less detailed and less useful than reports on similar activities in the past. And on large open questions, like who was responsible for the dissemination of deadly anthrax spores in the nation's capital in mid–October 2001, the government can continue to make representations about the status of the case with little opportunity for the public to probe the government's claims because information associated with the investigation remains secret.[51]

IV. UNDERSTANDING PRIVACY AND SECRECY

What we have witnessed since September 11 is both the diminishment of personal privacy and the expansion of government secrecy. Now this is a significant development that bears some exploration however we may feel about the specific steps taken in the wake of September 11. It is my aim at this point to look more closely at the interplay of these two trends and to see if the traditions in privacy law help us understand the transformation taking place since September 11. Should it surprise us that as personal privacy is diminished, government secrecy expands?

We can begin with the observation of some commentators that there is a trade-off between privacy and transparency or privacy and openness. According to this view, privacy stands in opposition to these values, and we may give up some privacy to gain greater public accountability.

The communitarian scholar Amitai Etzioni, for example, has argued that privacy must be balanced against competing interests.[52] Since September 11, Etzioni has endorsed a number of proposals to expand surveillance, including adoption of a national ID card and new airport screening procedures.[53] It is Etzioni's view that these measures will promote public safety and reduce the risk of future terrorist acts.[54]

David Brin, author of *The Transparent Society,* argued in similar fashion that privacy should give way to other social interests, particularly the need for greater openness and transparency that characterizes democratic society.[55] Brin has also argued since September 11 for greater tracking and monitoring procedures.[56]

Corporate leaders such as Scott McNealy and Larry Ellison also have argued that the interests of privacy must be traded against the interests of openness, and both have argued since September 11 for the creation of a system of national identification.[57] Ellison has specifically proposed that software and services developed by his company could provide the basis for greater information sharing across federal agencies.[58]

In my view, none of these scholars, writers, or business leaders properly understands the relationship between privacy and secrecy. For privacy scholars and advocates, the relationship between privacy and transparency is well understood. It was expressed most famously, and a bit paradoxically, by the European scholar and early architect of data-protection laws Jan Freese, who said, "We must protect privacy to enable the free flow of information."[59] But whereas many have seen a sharp contrast between the U.S. privacy and the European privacy traditions, the similarities are significant, particularly in understanding the proper relationship between privacy and secrecy.

I would like to turn now to the American tradition of seeking to protect privacy while limiting government secrecy. It is my contention that this tradition, the one that sees privacy and openness as complementary values, is most at risk after September 11. To make this point, I will point to three critical historical references: the opinions of Justice Louis Brandeis, the post-Watergate reforms of the U.S. Congress, and the establishment of the OECD Privacy Guidelines in 1980.

To understand the complementary nature of privacy and openness, it is useful to look briefly at the legacy of the jurist most responsible for the legal right of privacy in America. Louis Brandeis is well known for the publication of the 1890 article "The Right to Privacy,"[60] which became the basis for the American privacy tort, and almost as well known for the 1928 dissenting opinion in *Olmstead* v. *United States,* in which he described privacy as "the most comprehensive of rights."[61] But Brandeis is less well known, at least in many of the popular debates on privacy, for his views on the First Amendment and open government. It was Brandeis who said, "Sunlight is said to be the best of disinfectants."[62] It was Brandeis who, together with Justice Oliver Wendell Holmes, wrote opinions that challenged the World War I convictions for unpopular speech under the Sedition Act.[63] In these opinions and others, Brandeis championed a view of the world in which both a secure private sphere could be protected in law and a robust public sphere of debate and democratic activity could be achieved.[64]

My second piece of historical evidence are the statutes enacted by Congress in the post-Watergate era that sought to protect the rights of citizens and to limit abuse by government, particularly in the context of new information technologies. In enacting both the Privacy Act of 1974[65] and adopting that same year the amendments that significantly strengthened the Freedom of Information Act, Congress sought to ensure that personal information collected and maintained by federal agencies would be properly protected, while also seeking to ensure that public information in the possession of federal agencies would be widely available to the public.[66] The complementary goals of safeguarding individual liberty and ensuring government accountability were enabled by legislation that protected privacy on the one hand and promoted government oversight on the other. To this day, the twin goals of limiting disclosure of personal information held by government agencies and enabling access to public information have been followed by nations around the world.[67]

Finally, let us consider the OECD Privacy Guidelines of 1980,[68] considered by many the most widely adopted articulation of privacy rights in the world.[69] The OECD Guidelines clearly impose restrictions on the collection and use of personal information.[70] Indeed, one of the critical contrasts between the OECD Guidelines and other less robust means for privacy protection, such as the FTC articulation of Fair Information Practices, is the failure to specifically include such concepts as "use limitation," "collection limitation," "disclosure limitation," or "secondary purposes."[71]

But it is equally clear that the other metric by which privacy policies often fail to match the standards set out by the OECD Guidelines is the absence of corresponding requirements for transparency. The OECD Privacy Guidelines make clear that for privacy protection to be effective, transparency and access concerns are paramount.[72] In many respects the OECD Guidelines mirror the goal set out in the 1973 report that gave way to the adoption of the Privacy Act in 1974: to ensure that there were no secret databases in government tracking the lawful activities of citizens.[73]

In outlining this argument that privacy and openness are complementary values, I do not intend to deny that there are hard cases that may place these interests in conflict.[74] This was clear in the Court's consideration of *Bartnicki* v. *Vopper* last term, in which the Court held that the First Amendment precluded liability under the federal wiretap statute for publication of information obtained by means of illegal wiretap where the publisher was not the person who had committed the unlawful interception.[75] Although it is fair to note that there are competing free-speech values for the participants in a conversation who wish to make use of new technology to exchange information that might not otherwise be disclosed absent the statutory protection, for those who wish to publish the contents of the conversation, their right to publish conflicts directly with the privacy interests of the parties to the conversation.

There are similar clashes over access to court records in electronic form and the publication of private matters by the press.[76] Even the Electronic Privacy Information Center (EPIC) faced the difficult question of whether to proceed with a Freedom of Information Act lawsuit against the Department of Justice to determine the status of those who were detained after September 11.[77] Clearly that case illuminates the concern that the disclosure of a person's detention could be stigmatizing and could create actual harm as to future employment and economic opportunity for the individuals whose status was disclosed. But it was also out of recognition that the privacy interests of the detainees could not become a proxy for the desire of government to maintain secrecy surrounding these possibly unlawful detentions that we at EPIC decided to go forward. It was and is our view that mechanisms could be created to enable disclosure of detainees' status that would minimize the privacy risk while maximizing the likelihood that some light would be shed as to the government's conduct.[78]

More broadly, we might say about modern privacy law that the aim is to enable both personal privacy and government accountability in the use of new technology by limiting the collection and use of personal information where possible and by imposing disclosure and reporting requirements where such collection occurs. Privacy law has made clear the particular importance of this goal in the area of new technologies where systems of surveillance dramatically amplify state authority.[79]

But these hard cases typically arise where there is a specific matter in dispute, a specific claim before a court. They rarely speak prospectively, as statutes do, to the ordering of privacy claims and publication requirements. And most significantly, the disputes outlined above do not require the simultaneous diminishment of personal privacy and expansion of government secrecy.

Privacy is, as Professor Raymond Shih Ray Ku suggests in his article, about power.[80] And privacy law is established to rectify asymmetries in power and to protect the rights of individuals against institutions that are able to delve deeply into our private lives. Viewed in this light, the developments since September 11 should be seen as an expansion of state power and a consequential limitation on the freedom of individuals. The balance between the authority of the state and the rights of the individual has shifted. There has been no beneficial trade-off between privacy and openness, as Etzioni, Brin, or Ellison have suggested.[81] There has simply been greater exposure of private life and greater secrecy surrounding the actions of government.

WHAT ARE WE TO DO?

It might be tempting at this point to stop and congratulate ourselves for this important insight about the relationship between privacy and secrecy and the underlying purpose of privacy protection in law. Much of legal study is indeed the careful consideration of doctrine, an examination of key concepts, decisions, and statutes. But I would argue today that after September 11 we have a greater obligation than just the production of a descriptive model that is intellectually satisfying.

As law students, teachers, and advocates, we should build on our legal tradition, on our constitutional democracy, and participate in the public debates that affect us not simply as experts in the field but also as citizens who will live with the consequences of action taken or not taken by the government that we have created. We should understand that in the battle to protect privacy lies also the struggle to maintain constitutional democracy, to safeguard the rights of citizens, and to hold government accountable. Privacy remains today as fundamental a measure of democratic society as it was when democracy was born.[82]

If there are to be proposals to establish new systems of public surveillance, then the legal community has an obligation to assess these developments and to determine their impact on current law and the rights of citizens.[83]

In going forward with this effort, I would like to make three points. First, we should understand that the balance to be achieved here is not the one too often stated as between security and freedom. Benjamin Franklin rightly cautioned that those who would sacrifice "essential liberty for temporary security" will have neither liberty nor security.[84] The balance that must be achieved is between the authority created for government and the means of oversight to ensure that these new powers are not misused. This tradition is well established in law, and it remains critical that every proposal put forward by Congress after September 11 explain how new state authority will be balanced by new means of oversight.

Second, we must avoid the risk of allowing the descriptive to collapse into the normative. By this I mean that we should not simply restate the observation that during times of national crisis, the authority of the government is necessarily expanded and the rights of the citizens are necessarily diminished. It is descriptively correct to say that Japanese Americans were interned during World War II. It is also normatively fair to say that the internment was wrong and should not have occurred. Those who cite the internment of the Japanese during the Second World War, the prosecution of pacifists during the First World War, and arguably even the suspension of habeas corpus during the Civil War in support of new restrictions on the rights of citizens should not go unchallenged. Many injustices occur in times of crisis, and the fact of prior injustice should not justify the commission of new injustice.

Most critically, we must oppose the fatalism that has captured the minds and hearts of too many Americans. We should reject the premise that after September 11 we can no longer afford the privacy or freedom that we previously enjoyed.[85] The United States has survived world war, presidential assassination, domestic riots, and economic depression. We have had nuclear weapons targeted on the nation's capital by foreign adversaries for much of the twentieth century. But none of these developments has required a permanent sacrifice in the structure of liberty established by the Constitution or by law, or, specifically, a sacrifice of the individual's freedom to limit the oversight of government. To allow crisis, even of the magnitude of September 11, to necessarily diminish the rights of citizens or the responsibility of government is a path without end.

And that remains our challenge today, after the events of September 11, and that remains the special obligation of the legal profession and legal educators. Alexis de Tocqueville told us that in the American form of government, lawyers come forward when there are great challenges.[86] We are at a similar point in history. We have a duty to safeguard privacy, to oppose secrecy, and to ensure the protection of constitutional freedom.

EXHIBIT: OBSERVING SURVEILLANCE

MARC ROTENBERG
MIHIR KSHIRSAGAR
CEDRIC LAURANT
KATE REARS

The Observing Surveillance Project documents the presence of video cameras placed in Washington, D.C., after September 11, 2001. The project was undertaken by the staff of the Electronic Privacy Information Center (EPIC) in Washington, D.C. Many of the images displayed in the exhibit may be viewed online at www.observingsurveillance.org.

FIGURE 1: The Observing Surveillance Project documents the presence of surveillance cameras in Washington, D.C. The image above was taken in front of the United States Department of Justice.

WHO WATCHES THE WATCHERS?

Historians debate the true meaning of Juvenal's maxim "*Sed quis custodiet ipsos custodes?*" The Roman satirist often poked fun at the ruling elite. According to one commentator, Juvenal's guardians were the eunuchs left with the women of Rome while the men traveled beyond the city. Perhaps there is no need to guard such guardians.

But in the modern era, the words are a call for greater transparency and greater accountability of those in power. Leading economists ask who will oversee the overseers of corporate governance.[1] Human-rights groups ask who will police the police. Commentators on technology ask who will observe those who have the means to observe others.

PANOPTICISM

The eighteenth-century utilitarian philosopher Jeremy Bentham described the perfect prison as the "Panopticon," a place where prisoners could be under constant surveillance. The Panopticon placed prisoner cells around a central observation tower. From the tower, prisoners could be observed but could not see who was watching. Bentham was impressed that the threat of surveillance would be enough to coerce the inmates such that actual observation would no longer be necessary.[2]

Modern social philosophers from Michel Foucault and Erving Goffman to Oscar Gandy and Gary Marx have noted that observation plays a similar function as a means of social control. In *Discipline and Punish: The Birth of the Prison,* Foucault wrote, "Hence the major effect of the Panopticon: to induce in the inmates a state of conscious and permanent visibility that assures the automatic functioning of power."[3] Surveillance thus becomes a means of social and political control. It is a way for those in power not only to observe, but also to coerce.

PRIVACY AND PUBLIC PLACES

Central to the debate about video cameras is the question of whether one has a reasonable expectation of privacy in a public place. Proponents of the camera systems say that if you can be observed by others, you have no expectation of privacy. But such a view ignores the role that technology plays in enhancing observation.

One person can easily obtain privacy against another by turning away or by speaking softly. But how do people obtain privacy against technology that seeks

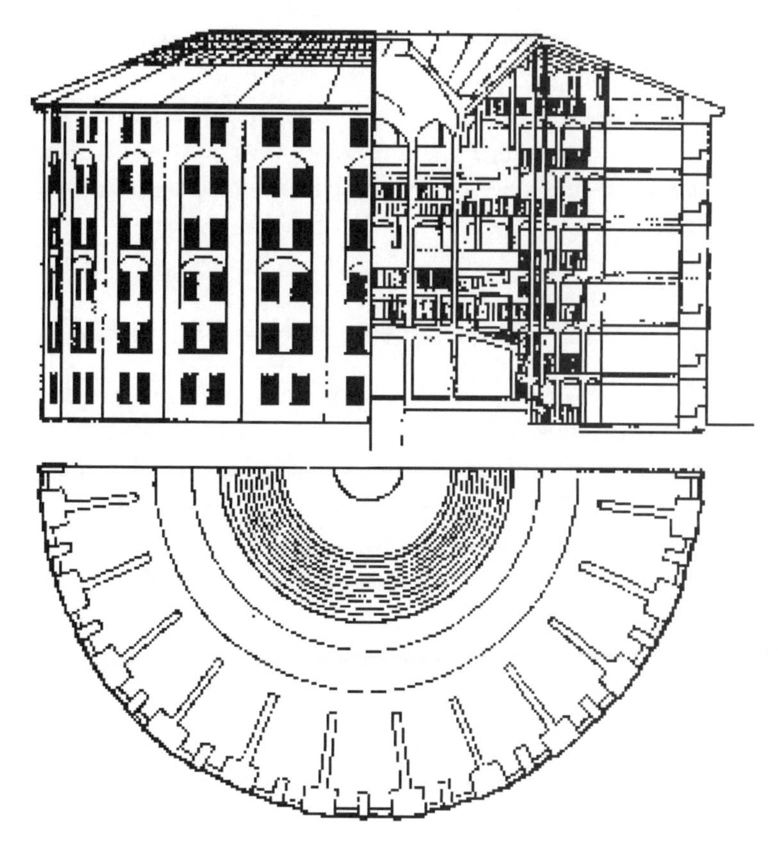

FIGURE 2: Image of Jeremy Bentham's Panopticon, the perfect prison.

to observe and to record all? And what if such technology is eventually designed to target those who desire privacy?

More than a century ago, Louis Brandeis said that the law must evolve to safeguard individuals from the encroachments of modern technology that made surveillance easy and inexpensive. The Brandeis article, credited fors the modern right of privacy, concerned observation in a public space.[4]

THE DEBATE IN WASHINGTON, D.C.

The mayor of Washington, D.C., Anthony A. Williams, has argued that increased government surveillance is a necessity after September 11, 2001. He has argued for the adoption of elaborate camera systems, similar to those now in place in London and Sydney, Australia.

The D.C. City Council has resisted the mayor's proposal. Council members and witnesses raised questions about the video camera system at a public hearing in June 2002. Residents asked whether their front doors and windows would fall within view of the police camera networks. Legislation is currently under consideration that would limit the use of the video camera system. The United States Congress has also questioned the unregulated use of video surveillance in Washington, D.C.[5]

TRANSPARENCY AND OPEN GOVERNMENT

The work of the Observing Surveillance Project has been undertaken in cooperation with the Freedom of Information Act litigation pursued by the Electronic Privacy Information Center.[6] EPIC has filed a series of FOIA requests with the Metropolitan Police Department and the Park Police to determine the scope and operation of the D.C. video surveillance systems. Material obtained from the litigation is incorporated in the Observing Surveillance exhibit.

PUBLIC PROTEST AND CONSTITUTIONAL FREEDOM

Washington has long been the center of political expression in the United States. Martin Luther King Jr. delivered the "I Have a Dream" speech from the Lincoln Memorial in 1963. Over the past thirty years, millions of Americans from all across the country have come to the nation's capital to express their views on important political matters. Documents obtained by EPIC under the FOIA indicate that in the past few years the Metropolitan Police Department used video surveillance from helicopters to monitor political demonstrations in Washington, D.C.

OBSERVING SURVEILLANCE AND ADVOCACY

The goal of the Observing Surveillance Project is to promote public debate about the presence of video cameras in Washington, D.C. Many systems of surveillance arrive quietly. A video surveillance system in the capital of the United States requires public debate. A second goal of the project is to explore the use of media to promote public dialogue. Most policy debate is based on text. The prevailing paradigm is the argument. It appears in legal briefs, congressional testimony, and policy papers. But most people do not read briefs, testimony, or policy papers. They view images.

United States Park Police Aviation
00 290 Mission Report
Date: Monday, October 16, 2000
Case Number: 00-31850
Nature of Mission: 301
Shift: 2nd
Jurisdiction/ Agency: USPP SFB
Location: National Mall
County: SW
Agency: Police
Check if YES: Narcotics; Mission Cancelled; FLIR Located; Arrests 0; 0.0 Terrorism Flt. Tim; USPP/NPS Jurisdiction
Next Mission; Print Daily; Close
Aircraft: 1 412EP
Cost: $320.00
Last Audit; Audit #: 824
overflight and downlink of areas for Million Family March
Start Time: 12:20
End Time: 12:44
Mission Time: 0.4
Reimbursable mission time:
Pilot: Bohn, Keith
Co-pilot:
Lead Medic: Stallman, David
Medic:
Pilot OAS2 time:
Copilot OAS2 time:
Lead Medic OAS2 time:
Passengers:

FIGURE 3: Helicopter log of surveillance of Million Family March on the National Mall on October 22, 2000, obtained by EPIC under the Freedom of Information Act.

PROLOGUE: THE ROLE OF IDIOMS AND ICONS IN ADVOCACY

Earlier projects undertaken by the staff of EPIC have made use of a wide range of political images and idioms. Mouse pads titled "Clipper 2.1," designed with the assistance of Phil Zimmerman, helped launch a campaign against a government effort to regulate encryption. Stickers labeled "Suitable for government surveillance" placed on hotel telephones drew attention to FBI surveillance proposals at a conference on Computers, Freedom, and Privacy. Buttons with the slogan "Privacy is a RIGHT not a PREFERENCE" helped shape the public debate over self-regulation. Bumper stickers that proclaimed "privacy.org, the site for news, information, and action" announced the arrival of a new privacy-advocacy website. The challenge in the digital world is to find idioms and icons that are familiar and accessible.

THE TRAVEL POSTCARD

One of the first new forms of inexpensive media in the twentieth century was the travel postcard. All across America and Europe, travelers purchased penny post-

privacy.org
the site for news, information, and action

FIGURE 4: A bumper sticker to announce the creation of a new website can also be considered a privacy-enhancing technique if it is placed over a camera lens.

cards with colorful images to send to friends and relatives back home. The postcards captured images of monuments and parks, beaches and famous hotels. The Observing Surveillance Project adapted the metaphor of the travel postcard. The first image published was of two American flags against a cloudy sky with a half-dome, lamppost-shaped video camera in the foreground. The font was selected to mimic a classic travel card—bold italics proclaim "Washington, D.C." The title across the top: "Observing Surveillance."

FIGURE 5: The vacation postcard is adapted to make a political statement.

FIGURE 6: This four-panel postcard mimics a popular vacation postcard available in Washington, D.C.

Subsequent cards incorporated the custom of a caption on the obverse of the card to identify location. For Observing Surveillance, the location is the position of the video surveillance cameras depicted on the card. The choice of cameras is not accidental. Several may be found in front of FBI headquarters and the U.S. Department of Justice. The montage is a popular way to capture several images on a single card. Observing Surveillance parodied the montage of Washington with a series of images showing several surveillance cameras.

THE TOURIST MAP

Washington is one of the most popular tourist locations in the world. The Washington tourist bureau provides colorful maps for visitors to locate museums, metro stops, and other sites. The Observing Surveillance Project modified a Washington tourist bureau map to indicate the location of video surveillance cameras. Tourists can then decide whether to visit or to avoid these new Washington landmarks. On the website it is possible to click on specific camera locations and "zoom in" on the cameras that are designed to zoom in on the street below.[7]

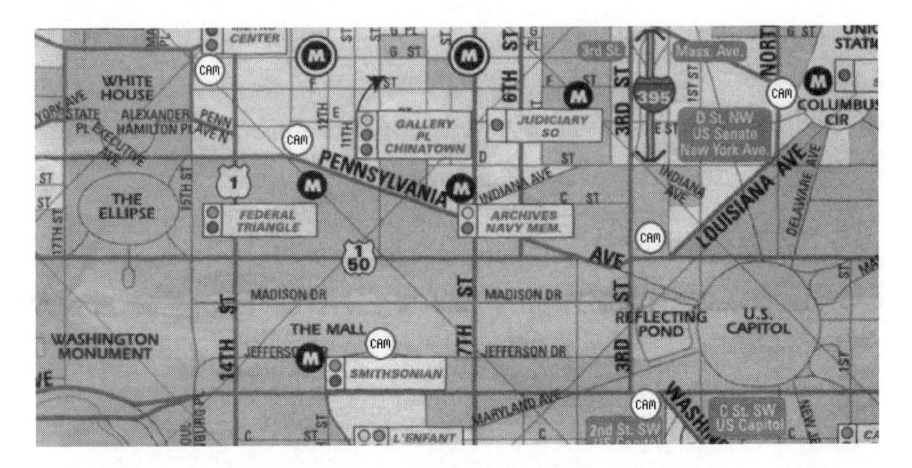

FIGURE 7: The image above is based on a popular tourist map in Washington, D.C. The circles with "CAM" inside were incorporated to identify the presence of video cameras in the nation's capital.

THE POP-UP WINDOW

For users of the Internet, the pop-up window is a genuine annoyance. It obscures the primary image screen and breaks the simple point-and-click routine of Inter-

ACT NOW! Stop Surveillance Cameras in Washington, D.C.

- The cameras will monitor DC residents, visitors, tourists, and peaceful protesters
- The **D.C. City Council** needs public comment on this proposal now
- **Send e-mail** "Stop Video Surveillance" to **dccouncil@dccouncil.washington.dc.us** with comments and cc: cameras@epic.org

1. **Urge strong legal safeguards**
2. Require a detailed cost/benefit study
3. Oppose all recording without judicial authority and proper public oversight

DC City Council www.dccouncil.washington.dc.us
Electronic Privacy Information Center (EPIC)
www.epic.org/privacy/surveillance

FIGURE 8: Text of a pop-up window urging Internet users to take action.

net surfing. One major Internet service provider that offered to block pop-up ads is currently running a campaign with pop-up ads with the simple claim "Get rid of this advertising!" Observing Surveillance embraced the pop-up ad to promote public participation in the D.C. City Council hearing on video surveillance. The goal is clear—focus the user's attention on the statement, and encourage a response. Protest has always had this character.

FIGURE 9: This image appears in a pop-up window which announces the Observing Surveillance photo exhibit. The image is of the L'Enfant Plaza administrative complex at the intersection of 7th and D Streets, NW, in Washington, D.C. A surveillance camera can be seen near the right edge of the image.

FIGURE 10: Image taken from a pop-up window drawing attention to the American flags and the surveillance cameras outside the FBI building in Washington, D.C.

THE VACATION ALBUM

Apple computer has released a new software program called iPhoto that makes possible the production of handsome, "linen-bound" photo albums. The Apple advertising promotes the use of the program to record vacation memories. The images feature young children splashing in the water at the beach, the parents smiling close by. But the technology that makes possible the transfer of digital images to vacation albums also makes possible digital documentaries. Text can be joined with photographs, monochrome substituted for color, citations incorporated.

FIGURE 11: Image from cover of iPhoto album "Observing Surveillance."

DIGITAL DOCUMENTARY

The Observing Surveillance Project visually demonstrates the impact of surveillance. Images of liberty, freedom, and travel are juxtaposed with images of surveillance and control. The images of surveillance cameras suggest also the construction of a Panopticon in the nation's capital. Observing Surveillance attempts to communicate ideas through images.[8] Watch the watchers.[9] The battle over control of the technology of observation has just begun.

PART III

DIGITAL WAR-MAKING

7. SOCIAL AND ELECTRONIC NETWORKS IN THE WAR ON TERROR[1]

RONALD J. DEIBERT AND JANICE GROSS STEIN

WAR BY A NETWORK

That we in North America face a new kind of threat is beyond question. The attacks against the heartland of the United States, its corporate and military icons, and the killing of over 3,000 civilians mark a watershed in thinking about security. Rarely in the last two hundred years have civilians in North America been the object of systematic attack,[2] and even longer since the core of the hegemonic power was struck from the periphery. The important analytical and political questions are: What kind of threat do we face? What is the appropriate response to that threat? In other words, what are the appropriate ways to think about dealing with a threat from a nonstate actor with no fixed location or permanently defined territorial assets?

President George W. Bush claims that the threat is from "evildoers" who seek to destroy Western civilization. This is a struggle of good against evil, of the forces of darkness against light. These forces of darkness are themselves threatened by the openness, the affluence, and the cultural diversity of postindustrial democratic society. Here, we come close to an argument of a clash of civilizations.[3] Others claim that the attacks are the work of a small, maniacal group of terrorists, unrepresentative of the mainstream of their societies, and isolated in small, disorganized, conspiratorial units. While both analyses capture part of the more complex character of the current threat, neither analysis can stand close scrutiny and the weight of evidence. And, more important, the conceptual language is wrong.

We are in a new kind of struggle, one against a network with global reach. We need to understand who organizes and manages this particular network. And we need appropriate conceptual language to understand what a network is, how it operates, how it thrives, and how it withers, if we are not to misunderstand the threat and misconceive the response.

For those seeking answers to these questions, most theorizing on security—both rationalist and reflective—offers only limited help. Mainstream rationalist approaches to security treat states as unitary, rational actors—billiard balls with hard outer shells and a sharp division between "inside" and "outside."[4] The group that organized the attacks on the United States, however, is part of a decentralized and transnationally dispersed network of religious extremists. Even if the terrorists are considered to be a "conflict group" equivalent to a state, their decentralized operational structure prevents them from acting in a unitary, rational way with clearly defined preferences that are knowable *ex ante*.[5] One of the characteristics of the terrorist network that organized the attacks was that local units operated with a significant degree of autonomy.

Not only are actor models misleading, but so is the way in which power is conceived by traditional theories of international relations. Realist approaches to international relations treat concentrated military and economic capabilities as the indicators of power.[6] But the military instruments that were employed by the terrorists—hijacked jets as ballistic missiles, public Internet terminals, cell phones, and rental cars—were plucked from the postindustrial fabric of the society that was targeted, rather than developed through a traditional process of national-military industrialization. How does a state "balance" against power assets and material resources that are part of its own society? And how do we theorize about a threat from actors whose capabilities are not only dispersed but also unpredictable, and hence cannot be measured?

"Reflective" or "critical" theories, on the other hand, can help decipher and deconstruct the paradigms through which threats to security are defined.[7] They offer little help, however, on how to deal with specific threats once they are identified and agreed upon. Admittedly, reflective approaches to security are forms of "critical," as opposed to "problem-solving," theory.[8] They stand outside the present order and ask how it came to be, while pointing the way toward alternative paths of development for the future. They help develop an understanding of why some threats are given attention and others are marginalized. But they are less useful in developing strategic concepts for a mutually agreed-upon construction of a threat and the appropriate response.

The network as an organizational form and "actor" in world politics requires a different set of conceptual tools than those found in traditional and reflective approaches to world politics. Different tools are required not because networks are new per se but because they differ from hierarchical forms of organization, such as states, that are the core unit of analysis in most theories of international relations. Although networks are often associated with postindustrial society, the network as an organizational form is an ancient practice.[9] Maritime trading networks were common in archipelagos in ancient Greece and the islands that now make up Indonesia. Christian religious scholars based in relatively isolated monasteries of western Europe in the early Middle Ages organized a very effective form of interaction through distributed social networks. Likewise, the Maghrebi traders of the eleventh-century Muslim world employed networks of information exchange.[10] Families, ethnic diaspora groups, and communities around the world can all be seen as variants of social networks.[11] Networks have always coexisted with hierarchical forms of social organization, sometimes prominently, other times submerged, depending on the historical and cultural context.

Nor is the study of networks new. Social network analysis came to prominence in the anthropologist A. R. Radcliffe-Brown's seminal 1940 article, "On Social Structures."[12] Ever since, many sociologists and anthropologists have employed network analysis to understand the linkages between people across domains. In international relations, the concept of the network, if not the formal term, is embedded in the work of functionalist and integration theorists, and in the "cobweb" theory of world order of John Burton.[13] More recently, networks form the core analytic concept of research on transnational advocacy groups and citizen activists.[14]

In this chapter, we use concepts derived from analyses of networks to investigate networks of terror and to help understand how they operate and function. Since 9/11, and even before that time, it has become increasingly common to describe nonstate terrorist actors as networks. What is needed now is to move beyond the metaphorical use of the term to systematically explore what type of network Al Qaeda is and how it functions. We set out to do this in the first half of the chapter. However, our goal is to understand not only how networks function but also how they can be debilitated. As we point out below, analyses of networks have examined how they arise and function but have paid less attention to how they decay and to their deliberate disruption. In the second half of our chapter, we draw from theories associated with warfare and hacking in computer networks to develop a new set of tools to fight networks of terror. We argue that the use of information and communication technologies (ICTs) by Al Qaeda and other terrorist groups was limited and that efforts to control or increase surveillance of ICTs are of questionable utility. However, network warfare concepts can provide the basis for useful *analogies* for military campaigns and intelligence operations against terrorism. At the same time, however, we recognize that all analogies, including those to hacking and network war, have limits. We attempt to make these boundaries clear in our analysis.

THE NETWORK AS THE BASIC FORM OF POSTINDUSTRIAL ORGANIZATION

We have witnessed the first large-scale violent attack against postindustrial society through its signature form of organization: the network. The network has become the most pervasive organizational image and the dominant form of social organization in postindustrial society. "As a historical trend," observes Manuel Castells, "dominant functions and processes in the information age are increasingly organized around networks. Networks constitute the new social morphology of our societies, and the diffusion of networking logic substantially modifies the operation and outcomes in processes of production, experience, power, and culture."[15] Networks also shape processes of terror and violence. We need to understand the structure of a network, its application, and its resiliency in the face of disruption.

A network is a collection of connected points or nodes, generally designed to be resilient through redundancy. It can be one terminal connected to the Internet, or one expert communicating with another expert in a common network devoted to a shared problem. Networks, in other words, can be both technological and social. The design of the network determines its resilience, its flexibility, its capacity to expand, and its vulnerability.

The first and still archetypal electronic network is, of course, the Internet. Apparently developed simultaneously by three different sources in the early 1960s—Larry Kleinrock, David Davies, and Paul Baran—the central feature of the Internet is a distributed form of communication without central control.[16] In a distributed network, messages are broken into individual "packets" that then take multiple different paths to reach their destination. Such a mode of transmission allows communication exchanges to continue even if parts of the node are destroyed or inoperative. The network is resilient because of its built-in redundancy; the more nodes are added to the network, the more resilient the network as a whole becomes. Built upon principles antithetical to centralized broadcasting modes of communication, the Internet builds strength through dispersion and multiplication of individual nodes. It is precisely for this reason that centralized forms of political authority find the task of censoring Internet communications so difficult. With the Internet, there is no single node from which all information emanates or through which it passes. Removing a single node, or even several, will not destroy the network. The network adjusts, reroutes, and reforms as everything from dissident websites in China to the trading of MP3 files demonstrates.[17] In the pure model of a network, such as the Internet, eliminating one node of a network does not imperil other nodes.

SOCIAL NETWORKS

Social networks mirror their electronic counterparts in important ways. They too are highly decentralized, with different leadership branches that operate with a large degree of autonomy. Unlike the tight pyramids of command-and-control political structures, the hallmark of industrial society, networks are "flat," with leaders who are empowered to act with minimal direction and supervision. Using advanced electronic forms of communication, social networks of every kind have multiplied in the last decade: businesses, civil society networks, journalists, scientists, physicians, lawyers, scholars, and environmentalists. These networks differ in how they are organized and, consequently, in their flexibility and resilience.

Most networks generally do not approximate the pure forms. Perhaps the most advanced networks can be found in the financial sector, where capital flows relatively seamlessly around the world through integrated electronic trading networks. Another can be found at the opposite end of the political spectrum, among so-called antiglobalization activists.[18] Linked through thousands of websites, e-mail lists, and Internet relay chats, citizen activists from around the world have been able to coordinate mass protests at major international events without a hierarchical mode of organization—a capability that seemed to escape the notice of many of the movement's critics who lamented the lack of overall "direction." Such pure network models are rare, however. A study of global knowledge networks found, for example, that the most successful networks require a center or a "hub," financial support, and a secure environment for the "host," which serves as the temporary organizational focus. There is an element of "place," even if that place is temporary, within which almost all successful networks function.[19] Even among global financial networks, major urban centers act as crucial, central nodes where financial expertise and personnel are located. It is for this reason that the city of London, for example, occupies such a central role in the global financial economy.[20]

Most social networks build some elements of a "web" into their design, even those that have major nodes within them. Analysts have suggested, for example, that one of the reasons why complex financial networks were able to resume operations so quickly after the attack on September 11 was that the "corporate headquarters" of many of the firms in the World Trade Center had been moved off-site after the first attack in 1993. Within hours, many had resumed operations because of the redundancy they had built into their information systems. Such redundancy also explains why e-mail traffic continued to move unimpaired on September 11, whereas telephone traffic ground to a halt in the northeastern United States.

GLOBAL NETWORKS OF TERROR

Global networks of terror bear an uncanny resemblance to their generally benign and productive counterparts. Unlike legitimate global networks, of course, they work in secrecy and through illegitimate practices and violence to advance their political purposes. Often with life cycles lasting decades, networks of terror thrive on the openness, flexibility, and diversity characteristic of postindustrial society, crossing borders almost as easily as do goods and services, knowledge, and cultures. They have global reach, particularly when they can operate within the fabric of the most open and multicultural societies, and through postindustrial organizational forms.

Global networks of terror are enabled by conditions unique to our times. They are conceivable only in a world that is tightly interconnected and in societies that are moving through the processes of postindustrialization. Without global markets and communications, the widespread mobility of people, and multicultural, diverse societies, these networks of terror could not survive, much less succeed. Many, though not all, "hosts" of networks of terror are weak states that can provide a secure environment for the infrastructure and resources they need. They often depend on states for infrastructure, logistics, and training sites. In exchange for the shield the state provides, a network delivers complex political and financial rewards that help a regime to stay in power. Some have argued that an ideal environment for a "host" of a network of terror is a weak, failed, or fractured state where a network can provide critically needed assets in exchange for the capacity to operate "in place." Even without a secure physical environment, however, networks can survive; a node can use mobile headquarters, but training, operations, and recruitment become more difficult. Likewise, networks can flourish in strong states with open societies, but operations become difficult for contrary reasons of social transparency and relatively capable law enforcement and intelligence.

The existence of Al Qaeda was well known to intelligence analysts and experts in the region long before September 11. Its organizational structure, according to the best available knowledge, in large part resembles a network. It is organized in self-contained nodes that function autonomously with limited communication and support from the center. Responsibility and decision-making authority are devolved down to the lowest possible level. Unlike open networks, however, each node is unaware of the identities and attributes of others.

The Arabic word *al-Qa'eda* means "base." Historically, the network has had only temporary bases, first in Sudan and then in Afghanistan. It is better described as "a distributed, roaming, nonterritorial network, operating through its combined use of advanced information technologies and traditional *halawa* exchanges."[21] Its nodes communicate through the Internet, funds are transferred through local exchanges with global connections, and its members move freely across the borders of diverse, multicultural societies.

Al Qaeda is also a network of networks. In the last three years it successfully interlinked with other networks led by Egyptian and Algerian dissidents and exiles. The Egyptian network brought a significant increase in the level of operational planning, competence, and logistics to the broader network. As Al Qaeda connects with other networks, it more closely approximates a pure network with very flexible, insulated, and redundant connections.

It does, however, have a center—the equivalent of a small corporate headquarters—and it operates in place. Both these attributes merit some attention. It has a hub, which is led by Saudi and Egyptian dissidents, and is organized as a "corporate" structure, with a *shura* (council). It has a finance committee, a military committee responsible for training and arms purchases, a committee on Islamic study, a media committee, and a travel committee.[22] Leaders are important but, as in other network structures, not all-important.

It is consequently misleading to personalize the threat as Osama bin Laden, for in this kind of hybrid network-corporate structure, others can replace him were he to disappear. On the other hand, it is also misleading to claim, as some do, that bin Laden is a social construction, that he is the creation of those who seek to personalize and demonize the enemy. His leadership, and his charisma—expressed in part through piety, asceticism, and commitment—has been significant. As in other kinds of social and political organizations, leaders matter in networks. They may matter far less than they do in command-and-control hierarchies, but, even in networks, they still matter. Al Qaeda approximates "a hybrid peer-to-peer network, in which a central source triggers the actions that are carried out by individual nodes."[23] Denying the major nodes a secure environment would weaken the network, but the nodes can find other, less attractive hosts. Destroying the center and removing the leader would weaken it even more but would not necessarily disable the network.

Al Qaeda is a network that also functions partly "in place." In its earliest phase of development, it used Sudan as a safe host environment. When Sudan expelled bin Laden, he secured his headquarters behind the shield provided by the Taliban in Afghanistan. Here, the network becomes a more familiar and vulnerable organizational form as it organizes training camps, recruits members, and draws on a pool of sympathizers to form a guard around its assets. These assets are potential targets and can be disrupted more easily than a pure network without the organizational apparatus of a corporate headquarters.

Paradoxically, this network organized in postindustrial form is committed to a preindustrial project of religious monopoly and intolerance. It rejects the postindustrial project even as it adapts its organizational forms and technology to pursue its purpose. Al Qaeda rejects not only postindustrial society but also the hierarchical command-and-control state characteristic of the industrial era. It seeks a return to an earlier community of the faithful uninterrupted by the borders and the divisions of the modern state.

THE CHALLENGE OF WAGING WAR AGAINST A NETWORK

A struggle against a network is asymmetric: states must fight a global network that is not designed around dominant power centers but is dispersed, flat, and flexible. It is easier, for example, to destroy a weblike structure, with a controlling hub, connected through strands to the points of the web. Destroy the hub, and the web is fatally weakened. Not so with a network. It is for this reason that the concepts and tools of traditional security studies and international relations theory are not much help in this struggle. Networks of terror are non-state-centric, nonterritorial, and largely distributed.

When we think about Al Qaeda as a network, it becomes clear that existing military doctrine, based on concepts of mass and maneuver reinforced by heavy strikes from the air, is only the first phase in a much longer struggle. At best, conventional military force can reduce the number of available host environments, degrade the capacity of a network to train members, and force the nodes to become mobile. A military attack to disable those who provide safe haven for the network is a first but limited response to a network of terror. Its purpose is to deprive Al Qaeda of the secure geographic environment that the Taliban had provided. Since the bombing campaign in Afghanistan, for example, the Al Qaeda membership has been scattered into hiding, but it has also slowly repenetrated Afghani territory and established new footholds in remote regions of Pakistan and Iran.[24]

Military attacks, conducted through a command-and-control structure, are designed to be effective against hierarchical state structures with conventionally structured and consolidated forces. Here the purpose must be not only to destroy the capacity of this host to act as a secure environment but also to disrupt and eventually disable the network. Military doctrine will have to change to decentralize intelligence and command to the lowest possible levels and to provide as much flexibility as possible to give local area commanders the capacity to launch continuous pinprick attacks from multiple directions to confuse and overwhelm the network.[25]

To return to the analogy of computer networks, terrorist groups often have more than a single server. Increasingly, application processing is distributed across a network of hosts that are geographically dispersed. Client workstations, or nodes within the network, access the network for application software and communication with other end-user workstations and with databases that are themselves often distributed in peer-to-peer networks. This analogy is a reasonably good fit with the way those who hijacked commercial flights communicated with nodes of the network that were dispersed. Although the node has no knowledge of which server is supporting which part of the task at any moment, it still needs to have sufficient servers intact and in touch to continue its work.

How then can the capacity of a network be impaired? It is unlikely that networks, organisms with rudimentary central nervous systems, can be completely destroyed. A network has no powerful central "brain" that can be targeted to lead to a "quick kill." Paradoxically, actions designed to "kill" a part of the network identify the part that has been damaged. Like other lower-order organisms, the network then sheds that part and regenerates elsewhere.[26] To destroy the organism, its capacity for regeneration must be gradually degraded, through suffocation and starvation. Similarly, to impair a network's functioning, the capacity of its servers must be degraded, the connections among nodes slowed, and the links between the workstations and the servers interrupted and eventually damaged.

Drawing from the extant literature on social and electronic networks and computer network warfare, in the following section we clarify the different modes by which networks of all types decay or can be debilitated. We then extend each of these modes to terrorist networks and develop accompanying strategies that might be employed to foster decay and debilitation. We outline how those strategies compare to the present configuration of intelligence and law-enforcement agencies and the United States–led "war on terror," and suggest how the latter should be modified. We also discuss some of the potential drawbacks, both practically and normatively, that such modifications would entail and the practical steps that would have to be taken to adjust institutional settings to a new networked reality of intelligence, law enforcement, and war fighting.

HACKING NETWORKS OF TERROR

Much is known about the operations and characteristics of networks, but comparatively less is known about how they break down. There are at least two fundamentally different modes of breakdown that are important to keep distinct, since they involve different processes and dynamics. First, networks can break down because of *decay*.[27] These are processes largely internal to a network itself, although the environment within which the network is embedded can play an important facilitating role. One example that should be familiar to most social scientists is the decay of academic e-mail lists. Many lists begin with great expectations and a flurry of e-mail exchanges only to get bogged down in recrimination, insults, and flaming. As list members unsubscribe, the positive "network effects" of combined numbers decreases, undermining the attractiveness, dynamism, and utility of the list, causing further erosion and spiraling deterioration. E-mail lists may also decay simply because the causes or issues around which the network was formed in the first place begin to disappear. Networks display a variety of forms of decay, each of which shares the common feature of being largely unintended by-products of circumstances beyond the network participants' direct intent or control.

Second, networks can break down because of *debilitation*. Unlike network decay, debilitation is a process that works largely from the "outside in" and is the product of a deliberate set of attack strategies. The best example of network debilitation is, of course, computer network warfare, including the use of viruses, Trojan horses, worms, and denial-of-service attacks. Network debilitation forms more out of a concerted plan than as the by-product of unfortunate circumstances, as in network decay. Both forms of network breakdown are important to understand because they exhibit different dynamics and require different strategies. Even though network decay is largely an internal process, distributed terrorist networks may be especially vulnerable to strategies designed to facilitate it. Lacking a territorial infrastructure, if the causes or ideologies and project-based activities around which terrorist networks form can be removed, little else will remain to hold them together.[28]

OVERFLOW, CONGESTION, AND THE BREAKDOWN OF TRUST

The most direct assault leading to network debilitation would be an attack on the network itself. The activities of Al Qaeda and other terrorist networks cannot be reduced to electronic means alone, as will be explained in more detail below, so those cannot be the prime focus of a network debilitation strategy. Indeed, they may be among the least important. Nonetheless it is useful to turn to computer network warfare to develop *analogies* that can be employed in strategies to debilitate terrorist networks.

In computer network settings, one of the more prevalent forms of network warfare used by both states and hackers has been distributed denial-of-service (DoS) attacks. DoS attacks employ the decentralized character of the Internet to organize an overwhelming and disabling flood of information to attack selected servers. Key to the launch of a DoS attack is a multiplier effect achieved by the control of "zombie" computers spread throughout the Internet, typically through backdoor access of computers with fixed Internet Protocols (IPs). At prearranged times, the linked zombie computers make repeated requests for fictitious files. The flood of information requests eventually overwhelms the capacity of the server to respond, shutting it down.

The software to organize DoS attacks is widely dispersed on the Internet, and depends on relatively minimal knowledge of network codes and operations. The most well known DoS attacks have been organized by nonpolitical hackers and crackers targeting large commercial websites, such as Yahoo and eBay. But DoS attacks have also been employed for political ends. One of the first DoS attacks was organized by a pro-Chiapan group called the Electronic Disturbance Theatre based in New York City, directed at the servers of the Mexican government. More recently, DoS attacks against an Internet service provider based in Toronto, Canada, that hosted websites of the dissident religious group Falun Gong were traced back to government computers in China.[29]

Another form of network warfare is the use of viruses, Trojan horses, and worms. These tools are programs or pieces of code that are loaded onto computers without the users' knowledge. Viruses can replicate themselves to the point of using all of a computer's available memory and resources. They can also transmit themselves across the network affecting multiple nodes and users and slowing down the network. Viruses can be extremely disabling, causing random damage to data files as well as compromising private or sensitive information. The ILOVEYOU virus of 2000 spread globally within days, causing upwards of $1 billion in damage to computers, lost business, and corrupted data.

How can the methods of *computerized* network attacks be translated into a broader fight against a network of terror? To extend the analogy, the objective would be to overwhelm the nodes of the terrorist network through a multiplier effect, making it more difficult, more time-consuming, more expensive for users in the field to get what they need from the network's "hosts" and to discern credible, useful information from "noise." One way to achieve this would be through more rigorous requirements for documentation, more frequent checks on existing documentation, more frequent checks on compliance with existing regulations, all of which increase the transactions costs for users. This kind of strategy does not necessarily require new powers of enforcement, but a different approach to the implementation of existing regulations. The strategic use of disinformation, misleading signals about possible targets, frequent and at times deliberately misleading messages about information at hand, organized and channeled through multiple media can all make it more difficult for end users to communicate with hosts and vice versa.

Essentially, such a strategy targets, and begins to break down, the system of trust (and their functional equivalents) upon which all social networks rely to flourish. To understand how this takes place, two different dimensions of trust are of significance to terrorist networks in this respect.[30] First, and perhaps most important, are relations of *personal* trust that bind network members together. Such networks can be found among the main inner core of Al Qaeda and would obviously be extremely difficult to infiltrate. Second are relations of trust based on *procedures* and *impersonal* modes of communication—essentially the functional equivalents to personal trust. Public key infrastructures are a good example from computer networks of the latter form of trust. Public key infrastructures, such as digital certificates, verify and authenticate the validity of each party involved in Internet communications, even if they have never met face-to-face. Such systems of procedural or impersonal trust are essential for a variety of transactions on the Internet, perhaps the most significant of which is electronic commerce.

Within terrorist networks, a very similar form of impersonal or procedural system of trust underpins the *halawa* exchanges described earlier in the chapter. Not everyone within the terrorist network has to know everyone else for the network to function. Instead, a series of intermediaries perform the roles of impersonal routers, keeping the information flowing without having to know the full nature of the information being relayed or the author of the information. Secret codes supply the encryption to ensure authenticity and verification. Although, as described above, an architecture of impersonal relations such as this provides enormous flexibility, it also creates a potential vulnerability. If the system of trust can be gradually compromised, if the authenticity of information and exchanges traveling through the network becomes increasingly difficult to verify, then the network itself will begin to unravel.

Much like the use of Trojan horses and viruses, such a strategy would require covertly penetrating as much as possible networks of terror—admittedly a difficult task given the closed nature of terrorist networks but one that can greatly facilitate the circulation of misinformation. Misinformation circulated through networks from both inside and outside could undermine the effectiveness of the organization and the credibility of information circulating within. Although difficult, it is important not to overestimate the difficulties either. Given the nature of the impersonal system of trust that underpins the *halawa* exchanges, not every node in the network needs to be penetrated in order for a compromise of the overall network to begin to take effect. Much as in the breakdown of trust in other types of social networks, only a selected few nodes or routers need be corrupted to begin the process of breaking down systems of trust for the network overall.

Among the reactions to perceived intelligence failures leading up to 9/11 has been precisely the inability of the United States to place operatives inside terrorist networks. To rectify such problems, it is widely perceived that more foreign-language skills and non-Western personnel are required among new recruits. But successfully penetrating such informal social networks would require moving beyond Western-based intelligence agencies to develop cooperative links with intelligence agencies in non-Western countries where nodes and routers are common. To move in the direction of a more distributed, networked architecture, in other words, nodes would have to be developed at local levels, "on the ground," so to speak. At the same time, however, such cooperative links across borders and with countries that may have dubious human-rights records—and the very practice of covert action itself—raise thorny issues of legitimacy and accountability, to which we will return below.[31]

ELIMINATION OF HOSTS

A second strategy is to starve and suffocate the hosts upon which nodes, routers, and ultimately participants depend. Networks that lack redundancy, as we have seen, are inefficient. The strategic objective in a struggle against a network of terror is to reduce its redundancy. Important in this respect are both identifying clearly the type of environments that are likely to provide suitable hosts and developing strategies to eliminate or minimize them. As mentioned above, one of the conventional wisdoms is that weak or so-called "failed states" provide the most propitious environment for hosts in networks of terror. The argument is that lacking law and order, failed states provide fertile ground for criminal organizations and terrorist groups to plant their main operations. Terrorist networks can more easily buy off corrupt politicians or local warlords, feed off grievous populations, and recruit discontented and impoverished personnel. Although logical, such an argument is not empirically valid in all cases and should not be assumed to be correct. For example, the Al Qaeda network did not take root in Afghanistan during the worst period of that country's civil war (1991–96) but only after the war had culminated in the victory of a sympathetic group, the Taliban, which provided them with a safe haven. Likewise, by all reports Al Qaeda is finding refuge today in cities such as Lahore and Karachi in Pakistan and across the sands of Baluchistan into regions of Iran. Though perhaps dangerous and remote, such regions cannot accurately be described as "failed states." Going further, Al Qaeda operatives were known to have located themselves (and perhaps still do) well within the heartland of Northern industrialized democracies, such as Germany, Canada, and the United States. Eliminating failed states will not necessarily eliminate the nodes that harbor networks of terror.

That is why the massive United States–led bombing campaign that obliterated the safe haven of Afghanistan, making at least one of the important hosts insecure, should not be held up as the model for eliminating hosts for terrorist networks altogether. There are less costly and ultimately more effective forms of suffocation that are and should continue to be employed. Multilateral efforts to coordinate among states across a range of policies—from standards on human rights to law enforcement—is a first and perhaps ultimately the most important step in eliminating host environments.[32] Coordination and even harmonization of banking regulations among states will help to stifle funding of terrorist networks. Stepping up international anti–money laundering regulations—which to date have been admittedly poorly applied—would do the same. Strengthening and widening the processes and institutions of accountable justice, such as through the International Criminal Court, would add another layer of protection. At the same time, states that provide an attractive "host site" or operational base for terrorists need to be identified and pressured into conforming with the standards of the international community *before* hosts take up residence. Pressure should be put on regimes that "export" or "deflect" their internal political problems to weaker regimes and refuse to open up their political space to legitimate political participation. Such a multifaceted effort goes beyond the admirable strategy of lifting failed states out of chaos to include pressures on strong, though perhaps illegitimate or corrupt, states to conform to multilateral standards of behavior.

To date, the war on terror has been carried out through an uncomfortable mix of weak multilateral approaches and an aggressive United States–based unilateralism. To fully shore up states and protect against the emergence of propitious host environments, law enforcement, intelligence, and ultimately military activities need to be multilaterally constituted—admittedly a long-term, difficult project for a deeply entrenched sovereign state system, but one not without precedent at other scales. Old institutions—such as Interpol, for example—may have to be re-formed, while new institutions will have to be created.

DENIAL OF TARGETS AND PROJECT-BASED ACTIVITIES

As outlined above, networks of all types can break down, not only by debilitation but by internal decay as well. While penetrating terrorist networks can help facilitate that process, other measures can be taken by actors outside of the network that have the same result. Most important are precautions taken to deny targets of opportunity, which in turn winnow away the number of project-based activities for terrorist networks. As the opportunities for terrorist targets thin out and as terrorist networks are frustrated in their aims, the appeal of terrorism as a mode of effective change may decline.

To frustrate project-based activities, targets must be protected and secured, reducing the number of opportunities for terrorist networks. Indeed, quickly following 9/11, states around the world have taken radical steps to do so through legislation and other means. The result has been a wide blanket of increased state powers at the cost of far-reaching infringements on civil liberties and debatable effectiveness in securing actual targets of potential terrorism. To give just one example, since 9/11, databases containing information on thousands of individuals on everything from grocery purchases to travel records, once legally segregated, have fallen within governments' surveillance web.[33] The most fundamental changes have occurred in the area of Internet surveillance, ostensibly because the Internet fuels the activities of terrorists, and intelligence and law-enforcement agencies can gather new information about terrorist networks if they are given new powers to eavesdrop and intercept.[34] Both are highly questionable.

First, although Al Qaeda and other terrorist groups undoubtedly employ the Internet, it is not entirely clear that such technologies are fundamentally important to their sustenance and operations. Nor is it clear that terrorists will turn to cyberspace as a means to carry out terrorist activities. For example, in spite of being the object of a massive international campaign, Al Qaeda still managed to move billions of dollars from one continent to another, not through electronic means, but by the material transshipment of gold bullion through sympathetic networks.[35] Although there is some evidence of Al Qaeda using sophisticated tools of encryption, there is also clear evidence that the network more often than not employed simple code words when communicating over e-mail—age-old methods of encryption that million-dollar computers do little to crack. And although threats to critical infrastructures are real, particularly in cases where poor security exists, many believe that a combination of advanced encryption and firewalls and de-coupling of critical systems from the public Internet could correct these vulnerabilities.[36] Moreover, it is far from certain that assaults conducted through cyberspace would provide as big a "bang for the buck" as would more kinetic forms of assault, such as bombs and converted missiles. It is just not that easy to bring down catastrophe through cyberspace.[37]

Second, it is not entirely clear that the actual intelligence failure of 9/11 was due to the lack of information per se, as it was the lack of proper *analysis* of data collected by the many disparate U.S. law-enforcement and intelligence agencies. More information may, in fact, lead only to information glut. A more significant problem was likely the *compartmentalization* of information among the various intelligence and law-enforcement agencies, both within the United States and around the world—a perennial problem. Interagency rivalry between the FBI and the CIA is widely cited as a substantial barrier to the proper analysis of threats.[38] And in spite of efforts to rectify such compartmentalization since 9/11, it appears that substantial compartmentalization among agencies still remains.

Rather than broad surveillance, denial of opportunities should focus instead on *targeted* security, much of which could be accomplished without radical infringements on civil liberties and sweeping intrusions on Internet communications. Common sense and practical measures—such as reinforcing cockpit doors, hiring more qualified security personnel at screening points, developing strong encryption and firewall technologies for electronic networks, controlling and accounting for access to critical technologies and materials—are steps that could be taken without introducing sweeping and excessive legislative powers. "Surveillance of means," Ashton Carter notes, "raises far fewer civil liberties issues than does surveillance of persons, and it might be much more effective."[39] Nor would it entail a drastic reversal of steps taken since the end of the Cold War to increase government transparency, as has occurred since 9/11. Smart "targeted" security, rather than blanket security, is the way to deny project-based activities against a mobile network of terror.

All of these strategies depend critically on intelligence, but our intelligence systems are not properly configured to wage this battle. Within the intelligence community, the emphasis is on secrecy, compartmentalization, and command-and-control structures. Forged during the Cold War, intelligence agencies are reflexively insulated from the outside world, both domestically and internationally. As Carter put it recently, "It is as though corporate America was managing the modern economy with the structures of the Ford Motor Company, the Bell System, and United Fruit."[40] The structure is poorly suited to the struggle ahead, as is the emphasis on closed channels and secrecy.

To disrupt a network of terror, we will need a reconfigured system of intelligence, one that is decentralized, network based, with a capacity to communicate and confuse in real time across borders. Sharing information across nodes, rather than controlling and limiting information in a hierarchical structure, increases its value and impact. To push further in such a direction requires the participation of citizens as well as states, nongovernmental organizations as well as international institutions. A model of "open-source" intelligence, analogous to the open-source software movement, is more appropriate to the network form. As with open-source software, open-source intelligence thrives on expanding and increasing flows of information and knowledge—the antithesis of the traditional intelligence model. Yet it is precisely such distributed flexibility that is suited to the decentralized nature of the threat.

CONCLUSION

New forms of social organization require new ways of thinking, particularly in response to threats to security that use these new forms. However, traditional international relations theorizing is notoriously conservative about conceptual experimentation. At a time of significant structural change and crisis, such experimentation needs to be encouraged. While the analogies we have put forward here are tentatively drawn, they suggest a new framework for addressing and responding to network-based terrorist threats. Networklike thinking is suggestive for the reconfiguring of strategies of military and intelligence. It privileges flexibility and local initiative over centralization and command-and-control, partnering rather than monopoly, and at times openness rather than secrecy. It will require a renewed emphasis not only on electronic but also on human intelligence, a resource neglected for years by intelligence agencies around the world. And, most important, it points toward an increasing dispersion, rather than consolidation, of authority in world politics to deal with networks of terror.

At the same time, however, moving in the direction of the network model to fight new threats raises significantly novel issues of governance, legitimacy, and accountability. Many of the recommendations to move in the direction of the network model entail moving into uncharted waters or undeveloped institutional settings. Who's accountable for performance at what stage and what level? Practices of information sharing at both local and global levels, as outlined above, often happen in ad hoc and even clandestine ways today. Although new laws passed since 9/11 mandate law-enforcement and intelligence agencies to do so more formally, what remains is to develop publicly accountable, transparent procedures of accountability that cut across territorial and bureaucratic divisions in step with the new networked models of intelligence, law enforcement, and war fighting that are beginning to emerge.

Legislators preparing new guidelines for the war against networks of terror would do well to keep these imperatives in mind. Legislation being passed now is reflexively turning to old strategies and methods of surveillance, secrecy, and closure. To respond to the new threat of network terror, however, new tools need to be adopted and employed that deal effectively with the threat while preserving the mix of rights and constraints on power that define liberal democracies around the world. Hacking networks of terror may not be as spectacular as a massive military campaign, but it may be more effective in the long run. Because these hacking strategies depend on targeted covert operations, intelligence and law-enforcement cooperation, and the application of legal instruments and practical safeguards, there will likely be fewer civilian casualties and highly visible destruction of state infrastructures in host states. In this respect, hacking networks of terror can degrade their capacity to function while minimizing potential resentment and "blowback."

8. PROGRAMMING THEATERS OF WAR: GAMEMAKERS AS SOLDIERS

TIMOTHY LENOIR

In 2002, on July 4 (the entertainment industry's traditional date for premiering the summer's movie blockbuster), the U.S. military released its new videogame, *America's Army: Operations.* Designed by the Modeling, Simulation, and Virtual Environments Institute (MOVES) of the Naval Postgraduate School in Monterey, California, the game is distributed free on the Internet and is intended as a recruiting device. Produced with brilliant graphics and the most advanced commercial game engine available at a cost of around $8 million, the game is a first-person multiplayer combat training simulation requiring players to complete several preliminary stages of combat training in an environment that simulates one of the military's own main training grounds—in other words, it is cyber–boot camp. The military had to add supplementary servers to handle the demand for the game, a reported 400,000 downloads the first day. As of late August 2002, the site continued to average 1.2 million hits per second. *Gamespot,* a leading computer gaming review, not only gave the game a 9.8 rating when it first appeared but also regarded the business model behind the new game as itself deserving an award.[1]

Contrary to initial expectations, the military-industrial complex did not fade away with the end of the Cold War. It has simply reorganized itself—in fact, it is more efficiently organized than ever before. Indeed, a cynic might argue that whereas the military-industrial complex was more or less visible and identifiable during the Cold War, today it is invisibly everywhere, permeating our daily lives. The military-industrial complex has become the military-*entertainment* complex. The entertainment industry is both a major source of innovative ideas and technology, and the training ground for what might be called post-human warfare. How has this change come about?

DISTRIBUTED NETWORKS: SIMNET

The historical answer to this question begins with the construction of the Defense Advanced Research Projects Agency (DARPA)–funded SIMNET, the military's distributed SIMulator NETworking project. Simulators developed prior to the 1980s were stand-alone systems designed for specific task-training purposes, such as docking a space capsule or landing a jet on the deck of an aircraft carrier. High-end simulators typically cost twice as much as the systems they were intended to simulate: for example, in the late 1970s an advanced pilot simulator system cost more than $30–35 million and a tank simulator $18 million, at a time when an advanced individual aircraft was priced around $18 million and a tank considerably less. Air Force Captain Jack A. Thorpe, serving as a research scientist in flight-training research and development at Williams Air Force Base east of Phoenix, Arizona, was brought into DARPA to address this situation.[2] In September 1978 Thorpe had presented the radical idea that aircraft simulators should be used to *augment* aircraft, teaching air-combat skills pilots could not learn in peacetime flying but could learn on simulators in large-scale battle-engagement interactions. Thorpe proposed the construction of battle-engagement simulation technology as a twenty-five-year development goal.[3] Concerned about costs for such a system, Thorpe actively pursued technologies developed outside the DOD such as videogame technology from the entertainment industries.[4] In 1982, upon approval for SIMNET from DARPA, Thorpe hired a team joining military personnel with industrial and computer-graphics designers to develop a network of tank simulators suitable to collective training.

The main reason that pre-SIMNET simulators were so costly was that they were typically designed to emulate the vehicles they represented as closely as engineering technology permitted—a flight simulator aimed to be "an airplane on a stick." SIMNET's contrasting design goal was *selective functional fidelity* rather than full physical fidelity; it called for learning first what functions were needed to meet the training objectives and only then specifying the needs for simulator hardware. As a result, many hardware items not regarded as relevant to combat operations were not included or were designated only by drawings or photographs in the simulator. Furthermore, the vehicle simulator was viewed as a tool for the training of crews as a military unit; the major interest was in *collective,* not *individual,* training. The design goal was to make the crews and units, not the device, the center of the simulation.[5] This approach helped make possible the design of a relatively low-cost device.[6]

Combining these concepts with newly available technology for visual displays and less costly networking architecture, SIMNET was constructed of local and long-haul nets of interactive simulators for maneuvering armored vehicle combat elements (MI tanks and M2/3 fighting vehicles), combat-support elements (including artillery effects and close air support with both rotary and fixed-wing aircraft), and all the necessary command-and-control, administrative, and logistics elements.[7]

The terrains for battle engagements were simulations of actual places, fifty square kilometers initially, but eventually expandable by an order of magnitude in depth and width. Battles were fought in real time, with each simulated element—vehicle, command post, administrative and logistics center, etc.—operated by its assigned crew members. Scoring was recorded on combat events such as movements, firings, hits, and outcomes, but actions during the simulated battle engagements were completely under the control of the personnel who were fighting the battle. Training occurred as a function of the intrinsic feedback and lessons learned from the relevant battle-engagement experiences. Development proceeded in steps, first to demonstrate platoon-level networking, then on to company and battalion levels, and later on to higher levels.

The prototypes and early experiments with SIMNET elements were carried out from 1987 to 1989, and the system was made operational in January 1990. The Army bought the first several hundred units for the Close Combat Tactical Trainer (CCTT) system: an application of the SIMNET concept, the CCTT was the first building block of a system that would eventually contain several thousand units at a total cost of $850 million.[8]

THE BATTLE OF 73 EASTING

The value of the SIMNET as a training system for preparing units for battle became apparent almost immediately during the Gulf War. Hailed as the most significant victory of the war, the Battle of 73 Easting took place on February 26, 1991, just three days into the ground war, between the U.S. 2nd Armored Cavalry Regiment and a much larger Iraqi armed force (armed elements of the 50th Brigade of the Iraqi 12th Armored Division). The battle was named for its location: 73 Easting is the north-south grid line on military maps of the Iraqi Desert. The battle lasted from about 3:30 PM until dusk fell at 5:15 PM, and took place in a swirling sandstorm. The U.S. 2nd Cavalry consisted of M1A1 Abrams battle tanks and M3 Bradley fighting vehicles. During the action, the cavalry troops destroyed fifty T-72/T-62 battle tanks, more than thirty-five other armored fighting vehicles, and forty-five trucks. More than 600 Iraqi soldiers of the 12th Armored Division and Tawakalna Republican Guard Armored Division were killed or wounded and at least that number were captured. After the battle, General Franks, the VII Corps commander, praised the action of the 2nd Cavalry as a classic instance of the cavalry mission to find, fix, and fight the enemy. The 2nd Armored Cavalry had trained intensely before the battle both in the field and on the SIMNET preceding the battle. Immediately, 73 Easting's potential as a simulation for network training on the military SIMNET was appreciated.[9]

A few days after the battle the military decided to capitalize on the SIMNET experience and technologies to record the Battle of 73 Easting for use in future networked training. For the 73 Easting simulation, most of Jack Thorpe's original team, builders of the SIMNET, combined with the staff of the Institute for Defense Analyses Simulation Center (IDA) under the leadership of Lieutenant Neale Cosby as prime technical contractor. Additional expertise was furnished by the Army's Engineer Topographical Laboratories.

Early military simulations had incorporated rote behaviors and did not capture "soft" characteristics well. IDA's effort to go beyond this limitation resulted in a computer-generated simulation of the Battle of 73 Easting, based on in-depth debriefings of 150 survivors.[10] The goal of the project was to get timeline-based individual experiences in response to the dynamic unfolding of the events—soldiers' fears and emotions as well as actions—and to render the events as a fully 3-D simulated reality, which any future cadet could enter and relive. Data gathering for the simulation began one month after the battle itself. The team assembled battle-site surveys and interviews with participants. Troopers from the 2nd Cavalry accompanied the DARPA team members to reconstruct the action moment by moment, vehicle by vehicle. They walked over the battlefield amidst the twisted wreckage of Iraqi tanks, recalling the action as best they could. A few soldiers supplied diaries to reconstruct their actions. Some were even able to consult personal tape recordings taken during the chaos. Tracks in the sand gave the simulators precise traces of movement. Every missile shot left a thin wire trail, which lay undisturbed in the sand. A black box in each tank, programmed to track three satellites, confirmed its exact position on the ground. Headquarters had a tape recording of radio-voice communications from the field. Sequenced overhead photos from satellite cameras gave the big view. A digital map of the terrain was captured by lasers and radar.[11]

With these data a team at the IDA Simulation Center spent nine months constructing a simulation of the battle. A few months into the project, they had the actual desert troops, then stationed in Germany, review and correct a preliminary version of the re-creation by sitting in tank simulators and entering the virtual battle. Nine months after the confrontation, the re-created Battle of 73 Easting was demo-'ed for high-ranking military in a facility with panoramic views on three fifty-inch TV screens at the resolution of a very good videogame.

The Battle of 73 Easting confirmed Jack Thorpe's original vision for the SIMNET: networked simulation technology using history to prepare for the future. The simulation provided both a link with history and at the same time served as a dynamic interactive training vehicle for the future. As a computer simulation with programmable variables, the scenario could be replayed with different endings. The next step after creating this detailed, accurate historical simulation was to couple it with Project Odin, a wargame-simulation engine developed in preparation for Desert Storm by Neale Cosby and the IDA staff.

The goal of Project Odin was to create a simulated electronic environment housed in a moving van–sized truck with generator trailer. Odin was intended for use in the field, its knowledge base supplied by up-to-date intelligence. It would allow officers to see the battlefield in three dimensions and enable them to zoom to any location to review the arrangement of forces. By adopting various perspectives of the opponent, one might infer the counterpart's intent and more easily gain mastery of the battlefield.[12] Odin was designed not to destroy targets but to assist in visualizing the battle about to be entered or, ideally, already joined. SIMNET technology was at the core of Odin. Like other SIMNET simulation units, Odin combined a digital-terrain database of any part of the world; intelligence feeds of friendly and enemy orders of battle (through another DARPA program called Fulcrum); an order of battle generator; a wargaming engine with semiautomated forces using AI components; and an extremely flexible visual display (the "flying carpet").

The "flying carpet" was the most innovative aspect of the SIMNET machine, allowing zooming to any part of the battlefield as well as forward or backward jumping in time, from any perspective. The simulated battlefield could be visually displayed from any viewpoint, air or ground, in two or three dimensions, and the overall situation at any moment could be seen on a digitized map. In 3-D mode a pop-up "billboard" display permitted a commander to click on an aggregate of battalions of armor, for instance, and get a selective representation of different classes of weapons: a useful feature for rapidly inspecting the force layout on the battlefield without all the clutter.

Once the 73 Easting project was completed, Project Odin provided a perfect platform for an interactive, predictive simulation. With the simulation database plugged into Odin, it was possible not only to rerun the historical simulation, but also to change the equipment used by the enemy to test out tactics for other scenarios. For example, it was hypothesized that infrared vision systems enabling navigation in the sandstorm favored the 2nd Cavalry, whereas the Iraqis had only optical sights on their equipment. The simulation allowed the addition of infrared to the Iraqi equipment in order to gauge its effect on the battle's outcome. In addition, multiple Odin simulators could be hooked up to the network, all running the 73 Easting database. Soldiers in the simulators and commanders at workstations could break into the simulation and add new tactics. Once improvements in processors and graphics cards became available, it was imagined that the size of simulation units could be reduced and actually embedded into

M1 tank units, attack helicopters, or F-16s themselves, allowing real soldiers to train for an impending mission right up to the hour of the engagement.

FROM DARPA TO YOUR LOCAL AREA NETWORK

In contrast to popular perceptions of the post–Cold War dismantling of the military-industrial complex, the major defense contractors receive more funding today than they ever have. According to William Hartung, as a result of a rash of military-industry mergers encouraged and subsidized by the Clinton Administration, the "Big Three" weapons makers—Lockheed Martin, Boeing, and Raytheon—now receive among themselves over $30 billion per year in Pentagon contracts. This represents more than one out of every four dollars that the Defense Department expends on everything from rifles to rockets.[13]

While defense spending has not diminished and seems destined not to in the immediate future, the relationship between defense contracting and the commercial sector has shifted radically. In the early years of the Cold War, when Eisenhower first called attention to the phenomenon of the military-industrial complex, attempts were made to keep relations between defense contractors and commercial firms either rigidly separate or delicately balanced in a complicated dance. During the late 1980s and early 1990s, following the collapse of the Soviet Union and the debates surrounding large government research projects such as the Superconducting Super Collider, policy discussions focused on reorienting defense research spending so that research not only served national defense but also ultimately benefited the commercial sector. The military-entertainment complex is one of the effects of this shift.

In the 1990s, the end of the Cold War brought an emphasis on a fiscally efficient military built on sound business practices, with military procurement interfacing seamlessly with industrial manufacturing processes. The Federal Acquisitions Streamlining Act of 1994 directed a move away from the DOD's historical reliance on contracting with dedicated segments of the U.S. technology and industrial base. In Secretary of Defense William Perry's mandated hierarchy of procurement acquisition, commercially available off-the-shelf alternatives should be considered first, while choice of a service-unique development program has lowest priority. In effect, these changes have transformed military contracting units into business organizations. In keeping with this new shift in mentality, "Company" websites now routinely list their "product of the month."

This shift in policy radically transformed the fields of computer simulation and training. Throughout the thirty-year history of these fields, developments in computer graphics, networking, and artificial intelligence (AI) had always been driven by demands of military and aerospace contractors because of the importance of simulation technology to military training. The perceived importance of simulation to the outcome in the Gulf War provided stimulus for increasing DARPA-supported research-and-development efforts around SIMNET (see Chart 1). Given the enormous expense of military aircraft and other armed systems, and given both the cost and the political difficulties in arranging large-scale training maneuvers, an effective campaign was mounted in the name of cost-effectiveness in support of military investment in simulation technology. STRICOM, the Army's Simulation Training and Instrumentation Command, was founded in order to manage and direct the DOD's simulation efforts in the newly streamlined, flexibly managed military of the nineties. In this role STRICOM has played a pivotal role in developments that have led to the current synergism of military simulations and the entertainment industry, the new military-entertainment complex.

The shift in procurement policy led to a loosening—indeed in many ways an erasure—of the boundaries between military contractors and the commercial sector. As a result, many important technologies in the area of networking, simulation, virtual reality, and artificial intelligence have moved from behind the walls of military secrecy into the commercial sector; and even more importantly, technology has flowed freely from the commercial sector, particularly the game industry, into the military. Several concrete examples show clearly how this has worked. One of the most instructive early examples is provided by Real3D of Orlando, Florida, a relatively short-lived company formed through merger and spinoff in 1995 and dissolved in 1999.

Developments connected with companies like Real3D are seminal in the historical evolution of the post–Cold War effort to create a seamless environment in which research work carried out for the high-end military projects can be integrated with systems in the commercial sector. The history of Real3D can be traced back to the first GE Aerospace Visual Docking Simulator for the Apollo lunar landings. In 1991, GE Aerospace began exploring commercial applications of its real-time 3-D graphics technology, which led to a contract with Sega Enterprises Ltd. of Japan, the world's largest manufacturer of arcade systems. Sega was interested in improving its arcade graphics hardware so its games would present more realistic images. GE Aerospace adapted a miniaturized version of its real-time 3-D graphics technology for Sega's arcade systems, providing a visual experience far exceeding expectations.[14] By the time Real3D closed its shop in 1999, Sega had shipped more than 200,000 systems that included Real3D technology.

CHART 1.

Large DOD Development Programs in Modeling and Simulation

Project Name	Description	Estimated Program Cost (millions)
Close-Combat Tactical Trainer	Networked simulation system for training Army mechanized infantry and armor units. It is composed of various simulators that replicate combat vehicles, tactical vehicles, and weapons systems interacting in real time with each other and semiautonomous opposing forces.	$ 846
Battle-Force Tactical Training	Tactical training system for maintaining and assessing fleet combat proficiency in all warfare areas, including joint operations. It will train at both the single-platform and battle-group levels.	165
Warfighter's Simulation 2000	Next-generation battle simulation for training Army commanders and battle staffs at the battalion through theater levels. It has a computer-assisted exercise system that links virtual, live, and constructed environments.	172
Joint Tactical Combat Training System	Joint effort by the Navy and Air Force to create a virtual simulation at the battle group level in which combat participants will interact with live and simulated targets that are detected and displayed by platform sensors.	270
Synthetic Theater of War (STOW) Advanced Concept Technology Demonstration	Program to construct synthetic environments for numerous defense functions. Its primary objective is to integrate virtual simulation (troops in simulators fighting on a synthetic battlefield), constructive simulation (war games), and live maneuvers to provide a training environment for various levels of exercise. The demonstration program will construct a prototype system to allow the U.S. Atlantic Command to quickly create, execute, and assess realistic joint-training exercises.	442

Project Name	Description	Estimated Program Cost (millions)
Joint Simulation System (core)	A set of common core representations to allow simulation of actions and interactions of platforms, weapons, sensors, units, command, control, communications, computers, and intelligence systems, etc., within a designated area of operations, as influenced by environment, system capability, and human and organizational behavior.	$154
Distributed Interactive Simulation	A virtual environment within which humans may interact through simulation at multiple sites that are networked using compliant architecture, modeling, protocols, standards, and databases.	500
TOTAL		**$2,549**

SOURCE: U.S. Department of Defense, Office of the Inspector General, 1997, *Requirements Planning for Development, Test, Evaluation, and Impact on Readiness of Training Simulators and Devices,* a draft proposed audit report, Project No. 5 AB-0070.00, January 10, Appendix D.

In 1993, GE Aerospace was acquired by Martin Marietta, the largest U.S. military contractor and a leader in the field of visual simulation. Martin Marietta not only advocated expansion of their relationship with Sega, but also encouraged further research and analysis to look at other commercial markets, such as personal computers and graphics workstations. In 1995, Martin Marietta merged with Lockheed Corporation to form the mega–defense contracting firm Lockheed Martin, and shortly thereafter launched Real3D to focus solely on developing and producing 3-D graphics products for commercial markets. Finally, in December 1997, Lockheed Martin established Real3D, Inc. as an independent company and at the same time announced that Intel had purchased a 20% stake in the firm. While it got off to a roaring start, Real3D went out of business just four years later, with Intel purchasing its numerous (roughly forty) patents and many of its employees returning to contracting with Lockheed Martin.[15]

Three-dimensional graphics capabilities were not the only Martin Marietta spin-offs made more widely accessible through the streamlining of military procurement. High-level research on distributed simulation environments such as

SIMNET and on the use of AI in generating synthetic agents, high-priority research problems in both the gaming and film industries, are other examples of federally funded research work that have been more rapidly disseminated through the military's new integrated product teams.

The employment trajectories of individuals who have participated in both the military simulation community and the entertainment industry suggest paths for the dissemination of research ideas across these seemingly different fields. An illustration is provided by the career of Steven Woodcock, Real3D's senior software engineer from January 1995 until 1999. Woodcock began his career in the development of game simulations for Martin Marietta. From October 1989 to January 1992 Woodcock was senior software engineer, and from 1992 to 1995 lead software and technical engineer for Martin Marietta Information Group, National Test Bed, where he was responsible for all weapons code development, testing, integration, and documentation for ARGUS, the Advanced Real-time Gaming Universal Simulation.[16] ARGUS is a real-time, distributed, interactive command-and-control simulation focusing on missile defense, running on a TCP/IP network consisting of a Cray-2 supercomputer and more than fifty Silicon Graphics workstations. During this time, Woodcock also worked on developing the Martin Marietta/Sega arcade platform. From March 1995 to March 1997 Woodcock shifted his venue completely from military network simulations to the interactive game industry, where he was lead programmer and oversaw all aspects of game development on the Sega-produced arcade game *Behind Enemy Lines,* featuring a true 3-D environment and use of AI. Woodcock has noted that his previous experience at Martin Marietta in distributed applications, real-time simulations, and artificial intelligence has proven invaluable in designing the real-time, 3-D, multiplayer game environments he has worked on since 1995. From January to June 1996 he was AI and game-engine developer for a Sony PlayStation project named *Thundering Death.* On this project Woodcock implemented the first goal-based AI on the PlayStation using neural networks to provide an ever-learning opponent. Such techniques are now stock-in-trade of every videogame.

If the career of Steven Woodcock illustrates the ways in which personnel, ideas, and technologies have flowed from military simulation efforts to the entertainment industries, the "careers" of *Doom,* a videogame produced by id Software, and *Falcon 4.0,* one of Spectrum Holobyte's videogames, provide glimpses into how the exchange has also gone in the opposite direction—from the game industry to the military.

The shift in military culture reflected in procurement policies is evident in new military approaches to developing critical thinking. Emblematic of this shift was Marine Corps Commandant General Charles C. Krulak's 1996 directive aimed at implementing improvements in what he termed "Military Thinking and Decision Making Exercises." General Krulak wrote: "It is my intent that we reach the stage where Marines come to work and spend part of each day talking about warfighting: learning to think, making decisions, and being exposed to tactical and operational issues." He identified an important way to exercise these skills:

> The use of technological innovations, such as personal computer (PC)–based wargames, provide great potential for Marines to develop decision making skills, particularly when live training time and opportunities are limited. Policy contained herein authorizes Marines to use Government computers for approved PC-based wargames.[17]

General Krulak directed the Marine Combat Development Command to assume responsibility for the development, exploitation, and approval of PC-based wargames. In addition, the Command was charged with maintaining the *PC-based Wargames Catalog* on the Internet.[18] In response to this directive, a group of Marine simulation experts from the Marine Corps Modeling and Simulation Management Office in the training and education division at Quantico, Virginia, tracked down a shareware copy of the commercial game *Doom* produced by id Software and began experimenting with its game engine. *Doom* was a milestone in the history of software distribution—the first level was released as shareware, uploaded to the University of Wisconsin server on December 10, 1993.[19] Gamers attracted by this first level would then purchase the full version from id. So many fans were taking the shareware copies and modifying them in various ways that id decided to release the *Doom* level editor as open source in 1994. General Krulak's marines acquired the shareware version and level editor and adapted the game as a fire-team simulation, with some of the input for the Marine version coming from Internet *Doom* gamers employing the same shareware software tools to build new levels.[20] Instead of using fantasy weapons to face down monsters in a labyrinthine castle, realistic images of sites, weapons, and soldier action characters were scanned into the game's files. The game was also modified from its original version to include fighting holes, bunkers, tactical wire, "the fog of war," and friendly fire. *Marine Doom* trainees used Marine-issue assault rifles to shoot it out with enemy combat troops in a variety of terrain and building configurations. The simulation could also be configured for a specific mission immediately prior to engagement. For example, Marines tasked with rescuing a group of Americans held hostage in an overseas embassy could rehearse in a virtual building constructed from the actual floor plans of the structure.

While a number of military simulations and commercial airline flight simulators have been adapted to the commercial game market, Spectrum Holobyte's

Falcon 4.0 was the first off-the-shelf commercial flight simulation videogame to be adapted to military training.[21] *Falcon 4.0* is a network-based game that supports either single-player or multiplayer modes. The game's 600-page manual suggests the complexity of the game and indicates why the military finds it attractive for its own training purposes. As producer Gilman Louie explains, the *Falcon 4.0* is a detailed simulation re-creating the experience of an F-16 pilot operating over a modern battlefield. The simulation has a highly accurate flight model and avionics suite incorporating flight parameters conforming to real-world specifications. *Falcon 4.0* accurately re-creates such effects as deep stall (to escape, the player must use the real-world procedure of flipping the Manual Pitch Override switch and "rocking" the aircraft out—the standard game trick of simply lighting the afterburners won't restore normal flight in this simulation). Weapon modeling is equally realistic and, except for omitting a few classified details, provides an amazingly accurate representation of weapons deployment. The simulation is so detailed, in fact, that reviewers of the game report consulting a real-world "Dash I" manual for the F-16 when playing the game. The realism of *Falcon 4.0* is further enhanced by graphics generated from actual aerial photographs and map data from the Korean peninsula. In its current version, the game only requires a computer with a processor of 400 megahertz or higher.

The extreme realism in this videogame led Peter Bonanni, graduate of the F-16 Fighter Weapons School and pilot instructor of the Virginia Air National Guard, to work with Spectrum Holobyte to modify the *Falcon 4.0* flight simulator game for military training. According to Bonanni, *Falcon 4.0* mimics the look and feel of real military aircraft and allows users to play against computer-generated forces or, in a networked fashion, against other pilots, which facilitates team-training opportunities. Another reason for Bonanni's enthusiasm is the virtual world around the player. Although the product features scripted Tactical Engagement missions as well as an Instant Action mode for newcomers, the heart of the product is the dynamic campaign mode, where the player assumes the role of a pilot in an F-16 squadron during a conflict on the Korean peninsula. The campaign engine runs an entire war, assigning missions to units throughout the theater. A list (displayed either by priority to the war effort or by launch time) shows the missions available to the player's squadron. The player can fly any of these missions, with the freedom to choose air-to-air or air-to-ground sorties. Unlike games with prescripted outcomes, the campaign engine allows story lines, missions, and outcomes to be dynamically generated. For instance, if a player is first assigned a mission to destroy a bridge but fails, the next mission may be to provide support to friendly tanks engaged by an enemy that just crossed the bridge. Each play of the game influences the next.

Like Steven Woodcock, Peter Bonanni moves seamlessly between the military and entertainment worlds. Bonanni not only helps adapt the videogame to military training needs but also writes a regular column for the www.falcon4.com website on tactics and has designed several of the thirty-one prebuilt training missions included with the game. He is author of two best-selling books on *Falcon 4.0,* one co-written with colleague James Reiner, also an F-16 instructor pilot and graduate of the F-16 Fighter Weapons School, and like Bonanni a consultant on the game. Beginning with some basics on the game and the various gameplay options, *Falcon 4.0: Prima's Official Strategy Guide* gives readers a guide to instant action missions, multiplayer dogfights, and full-fledged campaigns. The book is a serious no-nonsense manual, devoting separate chapters to laser-guided bombs and even the AGM-65 Maverick missile. Bonanni's second book, *Falcon 4.0 Checklist,* was already high on the Amazon.com sales list before it even hit the bookstores.

The scenarios depicted here have mutually benefited both the military simulation effort and the videogame industry through their two-way flow of people and technology. The military profited from id Software's release of *Doom*'s code and level editor for creating the first military first-person shooter training simulation; and at the same time the game industry benefited from people like Woodcock and Bonanni, with their various skills, who added whole new dimensions to commercial games.

Among the numerous similar accounts of spin-off groups who were involved with the design of SIMNET and subsequently left military contract projects to launch commercial simulation and videogame companies, MÄK is one of the most interesting, because it adds a new dimension to the military-entertainment complex; namely, the simultaneous release of a product as a commercial videogame and a training simulation for military purposes. MÄK (pronounced "mock") Technologies (Cambridge, Massachusetts) was founded in 1990 by two MIT engineering graduates, Warren Katz and John Morrison. After graduating from MIT, both were original members of Bolt Beranek & Newman's SIMNET project team from 1987 to 1990, where they participated in work on network interconnectivity for distributed simulations. MÄK's corporate goal is to provide cutting-edge research and development services to the Department of Defense in the areas of distributed interactive simulation (DIS) and networked virtual reality (VR) systems, and to convert the results of this research into commercial products for the entertainment and industrial markets. MÄK's first commercial product, the VR-Link™ developer's tool kit, is the most widely used commercial DIS interface in the world. It is an application programmer's tool kit that makes possible networking of distributed simulations and VR systems. The tool kit complies with the Defense Department's DIS protocol, enabling multiple participants to interact in real time via low-bandwidth network connections.[22] VR-Link is designed for easy integration with existing and new simulations, VR systems, and games. Thanks to such products, MÄK was ranked thirty-sixth in the 1997 New England Technology Fast 50 and 380th in the 1997 National Technology Fast 500 based on revenue growth between 1992 and 1996.

In addition to its work in the defense community, the company's software has been licensed for use by several entertainment firms, such as Total Entertainment Network and Zombie Virtual Reality Entertainment, to serve as the launching pad for real-time, 3-D, multiuser videogames. One such game, *Spearhead,* a multiuser tank simulation game released in mid-1998, was written by MÄK and published by Interactive Magic. *Spearhead* can be played over the Internet and incorporates networking technology similar to that used in the military simulations the MÄK cofounders first worked on with SIMNET.

The networking capabilities of distributed simulation technology developed by MÄK and other government suppliers are now enabling entertainment providers to create platforms for 3-D worlds supporting up to 100,000 participants simultaneously. Katz has described his vision provocatively in a chapter for the book *Digital Illusion: Entertaining the Future with High Technology.* The chapter is titled "Networked Synthetic Environments: From DARPA to Your Virtual Neighborhood."[23] In the near future MÄK co-founders Katz and Morrison are betting that Internet-based populations the size of a mid-sized U.S. city will be able to stroll through an electronic shopping mall, explore and colonize a virtual universe, or race for prizes in cyberspace's largest 3-D road rally.

The contract awarded by the U.S. Marine Corps to MÄK in 1997 has assisted this vision of vastly shared virtual reality; it further erodes the distinction between military simulation technology and the technology available to ordinary users. The contract called for a multiplayer, networked game/training simulation, *Spearhead II,* developed in cooperation with the U.S. Marine Corps in order to ensure that a high level of realism would be incorporated into the simulation. The special operations unit commander in this game will see a battle engagement from a 3-D tactical view, enabling him to select units, issue orders, and monitor the progress of his forces. Each player will be able to assume a position in the command hierarchy of either U.S. or opposing forces. Additionally, players of platform-level simulations will be able to assume their appropriate positions in the command hierarchy. MÄK will use the same game engine in both its military and civilian versions. The military version will add more accurate details about tactics and weapons, while the civilian game will be less demanding. But both versions will allow multiple players to compete against each other over a local area network or the Internet.

While many key developments in the area of networked games, artificial intelligence, and graphics during the mid 1990s were spin-offs of the military simulation efforts, the recent development in all of these areas has been more heavily weighted toward contributions from the game industry. Military technology, which once trickled down to civilian use, now often lags behind what is available in games, theme park rides, and movie special effects. As STRICOM Chief Scientist and Technical Director Dr. Michael Macedonia wrote in a recent article in *Computer:*

> As Siggraph—the computer-graphics community's showcase—has demonstrated over the past several years, the demands of digital film development are making way for computer games' even more demanding real-time simulation requirements. As a mass market, games now drive the development of graphics and processor hardware. Intel and AMD have added specialized multimedia and graphics instructions to their line of processors in their battle to counter companies such as Nvidia, whose computer graphics chips continue breaking new performance boundaries. . . .
>
> By aggressively maneuvering to seize and expand their market share, the entertainment industry's biggest players are shaping a 21st century in which consumer demand for entertainment—not grand science projects or military research—will drive computing innovation. Private-sector research-and-development spending, which now accounts for 75 percent of total U.S. R&D, will increase to about $187.2 billion in 2000, up from an estimated $169.3 billion in 1999. . . . [24]

Graphics is not the only area of computing innovation that bears out Macedonia's claim. The same pattern has been repeated in AI research. Artificial intelligence was once synonymous with military research. Since the birth of the videogame market, artificial intelligence had been a standard but minor feature of games. Emphasis was placed instead on other aspects of the game, from tuning 3-D engines to integrating last-minute sound effects. Design and coding the computer opponents was often deferred to the final phase of the project. But from the mid 1990s on, AI has been adapted by commercial game developers with striking success. And once mutual exchanges between military, academic AI researchers, and videogame design teams began, the successful game applications accelerated the field and created a reverse flow back into large-scale military projects.

THE INSTITUTE FOR CREATIVE TECHNOLOGY

Until the last two or three years, crossovers from military simulations and the entertainment industries have been unplanned and opportunistic. Recently several top officials in the military simulation command have sought more formal collaborative relations with the videogame and entertainment industries. In December of 1996 the National Academy of Sciences, acting on the initiative of Professor Michael Zyda, a computer scientist specializing in artificial intelligence at the Naval Postdoctoral Academy in Monterey and indeed the same director of the MOVES Institute behind the networked action game *America's Army: Operations* discussed in the opening paragraph of this paper, hosted a workshop on modeling and simulation to investigate the possibility of organized cooperation between the entertainment industries and defense.[25] Zyda was joined in this effort by Warren Katz from MÄK, Gilman Louie from Spectrum Holobyte, and several academic and industry leaders from the fields of computer graphics and virtual reality. Zyda's report and follow-up proposal stimulated the Army in August 1999 to give a $45 million, five-year grant to the University of Southern California to create a research center, the Institute for Creative Technologies (ICT), to support collaboration between the entertainment and defense industries, to apply entertainment-software technology to military simulation, training, and operations, and to leverage entertainment software for military-relevant academic research. The research center has enlisted film studios and videogame designers in the effort, with the promise that any technological advances can also be applied to make more compelling videogames and theme-park rides. Although Hollywood and the Pentagon may differ markedly in culture, they now overlap in technology: wargames are big entertainment. In opening the new ICT, Secretary of the Army Louis Caldera said, "We could never hope to get the expertise of a Steven Spielberg . . . working just on Army projects." But the new institute, Caldera said, will be "a win-win for everyone."[26]

While putting more polygons on the screen for less cost has certainly been one of the military's objectives at the ICT and in similar alliances, other dimensions of simulated worlds are even more important for their agenda. Movies, theme-park rides, and increasingly even videogames are driven by stories with plot, feeling, tension, and emotion. Military simulations have always been extremely good at modeling hardware components of military systems. Flight and tank simulators are excellent tools for learning and practicing the use of complex, expensive equipment. However, to train for real-world military engagements is not just to train to use the equipment but also to cope with the implementation of strategy in a fearful environment with uncertainties and surprises. As Marine Corps Commandant General Charles C. Krulak emphasized, decisions made in war must frequently be made under physical and emotional duress. His directive states that the PC-based wargame exercises in peacetime should replicate some of the same conditions: "Imaginative combinations of physical and mental activities provide Marines the opportunity to make decisions under conditions of physical stress and fatigue, thereby more closely approximating combat."[27]

How has the pursuit of this line of development in new settings like the ICT taken shape? Prior to the ICT's launch, the work by several key ICT members focused on constructing semiautomated forces and multiple distributed agents for virtual environments, such as training programs. Others in the ICT worked on building models of emotion for use in synthetic training environments. Still others constructed intelligent agent technology for incorporation into state-of-the-art military simulation systems. At the opening ceremonies of the ICT, Executive Director Richard Lindheim outlined several projects for the institute. Among them was a construction of what he referred to as "the holodeck": immersive virtual environments with interactive synthetic agents, *synthespians,* for the staging of simulation- and game-based learning exercises. Some examples of the programs under way at the ICT that partially realize the mission of creating the holodeck are the Advanced Leadership Training Simulation and the Mission Rehearsal Exercise.

One of the Mission Rehearsal Exercise scenarios presents a situation to train soldiers heading for combat, peacekeeping, and humanitarian missions. In this interactive scene, you are an American soldier in Bosnia-Herzegovina whose Humvee has accidentally struck a civilian vehicle and injured a child. A soldier stands, awaiting orders to continue with the mission or to call for medevac assistance. "Sir, we should secure the assembly area," he says—a platoon already in position is expecting your arrival as backup. Along the cobbled streets, a crowd has gathered. A TV crew is now on the scene. A helicopter circles overhead. Tension mounts.

The five-minute scenario is projected onto a 150-degree movie screen, complete with 10.2-channel audio that creates floor-shaking sound effects. To enhance the sense of reality, smells including burned charcoal can be pumped into the room. Participants can gesture and touch objects and elicit responses in the simulator. The machine also uses voice recognition technology and different languages to allow participants to converse with the characters they encounter. The designers of this simulation, led by Jonathan Gratch, have spent considerable time trying to make this artificial intelligence respond in unpredictable ways so the experience is slightly different each time the system is used.

Other simulations are being constructed to train soldiers for circumstances too dangerous for real-life training—for example, a chemical spill. The goal of constructing the holodeck is to create the type of technology that allows teams of soldiers to be embedded in any environment. By 2008, ICT hopes to take the experience off the movie screen and compress it into a helmet, which users can wear to experience virtual reality anytime, anywhere.

Directly related to the game-based mission rehearsal exercises is the ICT games project, which will release two games, *Combat System XII* and *C-Force,* by the end of 2002. The games are intended to have the same holding power and repeat value as mainstream entertainment software and will be available commercially as well as for military training. The goal of the ICT games project is to create immersive, interactive, real-time training simulations to help the army teach decision-making and leadership skills. The first game, *Combat System XII,* is a PC-based company command simulator scheduled for completion in December 2002. As the commander of a U.S. Army light infantry company, the student must interpret the assigned mission, organize his force, plan strategically, and coordinate the actions of about 120 men under his command. The second game, *C-Force,* will run on the Microsoft XBox and places the student in the role of a squad leader. The student is at the tip of the spear, leading and coordinating about a dozen men to complete a series of missions and come home safely. The games are being designed in a collaboration involving STRICOM and commercial game development companies and will include state-of-the-art technologies in artificial intelligence and physics modeling of military equipment as well as an extensive pedagogical evaluation module.

SHAREWARE: MODS ROCK THE GAME INDUSTRY

At the same time that developments like the ICT have formalized the mergers and crossovers in the military and the entertainment industry, the previously distinct roles of videogame makers and videogame players have become increasingly complex and commingled. Since id Software released the *Doom* level editor in 1994 a number of videogame companies have released editors allowing users to modify various game-related parameters. (In fact, as noted above, *Marine Doom* was a product of the adapted shareware version of *Doom.*) id Software's John Carmack was simply noticing a phenomenon that had been around since the beginning of computer games, going back to 1983 with Andrew Johnson, Preston Nevins, and Rob Romanchuk's parody of Silas Warner's original game *Castle Wolfenstein*—the mod (a user-constructed game modification) was called *Castle Smurfenstein*—for the Apple II and the Commodore 64.[28] By 1990 players of *Duke Nukem* began to build their own editors to make modifications of games and share them with other players. With the takeoff of the Internet, this phenomenon, called "modding," began to assume massive dimensions. Many game mods were extremely professional and were great additions to the game. Realizing the importance of this phenomenon for building a fan base for games as well as the potential value of incorporating such mods into the commercial game itself, Carmack released *Final Doom* in 1996 with a compilation of user-built mods, and he allowed the mod builders to share in the proceeds from sales.[29]

The next phase of the mod movement, and indeed some would maintain its high-water mark, began in 1996 with id Software's release of *Quake,* which was written in Quake-C, a subset of the computer language C, designed by Carmack especially for *Quake. Quake* was not only the first true 3-D game: Quake-C enabled an unprecedented degree of interactivity in a first-person-shooter videogame. Immediately *Quake*-mods began to spring up, and a vibrant Internet community devoted to creating mods for all aspects of *Quake,* including its AI components, emerged. Players who were not highly trained computer programmers were able to acquire guidance not only in how to build their own levels and fill them with monsters, but also to specify how the monsters would act in some situations. If players didn't like the standard-issue game monsters, they could build their own—and they did. Extensive websites, such as www.planetquake.com, www.actionnation.com, www.botspot.com, and later the Modsquad's www.planetunreal.com, began to provide interviews with mod creators on how they constructed their patches, open forums, and tutorials for would-be game AI builders to create new scripts and modify their games with tools posted on the website and promoted by commercial gamemakers.

Among the literally millions of mod builders worldwide, a number have achieved legendary status for having changed the way games work. One of the most famous mod careers of this generation is that of Ben Morris,[30] who, as a teenager in 1994, built the most widely used level editor for *Doom,* called the *Doom Construction Kit.* Morris's utility was celebrated in the modding community as a resource for crafting complete conversions of games to generate an entirely different look and feel from the original. In 1996 when id's fully 3-D game *Quake* came out, Morris set to work on building a level editor called *Worldcraft.* Morris made *Worldcraft* publicly available as a free download in December 1996. Marc Laidlaw described the wonders of *Worldcraft* in his regular feature "Street Cred" for *Wired,* as follows:

> So you want to be a god? Nothing to it. If you already have a fairly powerful PC and a registered copy of Quake (id Software's cutting-edge 3-D game), all you need is the powerful level-design shareware Worldcraft. This week, using Worldcraft, I made a brand-new world. Not a huge one—but it's all mine. It has teleporters and magical floating platforms, gold keys, hidden tunnels, secret elevators, vast dark chambers rimmed by molten lava, and, at the center of it all, an inside-out ziggurat full of luminous golden orbs and a lovely blue bridge. . . . Last week I could hardly draw a line with a straight edge. And clarity is crucial when you're working in three dimensions at once, because the possibilities

> for confusion skyrocket as your map begins to sprawl. Starting with a handful of simple forms (blocks, wedges, and spikes, with more forms slated for future versions of Worldcraft), you add and subtract shapes to build just about any imaginable structure. Fill your map with secrets, infest it with monsters, and you're ready to upload a finished map to the Worldcraft Web site and invite your friends to share your nightmare. . . . Try your hand making maps for 3-D games, and you may discover a pastime more addictive than the games.[31]

Morris, a Victoria, British Columbia, native, was ultimately offered a position at Valve Software to join the team in creating a new game called *Half-Life.*

Valve Software has transformed the active involvement of an extensive mod community into a business model for commercial game development. The first step toward this new business model was *Half-Life.* Valve was founded by two Microsoft engineers, Gabe Newell and Mike Harrington. Their game project was based on a license of the *Quake* game engine from id Software. Newell and Harrington invited Ben Morris to join them in using *Worldcraft* to create the game. *Half-Life* appeared in 1998 and has been the most successful single-person, first-person-shooter game to date, with more than fifty "Game of the Year" awards from various organizations. In addition to the game content itself, factors contributing to the game's enormous success are its multiplayer component and its streamlined, extremely fast connection directly to a local area network. Valve also followed id's lead in providing the game source and a user mod builder to create stakeholder buy-in for *Half-Life* and subsequent Valve titles.

The next step in the formation of Valve's business model actually happened *outside* the company in the amateur gaming community, and it illustrates how, for the moment at least, the mod community has become both dedicated stakeholder and major generator of both the technology and content driving the industry. Enter Minh "Gooseman" Le, a computer science student at Simon Frasier University near Vancouver. The Gooseman got his start with building a mod for *Quake,* called *Navy Seals,* a project that occupied him during July and August of 1997. Using the software development kit issued by id with *Quake,* Le modeled some exceptional weapons and a stable of characters. He teamed with various other modders, most of whom he met only online, to build levels for *Navy Seals.* With the overwhelming success he enjoyed in the modding community, Minh Le decided to construct a complete mod of a game. He felt he had done everything he wanted to do with the *Quake* engine and decided to work with the new Valve game *Half-Life,* released in early 1998. Like id, Valve released a software development kit for *Half-Life* a few months after the initial game publication. Minh Le was already poised to build what has become the most spectacular mod of a game ever, *Half-Life: Counter-Strike.* Minh Le, now in his senior year, designed the first version of the game entirely on his own and assembled a team of mappers, modelers, and editors to collaborate in the construction.[32] The *Counter-Strike* team has eventually grown to about twelve persons distributed all around the globe.[33] Most of the team had never met face-to-face before launching the game. *Counter-Strike* transformed *Half-Life's* sci-fi adventure with biotech experiments gone awry into a team-oriented multiplayer military mod that pits a hostage rescue team against terrorists. (In the days following the World Trade Center attack on September 11, 2001, new mods began surfacing with the hunt for bin Laden as their theme.) The first beta version[34] of *Counter-Strike* went online in June 1999, and by late 1999 it had become the most popular online game in history with upwards of 65,000 people logged on at any one time. By 2000 *Counter-Strike* was included as one of the tournament games in the Cyberathlete's Professional League, and the CPL Pentium4 Processor Summer 2002 Event held in Dallas featured *Counter-Strike* as the main tournament game, with prizes totaling $100,000.[35]

Early on, Valve recognized the value of the mod community around *Half-Life* and in 1999 began organizing an annual *Half-Life* mod expo, where mod builders could come to show off their creations.[36] As the popularity of *Counter-Strike* continued to grow, Gabe Newell approached Minh Le to release *Counter-Strike* as a commercial game. By creating a symbiotic relationship with the mod community, Valve extended the life of *Half-Life.* While *Counter-Strike* still goes on as a freely downloadable online game, the retail version comes packaged with *Half-Life.* The retail version came out in the fall of 2000 as *Half-Life: Counter-Strike,* and included the *Counter-Strike* mod as well as several other popular *Half-Life* mods. Valve repeated this same scenario with another extremely popular *Half-Life* mod, *Day of Defeat,* a game that transforms the original biotech nightmare into a battle zone for ultrarealistic squad-based combat set amid the ruins of World War II's European theater. In March 2002, at the annual Game Developers Conference (GDC), Valve announced that it had contracted with the team behind *Day of Defeat* to release a retail version. At this same GDC event Newell announced the formation of a new company, Steam, that aims to recognize the importance of the symbiotic relationship to the user community for commercial game development. Steam is a broadband distribution network that will offer instant updates—many built by modders—to recent Valve games and serve as a distribution point for new mods.[37] Mod teams will be offered a $995 engine license plus royalty to allow them to distribute their mods over Steam. Valve co-founder Newell announced the new broadband distribution enterprise: "Once a mod team has developed an audience, they could think about either being aggregated into some other offering or going all the way to publishing their game over Steam."[38]

Just as the military has leveraged the commercial sector for advanced technology, the game industry has pursued the open source community for some of its hottest developments. The examples of id and Valve demonstrate that these developments have already had enormous implications for the industry. Since the mid 1990s the military too has been deploying newly minted best practices of game design and business models to compete in the arena for young highly trained cyber-warriors. The launch on July 4 of *America's Army* as a free online download and the commercial/training simulation projects at the Institute for Creative Technologies are just some of the most salient examples of how the new military is adapting to the cyber-economy. But to date the military has not announced that it will bite the bullet and release software development packages for its new products analogously to Valve, id, and other fast-moving game companies. In her contribution to the ICT's May 2002 Inside Games Workshop, J. C. Hertz urged that, in terms of practices stimulating innovation, the military has been leagues behind the commercial game industry, "because of [the game industry's] development process and cultural infrastructure: extensible applications, constantly modified and improved by the player base, a highly motivated, globally networked, self-organizing population of millions, all striving to out-do one another."[39] Hertz argued that in order to fully transform itself the military will have to adopt two key features of the cultural infrastructure that drives the commercial game industry: continuous, user-driven innovation as a conscious principle of software design; and the social ecology that drives online multiplayer games.[40]

In a sense, whether they like it or not the military is now part of the ecology Hertz describes. To see this, consider the game engine at the core of *America's Army*. It is the *Unreal* game engine designed by Epic Games, considered by everyone in the industry to be the premier game engine for its amazing artificial intelligence and game physics engine. The engine, originally designed for Epic Games' *Unreal*, released in 1998, has been licensed for all sorts of applications, including many games as well as architectural and historical re-creations. While it cost $3 million to produce and licenses for $350,000, this game engine has important roots in mod culture, or more specifically "bot" culture,[41] which is devoted to the design of computer opponents in games.[42] One of the principal designers of the AI components of *Unreal* is Steven Polge, who before joining Epic was famous in mod culture as the author of the "Reaper" bot for *Quake* that introduced unprecedented learning capability and precision targeting into a computer opponent.[43]

It is not just the presence of high-level talents on a par with Ben Morris, Steven Polge, and Minh Le out there in mod culture that gives one pause—and perhaps a bit of a chill—in thinking about what it means for the military to be out there too. As the example of Polge reminds us, Epic is one of the new-styled companies exploiting user-driven innovation. Indeed, as might be expected, a vibrant and enthusiastic mod culture has grown up around *Unreal* and its highly acclaimed multiplayer *Unreal Tournament.* Exactly parallel to the other games I have discussed, a number of sites provide portals to the extensive *Unreal* mod community. Gamespy's *Planet Unreal,* which might be considered the "official" *Unreal* mod site, has access to tools, tutorials, discussions, and downloads for modifications, editors, textures, models, and skins, as well as reviews and much more. Given our theme, one of the more interesting recent mods is *Terrorism: Fight for Freedom.* Like the other mods I've discussed, *Fight for Freedom* recruits its team members online from around the world. In the original single-player version of *Unreal,* the player is cast as a prisoner aboard a ship en route to a penal colony. The ship crashes on a mysterious planet where the mystical Nali race is victimized by the cruel and technologically advanced Skaarj. As you journey through the many environments on the planet, you must find a means of escape from the planet and help the Nali defeat their oppressors. The game has stunning graphics contrasting medieval Nali architecture and culture with the sci-fi design of the weapons and the Skaarj warriors. The architects of *Terrorism: Fight for Freedom* describe their project in an update from August 11, 2002:

> *Terrorism: Fight for Freedom* is a modern-day, small-scale warfare Total Conversion for *Unreal Tournament 2003.* The mod is based upon wars that are currently occurring in the world.
>
> The armed forces involved are the Special Forces, comprised of soldiers from armies across the world, and the Tangos. *T:FfF* has many of its maps loosely based on locations around the world where there are conflicts currently occurring. *T:FfF,* along with these "Wars Of The World" Campaigns, will feature a set of maps called "Single Black Ops" which are maps that don't have any particular theme but give the player a wide variety of stipulated situations. Single Black Ops can include things such as Hostage Rescue operations to things such as Terrorist weapon dump raids.[44]

The beta version is expected to launch in December 2002 or January 2003.

Given this rich scenario, we might best consider *America's Army: Operations* itself as a highly developed *Unreal* mod. Indeed, it already seems to suffer from some of the issues that fill the forum pages of *Half-Life: Counter-Strike;* namely, cheat codes and hacks. For instance, in one of the features of *America's Army,* to be "authorized" to play the highest levels of the game, you need to train in a cyber–boot camp that actually replicates facilities at Fort Benning, Georgia. It took only a few days before a cheat appeared allowing players to bypass the training sessions. More are sure to follow. In a post–9/11 world where distributed collaboration in a military context has come to signify "terrorist cells," the potential mods based on the *Unreal* engine conjure up an all-too-frightening potential *reality.* No doubt somewhere, either in the game industry itself or among the worldwide community of mod builders, a group is currently developing a cyberterrorist game based on attacking the computer infrastructure of a country, disabling its power grid, infiltrating its financial networks, and hacking into mainstream news media such as the *New York Times* to confuse the public about what's going on. Will this be a market in which the U.S. military can choose (or afford) not to compete?

9. PERPETUAL REVOLUTION IN MILITARY AFFAIRS, INTERNATIONAL SECURITY, AND INFORMATION

CHRIS HABLES GRAY

THE PERPETUAL REVOLUTION IN MILITARY AFFAIRS

> The revolution in military affairs is but a name that has been given to a portion of the long running continuum in military technical development.
>
> —MARK HELPRIN[1]

There has been a great deal of discussion in the last few years about how a "revolution in military affairs" (RMA) is fundamentally changing war. Sometimes it is electronics that drives this RMA, sometimes information, sometimes biology; the specifics seem to vary. The new types of RMA-generated war vary as well: amorphous virtual war, devastating precision-munitions conflicts, and messy street fighting are just a few of the candidates. But a closer look at recent history suggests that today we have all of these RMAs and all of these wars—and actually there has been no single RMA. Rather, since 1945 at least, we have been experiencing a perpetual revolution in military affairs (PRMA).

Why a perpetual revolution as opposed to a single revolution or a set of revolutions? Because we are not experiencing one basic change in military policy and practices, nor really a series of discrete changes as marked the history of modern war. Since 1945, when the use of two atomic bombs by the United States on Japan rendered the basic idea of modern war (total mobilization for total war) absurd, the very nature of war has been in constant flux. The different RMAs that have been postulated are really part of a system of continual fundamental changes in military technology and doctrine that represent a futile attempt to overcome the basic contradiction of war today: modern principles in the context of postmodern technologies. This means that the famous slogan of the Prussian general and philosopher of modern war, Baron Carl von Clausewitz, that "War is politics by other means," no longer applies. If anything, politics has become an extension of war, as Michel Foucault, the controversial French thinker, claimed, because since 1941, the main superpower, the United States, has been in a constant state of national emergency, partial mobilization, and political militarization.[2] The first cold war against the Communists has been replaced by a more amorphous second cold war, ostensibly against terrorism. But the basic structure of the postmodern war system remains the same: no total war but all other types of war, continual technological innovation, increasing speed and lethality (including the proliferation of weapons of mass destruction), the militarization of technology and science, more intimate human-machine systems (cyborgization), and the fetishization of information, wanting it more for itself than for its real use value.

Even though this system of postmodern war is now fundamentally at conflict with itself, it is still dynamic. The dominant doctrines call for continual military innovation, bureaucracies are dedicated to it, and the key engine of technological advance, the computer chip, doubles in power every dozen months or so. The "institutionalization of innovation" has met Moore's Law (the geometric increase in computer chip power) with startling effect, producing major military innovations continually.[3] Michael O'Hanlon, a researcher at the Brookings Institution, summarizes it clearly:

> The list of military technologies that have emerged since World War II includes helicopters, reconnaissance satellites, infrared-vision devices, laser range finders and target designators, electronically steered radars, high-performance air-to-air and surface-to-air missiles, the modern jet engine and supersonic aircraft, the cruise missile, the global positioning system, stealth materials and designs, the thermonuclear warhead, and the intercontinental missile.[4]

O'Hanlon actually goes on to describe these innovations as having an "evolutionary, not revolutionary" impact, but this is not logical. Perhaps his conclusion is based on leaving out nuclear submarines, interactive armor, incredibly powerful munitions, extraordinary medical services, drones and remote-controlled aircraft, the militarization of space, and the development of new and more effective biological, chemical, and nuclear weapons of mass destruction. If this isn't a perpetual revolution in military affairs then nothing could be.

Consider the earlier RMAs. Andrew Krepinevich, the noted historian, has given one account of military revolutions throughout history that includes the infantry revolution (fourteenth century), the artillery revolution (fifteenth century), the revolution of sail and shot at sea (fourteenth to seventeenth centuries . . . a slow one), the fortress revolution (sixteenth century), the gunpowder revolution (sixteenth and seventeenth centuries), the Napoleonic revolution (eighteenth century), the land war Revolution (nineteenth century), the naval revolution (nineteenth and twentieth centuries), and then a series of revolutions between the world wars (mechanization, aviation, information) and the nuclear revolution afterward.[5] Notice how at first revolutions followed one after another, century after century, as infantry supplanted cavalry, artillery took over the battlefield, gunpowder smashed fortresses, and so on. An evolution in effective carnage. But then comes the twentieth century and the pace of change accelerates markedly with revolutions running into each other and overlapping until we have today's cycle of constant innovation.

The PRMA is a major part of the postmodern war system that since World War II has been continually producing deep, if uneven, changes in military doctrines and practices (affairs, if you will) without producing complete military superiority on even a temporary basis, let alone permanently. As for perfect security, we know today there will be no such thing no matter what the RMA, for three fundamental reasons that will be discussed at length below: the fog of war, the limits of information technology, and the postmodern war system.

Since the middle of the twentieth century over thirty new labels have been offered for how war has changed. Electronic war, pure war, computer war, and information war are just a few of these. The related confusion about what is the "real" RMA is clear in the profusion of different definitions. Is it precision weapons? Electronics? Biomaterials? Nanotechnologies? No, it isn't any one of these, but the various proposed RMAs do make a map of the PRMA, and it shows that from the depths of the sea to the orbit of the moon, new weapons are constantly being introduced. They lead to, or come from, new theories on war-fighting based on new illusions of intelligent weapons and super-effective computerized systems. Meanwhile, in the real world, a handful of hijackers can kill thousands, and hundreds of thousands continue to die the old-fashioned way in retro-wars—hacked with machetes, shot with guns, blown up with iron bombs—and weapons of mass destruction proliferate relentlessly.

Mikkel Rasmussen, a Danish political scientist, points out that RMAs "require a transformation of episteme as well as techne."[6] In other words, a true RMA has to change the way we think about war, not just how we wage it. Instead, new RMAs are put forward as solutions to the traditional problems of uncertainty and casualties, and the ways in which they might fundamentally change war itself are ignored. Yet war is changing, and these changes are related to a basic "social paradigm shift," as Rasmussen argues, that is revolutionizing the international system with profound implications for international security. War is no longer a separate and clear political instrument that can be used to provide a decisive victory between two state antagonists. It is a messy and limited process where often even clear victories, such as the United States in Afghanistan, can lead to more problems and confusion and where many of the antagonists are not even states or even proto-nations. This is all the more true with our twenty-first-century PRMA. Instead of increasing war's utility as a useful political instrument, which is the dream of each new RMA, the continual development of new weapons and systems has become the central driving force of confusing, asymmetrical, and very indecisive postmodern war.

TWENTY-FIRST-CENTURY POSTMODERN WAR

Modern war can be defined as rational war: rational in the sense that science and technology are mobilized to provide the latest, most effective weapons, and rational in that going to war and using the best weapons can produce clear and decisive political advantages. In modern war the various RMAs (such as those listed above by Andrew Krepinevich) almost always produced usable weapons and real (if often only temporary) military superiority. But a point was reached where many weapons (especially weapons of mass destruction—WMD) could not be used, and even more surprisingly, military superiority did not always produce victory, as Vietnam, Algeria, and Afghanistan demonstrated.

Total (i.e., modern) war is impossible now, technologically first of all, but also because of the international paradigm shift alluded to above, which itself is driven by the information and other technologies that have led to an increasingly integrated world, economically and politically. Still, the established militaries of the world think in terms of modern war, and that includes a quest for technological answers to the political and moral problems of contemporary war. No such solutions are forthcoming, but new weapons are.

The context for the development of postmodern war was the first cold war, which used the unusable WMD as a basis for security and stability and which turned every conflict around the world into part of its own binary (two-sided) logic. While the collapse of the Communist side of that conflict at the end of the twentieth century did not end the postmodern war system, it did change it significantly.

So what is postmodern war in the early twenty-first century? It is suicide cyborgs in the Middle East and New York City, it is guerrilla groups such as FARC in Colombia bragging about their jungle computers being Y2K compliant, it is Green Beret political scientists. It is collateral damage to Afghanistan wedding parties and Palestinian families. It is the second cold war. The "Balance of Terror" that framed the first cold war has morphed into a War of Terror for the second. The enemy is "terror," the justification is fear (terror), and the strategic claims and the major doctrines are often based on terror—not of what is happening but on a fear of what might happen. Restrictions of civil liberties, the growth of security services, the expansion of the military, preemptive attacks and wars, are often based on the fear of a worst-case scenario in a simple evil/good world, as with the domino theory and Vietnam and CIA estimates of Soviet capabilities. In the few cases where fear isn't the motivation, there is vengeance.

What makes the current situation clearly another cold war is that just as in the twentieth century the use of many weapon systems is precluded, and decisive victory impossible, the search for new weapons to solve this problem escalates. It is a "cold war" because a "hot" war is total war, and that would include the significant use of chemical, biological, and/or nuclear weapons along with the total military mobilization of major powers. This may happen. Then postmodern war will be over and apocalyptic war will be here. But for now, conflicts may be horrific but they remain limited technologically and geographically, and no great power has fully mobilized since World War II.

War has always been terrible, and now that its political (practical) utility is severely limited, its horror is the single most important thing about it. The terror starts with the reality of WMD, whose threat of human extinction is seldom raised in polite company, let alone on official levels. However, it is permissible to argue that WMD threatens a nation-state in particular or, in extremis, a civilization, as with the U.S. justifications for a preemptive attack on Iraq. The goal is to save the United States, not the world, but that is a horrible enough scenario actually, and in a real sense the fate of the world is directly involved, and so it will be terrifying in that way as well, as all wars seem to be now. On the other end of the spectrum we have the ethnic and religious massacres of neighbors and the threat of a single shoe-bomb terrorist sitting next to you on the plane. But he is actually also part of a network, just a less formal one than the Delta Squad spotter hunting Osama bin Laden who can call in thousands of pounds of explosives from artillery, ships, and planes.

This increasingly important "terror" part of war is often more about perception than military objectives. War has always paid attention to perpetuating and confronting terror. But today, with each death potentially captured forever and broadcast to the world thanks to the magic of information technologies, perception is particularly important. This is why the WTO was attacked, of course, because it was built as a statement about the economic and political organization of the future.

Consider the decision of George W. Bush's administration to achieve and ensure strategic and tactical domination of space, a favorite RMA to many. This is put forward in the guise of an argument for a limited ballistic missile defense system to keep North Korea or some other small rogue state from attacking the United States with nuclear warheads. Notice the real policy underneath: to control space, the high ground.

Besides its destabilizing impact on the world politically, especially if China or

Russia perceive that the defense shield is too effective and therefore undoes their deterrent—the ability to launch an effective counterstrike after a U.S. first strike—and the balance of terror (mutually assured destruction—MAD) they currently have with the United States, such a policy is seriously flawed in any event. Once space assets become integral to all U.S. military operations, the very denial of these space assets could prove disastrous. The defense analyst Jonathan Lockwood rightly calls this the "Achilles' heel" of the major U.S. RMA doctrine.[7] Militarily, new technologies will never solve the fundamental political problems that now bedevil the world. No RMA is going to be the one sought-after "silver bullet" that will finally bring about real security; not controlling space, not having the smartest weapons, not even having the biggest computers. Security will have to come from a fundamental change in the world order, an order that in many ways has been shaped by postmodern war and the PRMA that defines it. To understand why this is, we have to look closely at the fog of war, the limits of information technology, and the constraints of postmodern war.

FOG, IT, AND POSTMODERN WAR

One of the common themes of RMA advocates is that the right RMA will do away with the "fog" of war, Baron von Clausewitz's term for war's uncertainty. Even Michael O'Hanlon, a critic of RMA advocates with their talk of achieving "complete situational awareness," "full-dimensional protection," "agile, rapidly deployable, automated, precise, and long-range strike force[s]," and "spacepower" anchoring the "reconnaissance-strike complex," claims, "We should not ignore the promise of high technology and resign ourselves to operate forever within Clausewitz's famous 'fog' of war."[8]

But the fog of war will never lift, because it is generated by the three main "problems" of war—your side's behavior, your antagonist's behavior, and nature (the weather, mainly). How will your soldiers act in the face of death? How will your machines perform? What will your enemy do and how will they react to what you do? How well will they perform? What will the weather be? These questions are not completely answerable, let alone predictable or controllable. They will never be. In terms of information theory, these are incomputable complex systems. War is an intractable problem conceptually; really the only way to know how a war is going to come out is to fight it.

Even as the military looks to better information technologies to dispel these uncertainties, it has become clear to the scientists and engineers who work with information technology that there are absolute limits to how much they can do.

The first thing about information we have really understood are the limits to our understanding.[9] Kurt Gödel, a twentieth-century mathematician, showed that any formal information system would either be incomplete, have paradoxes, or both. He did this by taking an old Greek philosophical conundrum and putting it into mathematics. What happens when you meet someone who always lies and they tell you something and add, "I'm lying"? If they are lying about lying, then . . . It turns out that *any* formal system for representing reality at a minimum is either incomplete or has paradoxes. It seems likely that such systems always have both problems, but that remains to be proven.

Gödel used mathematics to prove that mathematics was not perfect; Alonzo Church and Alan Turing soon showed that Gödel's proof applied to infinite computing machines as well. The perfect computer is impossible. In the 1980s, computer scientists debating the possibility of President Reagan's Strategic Defense Initiative (aka Star Wars) defined the boundaries of computing even more strictly, stressing the gap between models, as all computer programs are, and embodied reality ("The map is not the territory"), as well as other "limits of correctness."[10]

These proofs are related philosophically to the claims from quantum physics that in many cases to know one thing is to be denied the possibility of knowing something else (such is evident when studying electron behavior) and that the observer of an event is part of it, and therefore affects it (Heisenberg's Uncertainty Principle, named after the great German physicist who first formulated it).

Since these discoveries in the early twentieth century, there have been real advances in our knowledge of systems and other forms of complexity. Complexity theory, for example, has shown that small events can have incredible implications (the Butterfly Effect) thanks to the multiplying possibilities of feedback loops. Ilya Prigogine, a Belgian chemist, has contributed his elegant work on dissipative systems to show how in some very interesting cases particular systems can transition into more complex systems with profound implications for our understanding, not just of basic informational principles from physics, which are still only partially understood (like entropy and extropy), but also of such complex systems as life itself. What we know of such processes (termed, by some, "out-of-control" systems because we can't control them) is growing significantly. However, in broad terms our understanding of information, and its relation to reality, is still primitive.[11] Yet RMA theorists, such as those O'Hanlon criticizes, want to shape U.S. military policy around weapon systems that will give complete situational awareness, full-dimensional protection, precise targeting, and so on. Complete, full-dimensional, precise . . . in other words perfect information.

This impossible dream has inspired the militaries of the postindustrial nation-states to develop a whole range of specific technologies (electronic battlefield, robotics, intelligent munitions) and information-saturated doctrines (AirLand Battle, Info War, Netwar). War, however, remains stubbornly confusing and quite bloody. The experiences of the United States in the Middle East show this quite clearly; from the wounding of the USS *Stark* to the war-hunt in Afghanistan against the Taliban and Al Qaeda, things have never turned out as predicted. No plan or illusion survives contact with the enemy or even the future.

Once, so the story goes, battles were won by the god-favored and the brave. Effective weapons helped, but internal qualities or just blind luck were more important in most people's view. Yes, Sun Tzu, the ancient Chinese philosopher of war, and his commentators knew better, but history shows that few generals, let alone soldiers, fought war as intelligently as Sun Tzu analyzed it. Still, in mass hand-to-hand combat the dedication of individual soldiers did make quite a difference; it was often decisive. Even clever generals played their role. As modern war supplanted ancient, however, the power of the weapons (increased through a series of RMAs), especially their force-of-fire, became crucial. War became more a matter of logistics than elan, culminating in the industrial slaughters of the world wars, the mirror image of industrial production.

In postmodern war, information has become the ideal, the main "force multiplier," as the military likes to say. The approach to it has usually been industrial (more is better) and often it has succumbed to the illusion that there might some day even be enough (perfect) information, although one of the few things we know about the nature of information is that it can *never* be perfect, thanks to the various paradoxes of representation, meaning, and systems (i.e., information) in general, described above.

Adding to this are the constraints of postmodern war itself. All weapons, especially the most powerful, cannot be used. Politically, military operations are constrained even further, and genocide, colonialization, and aggressive regime-changing from outside are severely limited. In many cases the problem isn't destroying your enemy, it is finding him. War continues, but it is messy and confusing, with few decisive battles and no clear-cut victories.

BLEEDING REALITY

Technology has often proved decisive in war. Stone and wood weapons were replaced by copper, then bronze, then iron, then steel. Chariots, stirrups, longbows, guns, cannons, machine guns, planes, and submarines have all played crucial roles in bringing victory to the technologically advanced. But since World War II it is hard to find a clear case where technology has been decisive in war. The U.S.

victory in the Kuwait war, for example, owed much more to the corruption and incompetence of the Iraqis than to the advanced state of U.S. and European weaponry. As General Norman Schwarzkopf said, "I certainly don't give the Iraqis much credit."[12] High-tech RMA weapons kept allied casualties down, but they weren't needed for victory. And in some cases, as with the Patriot missiles, we now know they didn't work at all. In the French and American Vietnam wars and the Afghan–Soviet War, the technologically sophisticated sides lost, even though they had incredible advantages. Political will, often manifested in appropriate, not state-of-the-art, technology, won out.

But hope springs eternal, and the lesson the United States drew from Vietnam was that more technology was the solution, especially if it could keep casualties low enough to prevent the voting public from getting upset. Trapped in the confines of postmodern war, the military became more and more involved in effecting political change, through nation building, for example. Doctrines such as low-intensity conflict and, later, information war justified this, but for the military, their core mission was still combat, and more and more of their faith was put into the latest technologies.

Yet high-tech weapons systems failed quite often. Among the most notable examples was the death of thirty-seven sailors aboard the USS *Stark* when she was hit during the Iran–Iraq War with an Exocet missile fired by an Iraqi plane. Theoretically the United States was neutral in the conflict, but in actuality it was a close ally of Iraq, and at one point it seems the United States even tried to provoke Iran into attacking, which led to the shooting down of a commercial Iranian airliner by the USS *Vincennes*. In both these incidents, and in the fighter-jet assassination attack on Mu'ammar Gadhafi in Libya, which killed his four-year-old daughter and hit the French embassy but did not harm him. The most advanced and sophisticated systems the U.S. military deployed failed.[13]

The reasons for these failures were diverse, but all were related to the fundamental problems with expecting perfection, or even extremely high reliability, from information or technologies in the most unstable part of human existence—war. So in the case of the tragedies in the paragraph above: false scenarios are fulfilled, key software is faked, models of reality prove fallacious, fear overrides irrelevant training, hubris trumps humility, and you have dead U.S. sailors, hundreds of dead Iranian civilians floating in the Persian Gulf, and another international incident.

In Somalia it was the same: overconfident planning, a lack of understanding and an excess of information, high-tech flying command-and-control sending rescue teams in deadly circles, and finally military victory perceived as humiliation.[14] It seems that in the recent campaigns in the second (terror) cold war

(United States–Al Qaeda; United States–Afghanistan), the same patterns are emerging.

Hoping to keep the casualty rate as miraculously low as it was in the Gulf War, where the life expectancy of U.S. soldiers was higher than civilians of the same demographic set,[15] the United States tried to use high technology and human proxies at Tora Bora and other places, with less-than-satisfying results. Even the destruction of the Taliban, which collapsed under air bombardment, well-supplied Northern Alliance assaults, and its abandonment by most of the people of Afghanistan, produced U.S. casualties. In one case the programming of a targeting device that automatically reset itself to its own location was the problem, in another, the need to closely question many prisoners quickly resulted in a failure of security and the death of a CIA agent, the first soldier to die in the U.S. seizure of Afghanistan. The RMA in precision weapons and integrated command-and-control helped produce victory in the first battle of Afghanistan, but it didn't win the war against terrorism. In fact, now these systems are a problem in the second battle of Afghanistan, the battle to build a new nation.

After the elimination of the Taliban and the rout of Al Qaeda, the United States continued to seek out enemy concentrations, and in several incidents ended up producing more than optimum collateral damage—in other words, killing a number of innocent Afghans. The famous case of the bombed wedding party is instructive. After a lengthy investigation, the U.S. Air Force found itself blameless, even though it admitted killing scores of civilians accidentally. The point, the USAF thought, was that antiaircraft weapons were very possibly (but not certainly) firing at the U.S. craft (but not hitting them) from within a number of villages. The villagers claimed it was their celebratory shooting of small arms that was the purported antiaircraft fire.[16] In either case, does it make sense for U.S. air assets to shoot up every target that might be shooting at them just because they can, thanks to their great sensors and computerized weapons, especially considering that someone might even be trying to provoke this as a way of alienating the newly bombed villagers from the United States and the government it supports in Kabul? Using the technology seems to outweigh using simple common sense.

So right after winning the campaign, the United States had to start a much harder one, called nation building (just as in Iraq after Gulf War II). As the *Washington Post* reported in early August 2002 of the U.S. expeditionary force: "Their mission has evolved from a clear-cut effort to topple the Taliban and cripple Al-Qaeda into an increasingly uncertain operation mired in the complexities of Afghan politics." The brief moments of modern war that are sprinkled about in postmodern war had passed, as had the relevance of the RMA technologies, and things were no longer clean and simple. Colonel Roger King, chief U.S. military spokesman in Afghanistan, declared: "It doesn't fit into the living-room definition anymore of what war is supposed to be like. It's almost like deterrence during the Cold War."[17]

Just as in the first cold war, the second cold war is an unbounded conflict; everything is part of it. Its very logic insists on dividing the world into two competing groups, us and them, and there is no space for nuances or distinctions.[18] Yet the reality is more complex. Human civilization is now one global economic and political system, as the world is one ecology, even if it isn't uniform. There really isn't one simple dividing line between "the terrorists" and the "antiterrorists." It is not a symmetrical system, nor one of simple dichotomies, any more than postmodern war is.

Technology doesn't change this. The RMAs that make up the PRMA don't solve the problem of postmodern war, they are part of it, because postmodern war is about the continual development of new weapon systems. But it is human politics and human culture that determine the shape of war, not technologies. New technologies might open some options and close others, but they aren't determinate. They establish the context. This is particularly clear in terms of the international political system.

ASYMMETRICAL GLOBALIZATION

> The rules of the game in international relations are changing and the origins of an extraordinary number of those changes can be traced to the Information Revolution.
>
> —DAVID J. ROTHKOPF[19]

Human globalization has been happening since our ancestors first left Africa, but there is no doubt that today's globalization is quantitatively and qualitatively different than anything before. The level of communications, even integration, between the humans of the world is undoubtedly at the highest level ever, by an order of several magnitudes. And it is increasing. This would be impossible without the incredible new IT-driven transportation and communication technologies, the same technologies that lie behind almost every RMA being argued for in the U.S. military.

Of course, the amount any particular person, family, clan, village, or tribe is integrated into the global grid (net, community, economy) varies enormously. And there must be hermits out there, seeing almost no one. But still, the world (of people) is knit together today in a fundamentally new way. We can even talk now of one human polis, one political community, inhabiting our one world, which is indeed one living system. At this point this human polis is pretty chaotic. What coordination there is politically is through the UN and a few dozen other international networks that are usually military (NATO) or economic (WTO, IMF). The most important connections between people are personal and take place outside the established lines of political and economic authority. The lifeblood of the human polis is the constant movement of people and goods between the communities of the world.

But if the people of the world form one polis, then it is one of profound inequality. There is no need to rehash the incredible numbers here, but suffice it to say that the great wealth of North America, Europe, and a handful of Asian economies such as Japan makes it clear that it is a very asymmetrical world system indeed. It is these countries, and in addition China, that are pursuing military superiority through new technologies and doctrines, specifically RMAs, in the near term, around precision weapons, integrated surveillance and communications, information war, and space superiority, and in the long term based on nanotechnology, biotechnology, and artificial intelligence. The plan is that these will ensure military superiority and victory in war.

Wars are almost always asymmetrical; that is why somebody wins and somebody else loses. But when the conservative defense intellectual Colin S. Gray claims that therefore "asymmetry essentially is a hollow concept" he is being willfully obtuse.[20] What makes asymmetry such an important idea now is that many different types and approaches to war exist in the postmodern war system. The old solution of the militarily dominant combatant, total war even to the point of genocide, is no longer an option (not that is hasn't been tried even recently). So, more than ever, war is political, not technological. This is why the greatest military power in world history and the second greatest both lost wars to relatively tiny opponents (Vietnam, Afghanistan). The conflicts were so radically asymmetrical that the great military advantages (based on such revolutionary weapons and ideas as helicopters and vertical envelopment and the electronic battlefield) of the United States and the Soviet Union weren't enough to overcome the fundamentally political rules. When the political situation is favorable, as with the U.S. war against the hated (by the Afghans most of all) Taliban, easy victories are forthcoming. But the same opponent, in a different situation, can be deadly. We forget this lesson at our peril. Can terror also be asymmetrical?

Back in 1982, Edward Herman, a leftist academic, made a distinction between retail and wholesale terror.[21] As he rightly pointed out, most terror was (and is) perpetrated by nation-states, and the scale of difference Herman characterized as wholesale is opposed to the retail terror on nonstate actors. There are two problems with this distinction, though. First, many of us would condemn all terror, from the beating of a child to the bombing of a city. Second, with the increasing technical complexity of our society, it is now possible for a handful of terrorists to kill thousands. WMDs make this even clearer. Still, Herman's main point remains: the system of terror includes nation-states, not just nongovernmental organizations (NGOs) and individuals, and so far it is the states that have the resources to do the most terrible of things, thanks to earlier RMAs in such areas as aviation and missile development. Perhaps a central paradox of this second cold war is that the gap is closing between the different types of terrorism, thanks to information technology and the technosciences it fosters. A network such as Al Qaeda could not threaten the United States except for the sophisticated technologies it appropriates for communication, targeting, and destruction. The Al Qaeda RMA is that radically decentralized nonstate actors can kill thousands with major international effects thanks to the existence of global communications, commercial airliners, and skyscrapers. All of these exist only because of the same sophisticated IT that underlies the military's RMAs.

Almost every theory of the current globalization process implicates IT as its primary engine. IT is also the culprit in most of the numerous proclamations that we are experiencing this or that RMA, and it certainly underlies postmodern war. Yet the discourses that analyze globalization and contemporary war are seldom brought together. This has to change, for they are part of the same sociological and technological phenomena that have produced our so-called "information society."

One can look at the elements of postmodern war and see that they do map closely onto the current globalization process.[22] Among the most salient:

- The central role of information and information technology. IT underlies the RMAs and the global economy.
- An increase in the speed of transactions and processes, leading to an increase in the pace of globalization and in RMAs that hope to dominate battle through more, and better, information sooner.
- A bricolage of different forms of war and politics from the totally new to the very oldest. In modernity the nation-state and total war were the dominant forms; in postmodernity, corporations, regional alliances, tribes, nations-without-states, NGOs, international governmental institutions, networks, and ethnicities share power and propagate various types of organized violence from mass rape to nuclear coercion.
- Increased human-machine integration (cyborgization). This is at the heart of new business practices, many RMA proposals, and the self-conceptualization and actualization of many individuals and groups worldwide.

- The lack of any one unifying narrative, in politics, religion, or in military affairs, hence the proliferation of RMAs without any one RMA being clearly the answer.
- A complexification of gender. The proliferation of IT-driven systems has allowed the integration of women into most military occupations and civilian jobs. Physical strength is now much less important in war and in work than skill and intelligence.
- Peace as the main justification of war. So security becomes dependent on risking the whole planet (as with the nuclear arsenals and ideas such as preemptive war), and war proliferates into culture, structuring economic decisions and framing mass culture. These Cold War doctrines for achieving peace through making weapons (the nuclear arsenal, missile defense) and war (containing, preemptive) are almost always based on unrealistic expectations of RMAs, such as the nuclear RMA and now the precision-weapons RMA.

Clearly, the problem of postmodern war is the problem of our current globalizing process and the international system that is framing it. War is no longer an effective political instrument but it is used as if it were, often because of the promise that new technologies are going to produce some wonderful revolution in military affairs.

The only RMA we really need is Gregory Foster's idea that the ultimate RMA would build a military that worked toward "No War" or even Kant's "Perpetual Peace" instead of just a new type of war.[23] This is the only real security we can have. The idea of total security is actually in opposition to the concept of a real peace. You can't build nations, or any peaceful political institutions, with new weapons systems and new illusions about making war effective again with an ultimate revolution in military affairs in the sky. Here today, on earth, we can't afford to mistake peace and war. Total security is impossible. Real peace is a type of human culture, it is a civilization perhaps not yet born, but certainly it is possible, and certainly it is necessary.

The high-tech "shock and awe" approach of Gulf War II might have minimized U.S. and British casualties, but it was hardly necessary against the incompetent, unpopular Saddam regime. And the war itself turned out to be as much of a political disaster as a military success, so it is hard to call it a victory except in the most limited terms. The RMA promise of easy victories is seductive, but an illusion. The costs of war are complex and often hidden in the future. The United States will be paying for the overrunning of Iraq for many years to come.

PART IV

CIVIL VIOLENCE AND INFORMATION TECHNOLOGIES

10. BULLETS TO BYTES: REFLECTIONS ON ICTS AND "LOCAL" CONFLICT

RAFAL ROHOZINSKI[1]

We don't often associate places like Somalia or Chechnya with information and communication technologies (ICTs). Nor does Palestine usually prompt us to think of the global information society. Rather, we often think of these zones—like other areas afflicted by protracted violence and poverty—as "informational black holes," cut off from the information revolution and on the wrong side of the digital divide.

And yet, throughout the 1990s, the world's conflict zones became increasingly penetrated by ICTs, in keeping with the larger global process of their exponential growth and diffusion. In part, these technologies were "carried in" to conflict zones by the increasing legions of development and aid workers. Others arrived on the ether—a result of the growing reach of satellite-based systems, which brought telephony to the remotest areas, along with hundreds of radio and television channels—and became accessible to individuals as technological advances drastically reduced the size and cost of satellite receivers.[2] More remarkable, perhaps, is the indigenously spawned proliferation of advanced ICT infrastructures, financed and built by local entrepreneurs and investors, in many conflict zones.

To be certain, Mogadishu has not become London: there remains a deep unevenness in the distribution of, and access to, ICTs within developing countries, including those torn apart by strife. Nevertheless, and despite these internal inequities, the world's poorest and most unstable regions have been increasingly penetrated by communications infrastructures of all kinds—wireless telephony, the Internet, satellite television and radio. In Somalia, for example, the quintessential "failed state" of the post–Cold War era where clan-based militias rule by the barrel of a gun, three Somali cellular operators cooperate to provide telephone and Internet coverage to over 70% of the country, which has gained a reputation for the "best and cheapest telephone system in all of east Africa."[3] Likewise, in the farthest reaches of the eastern Congo, e-mail and Internet telephony are available in commercially run *tele-cabines.* In Palestine, at least five separate cellular providers—four Israeli and one Palestinian—blanket the region with telephone services. Even in Chechnya, whose capital city, Grozny, was bombed back into the Middle Ages under the full weight of the Russian military machine, a cellular phone operator vies for clients amidst the detritus of war. Indeed, of the handful of countries that remain unconnected to the Internet, all are controlled by authoritarian regimes who limit access for political reasons.

It is perhaps surprising that our knowledge about the degree of penetration of these technologies within conflict zones is not matched by an understanding of their usages and potential impacts, especially given the international community's increasing preoccupation with these zones. If we accept that ICTs are precipitating fundamental shifts in the material basis of life in advanced industrial societies, then surely we can assume that they are facilitating equally monumental shifts in countries outside the industrial core, including those embroiled in violence. And yet, on a *substantive* level, our knowledge remains sketchy. For example, while we know that in Taliban-controlled Afghanistan (a regime that eschewed all forms of modern communication) 85% of all male respondents in a 1999 survey replied that they owned a radio in working order,[4] we do not know how or in what ways radio influences decision making in oral or illiterate cultures and societies. On a different note, we *suspect* that ICTs are important in supporting a myriad of informal, private, and mostly hidden flows of goods and monies (especially remittances) that support the survival of ordinary people in zones of conflict.[5] Likewise, we *infer* that the "criminal entrepreneurs" of conflict zones—who export drugs, slavery, diamonds, timber, and gold, while importing arms, cigarettes, and *khat*—employ ICTs to ply their wares and source their needs on world markets. These suspicions have emerged because our knowledge of the drivers and dynamics of local conflicts has improved over the years through direct experience in places like Bosnia, Somalia, and West Africa (as well as recent research).[6] However, while we may think our comprehension of conflict dynamics has improved, our understanding of the ways in which ICTs may be altering these dynamics and/or reworking the material basis of life within these zones remains markedly underdeveloped and understudied.

Where we have derived some perspective on the appropriation of ICTs by actors in conflict zones is through their encounters with the representatives of the international community who have come to increasingly populate these zones. The scale and scope of the international community's interventions in conflict zones expanded greatly throughout the 1990s, an involvement driven in part by the enormity of human suffering caused by the cascading conflicts in sub-Saharan Africa, Asia, the Middle East, and the southern doorstep of Europe, and in part by hope for the "peace dividend" that was to accrue with the end of the Cold War. During the Cold War, international humanitarian relief and peacekeeping efforts were circumscribed by the bipolar balance, which carefully preserved the sovereignty and territorial inviolability of nation-states. The collapse of this system in the 1990s held out the (momentary) promise of global peace and a newfound role for the international community in stabilizing conflict zones and building that peace. However, as old conflicts continued to fester and new ones erupted, the scale of international interventions grew in size—encompassing ever larger numbers of United Nations agencies, nongovernmental organizations, and, increasingly, military forces from advanced industrial countries (who were bent on "peace enforcement" or, more recently "regime change"). At the same time, the objectives underpinning these interventions became ever more encompassing. They moved away from more limited exercises to halt violence, keep the peace, and provide humanitarian relief, and toward more comprehensive ambitions of social transformation—to apply the neoliberal levers of development, market reform, and good governance, in order to transform conflict zones from nests of Hobbesian atavism and poverty into modern, liberal, market-oriented democracies.

As some notable scholars have argued, the interventionist experiences and impulses of the past decade have resulted in a growing neoliberal consensus (at least among the dominant Western actors, donors, and the agencies of the UN system) about the linkages between underdevelopment, conflict, and regional/international instability: conflicts now spill over borders and threaten regional/international stability; conflicts result primarily from poverty, underdevelopment, and bad (read "illiberal") governance; the remedy to conflict, and to ensuring international stability, therefore is development (neoliberal style). These linkages, embodying what Mark Duffield describes as the "securitization" of development, have further strengthened the imperative for, and scope of, international intervention in conflict zones, which, because of their risks to international insecurity, must be, like a cancer, treated or excised, through development, or through military compulsion, or through both.[7]

For the purpose of this chapter, which seeks to illuminate the uses of ICTs in conflict zones, I will divide the international community's "relief-to-development-backed-by-firepower enterprise" into two broadly defined groups: the "peace-building and development" community; and the more military-minded interveners. Both of these groups consider ICTs to be an essential part of their organizational operations. However, they hold radically different assumptions about the nature and potential of ICTs within conflict zones. Development actors tend to see ICT infrastructure as "neutral," and its development/peace-building potential to be positive. By contrast, military actors see ICTs as a potential war-waging tool that can empower new actors and open up new terrains of battle; but they also believe these new challenges can be met largely through superior technology and organization.

This chapter seeks to highlight some of the ways that protagonists in conflict zones appear to be appropriating ICTs in the service of their locally defined objectives. It does this through illustrations drawn from various examples of the encounters between local, ICT-wielding protagonists and external development and military peace-building complexes. In so doing, this chapter will underscore the fallibility of certain received assumptions about the role and nature of ICTs in conflict zones, while suggesting the need for further, grounded research.

"DEVELOPING" PEACE: RATIONAL ASSUMPTIONS, SUBVERTED INTENT

ICTs play an increasingly central role in the operations and programs of relief/development agencies, especially in conflict/post-conflict zones. Operationally, ICTs help support the complex logistics and management of relief and development operations, helping to maintain the flow of information, supplies, and people. Like in other complex undertakings—business, government, trade, finance—ICTs are the "nerves and arteries" that sustain and enable coordinated action, in this case the wide and disparate range of development and relief actors. Programmatically, ICTs are increasingly perceived as specific tools that can help developing countries "leapfrog" over traditional barriers to development by enhancing governance, empowering citizens, facilitating regional development and national economic integration with the global economy, and offering new opportunities to combat poverty.[8] These tasks can take on added urgency in post-conflict zones where "development" is seen as the solidifier of stability and security. In addition, development actors have posited a special "peace-building" potential for ICTs: as a potential medium through which to link up the members of communities torn apart by war—to allow them to communicate and cooperate together, to thereby build bridges of peace.

Overall, development/relief actors consider the infrastructures of ICTs to be neutral—as rational communication tools creating open channels rather than contested spaces—while harboring strong expectations for the positive development and peace-building potential that they may enable. In fact, this view—of rational neutrality and positive potential—goes far beyond their perceptions of ICTs; rather it underpins the self-understanding of the development enterprise itself. Thus, the present-day theory and practice of relief/development is infused with positivism—a belief that the application of reason, rationality, and the scientific method can and should bring about expected and beneficial results. Politics and the chaos of the market is accepted as a necessary regulating mechanism for an otherwise scientifically ordered world where established "formulas" and "principles"—in development parlance, "programs" and "policy"—can be applied to bring about predictable and positive results. When applied to the role of ICTs, these rational self-assumptions become even further reified by a pseudo-scientism that considers tools that are themselves a product of scientific methods (as ICTs are) to necessarily be carriers of rationality.[9]

To date, the lack of evaluative evidence about the impact of ICT-enabled development/peace projects means there is no basis on which to "vindicate" the faith of their purveyors. However, there is some sobering counterevidence emerging from the field, evidence that reveals a somewhat more ambiguous truth about how ICTs are perceived and its infrastructures put to use by local actors in zones of conflict. A few examples follow.

Not So Neutral

Examples from Rwanda suggest that the imported ICT infrastructure, on which relief and development actors depend operationally for their own internal communications, is neither neutral nor inconsequential in the eyes of conflict protagonists on the ground.

The United Nations' radio network in the Great Lakes region (covering Rwanda, Burundi, Tanzania, Congo, and Uganda) attracted a great deal of interest from a range of local actors throughout the 1990s.[10] At the most benign end of the scale, UN radios were frequently stolen and regularly used by former (local) UN employees and other Rwandans, who pirated UN frequencies for long personal conversations between family and friends in different regions. UN radio room staff monitoring these frequencies would often find them more active at night, when UN operations where generally dormant, than during the day when they were used by upwards of thirteen UN agencies and their NGO partners. On a more worrisome level from the perspective of neutrality and peace-building, the network was also allegedly used by elements of the former Interhamwe militias (who were key perpetrators of the 1994 genocide) to pass coded messages between different regions of the country and elsewhere. In both cases, these uses were exploitative, opportunistic, and, in the case of the latter, potentially furthering violence. However, although senior UN staff were aware of this subversion of their systems, they took no action. The situation continued unchecked until late 1999, when the Rwandan government (which was actively monitoring UN frequencies) threatened to revoke the UN's license to operate a radio network, accusing it of aiding and abetting rebel groups.

Interestingly, there is evidence that in an earlier period the Rwandan government itself subverted the telecommunications capacities of the relief/development enterprise, to further its war aims and do so unimpeded by the displeasure of international opinion. The incidents occurred in 1996, when the Rwandan Army mounted a military campaign to eliminate the threat posed by Interahamwe militias that were operating from UN High Commission for Refugees (UNHCR)–run camps along Rwanda's northwest border, and to force the repatriation of over a million Hutu refugees. During the campaign, the Rwandan military monitored NGO communications (which were transmitted without encryption) to extract information passed by aid workers (to each other) about the locations of refugees fleeing the Rwandan troops. The Rwandan military then used this information to track down and kill large groups of Hutu refugees.

On a more strategic level, the Rwandan military waged a sophisticated disinformation campaign against the international community. First, it confiscated satellite phones and other means for international communication that belonged to the UN agencies and NGOs in the zone of fighting. Thus incapacitated, the development and relief workers were unable to report Rwandan military abuses to the outside world. Second, the army banned reporters from traveling freely in the region; "news" from the zone of combat was passed to selected journalists as "exclusives" by Rwandan military "minders," or presented at press briefings organized by military commanders. These strategies were so successful at ensuring Rwandan victory that Rwandan Minister of Defense (now president) Paul Kagame later boasted that the Rwandan military had "used information and communication warfare better than anyone," and thus, "invented a new way of doing things." [11]

Building Bridges or Building Walls?

As noted, many development actors are enamored with the potential of ICTs both to empower civil society actors (with the emphasis on "civil") and, especially in conflict/post-conflict zones, to build communication bridges between (formerly) warring communities in order to encourage reconciliation and consolidate peace.

The belief in ICTs' capacities to empower civil society actors does have some evidentiary support at the global level. For example, ICTs have played a significant role in facilitating the transnationalization and influence of NGO actors and networks in the global arena. These networks, as some scholars argue, are perhaps the nuclei of an emerging global civil society and public sphere, which may re-create on a planetary scale the civil society of Habermas's café society.[12] The success of NGOs in pushing governments on global issues ranging from the environment, debt relief, and, significantly, the campaign against land mines, is testament to the vitality of the new cosmopolitan politics that may be emerging.

However, whether ICTs can really help build lasting bridges between (formerly) warring communities, by overcoming fears and rebuilding trust, remains more of a theoretical proposition than a proven fact. Moreover, the liberal values that buttress this perspective—which suggest that through open communication alone the fears and grievances that underpin violent conflict can be overcome—may severely underestimate the various forms of structural violence that separate communities in conflict, and which often remain even after the cessation of physical violence.

Currently, there is research under way that seeks to examine how NGOs are using ICTs to build dialogue channels and communities of peace in active war zones, however, this research is in its nascent stages.[13] It is perhaps surprising, therefore, that despite the lack of any concrete proof concerning the ICT-for-peace equation, the international community has dabbled in large-scale experimentation using ICTs in post-conflict settings, including East Timor and Kosovo. In both places, substantial resources were invested in creating an Internet infrastructure as part of the relief and reconstruction effort. In both cases the hope was that these infrastructures, in addition to servicing the operational needs of relief and development actors, would also provide a space and channel for local NGOs and civil groups to communicate, coordinate, and hopefully support the construction/consolidation of civil peace. These initiatives have not yet been evaluated or comprehensively reviewed.

While the jury is still out as to whether ICTs will substantially empower the forces for peace in these places, it is important to underline that "civil minded" actors are not alone in exploiting ICTs in these regions. In the Balkans, for example, organized criminal gangs have taken to cell phones and the Internet with equal vigor, using them to sustain criminal enterprises and networks that penetrate the larger region and range across sectarian lines. Moreover, we should recall that rebuilding trust and assuaging fear among communities in a post-violence situation is infinitely more difficult, and more fragile, than the task of sowing mistrust and terror. Thus, we have well-documented evidence of how the "old" ICT broadcast medium of radio has been used to reinforce communal fears, hatred, and violence in many of the world's protracted war zones. In Lebanon, for example, each sectarian militia operated its own radio station—targeting its own community with messages of internal solidarity and external fear of the "others"—while larger factions ran small media empires that included television and print media.[14] In Bosnia, over 280 radio and television stations (a concentration higher than that of the United States, the world's most saturated media market) competed for command of the airwaves. So significant was the perceived incendiary power of these media that the Dayton Accords that ended the war called for the creation of an international media commission to ensure that local stations did not undermine the peace.[15] And perhaps the most heinous example comes from Rwanda, where the genocidal directives broadcast by Radio "Mille Collines" penetrated into every *cellule* of the country; its messages of hatred, fear, and national duty (to cleanse the country of the Tutsi "cockroaches") are thought to be one of the major proximate factors inciting thousands of Hutus to turn on their Tutsi neighbors, relatives, and friends.[16]

Against this grim backdrop, we should note that technological developments of the 1990s may be furthering the use of ICTs to build intercommunity walls rather than bridges. What is new in the past decade is the *convergence* of "old" broadcast technologies (radio and TV) with "new" interactive ICTs. What this has meant is that broadcasting capabilities no longer require huge capital investments in equipment and people; sophisticated multimedia content can be compiled cheaply and easily, and widely distributed at marginal cost via the Internet or compact disc. Thus, it is now possible for anyone armed with an inexpensive digital camera and a PC to become a potential Spielberg (or Riefenstahl). The net effect of this technological convergence has been twofold: first, the power to create content has shifted downward to a new range of small producers; and second, the reach enabled by new media (such as Internet and satellite channels) has shifted outward, with small actors now able to transmit their content to far-flung audiences of planetary proportions.[17]

The potentialities unleashed by this technological convergence have not been lost on small politically motivated actors in the world's zones of conflict. Indeed, one of the most successful exploiters is found in South Lebanon, namely Al-Manar television (the official media organ of Hizbollah, "The Party of God"), whose self-proclaimed role is to combat the Zionist state.[18] Al-Manar's sudden rise in popularity in the Middle East region derives, in part, from its strategy of preparing content in three formats: terrestrial and satellite broadcast, news wire, and streamed video (for broadcast on the Internet). Al-Manar's website hosts a large archive of downloadable video clips that portray Hizbollah guerrillas attacking Israeli Defense Forces along the disputed border zone between Lebanon and Israel. While the strict military value of these attacks is dubious, their propagandistic value is enormous. Thus, guerrilla actions are videotaped and set to inspirational music; the resulting "music videos" are widely circulated and have turned Al-Manar itself into a popular symbol of resistance against Israel. Indeed, Al-Manar has become the "media of choice" for non-Hizbollah groups claiming responsibility for suicide attacks in Israel.[19]

While it is easy to dismiss these kinds of video-vignettes as cheap propaganda, it is worthwhile to consider how new and different they are when compared to the government-controlled fare previously available to "the people" of the Middle East region. While it is true that many Middle Eastern governments were prone to incite and manipulate their respective population's sympathies with respect to the Palestinian situation, these activities were strongly controlled to strike a careful balance between encouraging street protest when this suited the regime's interest and calming these sentiments when the regime's interest calculations changed. There is no such strategic braking mechanism in the new media enterprise of Al-Manar. During the June 2002 Israeli reoccupation of the West Bank (and portions of the Gaza Strip), for example, Al-Manar (among other regional media broadcasters) ran uncut images of Israeli military operations. This brutal portrayal of Israeli violence across Arab TV and computer screens—what some U.S.–based critics characterized as the "greatest hits from the Israeli-Palestinian conflict: nonstop film of Israelis hitting, beating, dragging, clubbing and shooting Palestinians"[20]—has contributed to new levels of anger throughout the Arab world. As one observer noted: "Real rage has replaced what was often the sometimes routine anger of the past"—Al-Manar broadcasts have had an effect on Arab audiences and on Arab public opinion similar to that elicited by U.S. networks two decades earlier, when they brought the brutality of the war in Vietnam into American homes.[21]

Al-Manar's ability to speak directly to the Arab "street" is in its nascent stages and thus its potential trajectories and impacts are as yet unknown. But the lesson of the Al-Manar example is that the convergence of broadcast technology with new ICTs has given voice to a new constituency of actors whose interests may not lie in building bridges; whose "agency" has been amplified by a technology that allows them to speak over the heads of existing regimes; and whose incendiary capacities will not be tempered by the "stability concerns" of state broadcasting entities.

In conclusion, the paucity of research and evidence means we have very little basis on which to predict the likely social trajectories that these technologies may engender within the context of building global/local peace (i.e., global civil society? transnational criminal networks? intercommunity bridges of peace? intercommunity walls of hatred?). What we can assert, however, is that the development community's unreflective assumptions about the "neutral, liberal, and positive" potential of ICTs in conflict zones are both fallible and potentially dangerous. They are fallible because they underestimate the networked complexities of conflict zones, as well as the growing sophistication of local actors who have appropriated these technologies to suit their own realities, which are often antithetical to the project of "liberal peace." They are dangerous because, as the Rwandan example demonstrated, the development enterprises' own informational infrastructures have been subverted to service highly illiberal ends. In this light, it is useful to recall that it took the better part of a decade for development actors to recognize that food aid could be a powerful weapon in the hands of local warlords and not the benign humanitarian gesture that they understood it to be. Unfortunately it may take several more "Rwandas" before a similar, critically informed understanding of ICTs finally takes hold.

MILITARY: ENTER THE JEDI KNIGHTS

Not all parts of the international complex that intervenes in conflict zones share the same degree of naïveté concerning the war-fighting potential of ICTs. Thus, as noted above, military representatives of the "international order" have been making more frequent appearances in these zones as traditional peacekeeping has given way to more aggressive forms of "peace-imposing." While Afghanistan represents the most recent example of the increasingly aggressive way in which military forces have become involved in creating "facts on the ground" and in "settling" local wars (to remove the "threat" that these conflicts are perceived to pose to international order and stability), it is by no means the first or only one. The 1990s saw the Gulf War, the aggressive deployment of U.S. troops in support of a peace-enforcement mission in Somalia, the NATO air campaign against Serbia, and the introduction of ground forces to end open fighting in the Balkans. Meanwhile—and more controversially—military interventions to supposedly "force" peace have been launched in both the Occupied Territories and Chechnya.

Conventional wisdom suggests that a contest that pits the overwhelming technological, material, and organizational resources available to the armed forces of advanced industrial nation-states against small irregular actors would favor the former. However, experience suggests that these seemingly superior capabilities are no longer sufficient to ensure victory over small actors who know how to leverage the asymmetric advantages accrued through the appropriation of ICTs and ICT-enabled war-fighting strategies.

To appreciate the magnitude of this simple observation, it is useful to note that the military establishments of both East and West share a similar obsession with trying to understand how ICTs are fundamentally transforming the art and science of war. In a nutshell, ICTs are seen as precipitating a revolution in military affairs, on par with the magnitude of changes wrought by the invention of gunpowder, the stirrup, or steel. The main idea revolves around the criticality of information and communication to war-fighting. Thus, the thinking goes, the side that can dominate the infosphere, while denying the same capability to its opponents, will successfully dominate the physical field of battle. The objective, therefore, is to command a "full situational awareness" of the entire battle space, to channel destructive resources where and when needed, to blind the enemy while rendering oneself capable of seeing through the "fog of war," and to thereby maintain a godlike perspective on the conflict. In many ways, the modern military desires to transform itself into "Jedi Knights" (of *Star Wars* fame)—a professional breed of highly trained and capable forces, guided by an all-seeing power (i.e., command-and-control warfare supported by a wide array of surveillance and intelligence systems) that allows them to "intuitively" (via network approach) organize and apply force where and when needed to overcome the forces of "darkness" (the Enemy).

Especially in the United States, the military establishment's concerns and motives have prompted staggering investments in the development of modern ICTs and their potential military uses. In the physical realm, whole categories of modern technologies—from the invention of solid-state electronics to supercomputing, networking, and branches of applied mathematics such as cryptology—have emerged largely from research funded through the Department of Defense or the intelligence and security community.[22] Similarly, most of the key concepts that inform the thinking of social scientists exploring the new forms of military organization and warfare enabled by ICTs have emerged out of research sponsored by military think tanks.

However, despite the energy and resources expended on understanding these issues by state military machines (such as the United States)—and the resulting sophistication of their technology and forms of organizational change—it seems that the big state actors are still limited in their abilities to combat small, ICT-empowered local actors and "irregular" forcers in conflict zones, who themselves are increasingly sophisticated or just plain imaginative in their uses of communication technologies to wage war, as the following examples illustrate.

Early on in the U.S. campaign in Afghanistan, the "Jedi Knight" approach—using mobile highly networked special operations troops to target concentrations of Taliban forces—caused a devastating effect. However, effectiveness dropped precipitously when the task became sorting, finding, and tracking down the diffuse networks of actors linked to Al Qaeda. The lesson here is that, while networks are effective at countering hierarchies, they are not necessarily effective against other networks.

Similarly, in 1994, in the breakaway Russian republic of Chechnya, Chechen irregulars who opposed the entry of Russian federal troops into Grozny precipitated the worst military defeat suffered by the Russian military since World War II. The key to Chechen success was the use of cell phones, which rebel commanders employed to communicate quickly in the urban terrain and to thereby effectively maneuver their small units into positions for ambushing the Russians as they advanced into the city center. By contrast, Russian military radios had difficulty working among the high buildings and narrow streets of Grozny. Moreover, messages between Russian commanders had to be passed up and then down several chains of command, which incurred long delays and confusion. At the same time, the Russian use of unencrypted radios enabled Chechen fighters to "listen in" and thereby anticipate the movements of Russian troops and the intended location/timing of Russian air and artillery strikes. The net result was that, in a little over two days, Chechen fighters managed to decimate several complete units of the Russian army, killing over 4,000 troops and destroying over 250 armored vehicles.[23]

Another example comes from the U.S. debacle in Somalia. During the 1993 UN mission, local militia forces that opposed the "robust" peacekeeping stance taken by the U.S. contingent (Task Force Ranger) were able to successfully track the whereabouts and movement of both UN and U.S. military forces. They did this by eavesdropping on NGO and UN traffic, while themselves using more primitive but robust signaling systems that relied on burning tires, Motorola radios, and a jury-rigged and limited analogue cellular phone system.[24] By contrast, according to sources close to the U.S. operation, U.S. intelligence was unable to successfully interpret Somali communications, and the intelligence gathered was of limited value. Consequently, despite possessing a vastly superior military force and full freedom of movement (via helicopters), U.S.–UN forces lacked the all-important element of surprise. As a result, in one well-known raid aimed at capturing a senior militia warlord (Farah Aideed), elite U.S. forces were quickly surrounded and drawn into a running firefight that lasted through the night and into the following day. U.S. forces lost two helicopters, shot down by militia forces, and suffered more casualties in a single day than in any other engagement since the end of the Vietnam War.

From a military perspective, it is fair to say that U.S. forces eventually "prevailed," largely as a result of their superior firepower (it is worthy to note here that over 500 Somalis were killed as a result of the U.S. action, and well over a thousand injured). However, the political fallout of the raid—caused in part by the high number of U.S. casualties and the video images of a dead U.S. airman being dragged through the streets of Mogadishu, an image repeatedly shown on television in the United States—rendered the military victory pyrrhic. Within weeks, U.S. political will to carry the fight forward disappeared, prompting the U.S. withdrawal and collapse of the UN mission.

The above examples illustrate how ICTs have been used tactically by small but sophisticated actors to "route around" large military machines. Beyond these new forms of empowerment in still fairly "conventional" forms of warfare, however, ICTs are also being used to define new terrains for battle. These new fields for battle are a source of great insecurity and worry to conventional military establishments, for they completely eliminate the possibility of being able to define the time and place of engagement (thereby contravening an important principle of military operations). To date, these new terrains of battle have surfaced in two primary ways: "Netwars," referring to battles waged against ICT infrastructure; and "Social Netwars" referring to ICT-enabled campaigns that mobilize and organize large groups of dispersed actors for political ends.[25]

Netwar: New Terrains (Hacking for Kin and Country)

Netwar occurs when actors take the struggle away from the physical field of battle and into the realm of "cyberspace" (that is, the "virtual" information space created by the dense interconnection of computer and communications systems). Netwar seeks to disable or disrupt the opponent's "critical" information systems, effectively rendering them deaf, blind, mute, or unreliable. At its most extreme (and hence the way in which it is presented in many post–9/11 publications) the image is of an electronic "Pearl Harbor," where the critical national systems—from the electrical grid to stock markets and air-traffic control—are taken over by legions of unknown hackers (perhaps state-sponsored, perhaps not), thereby crippling the national economy and severely degrading the ability of the military to conduct war operations. Although this particular image most likely remains in the realm of the theoretical (if not science fiction), some security sources claim that "red team" exercises, allegedly carried out by the U.S. National Security Agency against U.S. military and civilian targets (to explore their vulnerabilities), demonstrate that considerable damage could be caused by hackers manipulating relatively open computer systems.[26]

To date, the experience with Netwar is largely limited to its use as "a weapon of mass disruption"—high on symbolic value, but whose actual military value is still largely theoretical. That being said, more and more of the groups and actors that are directly or indirectly involved in local conflicts have taken to the Internet to highlight their respective causes or participate in the struggle within the confines of cyberspace. The significance of their actions—besides the disruption they cause and publicity they gain for their "side"—resides in the fact that the kind of "warfare" they pursue is neither strictly military nor neatly confined to any one jurisdiction.[27]

However, this is not to argue that these cyber-struggles are not of consequence to actors on the ground. As Netwar becomes ever more enmeshed with actual physical struggles, retaliation for acts committed in cyberspace is increasingly meted out physically, directly against parties within zones of conflict, including those whose struggles have only a fleeting connection to a Netwar being waged in their name. This interplay between physical and virtual arenas is well evidenced in the multilevel struggle between Israelis, Arabs, and Palestinians, particularly in recent years.

The opening shots of the regional Netwar—the "Inter-fada"—occurred in the autumn of 2000 when a group of Israeli hackers successfully crippled a website run by the Lebanon-based Hizbollah. The attack was ostensibly launched in response to Hizbollah's capture of three Israeli soldiers on Israel's northern border with Lebanon earlier that fall. According to the Hizbollah webmaster, a total of 8,521 servers from Israel and the United States (and to a smaller extent Canada and the South Africa) were marshaled by pro-Israeli hackers to launch a concentrated "denial of service" attack against Hizbollah's website.[28] In response, various anti-Israeli groups across several countries (including Gforce Pakistan, Xegpyt, and UNITY) launched a massive, coordinated counterstrike that took down over 166 Israeli websites, including those of the Office of the Prime Minister, the Israeli Foreign Ministry, the Knesset, and the Israel Defense Forces, while creating difficulties for Israel's leading ISP, Netvison (which hosted many of the affected sites).[29] One Internet security firm reported that at the peak of the engagement upwards of twenty groups from Israel, Palestine, Lebanon, Egypt, the U.K., the United States, Pakistan, and Brazil were involved in the conflict.[30]

This cyber-engagement had potentially important symbolic as well as material consequences. According to an Israeli group monitoring the Netwar, the autumn 2000 engagement may have been responsible for an 8% dip in the Israeli stock exchange.[31] Moreover, while this first encounter largely involved taking down websites, a spokesperson for one Arab hacker group (UNITY) predicted that future phases would target Israel's banks, stock exchange, and e-commerce sites.[32] The sheer technical effort in launching these attacks is worth noting. Upwards of sixteen new attack tools, including mass mailers, ping scripts, word macros, and other computer viruses were deployed in the struggle. The anti-Israeli hackers (most of whom were under twenty years old) methodically worked their way through all of the ".il" domains.[33] By the time this round of "fighting" petered out in early 2000, the anti-Israeli coalition, which had been more aggressive throughout, was said to have had the upper hand—a fact that did not go unnoticed or unadvertised in Arab cyberspace.[34] Consequently the "Inter-fada" became seen as a successful way to fight back against Israel's military and technological dominance of the region.[35]

The extent to which Israeli authorities considered the Inter-fada Netwar to be a fundamental threat has never been publicly revealed. However, it is worth noting that, when the opportunity presented itself during the Israeli reoccupation of the Palestinian Territories (spring 2002), Israeli forces deliberately and systematically destroyed the communication and information infrastructures on which the Palestinian Authority, and thousands of community and civil groups, depend for their daily work. Reports document how hard drives were systematically stripped from PCs in ministries and cyber cafés, how Internet service providers (ISPs) were destroyed, and how Israeli Defense Force (IDF) experts systematically disabled certain telephone switchboards, thereby cutting services to specific areas of operation.[36] The scale of destruction of Palestinian ISPs led to the knocking out of many websites from the ".ps" domain.[37] In addition, television and radio stations were singled out for destruction. In Ramallah alone, eight TV and radio stations were reported damaged and/or rendered inoperable.[38] Even the nonpartisan educational channel, Al Quds Educational Television, was destroyed.[39]

There are several aspects of the Inter-fada worthy of note. Most of the primary actors on the "anti-Israeli" side, were themselves neither Palestinian nor necessarily committed to the Palestinian cause in the same way as Palestinians were. Rather, their concerted action, which in some dimensions symbolically appropriated the Palestinian cause, was undertaken because it was possible to do so with relative ease and at relatively low cost (with no real risk of personal or organizational harm through retaliatory measures). Subsequently, many of the groups involved have moved on to other causes, including, most recently, a "cyber-jihad" against the U.S. war on terrorism. However, despite the fact that few if any of the attacks emanated from the West Bank and Gaza, the IDF nevertheless deliberately targeted the ICT infrastructure of the Palestinian territories. Whether or not this systematic targeting was fueled by Israeli fears raised because of the Inter-fada (meaning fear of the Palestinian potential to support their very grounded struggle through greater use of Netwar strategies) is not known.

Overall, the evolution of Netwar reveals something of how the global diffusion of ICTs has lowered the costs, while increasing the capability, of new actors—including loosely associated and often submerged networks—to wage coordinated and disruptive attacks. As the ability of disparate hackers worldwide to come together, coordinate their activities, and then disperse aptly demonstrates, these technologies greatly increase the potential for individual and collective *agency* on a global scale.

Social Netwar: Leveraging Networks

The social aspect of networks (and particularly the power that can be exercised by and through networks) is key to the other axis along which the ICT-enablement of conflict has developed throughout the 1990s. "Social Netwar" describes a means by which technical networks serve as a channel through which large groups of actors can be mobilized to political ends.[40] Unlike Netwar, where hackers turn their attention toward disrupting the technical capabilities of foes, Social Netwar sees the technical network as merely the vehicle through which otherwise weakly linked networks can mobilize around issues and actions of common concern. For big military actors, Social Netwar is problematic because it elevates the level of conflict beyond the military sphere and into the realm of politics, an area in which, for most NATO countries, military establishments are unwelcome.

The most celebrated example of Social Netwar—indeed, one that helped define the concept—was applauded by believers in the potential for Global Civil Society, because it was seen to support a "legitimate" cause. The "war" involved the Zapatista rebels in the Mexican state of Chiapas, who were able to attract the support of extensive networks of Mexican NGOs, while building bridges with networks of NGOs in Europe and North America. These networks in turn acted as channels for solidarity and information that over time created severe pressure on the Mexican government to withdraw its military forces from the Chiapas region and negotiate terms with the Zapatista rebels. Thus, while the Zapatistas themselves were not particularly savvy in the technological aspects of ICTs, they were able to leverage them to mobilize global political support, which proved impossible for the Mexican military to ignore.[41]

Similar sorts of Social Netwar have been waged by the "smaller" actors in other conflict zones (although the specifics of the Zapatista case, with its engagement of northern NGO networks, remains unique). During the Russo-Chechen war (1994–96), for example, the Chechens pursued an information warfare strategy that targeted the Russian public and proved critical to securing the withdrawal of Russian federal forces in 1996. In part, the success of this campaign was based on the sophisticated "hearts and minds" policies adopted by Chechen commanders, who gave foreign and *Russian* journalists unfettered access to *their* side of the "front line." This access meant that the images and stories from the war were coming largely from the Chechen side. Russian TV screens were filled with grisly reports showing dead Russian soldiers and the atrocities committed by Russian forces. This "news" contrasted sharply with official Russian government statements that cast the war as being successfully waged "against bandits and terrorists" with relatively few casualties. Far from being portrayed as bandits, television reports portrayed Chechen fighters as romantic freedom fighters who had taken up arms against a foreign oppressor. The Chechen Minister of Information played a central role in the effort, working his satellite phone and fax machine to continually brief news services worldwide about the war from the Chechen perspective, including the legitimacy of their cause and their military capabilities. Overall, this "access" campaign proved a principle force in mobilizing Russian public opposition to the war and involved a wide range of Chechen and Russian networks of civic and political actors. Moreover, it undermined the credibility of the Russian government and faith in the professional capabilities of its armed forces. In the end, the Chechens' success in launching several high-profile military operations in combination with a looming presidential election in Russia forced the Russian government to sign a peace treaty with its breakaway republic and withdraw its troops.

The seeming political effectiveness of Social Netwar has led to wide-ranging speculation concerning its deeper meaning for the global polity. Analysts such as Harry Cleaver posited that the ability of actors such as the Zapatistas to organize local action on a global scale (and global action on a local scale) heralds the birth of a new kind of politics and a new kind of actor that transcends the level of the nation-state.[42] Similarly, the success of global protests against the WTO and GATT is seen as an indication that radical politics can transcend geography and challenge dominant global ideologies. However, more military-minded actors have also pondered the meaning of the experiences of Chiapas and Chechnya, and their conclusions are somewhat different. For the military, the surprising power exercised by the Zapatistas and the forced surrender of the Russian military underline the urgent necessity to be able to "counter" the strategies of Social Netwar by seizing and establishing dominance of the informational sphere of battle.

In the Russian case, these "lessons learned" played an important role in the second phase of the Chechen conflict (1999–to present day).[43] During this campaign, Russian forces deliberately targeted the Chechen information infrastructure. Just prior to the 1999 reinvasion, telephone service to the republic was cut and cellular towers and other communications facilities were targeted by air strikes while radio direction-finding equipment was deployed on the borders and in the air above the zone of conflict. To guard against interception of its own radio traffic, Russian forces were issued new encrypted tactical communications systems, and specialist communications troops were deployed to support the military operation. As a result, the tactical advantage enjoyed by the Chechens during the first conflict has been greatly diminished. The radio-electronic spectrum is "dominated" by the Russians, and Chechen commanders are forced to play "cat and mouse" to avoid detection and targeting by Russian troops.[44] On a more strategic level, the Russian government prepared the groundwork for the military onslaught with a carefully crafted public-relations campaign. Chechens were branded terrorists, and several large-scale acts of violence, including the bombing of apartment buildings in several Russian cities (causing appalling loss of life), were blamed on Chechen "bandits" (although suspicion has now fallen on the Russian secret services). A government press center was established to continually narrate the "war on terrorism," while the access of Russian journalists to the Chechen side of the conflict has been greatly reduced through threats and intimidation by Russian authorities. More ominously for Russian democracy, the government has been placing severe pressure on all media outlets, deliberately persecuting and closing down those who have taken a pro-Chechen line.[45]

However, the ability of small actors to find new ways to route around the superiority of resources and techniques available to big actors also continues to evolve. In the aftermath of the NATO intervention in Bosnia—eight years after having established a near-permanent military presence—NATO forces are unable to track down and apprehend indicted war criminals. One of the reasons suspected for this failure is the ability of local actors to successfully monitor Stabilisation Force (SFOR), UN, and NGO radio, which functions as an "early-warning system" of impending actions by NATO forces for the wanted suspects. Similarly, in the Occupied Territories—where Israeli dominance over information infrastructures and the means to monitor all communications is total—Palestinian militants are still able to harness the means made possible by ICTs to further their objectives. Cell phones have been used to remotely detonate explosives, while the combination of Internet and regional media agents (such as Al-Manar and Al-Jazeera) provide a means for Palestinians to continue to narrate their struggle—despite being branded by some as aligned with the wrong side in the "war on terror."[46]

What these patterns suggest is that the degree and depths to which ICTs and their infrastructures are being appropriated by forces directly engaged in conflict are only beginning to be plumbed. Despite the sophistication of their understanding, military actors still find it difficult to effectively deal with small, networked actors empowered by ICTs. Moreover, the ability of small actors to adapt in the face of countermeasures suggests these new forms of warfare can be expected to evolve as these technologies continue to make inroads globally and their reach extends and deepens.

QUO VADIS? SOME PARTING THOUGHTS

This chapter began with the observation that ICTs and ICT infrastructures are making deep inroads into the world's poorest and most unstable regions. And, in cases where the representatives of the international community—development actors or military actors—have encountered ICT-enabled local actors, the results have been either unexpected or, if not unexpected, then difficult to counter.

The examples suggest that our understanding of technology remains closely bound to our perceived assumptions regarding the kinds of transformations we expect them to engender and the trajectories we expect them to follow. This perspective is understandable, given that most of what we have experienced with ICTs to date in the West has been largely in keeping with the norms and behaviors of the liberal industrialized societies—meaning the societies in which these technologies were first developed and who continue to predominate *globally* as core users of these infrastructures and systems. However, as Mark Duffield argues, one does not have to embrace the neoliberal values of modernity to partake in the benefits that its artifacts and technologies make possible.

In this regard, it is important to recall that networks are nothing if not social. They make possible a degree of *connexity* unprecedented in the history of humanity. ICTs *do* empower human agency across time and space—whether those actors are NGOs seeking to ban land mines, or Chechen expatriates raising funds and support for their fight against occupation by Russian forces. What is more of an issue are the consequences of that agency, and whether the causes they "empower" are accepted or rejected as being "legitimate" by the politics of the day. And herein lies the danger.

The examples cited in this chapter suggest that as more societies build and appropriate ICTs, patterns of appropriation will tend to follow and support the behaviors typical to those societies, their customary cultural norms of social and economic interaction, and the political struggles in which they find themselves—whether or not these practices and struggles are judged as "acceptable" or "legitimate" by the rest of the world. Moreover, as research examining the phenomenon of conflict in the 1990s reveals, the context of "local" conflicts can be hugely complex, encompassing a myriad of economic, political, and ideological drivers and associated networks of actors. With increased population movements through emigration or forced migration, rarely are these drivers/actors neatly contained within the boundaries of a single nation-state. Indeed, just as NGOs have become *transnationalized,* so too have local conflicts, particularly through the thick networks of diasporas and other actors that in one way or another remain connected to these regions.

This brings us back to where this chapter began. In many ways our assumptions dictate to a large degree what we accept as being the *legitimate* uses of ICTs. Our inability to look outside our own "legitimating frameworks" is perhaps one of the main reasons we have been rather blind to the enormously creative use of ICTs in conflict zones. Moreover, when ICTs are used in ways that subvert our expectations, or support unwelcome resistance or "criminal" activities, these uses are either ignored or dismissed as *illegitimate.* But even the cursory examples cited in this chapter suggest that the appropriation of ICTs is well under way within these so-called "blackholes," energized by transnational networks of actors, not all of whom embrace the dominant liberal values that supposedly define globalization, and in this sense, perhaps, represent globalization's poorly understood "underbelly." While some have sought to dismiss aspects of this underbelly as "criminal" (which no doubt it is, in part), to label the entirety as such is akin to throwing out the baby with the bathwater. Instead, the argument here suggests that deeper, more complex processes are afoot, and these warrant our attention.

If we accept that ICTs have played a major part in globalization—supporting the growing integration of institutions and capital within a neoliberal framework—then perhaps we should reflect more deeply on how these technologies may be enabling alternative forms of integration, convergence, and value-driven action, especially in conflict zones. Excavating understandings of this "globalization of the local" (*glocalization*) is urgently needed. Otherwise, the tendency to label all of its manifestations as "illegitimate" could serve to further alienate the millions of individuals in the developing world who depend on these alternative networks (and their alternative value systems) for their livelihoods, their survival, and increasingly for highlighting the "legitimacy" of, and impetus for, their political struggles. In the long run such alienation may risk exacerbating the very insecurities that the securitization of aid seeks to address. More ominously, it may serve to radicalize those whom our well-meant interventions are intended to benefit, perhaps forcing us into military confrontation with an "enemy" who is difficult if not impossible to defeat in conventional military terms. As with those who live in glass houses, the solution does not reside in throwing stones, but in trying to understand and find commonality with our global roommates.

11. ICT AND THE WORLD OF SMUGGLING

CAROLYN NORDSTROM

THE XLEGAL

Perhaps no group has benefited as much from globalization and the advances in information-communication technology (ICT) as smugglers. Those who operate outside the law cannot "inscribe" in the classical sense designating progress in human society. The values, norms, and rules of behavior in the world of the extralegal cannot be published in texts, discussed in professional journals, taught in MBA programs, saved in libraries, shared in Lions Clubs and Chamber of Commerce meetings, and negotiated through unions. The very instrument of modernity—inscription—is the bane of the illegal.

Every extralegal—or, as I denote it, the xlegal—action depends on extensive information, requiring not only the same social, economic, and political knowledge upon which legal enterprises depend, but also facts on how not to get caught, arrested, double-crossed, or killed. For a legal businessperson, the failure to have or use information wisely results in, at worst, economic failure. For those working in the nonlegal universe, imprisonment, flight, and death can result from inadequate knowledge. The dilemma is strategic: business represents a set of institutions which endure over time and crises because they are codified in values, norms, and rules of behavior that are shared. The illicit, the informal, and the illegal are, in Latham's words, illegible: they are social and economic texts that are erased. How, then, does the uncodified flourish?

IN THE FIELD

When ICT was more primitive, traditional definitions depicted mafias, cartels, and triads as extended families and communities based on face-to-face interaction. In this view, the xlegal was comprised of close-knit groups that relied on hierarchy, fealty, and brutality to run their organizations. However realistic this may have been in the past, internationalization has redefined the illicit world to as great a degree as it has legitimate commerce. ICT has extended the "extended family" to global proportions: international networking, cross-global markets, and sophisticated multigroup enterprises are now the norm in the xlegal world. Smugglers today are more likely to be armed with a degree from a leading ICT/computer technology course than an assault rifle.

This point was brought home to me during eighteen months of fieldwork I conducted on illicit economies and globalization in 2001–2002.[2] Following unrecorded trade flows, I started in the war-torn interior of Angola and followed critical resources (from diamonds and oil to food and equipment) in and out of the country, through southern Africa, along international trade channels, and out to cosmopolitan centers in Europe. During Easter of 2002, I traveled to a legal border post in southern Africa that I will leave unnamed given the sensitivity of the story that follows. The site was located on a regional set of trade routes that link through both urban zones and impoverished war-torn areas. It is a corridor where smuggled pharmaceuticals can bring as much profit as the unrecorded diamonds and gold that pay for them.

The post is located in a remote, cinder-block and zinc-sheet town stretching along a single roadway that connects two countries. Hundreds of kilometers from any capital city or commercial port, the town looks like the quintessential African community on the margins of modernity. I was told there is a post office but could never find it. Barefoot children heading to school casually crossed the dirt road and single wire marking the international border. When I'd visited the town five years before, no hotel existed. Now a single one was open for business, barely visible across a muddy field, and a clump of trucks parked in front, populated by drivers waiting to negotiate deals, buy goods, and cross the border.

Entering the hotel, I was told that the hotel manager spoke no English, only the language of the country across the border. So in this language I told him only that my name was Carolyn and that I would like a room for some nights. He asked for no documentation or further information. It was ten o'clock at night, so after getting a key I went for dinner. Around midnight I stopped in the hotel's lobby—a pool hall. The hotel manager came up to me and handed me a refreshment, and, speaking in perfect English, said:

"I was born in the town of Sleeping Rock. In fact, I was the first person born in the hospital that was just built then." I had just come from Sleeping Rock and wondered at the irony: the town is now desperately war-ravaged; only the barest handful of people travel there. But with his next sentence, I questioned if this was irony.

"I was born in the same year you were, Carolyn."

His intention was not to threaten me but to let me know he had checked on me. I assumed, since we were having a relaxed conversation, that I checked out all right.

"You know, not everyone believes you are who you say you are," he said. That made me laugh: I imagined it was hard to believe that a professor from the University of Notre Dame would be in a truck-stop pool hall in a hot and dusty outpost on one of the continent's established illicit transit corridors asking truckers and businesspeople not for gems or a cut of some lucrative trade, but merely for their stories, for monetarily impoverished information.

"I run a business, and gems too," he said easily. He had apparently decided I was safe to talk to.

People from cosmopolitan urban centers tend to assume that the remote outposts of industrial humanity are equally remote from state-of-the-art technology and information. As this man had just demonstrated, this is no longer true. Logically there was no way he could have known my birth date, yet he had acquired it. Information, quite literally, is survival, and nowhere is information more critical than on the borders of legality and illegality, in dusty rural border outposts like this.

Commerce into this town crossed all lines of il/legality and numerous national borders, encompassed scores of languages and a vast spectrum of military, political, and business contacts. The traders came not only from all parts of the continent but from all continents. I spoke with merchants from Asia, South Asia, Europe, and the Americas. They told me they operated across myriad political and legal domains and through environments that varied from urban cosmopolitan to war-ravaged regions devoid of functioning services.

The day I left I went to pay the bill. The manager took me to his office in back, smiling as he unlocked and opened the door. In this backwater mud-and-cinderblock town stood an office that might rival a NASA command center.

"Need to e-mail? Phone?" he asked as he waved me over to the latest in information and communication technologies. "Oh, I've a sat-link if you need it. Anything else before you go? I'm going to send you to a friend of mine down the road about eight hours"—he named an infamous nonlegal border post. Picking up his cell phone, he punched in some numbers and told the person on the other end that I'd be in that night. He then handed me a map to the place, and gave me a pat on the back.

I wondered then if he had gotten online and read any of my work, as the information he gave me and the introduction to nonsanctioned border crossing was exactly what I was looking for.

After a hot eight-hour drive along potholed roads, I arrived at the town the manager had recommended and was graciously greeted by his friend. It was, if possible, more remote and basic than the town I had just left. After several days and a number of conversations with the businessman, he took a call while we were talking. A convoy of trucks was coming down an unmarked border road carrying a consignment of commodities for him, and one of the trucks had disappeared. I did not ask if this meant the truck driver had tried to abscond with a truckload of goods, if he was running from bandits or border guards, or if he had just had a blowout and was off the radar screen; he did not offer an explanation. But he did explain why it was important: the truck carried over $60,000 worth of merchandise, wholesale (unrecorded) price, guaranteeing a much larger street value. His response was immediate. He contacted an international group of associates by cell phone or sat-com (satellite-communication) gear. He pulled up his computer to check transit, flow, and routing channels, and swore as he found a glitch. His son, he explained, had a degree from a leading university in the U.K. and kept him in the latest technology and upgraded software programs—creatively tailored to suit his needs. But his son was out of town. Juggling his state-of-the-art computer, sat-com gear, cell phones, and a sheath of printouts, he called his son and had him walk him through a computer repair, simultaneously sending an e-mail to his lawyer in a major urban city, and to his "financial consultant." If the trucker thought he could just disappear with a fortune of commodities on a lonely stretch of outback savanna, he was, the businessman let me know, seriously out of date. ICT has changed all the equations. Taking a moment to relax, the businessman smiled and told me he was born in the same year I was. These men and their "offices" are a window on how unregulated economies have grown into a multitrillion-dollar global phenomenon.

GLOBAL NETWORKING AND THE WORLD OF SMUGGLING

There is a misperception that extralegal enterprises constitute a small fraction of the global economy. Trillions of dollars now circulate the world outside of legal channels, in operations involving millions of people. These enterprises range from small groups profiting from local resources to complex international networks that can command more economic and political clout than many small countries; the more successful have the power to shape emergent governments.[3] While I have never found a formal figure estimating the world's gross extralegal products, the sheer magnitude of the xlegal world can be indicated by a few figures. In this discussion, it is useful to keep in mind that the world's combined GNP (which considers only legal phenomena) is estimated at over $30 trillion per year.

The UN estimates that illicit drug earnings amount to $500 billion per year.[4] The illicit arms industry is estimated to be of comparable size. Human trafficking, considered to be the third-largest illicit activity after arms and drugs, brings in hundreds of billions of unregulated dollars a year. Of comparable size is the empire of gain from the unregulated sex trade and pornography industries.

At another level, in the United States alone, estimates of the costs of only three categories of *corporate* crime—consumer fraud, corporate tax fraud, and corporate financial crime—range between $247 billion and $715 billion annually.[5] The black economy in India was estimated in the early 1980s to amount to more than $60 billion, and has grown since then.[6] In Peru, 48% of the economically active population works in the informal sector. In Kenya the figure rises to 58%. Statistics place Italy's extrastate economy at up to 50% of gross domestic product.[7] In the United States estimates range from 10–30%; one-third of Canada's population participates in informal economic activities;[8] and some 60% of Russia's economy falls outside formal purview.[9] As much as 20% of the world's financial deposits reside in unregulated banks and offshore locations.[10]

Though trafficking in illegal narcotics and weapons gets most of the media's attention, unrecorded sales of more mundane commodities like electronic goods, computers, software, communications technology, pharmaceuticals, industrial supplies, precious gems, minerals, art masterpieces, and vehicles can rival profits from illegal narcotics and weapons. The items that fall into unrecorded trade are extensive.

Instead of tight-knit crime families, these networks are more likely to be loose associations of skilled specialists—computer literate and well versed in international trade policy and flows, people more likely to rely on techno-information than on violence. Such technical sophistication characterizes xlegal activity carried out not only in large developed population centers like Amsterdam, Shanghai, and Los Angeles but also in the interior of Angola, the outback of Australia, and the mountain passes of the Himalayas. With long stretches of unguarded borders, thousands of miles of sparsely populated territory, and sometimes vast resource deposits, these more remote sections of the globe have long been fertile ground for potential xlegal activity. Advances in information and communication technologies have greatly expanded the ability of criminal networks to exploit that potential.

FOLLOWING THE FLOW

During the final years of war in Angola (from the 1990s through 2002), the country provided an ideal locale to begin charting these complex economies: it is rich in resources central to urban and industrial life and thus links to the global economy. The country is home to rich deposits of oil, diamonds, minerals, hardwoods, fish, and agricultural products. During this time, the UN estimated that some 90% of the economy took place outside the formal legal economy.

The world campaign against "blood diamonds"—diamonds used by militaries to purchase arms in wars where civilian populations are decimated—was launched in Angola and Sierra Leone. This one example helps illuminate the deep complexities of extralegal trade and its links to ICT: diamonds do not travel alone, they are wed in a cycle of (il/licit) commerce where diamonds travel with arms . . . and as well with smuggled electronics, narcotics and pharmaceuticals, industrial equipment, food, and a veritable supermarket of unrecorded goods and services. By the time the campaign gained world force in the mid 1990s, the rebel forces in Angola alone were acquiring an estimated $500 million a year from these gems. Both legal and unrecorded diamonds also traveled out of the government-held zones.

Bringing an unrecorded diamond out of a mine in Angola (or gold out of the Amazon, or hardwoods or drugs out of Southeast Asia) is not a simple buy-sell transaction—it involves an extensive network of people. Start with the miner who extracts the gems; add in the toolmaker who makes the miner's tools, the cook who feeds him or her, the teachers who tutor the miner's children. The miners may be working independently, following their own commercial networks to broker the gems they find, or they may choose, or be forced, to work for a military. Militaries use resources like diamonds to raise foreign currency to buy arms and supplies,[11] but they also set in motion an extensive "barter" system that taps into global commodity exchanges—"barter," of course, avoids regulations and taxation, the classic foundations of legality. As the London-based organization Global Witness writes:

> In cash terms diamonds are cheaper in Angola at approximately US$100 upwards per carat, although UNITA seems keen to encourage barter for medicine, clothes, electrical equipment and other supplies. Again rates given for barter vary widely from a couple of pairs of trousers for a small diamond or a 'Sharp' cassette player for a larger stone from an individual seller, to the agreement of orders in advance with UNITA officials for quantities to be brought in by four-wheel drive vehicle, whilst placing a counter order for diamonds at the same time.[12]

An entire economy is set up to mine, to support the miners, and to transport the gems to profit; and this economy does not run on kwanza (Angolan currency) but on dollars, resources, and international commodities. Photo exposés on diamond mining may lead general audiences to think of tired men in tattered clothing braving hostile and primitive working conditions. This is part of the story, but the exposé seldom also depicts the unlicensed on-site diamond buyer who wields a laptop or net-linked cell phone to monitor global commodity prices, exchange rates, and market dynamics.

Diamonds do not exist in isolation any more than the miners do: both circulate, and gain worth, in a world of complex commodity flows with values that change in relationship to each other and global markets almost instantaneously. A miner does not sell a diamond for some arbitrary set price, but for its ability to be laundered into a formal economy where it will garnish a set amount of buying power in relationship to gold, to exchange rates, to other commodities, and to financial market relationships. The best illustration of this involves currency valuations. If the power of the xlegal remains in question, one need only consider currency exchange rates. The World Bank has shown time and again that currency exchange "street rates" are often more accurate than formal bank rates, and has recommended to a number of struggling governments that they take the street rates as the truer economic indices for their country. But who sets these street rates? They are set by businesspeople. In countries like Angola where some 90% of the economy takes place outside formal legal channels, or in Kenya, Russia, Peru, or Italy where some 50% of the economy is nonformal, this in large part means those who work outside formal reckoning. Of course, to work the street markets at all is technically illegal. The xlegal world is thus a major player in setting the currency exchange rates undergirding an entire country's economy.

When diamond merchants purchase a gem near the mines in the remote outback of a country, they must have access to the global factors that set "street rates" and commodity prices if they are to be successful in business. The diamond buyer sitting next to the tired miner in tattered shorts is likely to be checking financial indices in Antwerp on a sat-linked palm pilot (that was counterfeit in a factory half a world away and never saw a payment of tariffs or taxes). This merchant is not the only tech-literate specialist in the area. Miners require services: international trade circuits cross such mining zones to drop off food, clothing, drugs, alcohol, cigarettes, medicines, vehicles, industrial supplies, videos and the machines to play them, ad infinitum. Each merchant as well deals not merely in a commodity but in a transnational market and set of currencies, in transport timetables, in meetings and negotiated exchanges. The woman with untaxed clothing and medicines hopping an unrecorded flight on a private plane with less-than-regulated flight plans who will make sales stops at mining camps before crossing the border (without clearing customs or immigration) into the next country to use the diamonds and dollars she just made in the mining camps for new commodities may well take a cup of coffee at an Internet café run on a generator in a dusty town with zinc roofs covering cinder-block buildings—checking market prices, currency exchange rates, transport routings, and her e-mail. She may well share her ride with a sanction-breaking arms dealer who got his order over the Net.

To fully understand these associations and the role ICT plays in these exchanges, consider a few players along the lines:

- Leo, a businessman, is well aware of the international laws he "circumvents" but insists, with apparent sincerity, "I am helping my country. We all try to work amidst endless strangleholds. Ruined infrastructure, corruption, excessive taxes, contradictory regulations, slow and inefficient bureaucracy, loaded and slanted international trade policies, patronage—you name it, we struggle with it. Without development, this country dies; the people starve. We make things work, we're bringing goods, industry, employment into the country."
- The pilots who fly humanitarian runs, and who also find themselves asked to fly contraband, do not consider themselves "smugglers"—though there is no doubt in their minds that they are ferrying goods across both legal and international borders.[13] "We're paid to fly a plane," said one pilot. "From start to finish, we don't make the decisions—not what cargo to carry, not where to ferry it. You don't like something, you don't fly, you don't get paid. It's as easy as that. We fly in here where no one else in their right mind comes, and we keep people alive. That's what we take home at the end of a long day."
- A man who works for an international nongovernmental organization unofficially runs gems. He knows the laws and the penalties for breaking them, but war and money are greater forces in his life. "I was thrown into prison for being on the 'wrong side' of the war. And while they break us down, the rich ones become richer, profiting on war and politics. Why should they, and not I? I lost everything by joining the wrong side. I watch my friends on the 'right side' send their children to good schools, travel in nice cars, wear expensive clothes. And I watch my children go to a school that doesn't have enough chairs, not to mention teachers. I do what I have to do to survive and to provide for my family."
- A military official "raises money" through unrecorded trade and cross-border exchange and profits personally by controlling access to resource-rich areas. "What I do I do for the good of this country," he says. "We've been fighting a war. To do that, we need resources, supplies, infrastructure. My control over access to prime 'business' locations? You can't let just anyone have access to setting up business and industry—the wrong people can take their gain

and turn it to those who fight us. We oversee these things in the interests of keeping the country stable."

These people are all professionals. As likely as not, they trained at leading universities. They use cutting-edge technology to do their jobs. Given their international networks and their skills in unrecorded trade, they can get most anything they need from anywhere in the world; they can advertise on the Net for an ITC specialist, and their ad will travel worldwide. It will travel only slightly faster than the diamonds or other smuggled goods that pay the bills and salaries of everyone involved.

And consider those who grease the wheels of this business:

• The forger, who scans or downloads customs declarations, bills of lading, transit papers, preshipping inspections, and a host of other legal documents, then "manages" the information, and finally uploads it back to render the xlegal "legal," at least on paper.
• The shipping agents who use high-tech shipping tracking systems to monitor transit and commodity patterns to look for the best avenues to insert undeclared goods into transit. (The flight from South Asia makes stops in Dubai, Amsterdam, and New York; the morning flight is the busiest time for X airport, and a large quantity of Y cargo will be coming in at the same time that will tie up the customs officials, so our chances of being detected are lowest here. . . . Several Panama ships carrying 6,000 containers of Z product are scheduled for the following ports; we can use our contacts to arrange some of our containers for these ships that will be highly unlikely to be monitored.)
• The lawyer, whose state-of-the-art ICT systems help keep him or her in twenty-four-hour accessible contact with the diamond buyers at the mines, the businesspeople in dusty border posts, and the shippers who broach a few laws and sanctions.

Finally, in following the circulation of unrecorded goods from source to international cosmopolitan centers, a further network of people must be in place to smuggle the goods across controlled borders with maximum profit and minimum penalty. Cars, trucks, planes, drivers, pilots, mechanics, fuel, loaders—all these and more are needed to see the gems safely from a mine to, say, the diamond trading center of Antwerp, Belgium. Specialist consultants make a living advising smugglers on how to transport illicit goods. There are also worldwide "businesses" that make illegal but fully reliable insurance available to protect against the seizure or loss of contraband goods.[14] If the gems are to be sold on the open market, they must be "laundered" to legitimacy, and a further chain of players must link buyers with black-marketeers, to create legality from illegality in formal economic and political institutions. In the more successful cases, stocks, banks, airlines, and franchises will be purchased in the act of laundering as well. A chart of these associations would produce a map with linkages that move from the interior of Africa out into the world's major trade routes and cosmopolitan centers, channels that transect both legal and xlegal business. A cell phone, a laptop, and a sat-link are all that are needed today to coordinate all these levels of activity—to coordinate what was previously restricted more to the face-to-face relationships that extended out from close-knit mafias, gangs, cartels, groups, or triads.

ILLEGALITY AND INVISIBILITY

The only way to get goods and services, legal or otherwise, from production to consumption and profit is to insert them into the world's commodity flows. The best way to move xlegal goods in many cases is not to look for remote borders and unmanned crossings (as popular lore would have it), but to add your contraband to commodity flows so large they will be overlooked in the sheer magnitude of volume. Instantaneous access to information, afforded by computers and the Net, has enabled criminals to monitor crucial variables like transport arrivals and departures, customs and police inspections, and commodity flows, improving their odds for success. But the odds are overwhelmingly in their favor to start with.

"Look what we are fighting now—cell phones," said the head of an elite anti-crime police unit during a conversation about smuggling. "We plan a bust, and the gangs have a lookout. In days gone by, we might make it to the drop site before the lookout. Now the lookout spots us, and they just call their mates on a cell phone, and everyone simply melts into the night.

"A ship with illegal cargo only has to call other ships when it is in open waters in order to arrange a rendezvous to transfer cargo illegally, and then they sail off without ever coming into port. The land crew arranges pickups with the smaller vessels and then sets up cross-country transport. It's professional, it's smooth, it's almost impossible to stop, and it's based in the explosion in communications technology."

Consider Rotterdam, the world's largest port in terms of volume and among the largest in size; it covers 26,000 acres. In 2001, some 30,000 seagoing vessels and 133,000 inland ships visited this port-world. They carried 313,700,000 metric tons of cargo throughput, and over 6 million containers (twenty-foot by twenty-foot sealed metal shipping containers measured as TEUs). The port's managers boast that most of Europe is accessible within twenty-four hours. Simple math demonstrates that on an average day, eighty-two seagoing vessels and 364 inland vessels visit Rotterdam carrying 859,452 metric tons of cargo and 16,438 containers (TEUs). The port has developed portable, state-of-the-art scanning machines, but it takes several hours and a team of at least six people to scan a single container as it must be off-loaded, transported to the scanner, monitored by the appropriate authorities, and potentially unpacked and then reloaded. A single ship may hold 6,000 containers. Even a customs staff of tens of thousands could not inspect all the cargo entering the country, and no city in the world can maintain a custom's staff anywhere near such numbers. The problem is compounded, as an official of the Netherlands's Chamber of Commerce explained:

> If we want to stay the number-one port, we have to deliver. Businesses now plan to the day, and sometimes the hour, when they need critical supplies and when the shipments they require need to arrive. The calculations are straightforward: the ship arrives, the cargo is off-loaded onto inland road, rail, or sea transport, and it arrives at their door within, usually, twenty-four hours. So what happens if we hold up these shipments for inspection? Of course, security is a top concern. But so is staying competitive. If we hold up crucial cargo, then the business just moves to a port in the next country.

In addition 26,000 commercial flights take place each day in Europe (by comparison, 48,000 flights are handled by air-traffic control daily in the United States).

"What we've said holds doubly for air transport and cargo," the Netherlands Chamber of Commerce official added. "Air transport is obviously more expensive, so the goods that are carried tend to be the more valuable. They are not only valuable in cost, but in importance—they are needed immediately. Perishables. Crucial industrial parts. Sophisticated electronic equipment. Essentials. You fly them in, get them onto transport, and get them to where they are going with no delay. Inspections are delay."

Consider that the ten largest ports in the world handled 1.6 *billion* tons of seaborne cargo and eighty million containers (TEUs) in 2000. The top four rapid mail-delivery services (e.g., Federal Express, DHL) move twenty million packages *a day.* Anywhere in the world, the waiting times are short, the efficiency high, and the costs moderate—*if* cargo is not held up in inspections. It is this massive flow that provides the invisibility xlegal merchants seek. The additional resources of ICT make judging the best times and places to move illicit goods a science, not a shot in the dark.

ICT also has eased the paperwork of xlegal enterprise. Moving illicit goods through licit channels requires inspection papers, bills of lading, customs stamps, financial statements, transit schedules and authorization, and a host of other "legalities." Providing these requires expertise. The Net has made it a profession.

"You move 'stuff' around the world, you need certificates," said the smuggler. "Diamonds, stolen cars, weapons systems, the latest Hollywood releases—you name it. A good forger is worth his or her weight in gold, literally. It is a profession. A person gets a reputation, and people seek him or her out for their work. A master forger commands a great deal of respect. And money. The good ones now advertise on their websites."

During this fieldwork, I became curious as to whether powerful players in unrecorded trade might acquire and use their own satellites. Sat-phones and sat-net can be used from the most urban to the most remote locales, and ownership might allow control over communications. I spoke with a successful entrepreneur in this field, asking him if there was a way to use communications satellites to avoid government regulations, monitoring and control.

> It is not that you would want to set up your own satellite outside of governmental control—that would be most difficult. You just embed a message in the vast, an incomprehensibly vast, amount of information circulating at any time. Why buy a multibillion-dollar satellite and go to extreme lengths to try to avoid governmental detection when you can just buy a bit of airtime and send one of several million messages going out at any given time that says "pick it up at 7 P.M."

A review of the legal world of ICT alone gives a sense of the possibilities that rest in the explosion of information communication technology. As of June 2001, there were 118 million wireless subscribers in the United States[15] and 1.39 million mobile cellular legal subscribers globally.[16] They generated 135 billion international telephone traffic minutes annually. Some 605 million personal computers and 665 million Internet users span the globe. In the United States the average Internet user spends three hours per week online at home and five and a half hours at work.[17] The magnitude of these sales and uses allows for a large industry in illicit ICT. Computers are counterfeited in unregistered factories; they are smuggled; they are stolen and resold; they break sanction after sanction as they move across borders of contention and war. Fifty percent of the software computers depend on in South Africa is illicit, and 98% is illicit in Vietnam and China; the computer industry would be satisfied if these countries could achieve the "success rate" of the United States with only 30% illicit software.[18] Cell phones, sat-com gear, global positioning system units, hardware, and the latest jacked-up programs are common to "street markets."

Amid this massive communication spectrum, a secret signal like "Sunday, 3 P.M., lot 5" is likely to escape all detection. No security force in the world has the human resources to monitor even a meaningful fraction of this intercommunication, much less the intelligence services to follow up or field agents to act on it.

SECURITY

Current notions of security are fiction, pure and simple. The fiction that borders can be "secured" continues to function among governments and security agencies because most of what moves invisibly across borders is not a threat to national security. From interviews I conducted with police and customs officials in America, Europe, and Africa, a picture emerged of the most actively and profitably smuggled goods in the world today: technology, electronics, entertainment commodities, computing soft/hardware, clothing, food, endangered and restricted species, industrial equipment, precious metals and gems, vehicles, alcohol, and cigarettes. At the end of a discussion with Detective Richard Flynn of Scotland Yard, I asked what among all the nonlegal commodities and services found in the U.K. he considered to be the most serious, the most dangerous. Without a pause, he responded:

> Cigarettes. That simple everyday packet of tobacco that you see in about 40% of the population's pockets. Because they flow in from everywhere—on the ferry from France, in the car from Holland, in the container from Bulgaria, on the plane from India or the States. They sell them out of car boots. Take a walk in the local street markets, guys line the streets with cartons of every brand name. They sell them from under the counters of the local corner store. They are absolutely everywhere, in the middle of everything. They show up every porous hole in our borders, our customs, our laws, and our ability to enforce the laws. And it's not just the cigarettes, it's what they move with—the routes of cigarettes, their flow into just about every conceivable corner of a country—just about every dangerous commodity moves along these same channels, with cigarettes. And at the end of the day, millions in taxes are lost yearly to cigarette smuggling.

Few effective means exist to manage true threats to national security—bombs, terrorists, chemicals—buried in a shipment of cigarettes on a cargo ship with 6,000 containers arriving at a port with ten other ships of the same size with a twenty-four-hour delivery promise. If security forces rely on profiling and rapid transmission of information, the smugglers are even more adept at using these very ICT systems to embed their products invisibly in global transit networks. Logging on to a port site to get information useful to smuggling is child's play; hacking into security work schedules, profiling records, timetables, and strategic plans is a skill a number of teenagers can manage—the skills for smuggling have come prepackaged in the information era.

The threats, however, do not all involve direct or military violence. Contrary to much traditional economic analysis, extrastate economics are not marginal to the world's economies and politics, they are central. The trillions of dollars of unrecorded monies that circulate the world every year represent economic power capable of shaping international markets; of moving in and out of banking systems to configure financial institutions, of entering into legal enterprise and governing structures to affect econ-political process. Larger successful xlegal networks can, in the more advanced scenarios, topple governments.

The ability of xlegal networks to internationalize has allowed them to gain economic and political sophistication that in some ways is analogous to transnational corporations and sovereign states.[19] As Manuel Castells and Susan Strange[20] write, these organizations now operate much like multinational corporations and political organizations. They exchange resources, forge trade agreements, draft foreign policies, create monopolies or service empires, shape political processes. Xlegal networks span cultural groups, languages, continents, and areas of specialization. They employ lawyers, accountants, trade specialists, financial advisers, bankers, transport specialists, and information and communication experts. And do it all without benefit of formalized information resources.

While the illegal world must, by definition, remain uninscribed, it can still create empires of profit and power based on communication and exchange. The interlinkages of different criminal groups across continents, the forging of international foreign and trade policies, and the increasing reliance on legal, commodity, and financial experts are developments redefining not only il/legality, but governance in the twenty-first century. Yet such systems must bypass the formal institutions that governments and legal businesses rely on.

In a curious development, both xlegal exchange and ICT are defined as easily interlinking sets of flexible, nonterritorial network systems that mirror one another. These very characteristics that allow the xlegal to succeed in a state-dominated territorial world of international law are the characteristics that have led to the exponential boom in ICT in the twenty-first century. It is not a far reach to question whether the dominance of the nation-state model is facing a challenge in the most fundamental sense from these new associations of exchange and power.

Consider one final example in the analysis of the unrecorded commodity movements from the remote interior of countries like Angola to the world's cosmopolitan centers. Unrecorded monies are worth only the papers they are printed on until they are "laundered." Michel Camdessus, former managing director of the International Monetary Fund, estimates that $600 million is laundered annually in the world. That figure represented between 2% and 5% of the world's gross domestic product in 2001,[21] yet it is considered by most experts to be a vast understatement. This is because, by convention, the figures used are gathered from the dramatic and large-scale "illegal" mafia, cartel, and triad-generated monies from the arms, drugs, sex, and human-trafficking industries. Informal (unrecorded but not illegal) trade, illegal trade in legal commodities like pharmaceuticals and electronics, mundane trade (as in food and clothing), and white-collar crime are seldom factored in.

Laundering has become quite sophisticated today: launderers move illicit earnings through a series of legal business ventures and through investments and stock markets in a multiple-step process of cleaning the money. Banks looking for large and unexplained investments from questionable sources rarely notice monies laundered in this multitier process. But in the information era, banks and legal financial institutions may be bypassed altogether. Unrecorded "banks" move unrecorded money worldwide with a trunk line and a modem. A person can walk into a "store-front bank" in Asia and a "banker" with a cell phone and a laptop can move the client's money to the United States in the time it takes to transmit an electronic message. Launderers with a good computer and decent stock portfolio software can move ill-begotten gains through stock markets with ease.

Consider security in this context: a coalition of people with access to unrecorded monies can manipulate markets. The sheer ease of instantaneous communication and information technology wed to illicit profits and the process of laundering can wreak dire consequences for economies, especially in emergent markets.

> Unchecked, money laundering can erode the integrity of a nation's financial institutions. Due to the high integration of capital markets, money laundering can also adversely affect currencies and interest rates. Ultimately, laundered money flows into global financial systems, where it can undermine national economies and currencies. . . . In some emerging market countries, these illicit proceeds may dwarf government budgets, resulting in a loss of control of economic policy by governments. Indeed, in some cases, the sheer magnitude of the accumulated asset base of laundered proceeds can be used to corner markets—or even small economies.[22]

It is ironic that many of the advances in technology heralded as enhancing security in the world have benefited those who violate laws and security even more. In a world where xlegal networks are globalizing in a framework of power that can rival smaller countries and where terrorism can cause havoc with the foundations of economic and political processes, security is a chimera. Smuggling antibiotics into Angola may violate international law, but the benefits of such an act do not make this a serious security issue. But dangerous items follow these same routes, utilizing the same mechanisms of invisibility: imagine the transfer of one bomb among hundreds of thousands of shipping containers and millions of packages arriving in a larger country any given day. The best that today's security personnel can hope is that spot checks will discourage some portion of the illicit traffic and that they will occasionally net one of the bigger fish. As for participants in xlegal activities, they can rest reasonably assured in their ability to hide in plain sight within the massive universe of trade and extant ICT operations.

12. INFORMATION TECHNOLOGY AND THE WEB ACTIVISM OF THE REVOLUTIONARY ASSOCIATION OF THE WOMEN OF AFGHANISTAN (RAWA)—ELECTRONIC POLITICS AND NEW GLOBAL CONFLICT

MICHAEL DARTNELL

The RAWA website illustrates how the conditions for global conflict have changed in a situation marked by fragmentation of the bipolar international system, the rise of new information technologies, and the intensified battle for hearts and minds seen in the Gulf War of 2003. RAWA's website shows how information technologies can be used to mobilize global civil society and transgress the territorial rigidities of conventional political thought and practice. Where domestic conflict once occurred within physical limits based in a political version of the retail adage "location, location, location," RAWA turned to a web-based struggle for hearts and minds. Similar trends were also seen on September 11, 2001, when innovative tactics and weapons were used in unexpected ways to expose the vulnerabilities of the United States. Ironically, as 9/11 violently thrust global conflict into the continental United States, RAWA's web activism challenged the Taliban's autarkic vision. RAWA activism did not ultimately result in a clear-cut political victory for Afghan women so much as it affirmed their place on the global agenda. In another sense, web activism seems to have played a role in preventing an even more catastrophic turn in Afghanistan's still-daunting conditions.

AFGHANISTAN: A GLOBAL WASTELAND OF DRUGS, RELIGION, AND MISOGYNY

Prior to the civil war, Afghanistan's ethnically, religiously, and linguistically complex society and agricultural economy lingered in relative geostrategic tranquillity. However, various political and social cleavages were in place. Afghans were divided into four main ethnic groups: 38% Pashtun, 25% Tajik, 19% Hazara, and 6% Uzbek.[1] This ethnic diversity is matched by a multiplicity of languages: Afghan Persian (Dari/Farsi), 50%; Pashtu, 35%; Turkic languages, 11%; and another thirty minor (mainly Balochi and Pashai) languages, 4%. Religiously, the population is mainly Sunni Muslim (84%) with an 11% Shia minority.[2] Gender-based conflict emerged from post–World War II social transformations, where urban women in particular became educated, moved into professions, and gained some autonomy. Language, ethnicity, religion, and gender gave Afghanistan the groundwork for a conflict that raged for over twenty years.

Extremely poor and landlocked, Afghanistan's economic development has been pushed aside by over two decades of war, including nearly ten years of Soviet military occupation.[3] The fact that Afghanistan became one of the world's most mined territories intensified the economic disruption for this agricultural economy.[4] Labor shortages persisted as parts of the population repeatedly fled the country; Pakistan and Iran at one time hosted more than six million Afghan refugees. Despite the repatriation of 4.2 million persons by January 1, 1999, the United Nations High Commission for Refugees (UNHCR) reported before the World Trade Center (WTC)–Pentagon attacks that the number of refugees fleeing to Pakistan due to war and drought had increased;[5] one million people had moved internally to urban areas. After the WTC-Pentagon attacks, the population again fled the cities toward the frontiers. War, population movements, loss of labor and investment capital, as well as disrupted trade and transport have led to plummeting gross domestic product over the past twenty years. Afghans have insufficient food, clothing, housing, and health care. Along with economic disaster and land mines, the economy also faces the enormous task of integrating persons with long-term disabilities as a result of injuries from land mines and warfare. One of the most telling measures of devastation is the suffering of Afghan women and children, which has reached proportions of a humanitarian disaster. While human-rights abuses existed in all parts of society, the United Nations Children's Fund (UNICEF) says women and children were particularly harmed by:

> (a) the fact that Afghanistan is one of the least developed countries in the world; (b) the long-term trend of high levels of mortality for both young children and women; (c) the war has caused profound damage to the traditional coping mechanisms of families and communities; and (d) severe, institutionalized gender discrimination.[6]

In its report, UNICEF describes an especially troubling aspect of the Afghan children's plight. Infant mortality is 165 children per 1,000 births. The mortality rate for children under five years old is 257 per 1,000 births. Diseases easily prevented by vaccines account for 21% of child deaths, while diarrhea and acute respiratory infections kill another 42%. Almost half of Afghan children are malnourished. Girls' education was banned in the 90% of the country controlled by the Taliban, leaving only 36% of boys and 11% of girls in primary school. Furthermore, the maternal mortality is the second highest in the world.[7]

UNICEF says that drought left only 11% of the rural population, or an estimated three million Afghans, with access to clean water. It also reduced cereal production in 2000 to 44% of its 1999 level, forcing farmers and nomads to sell or slaughter herds and livestock. This allowed survival but diminished self-sufficiency and compounded the negative impact of drought. International aid must address the humanitarian catastrophe before starting to promote economic development.[8]

One area in which the economy has flourished is in the cultivation and production of illicit drugs. In 1999, Afghanistan became the world's largest opium producer, ahead of Burma, and a major source of hashish. The CIA alleged more and more heroin-processing laboratories were set up and that all major Afghan political factions profited from the drug trade.[9] A Six-Plus-Two Group[10] meeting in September 1999 expressed "deep concern at the increased cultivation, production and trafficking of illicit drugs in and from Afghanistan and discussed establishment of a mechanism to enable them to cooperate more closely on counter-narcotics issues."[11] The UN Office for Drug Control and Crime Prevention (ODCCP) formulated a regional plan to control the drug trade. Following a cultivation ban by the Taliban, the ODCCP reported in June 2001 that "farmers in Afghanistan, the world's number-one producer of opium poppy, did not plant the illegal crop this year."[12] In the post-Taliban era, poverty remains a factor that, in turn, positions opium as a tempting source of revenue.[13]

Once a kingdom, then a republic, the country's internationally recognized name is the Islamic State of Afghanistan (ISA). Overthrown by the Taliban in 1996, the ISA held the country's UN seat until the interim government that succeeded the Taliban took office on December 22, 2001. The Taliban called the country the Islamic Emirate of Afghanistan (IEA), but was recognized only by Pakistan, Saudi Arabia, and the United Arab Emirates. The Taliban Sunni Muslim fundamentalist regime followed Islamic law (Shari'a) by tacit agreement with all factions. After the ISA fled Kabul in 1996, the country had no functioning government structures. The Taliban's focus was defeating the other factions, consolidating its power, and forcing its international recognition as de facto government.[14]

While world attention focused on the Taliban's impact on global terrorism, regional stability, displaced persons, human rights, treatment of women, and the drug trade, less attention was paid to the role of the international community in preparing its rise and sustaining its position. A Human Rights Watch (HRW) report argued that

> The civil war in Afghanistan, a geopolitical battleground during the Cold War, is once again being sponsored by outside parties: Pakistan, Iran, Russia, and other neighboring

countries, with the United States and India working in other ways to influence the outcome.[15]

HRW called for a sustained arms embargo of all parties to the civil war, investigation of human rights abuses, an end to all military assistance, respect for international humanitarian law, and measures to defuse the conflict so rebuilding could begin and the catastrophic humanitarian crisis could be addressed.

After the WTC-Pentagon attacks, the international community focused on the Taliban. Some Taliban factions supported Islamic militants worldwide and provided Osama bin Laden with safe haven. In the aftermath of the September 11 attacks, the United States quickly blamed bin Laden and focused all its efforts on pursuing him. This obsession with capturing bin Laden detracted from human rights and humanitarian issues. In this way, U.S. policy recapitulates the heartland-thesis mind-set in which the region is central for global security but its inhabitants are denied tools to build the stable and peaceful environment needed to secure that end. After the Taliban unilaterally declared itself Afghanistan's legitimate government, its control of between 90% and 95% of the territory made it a revolutionary regime.

The UN deferred its decision on credentials for the existing General Assembly seat and organization membership. The Organization of the Islamic Conference left the Afghan seat vacant until the question of legitimacy can be resolved by negotiations between warring factions. The country was ethnically divided, and the ethnicized conflict became a key to the Taliban's defeat. Pashtun-dominated Taliban controlled Kabul and most of the country, being especially strong in predominately Pashtun areas in the south. Factions opposed to the Taliban formed a coalition, the United Front (UF), with a stronghold in the ethnically diverse north.[16] The Shia minority in the north received Iranian assistance. The struggle between the UF and the Taliban featured ethnic violence,[17] which was especially troubling in a territory with no institutions into which conflict could be channeled.

In addition to properly political organizations, several pressure groups are important. Tribal elders are traditional Pashtun leaders, but the conflict over the past twenty-five years weakened their effectiveness: in 2000, "peace efforts, including an initiative by the former Afghan king, Zahir Shah, to establish a government representative of all ethnic groups and factions through a traditional Loya Jirga (Grand Assembly), did not receive support from the Taliban."[18] Afghan refugees in Pakistan, Australia, the United States, Canada, and elsewhere are organized politically but could not influence the Taliban. Groups in Peshawar, Pakistan, include the Coordination Council for National Unity and Understanding in Afghanistan (CUNUA), the Writers' Union of Free Afghanistan

(WUFA), and Mellat (a social-democratic party). The diverse Afghan diaspora contrasts the political system that the Taliban built, which did not tolerate organized opposition or free expression of ideas. Opponents to the Taliban were imprisoned, tortured, and frequently executed.[19] In September 2002, post-Taliban Afghanistan features a central government in Kabul that is supported by the UN and other foreign troops and the redivision of the country through the rise of a new system of warlords in various regions.

THE AFGHAN POLITICAL ECONOMY OF INFORMATION

The impact of RAWA web activism is most clearly seen in relation to global civil society and it is particularly remarkable given the social, political, and information economy context from which it emerged. This Afghan political economy of information includes traditional print media (magazines and newspapers) and electronic media (radio, telephones, television, and the Internet), but differs from industrial societies that have not experienced such intense and prolonged conflict. By the time the Taliban took power in 1996, telephone and telegraph service were very limited due to war damage. The Taliban moved to redress this situation by repairing some international telephone links. By 1997, the regime had reestablished some domestic telecommunications links (i.e., between cities) by means of satellite and microwave transmission. Similar moves were taken in relation to international telecommunications, which were serviced by an Intelsat satellite earth station linked to Iran and an Intersputnik satellite earth station. As the regime tried to consolidate its hold on the country, a commercial satellite telephone center located southwest of Kabul in Ghazni was brought into operation.[20]

Beyond telephones, the information economy under the Taliban was very bleak. Television broadcasts, music, and images of the human body were outlawed in the name of Islamic "purity." In 2000, audiences for evening news on the Taliban-controlled radio were estimated at 70% of the population. One radio station covered the entire country with religious broadcasts (without music) and official propaganda. The ISA ran a national television broadcasting station and regional stations in a few provinces, but Taliban converted the Kabul TV center into barracks.[21] The country had approximately 100,000 television sets before the Taliban's 1998 campaign to destroy them.[22] In 2000, the Taliban's information minister told the BBC that a TV ban would remain in place.[23] The only television broadcasts in 2001 came from UF-controlled Badakhshan TV's evening news and endlessly repeated music, film, and cartoons.[24] TV broadcasts rapidly returned after the Taliban fell in late 2001.

Freedom of expression did not exist under the Taliban. Newspapers were monitored and had to follow Taliban principles. No photos, features, readers' letters, or editorials were allowed. The Taliban allowed the English-language weekly *Kabul Times,* Pashto-language magazine *Nangarhar,* and Farsi-language newspapers *Hewad* (Fatherland), *Anees* (Companion), and *Shariat.*

> All the news comes from ministries or the official news agency. Journalists are under orders from members of the Taliban who are assigned to editorial offices. The state pays badly and irregularly, and most journalists earn around 12 euros [$16.57 Cdn in August 2001] per month. In July 2000 the government launched *The Islamic Emirate,* an English-language monthly intended to "counteract the biased information put out by the enemies of Islam." The first issue carried the front-page headline "No terrorist camps in Afghanistan" and "Extraditing Osama bin Laden would be scorning a pillar of our religion."[25]

Foreign media were subject to Taliban control and image manipulation. In January 2000, CNN opened a Kabul office, but had no rights to film anywhere. Al-Jazeera also opened a Kabul office. The BBC and Reuters filmed Kabul street life so the world could see how UN sanctions impacted civilians, but operating under the Taliban was dangerous. In August 2000, Pakistani Khawar Mehdi, American Jason Florio, and Brazilian Pepe Escobar were arrested, accused of photographing a soccer match, their film confiscated, and they were questioned. After August 2000, foreign journalists received a Taliban "good behavior" list: no visits to private homes; no interviewing women without ministerial permission; and no photographing or filming people. Pakistani reporters in Afghanistan began to have trouble obtaining visas. BBC interpreter Saboor Salehzai was arrested in December 2000, charged with breaking regulations for Afghans who work for foreign media, and released after four days.[26] Murders of journalists after the fall of the Taliban in October–November 2001 as well as the execution-style killing of Daniel Pearl in 2002 illustrate the continuing tension in the region.

Aside from some administrators and VIPs, Afghans under the Taliban could not access the Internet, which was a potential site for debate, ideas, and resistance in a closed environment. With ordinary Afghans unplugged by poverty, foreign intervention, civil conflict, and technophobia, the Taliban tried to use the Net to cultivate an international profile. However, an IEA website[27] set up to court global opinion was out of service by August 2001. Ironically, the technophobic Taliban had a website,[28] where a hacker posted porn, denounced Islamic fundamentalism, and left a Russian e-mail address in August 2001.[29] Pakistan gave Taliban authorities Net access by hosting the Taliban and IEA websites. The Comsats server provided connections for several Taliban ministries, who apparently received "preferential prices." In 2000, a Taliban official in Peshawar told *Reporters*

Sans Frontières (RSF) that he received e-mail from the foreign affairs ministry and that several government branches used e-mail. Aside from Taliban, some NGOs and foreign correspondents in Afghanistan accessed the Net via satellite. A photographer traveling in Afghanistan in 2000 said that former UF commander Ahmed Shah Masood had an e-mail address that he occasionally accessed via satellite phone.

WWW.RAWA.ORG: POST-TERRITORIAL CONFLICT

The RAWA website,[30] based in Peshawar, Pakistan, embodies the web's potential utility for resistance, alliance-building, testimony, fund-raising, and counter-discourse. In this way, web activism embodies a new information-based form of conflict that shifts some attention for the conventional physical and coercive matrix of politics. Left-of-center RAWA radically challenged gender-based stigmatization and oppression by addressing global civil society on the web. The website illustrates how IT supplements activism in physical space with a virtual context marked by representation, images, emotional-moral appeals, and a battle for hearts and minds. Just as RAWA, an independent political organization of Afghan women set up in Kabul in 1977 to fight for human rights and social justice, empowers the disempowered, its website carries on activism that would be impossible in territorial space. RAWA's electronic transgression of conventional territorial politics started after civil war and the Taliban forced relocation to Peshawar.

The website focuses on the impact of fundamentalism on Afghan women. In August 2001, the homepage featured seventy-two reports, including appeals to the U.S. public through the *Oprah Winfrey Show* as well as to the UN, press conferences, accounts of protests, denunciation of an alleged Afghan war criminal living in the U.K., a statement on UN sanctions, photographs of atrocities, and information on RAWA activities.[31] Alongside text, the site has extensive multimedia (audio and especially photo images) that enhances its moral-emotional appeal through images of Taliban brutality and realistic portrayal of the oppression of Afghan women.[32] The large volume of hits on the site suggests that this activism drew a response from global civil society. On August 22, 2001, the website counter registered 824,617 hits. The number rose to 858,109 by September 2, 2001, an increase of 33,492. It had risen to 130,137 hits to 988,246 by September 15 (fours days after 9/11). On September 16, it reached 1,016,683 (an increase of 28,437 in 24 hours). By September 19, hits increased again to 1,144,531, an additional 127,848. On September 28, there was another increase of 415,281 hits to 1,559,812. The huge increase around 9/11 suggests how web use follows other electronic media[33] given the latter's blanket coverage of events. Prior to this, the high volume of hits at the original homepage had already necessitated a mirror site.

Website Analysis

The website's many text, video, and audio resources are cross-referenced to draw visitors to specific materials. The homepage covers RAWA, its activities, the situation in Afghanistan, and suggestions for a global response. In general, website documents are fewer than six pages long and are easily navigated. The site is multilingual: English, Italian, Spanish, French, German, Farsi, Catalan, and Portuguese. For this analysis, English-language materials were used to assess RAWA's use of a major international language and potentials of global communication. The homepage is organized around eighteen categories: About RAWA; On Our Martyred Leader; Our Publications; Our Social Activities; Patriotic Songs (MP3); Photo Gallery; Reports from Afghanistan; On Afghan Women; RAWA Documents; RAWA Events; RAWA in Media; Movie Clips; Poems; Links; How to contact us?; How to help us?; Search our site; and, Subscribe to mailing list. The homepage is structured around theme areas and a features area. Effective use of color, images, and sound communicates the brutal reality of Afghan women's lives, realizing in this way the moral and emotional promises of immediacy and authentic communication by representational imagery in a global setting.

Website texts include reports, statements, press releases, and some longer documents. The features section contains media articles from sources such as ABCNews, *The Toronto Star,* Tehelka.com (New Delhi), *Marie Claire* magazine, the BBC, and *La Vanguardia* magazine. Most reports on Taliban violence and human-rights abuses center on women and children. Abuses listed in the features section "Recent reports from Afghanistan" include public hanging, executions, arrest of foreign aid workers, destruction of TVs and VCRs, the Internet ban, population displacements, victimization of women in bride sales, destruction of rebel towns, school closings, religious intolerance against Shia Muslims, Sikhs, and Hindus, attacks on intellectuals, and widespread poverty.

Another features section focuses on RAWA's political activities: a message of "Afghan Solidarity," press conferences, celebrations of International Women's Day, a demonstration at Kofi Annan's arrival in Islamabad, an appeal to suspend Afghanistan's UN seat, a statement about an Afghan war criminal living in the U.K., photos of the French human-rights prize, and a statement on UN sanctions against the Taliban. An additional section includes nineteen documents on RAWA's wide-ranging social activism: distributing foodstuffs, medicines, and blankets in refugee camps, photo-documenting massacres, selling RAWA

T-shirts, participating in UNCHR sessions on human rights, home-based classes in Afghanistan, campaigns in the United States, Canada, and Japan, and examining the lives of those marginalized by the Taliban (especially beggars, prostitutes, and prisoners). Still another section has photos of atrocities, drought, refugee suffering, malnourished children, poverty, and fundamentalist terror.

"About RAWA" briefly outlines the organization's history and goals. The group was created to draw Afghan women into the struggle for human rights, social justice, women's rights, and democracy. RAWA says

> The founders were a number of Afghan women intellectuals under the sagacious leadership of Meena, who in 1987 was assassinated in Quetta, Pakistan by Afghan agents of the then KGB in connivance with the fundamentalist band of Gulbuddin Hekmatyar.[34]

From its early goal of establishing a secular, democratic government, RAWA moved into education, health, and antipoverty projects to secure women's rights and democracy.

After the Soviet-backed coup d'état in the April 1978 and December 1979 invasions, RAWA joined the resistance movement. However, its advocacy of democracy and secularism distinguished it from Islamic fundamentalist "freedom fighters." Under Soviet occupation, activists went to Pakistan to work with refugee women. They set up schools, hostels, and a hospital as well as women's nursing, literacy, and vocational training in Quetta, Pakistan. In 1981, RAWA began publishing the magazine *Payam-e-Zan* (Woman's Message) in Persian and Pashtu to raise Afghan women's social and political awareness. Some texts appear in English and Urdu. After the Soviet-backed regime was overthrown in 1992, RAWA's struggle centered on fundamentalism, Taliban atrocities against all Afghan people, and the latter's ultra-chauvinism and misogyny. RAWA wants to broaden its social and relief work, but says, "unfortunately we do not at the moment enjoy any support from international NGOs, therefore our social programmes are presently greatly reduced for lack of funds."[35]

The first category includes a May 1995 Amnesty International document, "Women in Afghanistan: A Human Rights Catastrophe,"[36] and a March 1999 AI call to protect an International Women's Day demonstration by Afghan women in Pakistan. A third AI text is an April 1997 condemnation of torture of a RAWA sympathizer in Pakistan. Another link documents award of "The French Republic's Liberty, Equality, Fraternity Human Rights Prize" to RAWA on April 15, 2000. A final link in the category specifies RAWA's aims:

- Struggle against the Taliban and Jehadi types of the fundamentalists and their foreign masters.
- Establish freedom, democracy, peace, and women's rights in Afghanistan.

• Establish an elected secularist government based on democratic values.
• Unite all freedom-loving and democratic forces and to struggle against all those who collaborate with the fundamentalists.
• Struggle against those traitors who want to disintegrate Afghanistan by causing tribal and religious wars.
• Launch educational, health care, and income-generation projects in and outside the country.
• Support the freedom-loving movements all over the world.[37]

"About RAWA" is also available in Persian, French, Italian, Spanish, and German.

"On Our Martyred Leader" features a biography of Meena, RAWA's founding leader. Born in 1957, Meena became an activist in the 1970s. After the Soviet invasion, she organized meetings and protests in schools, colleges, and at Kabul University. RAWA says her main accomplishments were starting *Payam-e-Zan* and Watan Schools for refugee children. Meena's biography is posted in Persian, Italian, Spanish, and French. The section also contains MP3/WAVE recordings of Meena, a translation of one of her poems, photographs, a song for her in English, and an article about her life and struggle from the March–April 1999 American girls' magazine *New Moon.*

"Our Publications" features links to *Payam-e-Zan* in Farsi, Pashtu, and Urdu.[38] Magazine covers hyperlink to articles in past and current issues. The second item is a two-issue English-language publication called "The Burst of the 'Islamic Government' Bubble in Afghanistan."[39] The third is a twenty-four-page color brochure outlining RAWA activities, viewpoints, and the situation in Afghanistan. The sixteen other items posted in this category include the seventy-two-page text "Afghan Women Challenge the Fundamentalists," four posters, a sticker, special bulletins for International Women's Day and demonstrations, greeting cards, audio cassettes of patriotic songs, AI reports on Afghanistan in Pashtu and Farsi,[40] and T-shirts. The items are sold to finance RAWA assistance to Afghan refugees and show the organization's sophisticated approach to presenting its ideas by marketing itself on the web.

"RAWA's Social Activities" outlines group activities in Pakistan and Afghanistan as well as future plans. RAWA activities in Pakistan range from primary and secondary schools for children, literacy courses for women, an orphanage, health care in refugee camps to a hospital that is near closure for financial reasons. In addition, RAWA provides news and reports on Taliban and fundamentalist abuses to human-rights NGOs and media, and produces antifundamentalist and educational cassettes, plays, poetry, and propaganda. It also organizes demonstrations and press conferences, issues press releases and leaflets, maintains the website, and sets up media contacts and interviews.

In Afghanistan, RAWA supports female victims of war and atrocities. Families that suffer violence are contacted so testimonies can be published in *Payam-e-Zan* or AI can be alerted. Where possible, post-traumatic counseling is offered, traumatized family or children are moved to Pakistan, missing family are located, basic needs are supplied, or sponsors are found. Regular activities in Taliban Afghanistan included education propaganda (home schools and literacy courses, discussion groups on women's rights, education, democracy and civil liberties), health care (health teams in seven provinces treat women who cannot visit doctors for fear of the Taliban or because of their poverty; the scope of health care includes treatment for children and for the wounded, first-aid classes, and polio vaccinations), and economic aid (chicken farms, carpet-weaving, embroidery, knitting, bee-harvesting, handicrafts, tailoring, and short-term loans to widows and families). RAWA wants to expand its activities to include more education; computer, English, and trade courses for women and girls; publications in main Afghan languages; and the publication of magazines that address "taboo" subjects.

"Patriotic Songs" and "Photo Gallery" employ the web's multimedia capacities with MP3 music and photographs. "Patriotic Songs" includes twenty-one songs in Pashtu and Dari, and one song in Urdu. The music varies from songs for Meena, condemnations of Islamic fundamentalism, appeals to fight for democracy and freedom, and laments for Kabul to children singing in a RAWA school. "Photo Gallery" links fifty-two photographs of Afghan society, the impact of conflict, and RAWA activities. Photos document Taliban massacres, hangings, and mutilations as well as poverty and drought. Photos of RAWA activities cover rallies, home-based classes, and distribution of food and blankets to refugees.

"Reports from Afghanistan" features nine types of documents, including recent reports from Afghanistan in English and Persian. Documents on what RAWA calls "fundamentalist criminality," the condition of women, fundamentalist destruction of Afghanistan's heritage,[41] two *Payam-e-Zan* reports, and a report from Herat City about life under the Taliban, and a photo gallery is also available. At this point, the website is complicated by cross-links between different categories. Links to "Afghan women under the tyranny of the fundamentalists" and "Photo Gallery" are also categories on the homepage. The difficulty in managing large amounts of information on small budgets and limited personnel is evident. Increased ease of global communication raises new complexities of information overload, management, and comprehension. The danger is that key information could be "buried" in a mass of texts. RAWA obviously weighed the merits of posting or not posting information, deciding to transmit information despite these limits.

"On Afghan Women" opens to "Afghan Women Under the Tyranny of the Fundamentalists," which has texts and photos of Taliban atrocities. At the top of the page, RAWA overviews women's conditions and lists some restrictions.[42] Information on the page comes from various sources. "Inside Afghanistan: Behind the Veil" presents journalist Saira Shah's account of a visit to the country to conduct interviews and take photographs for a June 2001 BBC News report.[43] Other documents describe conditions for Afghan women in a society in which they could not work or be personally secure outside the home. Rising drug addiction; a ban on female university students, civil servants, and teachers; trafficking in women; murders; rapes; house arrests; floggings; public executions; restrictions on female foreign-aid workers; polygamy and concubinage; beatings; and oppressive clothing are listed as some of the results of these restrictions. Photographs depict a mother of four who was raped and killed by fundamentalists, an Afghan widow, a woman forced into prostitution by poverty, women forbidden to attend a funeral, a woman speaking about her husband's death, public execution of a woman, and the wounds of an elderly woman attacked by fundamentalists. The images document Taliban gender abuse and highlight their relevance for international relations as a specific form of human-rights violation.

"How to help us?"[44] provides various ways for the global public to assist RAWA. In addition to donations, visitors may sign an electronic petition.[45] Fund-raising and awareness drives to assist RAWA have been organized on Quadra Island, British Columbia, in Santa Barbara, California, and by northern California high school students.[46] Other ways to take action are: demanding that the British government investigate and prosecute a war criminal living in the U.K., and sending donations to impoverished refugees in Peshawar, Pakistan. Another page requests donations to reopen Malalai Hospital, which specializes in land-mine injuries.

RAWA lists twenty-three ways in which citizens of the global community can help the organization: by introducing it to individuals, groups, schools, organizations, and congregations; staging protests and demonstrations to support RAWA and Afghan women; organizing meetings and seminars to highlight the situation in Afghanistan; writing to Pakistani authorities to protest government and non-government violence against RAWA; inviting RAWA members to speak; covering Afghanistan and fundamentalist crimes in publications; translating RAWA materials into English, Spanish, French, Portuguese, Italian, and Arabic; distributing RAWA publications and audiocassettes; sending money and supplies for RAWA schools; organizing fund-raising campaigns; sending medical supplies; donating computers, camcorders, cassette duplicators, sound and film mixing equipment, CD recorders, small photo and video cameras for RAWA documentation of fundamentalist crimes, miniature video and photo cameras to film and photograph atrocities in Afghanistan, and films, books, and materials with progressive and antifundamentalist themes; and sponsoring teachers in Afghanistan. The collapse of the Taliban will undoubtedly influence how RAWA activism develops over the coming years.

VIRTUAL POLITY, VIRTUAL COMBAT?

In a context in which globalization and information technology embody far-reaching processes, RAWA highlights the projection of once largely domestic issues of gender and gender-based oppression into the guts of global conflict. While its main concerns are gender-based discrimination and oppression, antifemale violence, brutality, and the killing of women and children by the Taliban, RAWA also highlights the deep-rooted poverty, fundamentalism, inequality, and violence in Afghan society. RAWA's proposed solution is a democratic, secular regime committed to social justice. It sees both the Taliban and the Northern Alliance as foreign "puppets" whose support for religious law is especially oppressive for women and is a factor that sustains violence, sociopolitical disintegration, and ethnic conflict.

Describing itself as an organization committed to freedom, democracy, secularism, and women's rights, RAWA advocates unity against groups and individuals allied to fundamentalists. It does not call for violence, but aims to generate awareness and spread its views through education, membership drives, and web activism. Characterizing Afghan women as not only politically and socially oppressed but also as leading a particularly oppressed existence, RAWA opposes foreign intervention in Afghanistan while it supports liberation movements in Palestine, Kurdistan, Kashmir, Iran, and elsewhere. RAWA support for these latter movements is based in its conviction that its conflict—the struggle to free Afghanistan from the influence of foreign Islamic fundamentalists—is like other struggles for national self-determination.

The RAWA website communicated information on political and social conditions under the Taliban to friends and supporters and raised awareness of its struggle. Unable to act domestically under the Taliban or the ISA, RAWA used web activism to circumvent gender oppression. Given the often hyperbolic claims as to the impact of information technologies, the issue is whether web activism advanced the cause of Afghan women and produced results. RAWA repeatedly emphasizes that finances hamper effective lobbying and participation in demonstrations. Web activism responded to these limits by promoting global awareness of the oppression of Afghan women and building ties to other women's groups and individuals.

While the Taliban was in power, RAWA's website was important to global witnessing as a venue for criticism, opposition, and resistance to a totalitarian ideology, movement, and regime. Witnessing is a major achievement in light of the success of twentieth-century totalitarian regimes in crushing feminism. The huge number of hits on the site hint at its impact on global conflict. While RAWA can be ignored, the plight of Afghan women has been comprehensively exposed on the website. The site's photo, audio, and visual media were an interactive springboard for a moral-emotional appeal, enhanced by use of numerous testimonies. Women's and other witnesses' personal experiences and extensive cross-documentation testify to a key social and political issue.

Given that RAWA operated with exceptional caution, that its target was the Afghan diaspora and global civil society, and that the Taliban also tried to maintain an extraterritorial web presence, the peculiarities of the case are evident. RAWA aims at the United States, the United Nations, NGOs, sympathetic activists, and donors. The nature of the Afghan conflict made the physical props of traditional politics unavailable to RAWA.

In this sense, the RAWA website uniquely demonstrates the relevance and applicability of new IT in a conflict setting of profound trauma, dramatic disenfranchisement of major segments of a population, and manipulation by great powers. It also encapsulates the limits and promise of electronic representation. The limits imposed on RAWA are many: no ability to conduct open politics in a physical space, no direct access to victims, no active aboveground organization in Afghanistan, activists exposed to extreme danger, no funds, and illegality in its territory of origin. On the other hand, RAWA embodies the promise of new Net-linked politics: articulating a counter-discourse to a savage regime, appealing to global civil society, witnessing, resisting by "thinking otherwise," and cross-organizational cross-ideological appeal.

In light of the Taliban's savage misogyny, the most remarkable feature of the RAWA website is its existence and relevance to an ongoing conflict with global import. It emerged from a society in which women began to break with traditional social structures in the last forty years of the twentieth century. The society experienced a coup d'état, revolution, foreign invasion, civil war, counter-revolution, and foreign intervention in a cycle from 1973 to 2001, a short time frame of twenty-eight years. The position of Afghan women is a key to the conflict, as women entered professions, assumed leading roles, and then saw advances brutally rolled back. As the voice of Afghan women was privatized by the Taliban, existence of a very public medium was a major achievement. RAWA web activism alerted global civil society and motivated the Taliban's efforts at an electronic response.[47] Ironically, a sign of web activism's power and relevance is that the public about which the RAWA website speaks (Afghans in Afghanistan in general and women in Afghanistan in particular) was not even online! RAWA shows the relevance of the web as a tool for disenfranchised, silent, or absent political movements. In this case, the web was a tool to fight a neototalitarian regime, bypassing location and altering the nature of security.

"SOME OF THE RESTRICTIONS IMPOSED BY THE TALIBAN ON WOMEN IN AFGHANISTAN"[48]

The following list offers only an abbreviated glimpse of the hellish lives Afghan women were forced to lead under the Taliban, and cannot begin to reflect the depth of female deprivations and sufferings. The Taliban treat women worse than they treat animals. In fact, even as the Taliban declare the keeping of caged birds and animals illegal, they imprison Afghan women within the four walls of their own houses. Women have no importance in Taliban eyes unless they are occupied producing children, satisfying male sexual needs, or attending to the drudgery of daily housework. Jehadi fundamentalists such as Gulbaddin, Rabbani, Masood, Sayyaf, Khalili, Akbari, Mazari, and their co-criminal Dostum have committed the most treacherous and filthy crimes against Afghan women. And as more areas come under Taliban control, even if the number of rapes and murders perpetrated against women falls, Taliban restrictions—comparable to those from the middle ages—will continue to kill the spirit of our people while depriving them of a humane existence. We consider Taliban more treacherous and ignorant than Jehadis. According to our people, "Jehadis were killing us with guns and swords but Taliban are killing us with cotton."

Taliban restrictions and mistreatment of women include the:

1. Complete ban on women's work outside the home, which also applies to female teachers, engineers, and most professionals. Only a few female doctors and nurses are allowed to work in some hospitals in Kabul.

2. Complete ban on women's activity outside the home unless accompanied by a *mahram* (close male relative such as a father, brother, or husband).

3. Ban on women dealing with male shopkeepers.

4. Ban on women being treated by male doctors.

5. Ban on women studying at schools, universities, or any other educational institution. (Taliban have converted girls' schools into religious seminaries.)

6. Requirement that women wear a long veil (burqa), which covers them from head to toe.

7. Whipping, beating, and verbal abuse of women not clothed in accordance with Taliban rules, or of women unaccompanied by a *mahram.*

8. Whipping of women in public for having noncovered ankles.

9. Public stoning of women accused of having sex outside marriage. (A number of lovers are stoned to death under this rule.)

10. Ban on the use of cosmetics. (Many women with painted nails have had fingers cut off.)

11. Ban on women talking or shaking hands with non-*mahram* males.

12. Ban on women laughing loudly. (No stranger should hear a woman's voice.)

13. Ban on women wearing high-heel shoes, which would produce sound while walking. (A man must not hear a woman's footsteps.)

14. Ban on women riding in a taxi without a *mahram.*

15. Ban on women's presence in radio, television, or public gatherings of any kind.

16. Ban on women playing sports or entering a sport center or club.

17. Ban on women riding bicycles or motorcycles, even with their *mahrams.*

18. Ban on women wearing brightly colored clothes. In Taliban terms, these are "sexually attracting colors."

19. Ban on women gathering for festive occasions, such as the Eids, or for any recreational purpose.

20. Ban on women washing clothes next to rivers or in a public place.

21. Modification of all place names including the word "women." For example, "women's garden" has been renamed "spring garden."

22. Ban on women appearing on the balconies of their apartments or houses.

23. Compulsory painting of all windows, so women can not be seen from outside their homes.

24. Ban on male tailors taking women's measurements or sewing women's clothes.

25. Ban on female public baths.

26. Ban on males and females traveling on the same bus. Public buses have now been designated "males only" (or "females only").

27. Ban on flared (wide) pantlegs, even under a burqa.

28. Ban on the photographing or filming of women.

29. Ban on women's pictures printed in newspapers and books, or hung on the walls of houses and shops.

Apart from the above restrictions on women, the Taliban has:

• Banned listening to music, not only for women but men as well.

• Banned the watching of movies, television, and videos, for everyone.

• Banned celebrating the traditional New Year (Nowroz) on March 21. The Taliban has proclaimed the holiday un-Islamic.

• Disavowed Labor Day (May 1), because it is deemed a "communist" holiday.

• Ordered that all people with non-Islamic names change them to Islamic ones.

• Forced haircuts upon Afghan youth.

• Ordered that men wear Islamic clothes and a cap.

• Ordered that men not shave or trim their beards, which should grow long enough to protrude from a fist clasped at the point of the chin.

• Ordered that all people attend prayers in mosques five times daily.

• Banned the keeping of pigeons and playing with the birds, describing it as un-Islamic. The violators will be imprisoned and the birds shall be killed. Kite-flying has also been stopped.

• Ordered all onlookers, while encouraging the sportsmen, to chant *Allah-o-Akbar* (God is great) and refrain from clapping.

• Ban on certain games, including kite-flying, which is un-Islamic according to Taliban.

• Anyone who carries objectionable literature will be executed.

• Anyone who converts from Islam to any other religion will be executed.

• All boy students must wear turbans. They say, "No turban, no education."

• Non-Muslim minorities must wear a distinct badge or stitch a yellow cloth onto their dress to be differentiated from the majority Muslim population. This is reminiscent of the manner in which the Nazis treated the Jews.

• Banned the use of the Internet by both ordinary Afghans and foreigners.

And so on. . . .

13. THE INTERNET'S MEDIATION POTENTIAL IN PROTRACTED CONFLICTS: THE CASE OF BURUNDI[1]

ROSE M. KADENDE-KAISER

Can Internet interactions contribute to peace in places like Burundi, Africa? This chapter considers the role that the use of the Internet has played in bringing together groups of Burundians of diverse backgrounds to interact with each other, and to explore together issues related to peace and security in their home country.

My main focus is on the electronic newsgroup referred to as the Burundi Youth Council (BYC), a recently developed online bulletin board where members raise issues that others can take on and discuss, if they are interested. BYC's active membership is dominated by young diasporic Burundians, and their discussions are accessible at www.burundiyouth.com. In order to better understand the effectiveness of BYC, I will also discuss a predecessor to BYC, Burundinet, a newsgroup established immediately after the onset of ethnic violence in 1993.

THE BURUNDI ETHNIC CONFLICT

The ongoing violence between the ethnic Hutu and Tutsi in Burundi has resulted in deep societal divisions and serious economic crises. Struggles for power since independence in the early 1960s culminated in the killing of over 100,000 people in 1972. The current conflict was triggered by the assassination of the first democratically elected Hutu president, Melchior Ndadaye, in October 1993. As many as 250,000 people have since lost their lives in revenge killings between the Hutu, who for decades were excluded from the leadership of the country, and the Tutsi, who until recently had a strong hold on political power in the country and who still dominate the national army. While the majority of the victims are innocent Hutu and Tutsi civilians, most of the violence is perpetrated by Tutsi-dominated military and security forces on one side, and armed Hutu-dominated opposition groups on the other.

In spite of the bloodshed and chaos, it is only since 1994, following the assassination of Ndadaye and subsequent killings, that the international community became involved in mediating the Burundi ethnic conflict. Peacemaking efforts resulted in recognition and guilt over failure to intervene in the Rwandan genocide of April 1994 and concerns that Burundi may turn to genocidal violence if appropriate measures were not taken to curb violent conflict. Concerns over the spillover of the Burundi and Rwanda conflicts to the rest of the region prompted careful attempts to intervene. Indeed, this concern became reality when, in post-genocide Rwanda, Hutu refugees who had fled to the eastern part of the Democratic Republic of the Congo (DRC) started attacking local inhabitants, as they were considered among Hutu refugees as well as by some DRC natives as brethren of Tutsi. Today, Rwandan, Ugandan, Zimbabwean, and (to a lesser extent) Burundian troops have been drawn into the war in the Great Lakes region, either supporting DRC's autonomy against this foreign invasion (as was the case of Zimbabwe) or, on the opposite side, Rwanda and Burundi in particular, seeking to keep Hutu rebels from attacking from outside their borders.

Peace-building initiatives in the Great Lakes region, including Burundi, have involved various regional and international actors. Despite progress, they are still far from reaching a destination on the long road to peace. In the case of Burundi, sporadic violence and hit-and-run attacks against civilian, military, or rebel targets continue to bring chaos throughout the country, as evinced by the recent violence in early September 2002, when approximately 200 women, children, and elderly were massacred.[2]

PEACE PROCESS: ITS STRENGTHS AND SHORTCOMINGS

Three main international actors have, since November 1993, been involved in the Burundi peace process. Ahmedou Ould-Abdallah preceded former president Julius Nyerere (Tanzania) and the current mediator, Nelson Mandela (South Africa), in searching for a lasting solution to the conflict in Burundi. They each had their own achievements, shortcomings, and challenges during the successive phases of conflict escalation. During his two-year tenure as the UN secretary general's special representative in Burundi between 1993 and 1995, Ould-Abdallah was able to establish contacts with various political institutions, foreign diplomats, representatives of international NGOs, as well as political party leaders and their proactive constituents on each side of the ethnic divide. Such contacts enabled him to prevent "a serious domestic crisis from exploding into a devastating, genocidal conflict."[3] Abdallah's experience in Burundi addresses mediation deficiencies as they relate to "coordination failures among the parties involved in peace and security." These failures had their roots in poor information circulation and/or coordination.[4]

Acting as an "international facilitator,"[5] Julius Nyerere's efforts resulted in constitutional amendments and the election of another Hutu president who unfortunately was killed in a plane crash in 1994 along with his counterpart, the president of Rwanda, to the north. With the support of the Carter Center, Nyerere's efforts sought to build confidence among regional actors and then ultimately resulted in his appointment as the regional and international mediator. When former president Major Pierre Buyoya took over in another military coup in July 1996 leading to the suspension of the constitution, economic sanctions were imposed by all the countries in the region and some in the international community, further isolating Burundi. Some would argue that the sanctions in fact undermined the negotiations, as many pro-Tutsi in Burundi became more suspicious of Nyerere's role as mediator, not only because the country suffered economically from the sanctions but also because Nyerere came from neighboring Tanzania (which hosts large numbers of Hutu refugees that fled the 1972 and 1993 violence). Nonetheless, constitutional political life was eventually reinstated.

Nyerere was succeeded by former South African president Nelson Mandela, who led a peace process that culminated in the signing of the Arusha Peace Process Accord in August 2000. While nineteen parties were signatories to the agreement, armed wings of Hutu opposition parties such as Coalition Nationale pour la Défense de la Démocratie-Forces pour la Défense de la Démocratie (National Coalition for the Defense of Democracy-Forces for the Defense of Democracy) did not take part in the peace talks, and they were not signatories to this agreement. Therefore, the transitional government resulting from the peace accord has not been able to stop the hostilities. These top-level, Track-One diplomatic efforts used a rather unusual mediation approach, leaving the cessation of hostilities and the achievement of a cease-fire to the end of the peace-building process.

While I recognize that in order for "peace to endure there must be profound social change . . . that transforms situations characterized by violence and fear into opportunities for social justice, participative democracy and reconciliation," protracted conflicts often require that cessation of hostilities or a cease-fire take place during early phases of negotiations. The "urgent cry in most situations of conflict is to silence the guns," and this often precedes substantive negotiations that lead conflict parties to an agreement and a political transition from war to peace.[6] Some interpreted Mandela's approach as a failure to recognize that Burundi's history was not the same as South Africa's. And some believe that he imposed his will on party representatives instead of allowing them to arrive at a jointly negotiated agreement. Mandela clearly indicated to the nineteen various parties that they would not take part in the transitional government if they failed to sign the peace agreement.

There is a consensus that coordinated conflict-prevention strategies are most effective in the early stages of the conflict cycle.[7] According to United Nations

Secretary General Kofi Annan, "preventive action should be initiated at the earliest possible state of a conflict cycle in order to be most effective."[8] Failure to intervene during the early stages of conflict escalation results in high-intensity violence and becomes "a proximate cause of the conflict's protractedness."[9] Violence sets in motion cycles of retaliation and retribution that are difficult to break as more and more people are drawn in or become direct victims of violent conflict. In Burundi, these acts of violence continue to cause hardship and suffering among the survivors, hence making mediation an extremely difficult task.

Opportunities for conflict intervention are more effective when parties "feel more secure in their relations with other groupings and when the level of violence is low." During this phase, formal ties still exist between different groups, and "*institutionalized channels of communication,*[10] though perhaps frayed, are available. During the early stages of the conflict cycle, there may well be more chances for mediation because attitudes and perceptions have not hardened and parties are still willing to talk to each other."[11]

Where initial waves of violence remind parties in conflict of the value of taking appropriate measures to prevent its violent escalation, communication channels can be used for de-escalation purposes, or to return calm to the situation. No assumptions should be made, however, that communication channels serve productive purposes intended for peaceful outcomes alone. Indeed, from Rwanda to Guatemala and the former Yugoslavia, the inflammatory role of the media is widely recognized. Through the radio or television, for example, inflammatory comments were made that increased cross-ethnic tensions. Such comments tend to become violence triggers.[12]

Once this happens, the channels of "open communication" will quickly close, hence limiting the scope and efficacy of conflict prevention and resulting in tremendous hardship, as well as a staggering loss of life of those involved in and affected by intensified conflict. Can productive communication be restored under such conditions of protracted conflict? What methods can be employed to achieve this?

I argue that when conflict has escalated to the level of massive violence such as in Burundi, new ICTs, and in particular the Internet, can be used as a tool for bridging communication gaps and engaging various parties in discussions regarding appropriate mechanisms for productive conflict transformation. It all starts with dialogue restoration, the greatest challenge of mediation. One of the initial phases of mediation requires bringing together the worst of enemies to sit at the same table and talk about peace-building. As threats to individuals' physical safety are actualized, fear and paranoia will keep victims of violent conflict away from their perceived or imaginary enemies.

THE POTENTIAL OF THE INTERNET: BURUNDINET AND BURUNDI YOUTH COUNCIL

The Internet has the potential to contribute to peace-building. However, attention needs to be paid to various phases of the conflict cycle so as to determine expectations about its contribution. For example, when the Internet newsgroup Burundinet was created in 1995, fresh memories of the killings that took place in the aftermath of the assassination of Ndadaye in 1993 and the 1994 genocide in neighboring Rwanda curtailed successful efforts at peace-building. Expectations were limited to achieving productive online communication where members could voice their opinions safely. When communication occurred, bias was often prevalent toward one or the other group.

Burundinet brought together different members of the Burundian community in the diaspora immediately following the onset of nation-wide violence. Members of this newsgroup were concerned with staying in touch with each other across geographic and ethnic boundaries in order to determine what went wrong in Burundi and what could be done to redress the situation. Not much emphasis was placed on what they could do themselves. In fact, messages whose focus was on intervention sought to call upon the main belligerents, namely the Burundi army and various rebel groups and gangs, to stop the senseless assassinations that continued to take the lives of innocent civilians. Burundinet was established and most active during an intensely violent phase of the Burundi conflict.

During this earlier phase of the "mobilization of conflict," which is when Burundinet was most active, discussions were centered on identity negotiation at the subnational, national, and international levels. Subnationally, Burundinet members explored the role of ethnic identity in political developments in Burundi. The "enemy" in this case was the ethnic "other," and the conflict could not be transformed productively until this "other" recognized its role in instigating violence. For those who recognized that Burundi was not an isolated case in the history of conflicts, a nationalist approach sought to call upon the different social, ethnic, and political subgroupings to transcend their differences and recognize that indeed a national identity still existed in Burundi. The goal for this group was to stimulate a discussion that refocused the attention on outside forces, the colonial legacy in particular. It was argued that colonial *divide et impera* policies ignited divisions and that recovery required a recognition of the destructive impact of colonialism on the country. Thus, the best way forward would be to return to precolonial realities of national unity.

A recent newsgroup, Burundi Youth Council (BYC), is more concerned with post-conflict reconstruction. BYC is as reliant on the Internet for brainstorming purposes as they are on face-to-face meetings with various national and international actors that can help them achieve their reconstruction goals.

In addition to fund-raising and supporting grassroots initiatives in Burundi, BYC continues to make contacts with high-powered individuals and organizations that might assist them in their pursuit of peace in the country, including members of the U.S. Congress. Efforts have included visits to BYC branches in Burundi, grant-writing to seek external support, engaging youth leaders in staying focused on cross-ethnic unity and reconstruction, public appearances at the United Nations, and interviews on CNN, VOA, and BET to emphasize the importance of enfranchising Burundi youth in rebuilding the country.

BYC's executive committee has developed a set of rules, posted online, that are aimed at encouraging productive interactions regardless of individual contributors' class, religion, educational level, or ethnic background. Although difference of opinion is permitted, issues that are primarily encouraged are those that both Hutu and Tutsi can relate to. Hence, the BYC site seeks to be conciliatory. A BYC executive committee member has the discretion to delete offensive messages.

If a user persists in challenging Net rules, the board members or executive committee reserve the right to terminate the user's membership. Understanding clearly and abiding by these rules of communication becomes every member's responsibility. Most of the rules are expressed in the form of a warning or a reminder that certain opinions will not be tolerated on the BYC bulletin board. Among them, ideas that represent ethnic and regional extremism constitute a threat to the moderate approach that the BYC executive committee is seeking to enhance and encourage among the network's constituencies.

Burundinet is no longer active. It was one of the first online resources that allowed Burundians in the diaspora to exchange ideas on mechanisms for violence de-escalation in their home country. When Burundians were engaged in war, those in the diaspora exchanged views and agendas on Burundinet.

BYC started its activities in March 2000. It remains active today with several successful initiatives to its credit. One of these achievements includes bringing together representatives of Hutu and Tutsi communities to initiate productive activities on behalf of the Burundi youth on the ground in the country.

WHY DO ONLINE DISCUSSIONS MATTER?

First of all, online interactions can open the way toward face-to-face meetings that would otherwise not be possible in an environment of high levels of tension and physical violence. Once some minimum trust is established online, face-to-face meetings become critical in helping bridge the spatial and ideological gap that was created in the construction of identity in Burundi. The first BYC Peace Summit that was held in Washington, D.C., on August 31–September 2, 2001, allowed young Hutu and Tutsi men and women to articulate their own visions of a peaceful Burundi. This very important step toward moving beyond the virtual world served as the foundation upon which face-to-face contacts were made, and individual members were able to take new leadership roles in the organization of future activities for BYC.

Second, online discussions allow for a freedom of expression that many BYC members are taking advantage of. According to one BYC board member I interviewed:

> Politicians have for many years claimed to represent the views and perspectives of the majority of Burundi citizens. The radio and television are medias of the government and are not open to criticism. The Internet allows us to challenge the dominant perspective that analyzes the Burundi conflict by focusing only on ethnicity. All of a sudden, we realized that we could voice our opinion in a safe environment and not worry about government censorship.

Third, where traumatic experiences have never been freely discussed, the Internet can open up the window of opportunity, allowing victims to come to terms with their past of pain and suffering. Online discussions can provide Hutu victims of 1972 and Tutsi victims of 1993 with a critical space to take first steps toward healing and reconciliation.

Open discussion, however, is not approached in the same manner by all discussants. My interviewee states that what has emerged online, via BYC, is an "ideological" split between "liberals" and "conservatives." Liberals represent those who are open and willing to discuss any issues. For example, the year 1972 is a highly controversial topic for Hutu and Tutsi. While some refer to 1972 as the year of gruesome atrocities and genocidal violence—where the majority of the victims were of Hutu origin—others view 1972 as representing only a tragic period of civil unrest that can be blamed on both ethnic groups. Others would rather not even discuss events surrounding April 29, 1972. The point is that liberals are open to various viewpoints whatever the implications are for established identities, histories, and traditions.

"Conservatives" support interethnic discussion, but they are concerned about the effects of radical liberalism. Hence, this group is supportive of freedom of expression provided that this does not undermine the specificity of Burundi culture and tradition. Recognized differences—including views about important historical events—should guide discourse and actions advocated for by BYC members. Failure to do this will result, according to this group, in cultural alienation and assimilation online.

Fourth, the Internet can enhance productive conflict transformation by connecting parties involved in or affected by conflict and serving as a *medium* through which the parties can communicate with each other and engage in the initial phases of productive conflict transformation. Mediation is crucial to transforming conflicts. With a mediator who is able to outline the rules of engagement, people can discuss their grievances online, minimizing offensive interactions that in face-to-face peace processes often lead to a standstill, particularly when disagreements force parties to shout and yell at one another and withdraw from the process.

Successful online conflict mediation requires engaging in the filtering process, delaying messages that do not support productive dialogue. In face-to-face mediation processes, one's views are communicated directly and promptly, hence making it possible for abusive interactions to occur. Online with a filtering process, messages can be postponed or permanently turned off, hence enabling parties in a conflict to save face or cool down before expressing their opinions. This is particularly possible so long as the online mediator for newsgroups is also responsible for the technical aspect of message coordination. On BYC, for example, messages are reviewed and approved by the board members before they are added online for public access. Throughout the online access, one becomes aware that certain messages will not be published, and where the message would be, one finds instead a note that "this message was deleted by the sender or BYC board." It is clear that those messages that do not follow the rules of interaction as stated on the BYC's code of conduct will not go past the board. The code itself is clearly stated and formulated, reminding users of the site to keep in mind the nature and aim of the organization to remain as apolitical as possible.

PROMOTING LIBERAL PRINCIPLES ONLINE

Research on online political engagement is based on the assumption that information technologies give citizens the freedom to participate in open debates about issues that are crucial to societal development. Ideally, online discussions would be part of a "public sphere" which, as John Keane perceives it, seeks to reinforce the "liberty of the press" and other publicly shared freedoms of expression and discussion, limiting the abuse of power.[13]

The public sphere constitutes an interesting vantage point from which to view what BYC represents. At its base, an effective public sphere assumes that participants feel personally secure to interact. So, do BYC members feel secure, and is BYC anything like the public sphere?

Bear in mind that BYC membership includes both Hutus and Tutsis in the

Burundian diaspora, and these are the same groups that have been involved in cross-ethnic violence, of which the most recent started in October 1993. It is thus not surprising that many BYC members "hide behind a nickname" and keep individual e-mail addresses inaccessible. As some have explained, the information they share online could be used for destructive purposes, and fears become even more real when guaranteed safety online for BYC web users cannot be extended to relatives or friends in the country. Until a complete trust between members of BYC online and offline in Burundi has been achieved, BYC Net users often choose to remain anonymous.

Several members express fear of possible betrayal because messages posted online can be accessed by anyone with Internet capacity, including Burundi authorities or other potentially harmful individuals. The concern that individual users could become targets of attacks online or of rejection in the "real world" suggests that online discussions are not guaranteed spaces of peaceful interaction.

It is in this light that Spears and Lea[14] question assumptions about virtual safety and the "equalization phenomenon"[15] of computer-mediated communication (CMC). While they agree that CMC has the potential to enhance the sense of anonymity by creating an environment that is conducive to the statement of "one's true mind and authentic self,"[16] they also warn that in relational contexts, "if power and influence are not outside, but are at least partly encoded within us, it becomes far less easy to argue that the source of power is necessarily displaced or diluted by the distanciation, isolation, and anonymity characteristic of CMC."[17]

After all, this search for a virtual space of freedom and fantasy would become irrelevant had the actual physical space of social interactions been fair and open to the achievement of human potential for men and women. Hence, entrance into virtual space cannot fully mask the benefits and drawbacks of interaction in the physical world but is often a mirror image of it. Nevertheless, a more comprehensive discussion of alternative mechanisms for conflict transformation is still better represented online by Burundians in the diaspora than is possible in face-to-face interactions on the ground in Burundi.

Far from being released from the pressures of the real world, BYC web users and messages conveyed on the BYC website continue to reflect on Burundian history and culture and its impact on the users' lives and the lives of their extended relatives in Burundi today. The use of alternative identity features seek to mask certain elements of the real self and sometimes their political views and lifestyle choices serve as a clear recognition among many BYC users that insecurity and discrimination based on difference in the physical world constitute adequate reasons for members to seek to conceal certain elements of their multiple identities to achieve progressive online exchange.

CONCLUSION

Endemic violence continues to pose a threat to peaceful cohabitation between the Hutu majority and Tutsi minority in Burundi as conflict escalation has led to losses that have amounted to over 250,000 deaths and deeper levels of animosity between the ethnic groups. Failures to prevent the escalation of conflict during the early years of independence in the 1960s have produced losses of life and unfruitful efforts at peace-building. Official mediation efforts to curb conflict escalation have not been able to achieve lasting peace agreements. The recent UN effort mentioned above—led by Special Envoy to Burundi Ould-Abdallah—did not result in any significant progress. When Ould-Abdallah left Burundi 1995, the more than dozen political groupings had not even reached an agreement as to the terms of the transitional government. While his efforts were well intentioned, they were overwhelmed by the complexities of conflict management in a country where violence has reached such an intense level of absurdity.

Appropriate techniques for effective mediation in a multiparty setting involve maintaining "open communication" across the lines of conflict and coordinating efforts at many levels. Coordination, open communication, and awareness of conflict phases can maximize mediation success. Information and communications technologies (ICTs) can be utilized at many levels during various conflict phases. As tools of communication, they have the potential to bring together parties to a conflict, enabling different sides to voice their opinions in a safe environment compared to face-to-face situations. They can also sustain the momentum during later phases of conflict, enabling groups to develop appropriate approaches to conflict reduction.

This chapter focused specifically on the use of the Internet by members of the Burundian community living in the diaspora, mostly in Europe, the United States, and Canada, who have used the Internet medium to communicate opinions regarding the nature of the Burundi conflict. By revising existing political practices and policies or developing new ones, BYC seeks to lay the foundation for a more peaceful Burundi. As the "practice of politics does not escape public notice."[18] BYC serves as an alternative forum of communication, a virtual space where the Burundian youth in the diaspora can contribute, albeit virtually, to contemporary debates on post-conflict peace-building and national recovery. Through the creation and participation in an electronic discussion and communication groups where government censorship is absent or limited at worst, the opinions of many marginalized views of civil society in Burundi are represented.

BYC site users are less inclined to blame Burundi's ills on ethnic differences. Their interest in redressing the "evil" acts of violence and retribution that were committed by previous generations of Burundi leaders led them toward full recognition of the wrongs of the past. In order to be productive, this recognition must mobilize the youth in productive undertakings that seek to amend the various conflicting fault lines of Burundi society. There are many problems that need to be resolved. As these are addressed, it is clear that cultural traditions and political practices that condone discrimination against various segments of Burundi society can no longer be reproduced, if peace is to be achieved. Challenging these well-entrenched traditions and practices might ensure that many of the marginalized communities in Burundi society will benefit from a full participation as equal citizens in the common struggle for national development. To the extent that BYC provides a space for such challenges and debates about them, it has the potential to facilitate productive conflict transformation in Burundi.

Whether or not BYC functions in ways that are similar to the "micro-public spheres" of the "coffeehouse, town-level meeting and literacy circle, in which early modern public spheres developed in Europe,"[19] may not be what matters. Instead, BYC's approach to online communication provides the necessary space for open and productive interaction across class, political, ethnic, and gender lines. While the freedom of expression and the development of ideas about moving toward peace can be a productive exercise for those involved, the ultimate benefit depends on the effects such discussions may have in the lives of those struggling to survive in the country. Therefore, online peacemaking becomes effective once actualized on the ground in Burundi, and begins to influence the degree to which peaceful interactions can be reinvigorated across the ethnic divide. Forced ethnic separation at the onset of the civil war that began in 1993 is part of the enigma that many Burundians, in the country and abroad, are still trying to come to terms with as they explore alternative approaches to conflict transformation and attempts to renew the sense of shared geographic space through the use of online bulletin boards and Internet newsgroups.

NOTES

Introduction

1. This transformation was traced by the military theorist Martin Van Crefeld, *Technology and War* (New York: The Free Press, 1989).

2. The long history of the relationship between military power and society is traced by historian William H. McNeil in *The Pursuit of Power* (Chicago: University of Chicago Press, 1982).

3. For an in-depth exploration of the role of IT in such networks, see Dieter Ernst, "The New Mobility of Knowledge: Digital Information Systems and Global Flagship Networks," in Robert Latham and Saskia Sassen, eds., *Digital Formations: Information Technology and New Architectures in the Global Realm* (forthcoming).

4. A good history of Internet development is Janet Abbate, *Inventing the Internet* (Cambridge: MIT Press, 1999).

5. Paul E. Cerrutti, *A History of Modern Computing* (Cambridge: MIT Press, 1998).

6. Richard Rosecrance, *The Rise of the Virtual State: Wealth and Power in the Coming Century* (New York: Basic Books, 1999).

7. For a recent discussion of these efforts, see Secretary of Defense, *Annual Report to the President and the Congress* (August, 15, 2002), Chapter 8. Available at http://www.defenselink.mil/execsec/adr2002/html_files/chap8.htm.

8. Yould in Chapter 3 labels threats from anywhere, anytime, or anybody distributed.

9. The implications of this blurring and the globalization of threats for the field of International Relations is discussed in Robert Keohane, "The Globalization of Informal Violence, Theories of World Politics, and the 'Liberalism of Fear.' " In Craig Calhoun, Paul Price, and Ashley Timmer, eds., *Understanding September 11* (New York: The New Press, 2002), pp 77–91.

10. For a discussion of the exercise, see Computer Science and Telecommunications Board, *Realizing the Potential of C4I: Fundamental Challenges* (Washington, D.C.: National Academies Press, 1999). Knowledge about the exercises, labeled "Eligible Receiver," have been controversial, with some claiming they are hype. See the 1999 Crypt Newsletter discussion at <http://www.soci.niu.edu/~crypt/other/eligib.htm>. See the Bendrath chapter (Chapter 2) as well.

11. See Charles C. Mann, "Homeland Insecurity," *Atlantic Monthly*, September 2002, 82–102.

12. U.S. National Security Council, 1947, cited in Andrew D. Grossman, *Neither Dead Nor Red: Civilian Defense and American Political Development During the Early Cold War* (New York: Routledge, 2001), p 28.

13. Critical Infrastructure Assurance Office, *National Plan for Information Systems Protection* (Washington, D.C., 2000), http://www.ciao.gov/publicaffairs/np1final.pdf.

14. But see David Lyon, *The Electronic Eye: The Rise of Surveillance Society* (Minneapolis: University of Minnesota Press, 1994).

15. An excellent discussion of this is in Eugene Weber, *Peasants into Frenchmen: The Modernization of Modern France, 1870–1914* (Stanford: Stanford University Press, 1976).

16. Cited in Matthew Frye Jacobson, *Barbarian Virtues: The United States Encounters Foreign Peoples at Home and Abroad* (New York: Hill and Wang, 2000), pp 51–52.

17. See Grossman, *Neither Dead Nor Red.*

18. The undersecretary for public diplomacy and public affairs of the U.S. Department of State defines public diplomacy as "engaging, informing, and influencing key international audiences," which it distinguishes from public affairs or "outreach to Americans." Quoted from <http://www.state.gov/r/>.

19. The importance of such support is described in Margaret E. Keck and Kathryn Sikkink, *Activists Beyond Borders: Advocacy Networks in International Politics* (Ithaca, N.Y.: Cornell University Press, 1998).

1. Cyber-security as an Emergent Infrastructure

1. The NIST website has information about best security practices for federal agencies. <http://csrc.nist.gov/fasp/>.

2. For a discussion of networks in the context of conflict and Net wars, see John Arquilla and David Ronfeldt, eds., *Networks and Netwars* (Santa Monica, Calif.: Rand, 2001).

3. David Noack, "Employees, Not Hackers, Greatest Computer Threat," *APB News Center* (January 4, 2000).

4. Dorothy E. Denning, "Is Cyber Terror Next?" The Social Science Research Council, <http://www.ssrc.org/sept11/essays/denning.htm>.

5. Ibid.

6. Barton Gellman, "U.S. Fears Al Qaeda Cyber Attacks," *The Washington Post,* June 26, 2002.

7. Tim McDonald, "CIA to Congress: We're Vulnerable to Cyber-Warfare," *NewsFactor Network* (June 22, 2001).

8. For the latest figures, see http://www.cert.org.

9. mi2g press release, London (January 8, 2002).

10. http://www.messagelabs.com/

11. http://www.truesecure.com/

12. David Moore, Geoffrey M. Voelker, and Stefan Savage, "Inferring Internet Denial-of-Service Activity," Proc. USENIX Security Symposium (August 2001).

13. Riptech Internet Security Threat Report (January 2002), http://www.riptech.com.

14. "Attack on Japan Airline Affected 15,000 Passengers," *Security News Portal* (August 11, 2001).

15. "Sewage Hacker Jailed," *Herald Sun* (Australia) (October 31, 2001).

16. Robert Vamosi, "Cyberterrorists Don't Care About Your PC," *ZDNet Reviews* (July 10, 2002).

17. "Wireless London Is Wide Open," *BBC News* (March 26, 2002).

18. David Moore, "The Spread of the Code-Red Worm (CRv2)," Cooperative Association for Internet Data Analysis (July 2001), http://www.caida.org.

19. Stuart Staniford, Gary Grim, and Roelof Jonkman, "Flash Worms: Thirty Seconds to Infect the Internet," *Silicon Defense* (August 16, 2001).

20. For a description of advanced hacking tools and how to counteract them, see Edward Skoudis, "Faster, Stealthier . . . More Dangerous," in *Information Security* (July 2002), pp 40–49.

21. http://66.129.101/top20.htm

22. Elinor Mills Abreu, "Gates Says Microsoft Security Push Cost $100 Million," Reuters (July 18, 2002).

23. Kevin Soo Hoo, Andrew W. Sudbury, and Andrew R. Jaquith, "Tangible ROI Through Secure Software Engineering, *SBQ,* 1:2 (Fourth Quarter, 2001), pp. 8–10.

24. Ross Anderson, "Security in Open versus Closed Systems—the Dance of Boltzmann, Coase, and Moore" (2002).

25. Lawrence A. Gordon, Martin P. Loeb, Lei Zhou, and Katherine Campbell, "Information Security Breaches: The Economic Effect on Corporations," the University of Maryland, School of Business, May 2002.

26. "How CloudNine Wound Up in Hell," Reuters (February 1, 2002).

27. The Computer Economics Security Review 2002 (April 2002); <http://www.computer economics.com>.

28. "CSI/FBI 2002 Computer Crime and Security Survey," *Computer Security Journal,* XVIII:2 (Spring 2002), pp. 7–30. For a summary, see http://www.gocsi.com/press/20020407.html.

29. @Stake Labs, "Defined Security Creates Efficiencies," *SBQ,* 1:2 (Fourth Quarter, 2001), pp. 10–13.

30. The Economic Impacts of Role-Based Access Control, prepared by RTI International for NIST, March 2002; http://www.nist.gov/director/prog-ofc/report02-1.pdf.

31. Robert Lemos, "Networking Report: No Slump for Security Biz," *ZDNET News* (August 22, 2001).

32. http://www.nsa.gov/isso/programs/coeiae/index.htm

33. See http://csrc.nist.gov/fasp/ for information about NIST's security projects.

34. The Economic Impacts of Role-Based Access Control, prepared by RTI International for NIST, March 2002; http://www.nist.gov/director/prog-ofc/report02-1.pdf.

35. Nicolas Chantler, *Profile of a Computer Hacker* (Seminole, Fla.: Inter.Pact Press, 1997).

36. Ibid.

37. See the Center for Democracy and Technology website, http://www.cdt.org/security/010911 response.shtml.

38. See, for example, http://www.fipr.org/rip/.

39. Will Knight, "Anti-Snooping Operating System Close to Launch," *NewScientist* (May 28, 2002).

40. William A. Arbaugh, William L. Fithen, and John McHugh. "Windows of Vulnerability: A Case Study Analysis," *IEEE Computer,* 33:12 (December 2000), pp. 52–59.

41. http://www.kb.cert.org/vuls/html/disclosure

42. Declan McCullagh, "DeCSS Allies Ganging Up," *Wired News* (January 26, 2001).

43. http://www.cs.cmu.edu/~dst/DeCSS/Gallery/index.html

44. http://conventions.coe.int

45. Abraham D. Sofaer and Seymour E. Goodman, "A Proposal for an International Convention on Cyber Crime and Terrorism," Center for International Security and Cooperation, Stanford University (August 2000).

2. The American Cyber-Angst and the Real World—Any Link?

1. Peter G. Neumann, review of *Pearl Harbor Dot Com* by Winn Schwartau, *Forum on Risks to the Public in Computers and Related Systems* 21:98 (March 29, 2002). <http://catless.ncl.ac.uk/Risks/21.98.html>

2. United Artists, starring Pierce Brosnan as James Bond and directed by Martin Campbell.

3. Tom Clancy and Steve R. Pieczenik, *Tom Clancy's Net Force* (New York: Berkley Publishing Group).

4. Winn Schwartau, *Terminal Compromise* (Tampa, Fla.: Inter-Pact Press, 1991); Winn Schwartau, *Pearl Harbor Dot Com* (Tampa: Inter-Pact Press, 2002).

5. John Arquilla, "The Great Cyberwar of 2002. A WIRED Scenario," *Wired* 6 (February 1998), pp. 122–127, 160–170.

6. National Academy of Sciences, Computer Science and Telecommunications Board, *Computers at Risk: Safe Computing in the Information Age* (Washington, D.C.: National Academy Press, 1991), p. 7.

7. Winn Schwartau of infowar.com already used the term "electronic Pearl Harbor" in June 1991 in a testimony before Congress, see: Winn Schwartau, *Information Warfare: Cyberterrorism—Protecting Your Personal Security in the Electronic Age,* 2nd ed. (New York: Thunder's Mouth Press, 1994), p. 43.

8. Michael A. Dornheim, "Bombs Still Beat Bytes," *Aviation Week & Space Technology* (January 19, 1998), p. 60.

9. "Cyberspace attacks threaten national security, CIA chief says," *CNN* (June 25, 1996).

10. Cf, for example, CIA Director George Tenet, "Remarks to the University of Oklahoma" (September 12, 1997).

11. George Smith, "An Electronic Pearl Harbor? Not likely," *Issues in Science and Technology* 15 (Fall 1998).

12. There is even a special term nowadays for the typical overblown threat warnings: "FUD," for "fear, uncertainty, and doubt."

13. As a seminal text, see John Perry Barlow, "A Declaration of the Independence of Cyberspace" (February 8, 1996), http://www.eff.org/~barlow/Declaration-Final.html.

14. David C. Gompert, "Keeping Information Warfare in Perspective," *RAND Research Review* 19 (Fall 1995).

15. Alan Shapiro, "The Star Trekking of Physics," *Ctheory* (October 9, 1997), <http://www.ctheory.net/text_file?pick=95>.

16. Ulrich Beck, *Risikogesellschaft. Auf dem Weg in eine andere Moderne* (Frankfurt/M.: Suhrkamp Verlag, 1986), p. 73, my translation.

17. For the cyber-threat discourse and its surprisingly small impact on policy decisions, see Ralf Bendrath, "The Cyberwar Debate: Perception and Politics in U.S. Critical Infrastructure Protection," *Information & Security* 7 (2001), pp. 80–103.

18. It was established by Presidential Decision Directive 39, "U.S. Policy on Counterterrorism" 21.6.1995; see: Louis J. Freeh, Director, Federal Bureau of Investigation, "Statement Before the Senate Appropriations Committee Hearing on Counterterrorism" (May 13, 1997).

19. John S. Tritak, Director, Critical Infrastructure Assurance Office, "Statement before the Senate Judiciary Committee Subcommittee on Technology, Terrorism and Government Information" (October 6, 1999).

20. White House, *Presidential Decision Directive/NSC-63, Critical Infrastructure Protection* (May 22, 1998).

21. William Clinton, *Defending America's Cyberspace. National Plan for Information Systems Protection Version 1.0. An Invitation to a Dialogue* (January 7, 2000).

22. George Smith, "Electronic Pearl Harbour," *Crypt Newsletters's Guide to Tech Terminology* (2001), http://sun.soci.niu.edu/~crypt/other/harbor.htm.

23. Wayne Madsen, "Teens a Threat, Pentagon Says," *Wired News* (June 2, 1998).

24. President's Commission on Critical Infrastructure Protection, *Critical Foundations. Protecting America's Infrastructures,* October 13, 1997, p. 14.

25. White House, *"Statement by the Press Secretary Review of Critical Infrastructure Protection and Cyber Security"* (May 9, 2001).

26. John Christensen, "Bracing for guerrilla warfare in cyberspace," *CNN Interactive,* April 6, 1999, http://www.cnn.com/TECH/specials/hackers/cyberterror.

27. Jack Kelley, "Terror groups hide behind Web encryption," *USA Today* (February 6, 2001).

28. United States Congress, *Concurrent Resolution, Expressing the Sense of Congress regarding Internet, Security and Cyberterrorism,* H. CON. RES. 22, introduced in the House of Representatives; Sponsors: Jim Saxton and Saxby Chambliss (February 6, 2001).

29. Currently, encrypting files is very simple and requires only the use of public available programs (see, for example, http://www.pgpi.com) whereas a digital break-in, especially into com-

puters critical for security, requires years of experience in systems and network programming. Additionally, only very few critical systems are connected to public networks. Furthermore, the defacement of websites and the construction of computer viruses are relatively easy to accomplish with only limited experience, especially because there are instructional tools available for this on the Internet. However, this does not pose a serious danger but rather an annoyance, and real hackers ridicule it as "script kiddie" behavior.

30. Peter Spiegel, "FBI warns on web terrorists," *Financial Times,* March 20, 2001.

31. Marc Lacey, "Clinton Gives a Final Foreign Policy Speech," *The New York Times,* December 9, 2000.

32. Lisa M. Bowman, "Cybercrime Fighters: The Feds Want You!" *ZDNet News* (December 11, 2000), http://www.zdnet.com/zdnn/stories/news/0,4586,2663288,00.html.

33. For a detailed analysis, see Ralf Bendrath, "The Cyberwar Debate: Perception and Politics in U.S. Critical Infrastructure Protection," *Information & Security: An International Journal* (2001), pp. 80–103.

34. The Clinton government later decided to call them "states of concern," which was immediately revised by George W. Bush when he became president.

35. United States Senate, Select Committee on Intelligence, *"The Worldwide Threat in 2001" Hearing* (February 7, 2001), transcript at http://www.cluebot.com/articles/01/02/08/1638232.shtml. See, as well, Declan McCullagh, "Feds Say Fidel Is Hacker Threat," *Wired News* (February 9, 2001), http://www.wired.com/news/politics/0,1283,41700,00.html.

36. Frank Tiboni, "Virtually Vulnerable. Civilian Board Warns Pentagon of Gaps in Computer Security," *Defense News* (June 25, 2001), p. 1; see also Office of the Undersecretary of Defense for Aquisition, Technology and Logistics, *Protecting the Homeland. Report of the Defense Science Board Task Force on Defensive Information Operations, 2000 Summer Study,* Volume II, Washington, D.C. (March 2001), ES-2.

37. Larry Wright, Memorandum for the Chairman, Defense Science Board. Subject: Report of the Defense Science Board Task Force on Defensive Information Operations, January 3, 2001.

38. Office of the Undersecretary of Defense for Aquisition, Technology and Logistics, *Protecting the Homeland,* ES-2.

39. Quotes after Kevin Poulsen, "Hack Attacks Called the New Cold War," *The Register,* March 23, 2001, http://www.theregister.co.uk/content/8/17820.html.

40. Bill Gertz, "Military Fears Attacks From Cyberspace," *The Washington Times,* March 29, 2001.

41. One example: Michelle Delio, "It's (Cyber) War: China vs. U.S.," *Wired News* (April 30, 2001), http://www.wired.com/news/print/0,1294,43437,00.html. More examples can be found in Florian Rötzer, "Banges Warten auf den Cyberwar," *telepolis* (May 1, 2001), http://www.telepolis.de/deutsch/special/info/7513/1.html.

42. Attrition.org, *Cyberwar with China: Self-fulfilling Prophecy,* press release (April 29, 2001), http://attrition.org/commentary/cn-us-war.html.

43. Michelle Delio, "FBI Warns of Chinese Hack Threat," *Wired News* (April 27, 2001), http://www.wired.com/news/politics/0,1283,43417,00.html.

44. Gerry J. Gilmore, "Rumsfeld to NATO: Prepare Now for Emerging Threats," in *American Forces Press Service* (June 7, 2001).

45. White House, Office of the Press Secretary, "Remarks by the President in Tax Celebration Event," Des Moines, Iowa June 8, 2001.

46. Andrea Stone, "Cyberspace Is the Next Battlefield. U.S., foreign forces prepare for conflict unlike any before," *USA Today,* June 19, 2001, p. 1. For an ironic reply see Thomas C. Greene, "USA Today as DoD cyber-war propaganda mouthpiece," *The Register,* June 21, 2001, http://www.theregister.co.uk/content/6/19884.html.

47. Lawrence K. Gershwin, "*Cyber Threat Trends and US Network Security.*" Statement for the Record, United States Congress, Joint Economic Committee Hearing. *Wired World: Cyber Security and the U.S. Economy,* June 21, 2001, p. 8f; see as well Thomas C. Greene, " 'Chinaman' dethrones 'Hacker' on cyber-terror hit parade," *The Register,* June 23, 2001, <http://www.theregister.co.uk/content/6/19922.html.>

48. Peter Dizikes, "Clear and Present Danger? Government Warns that Its Computer Systems Need Security Improvements," *ABC News* (August 29, 2001).

49. Kenneth A. Minihan, "Prepared statement before the Senate Governmental Affairs Committee" (June 24, 1998).

50. Leslie G. Wiser, Jr., *Cyber Security. Statement for the Record of the Chief, Training, Outreach, and Strategy Section, National Infrastructure Protection Center, Federal Bureau of Investigation, before the House Committee on Government Affairs Subcommittee on Government Efficiency, Financial Management, and Intergovernmental Relations.* San Jose, California, Field Hearing (August 29, 2001).

51. George I. Seffers, "Spacecom on alert for cyberattacks," *Federal Computer Week* (September 11, 2001), http://www.fcw.com/fcw/articles/2001/0910/web-cyber-09-11-01.asp.

52. InfraGard is a locally based public/private partnership run by the FBI and the private sector. See http://www.infragard.net.

53. Dan Verton, "FBI issues cyberthreat advisory," *Computer World* (September 12, 2001), http://www.computerworld.com/storyba/0,4125,NAV47_STO63755,00.html.

54. John Schwartz, "Computer Network System At Risk for Terrorism," *USA Today,* September 13, 2001.

55. National Infrastructure Protection Center, *ADVISORY 01-020 "Increased Cyber Awareness"* (September 14, 2001).

56. National Infrastructure Protection Center, *Daily Report* (September 9, 2001).

57. George W. Bush, *Executive Order, Establishing the Office of Homeland Security and the Homeland Security Council* (October 8, 2001); George W. Bush, *Homeland Security Presidential Directive 1. Organization and Operation of the Homeland Security Council* (October 29, 2001); George W. Bush, *Executive Order, Critical Infrastructure Protection in the Information Age* (October 16, 2001).

58. White House, Office of the Press Secretary, *Fact Sheet on New Counter-Terrorism and Cyber-Space Positions* (October 9, 2001).

59. Before, the post was called "Senior Director for Critical Infrastructure Protection" and had been held from 1998 until the end of the Clinton Administration by Jeffrey Hunker.

60. Kevin Poulsen, "Justice Department proposal classifies most computer crimes as acts of terrorism," *SecurityFocus* (September 23, 2001), http://www.securityfocus.com/news/257.

61. United States Congress, *Uniting and Strengthening America By Providing Appropriate Tools Required to Intercept and Obstruct Terrorism (USA PATRIOT) Act of 2001,* Public Law 107-56, 26.10.2001, Section 814.

62. John Schwartz, "Cyberspace Seen as Potential Battleground," *The New York Times* (November 23, 2001).

63. Patricia Daukantas, "Professors hash out emergency response, cyberterrorism strategies," *GovernmentComputer News,* December 14, 2001, <http://www.gcn.com.vol1_no1/daily-updates/17642-1.html>. The Powerpoint presentation of Dorothy Denning is available at <http://calder.ncsa.uiuc.edu/ACCESS/PPT/011212mscmc/Denning.ppt>.

64. Brian McWilliams, "Suspect Claims Al Qaeda Hacked Microsoft—Expert," in *Newsbytes* (December 17, 2001), http://www.newsbytes.com/news/01/173039.html.

65. See Ravi Visvesvaraya Prasad, "Hack the Hackers," *Hindustan Times,* December 19, 2000, and Ravi Visvesvaraya Prasad, "Generation Gap," *Hindustan Times,* December 24, 2001.

66. National Infrastructure Protection Center, Advisory 02-001, "Internet Content Advisory: Considering the Unintended Audience" (January 17, 2002).

67. "FBI: Al Qaeda may have probed government sites," in *CNN* (January 17, 2002).

68. Donald H. Rumsfeld, "Statement by the U.S. Secretary of Defense at the NATO North Atlantic Council (NAC-D)," NATO HQ, Brussels (December 18, 2001).

69. Dale L. Watson, "The Terrorist Threat Confronting the United States. Statement for the Record of the Executive Assistant Director on Counterterrorism and Counterintelligence, Federal Bureau of Investigation, before the Senate Select Committee on Intelligence," Washington, D.C. (February 6, 2002).

70. Robert S. Mueller III, "A New FBI Focus. Statement for the Record of the Director. Federal Bureau of Investigation before the Senate Committee on the Judiciary" (June 6, 2002).

71. George J. Tenet, "Worldwide Threat—Converging Dangers in a Post 9/11 World, Testimony of the Director of Central Intelligence, before the Senate Armed Services Committee" (March 19, 2002), p. 3.

72. Thomas R. Wilson, "Global Threats and Challenges. Statement for the Record of the Director, Defense Intelligence Agency, before the Senate Armed Services Committee (March 19, 2002), p. 14f.

73. Shawna McAlearney Amid, "Cyberspace Braces For Escalation and War," *Information Security*, November 29, 2001.

74. "Islamic Cyberterror. Not a matter of if but of when," *Newsweek*, May 20, 2002.

75. "Government Not Ready for Cyberattacks," *Internet News*, June 26, 2002. <http://www.internetnews.com/ent-news/print.php/1377081>.

76. Business Software Alliance, "Government at Risk for Major Cyber Attack in Next 12 Months. IT Pros Say," press release (June 25, 2002).

77. "Is Online Terrorism a Legitimate Threat?" *eMarkter.com* (August 20, 2002), <http://www.emarketer.com/news/article.php?1001517>.

78. "Al-Qaeda Wages Cyber War Against US," Agence France-Presse (June 30, 2002).

79. Ibid.

80. Farhad Manjoo, "The Case of the Missing Code," *Salon.com* (July 17, 2002), <http://www.salon.com/tech/feature/2002/07/17/steganography/index.html>.

81. Jack Kelley, "Militants Wire Web With Links to Jihad," *USA Today*, July 9, 2002.

82. Wesley Clark/Bill Conner, "Vulnerability on the Cyber Front," *The Washington Times*, August 19, 2002.

83. Business Software Alliance, "Government at Risk for Major Cyber Attack in Next 12 Months, IT Pros Say, Press Release" (June 25, 2002).

84. Giles Trendle, "Digital Backlash to War?" *IT-Director.com* (September 12, 2002), <http://www.it-director.com/article.php?id=3191>.

85. Thomas C. Greene, "Mock Cyberwar Fails to End Mock Civilization," *The Register*, August 14, 2002, http://www.theregister.co.uk/content/55/26675.html.

86. Ariana Eunjung Cha/Jonathan Krim, "White House Officials Debating Rules for Cyberwarfare," *The Washington Post*, August 22, 2002.

87. Dan Verton, "White House Cybersecurity Chief Defines Cyberthreat," *Computerworld*, June 9, 2002.

88. James Middleton, "9/11: Cyber Threats Fail to Emerge," in *Personal Computer World*, September 13, 2002.

89. The President's Critical Infrastructure Protection Board, "The National Strategy to Secure Cyberspace—For Comment, Draft" (September 18, 2002).

90. The sectors and their strategies are: Banking and Finance, <http://www.ciao.gov/resource/CS_Banking_Finance_Input_National_Strategy.pdf> and <http://www.ciao.gov/resource/CS_Banking_Finance_Input_National_Strategy_Appendices.pdf>; Chemicals, <http://www.ciao.gov/resource/CS_U.S._Chemicals_Sector_Cyber_Security_Strategy_FINAL.pdf>; Electric Power,

http://www.ciao.gov/resource/CS_Electric_Sector_05-09-02_final.pdf; Higher Education, <http://www.educause.edu/security>; Information Technology & Telecommunications, <http://www.ciao.gov/resource/CS_Information_and_Communications_5-20 02_final.pdf>; Insurance, <http://www.ciao.gov/resource/CS_National_Plan_I14_Insurance_final.pdf>; Oil and Gas, <http://www.ciao.gov/resource/CS_Oil_and_Gas_06-2001_final_version.pdf>; Law Enforcement, <http://www.ciao.gov/resource/CS_Emergency_Law_Enforcement_02-2001_final_input.pdf>; Transportation (Rail), http://www.ciao.gov/resource/CS_Rail_05-02-02_final_version.pdf; Water Systems, http://www.ciao.gov/resource/CS_Water_Sector_07-24-01_final_input.pdf.

91. The President's Critical Infrastructure Protection Board, "The National Strategy to Secure Cyberspace—For Comment, Draft" (September 18, 2002), p. 4.

92. Ibid., p. 3.

93. U.S. Department of Defense, "Quadrennial Defense Review Report," September 30, 2001, p iv.

94. The President's Critical Infrastructure Protection Board, "The National Strategy to Secure Cyberspace—For Comment, Draft" (September 18, 2002), p. 4.

95. See http://www.securecyberspace.gov.

96. Brian Krebs / Robert MacMillan, "White House Slows Cybersecurity Planning," *The Washington Post,* September 16, 2002.

97. Matthew Fordahl, "White House Cybersecurity Plan Avoids Calls For New Rules," Associated Press, September 18, 2002.

98. Dan Verton, "Feds Plan Cybersecurity Center," *Computerworld,* September 2, 2002.

99. mi2g Digital Solutions Engineering, "Link with Terrorism affects Global Hacking," press release, London, February 2, 2002, http://www.mi2g.com/cgi/mi2g/press/020102.php. See <www.mi2g.com/status> for detailed statistics since 1995.

100. *Riptech Internet Security Threat Report,* Volume II (Alexandria: Symantec, July 2002), p 15.

101. Niall McKay, "Cyber Terror Arsenal Grows," *Wired News,* October 16, 1998, <http://www.wired.com/news/politics/0,1283,15643,00.html>.

102. Richard Aldrich, Staff Judge Advocate of the Air Force Office of Special Investigations (AFOSI), "CNA and Law Enforcement," Presentation at the InfowarCon in Washington, D.C. (September 6, 2001).

103. Richard A. Clarke, "Memorandum. Implementation of PDD 63 Through Project Matrix," Critical Infrastructure Assurance Office, July 19, 2000.

104. Robert Lemos, "Data on Internet Threats Still Out Cold," *CNET News.* January 21, 2002, http://news.com.com/2100-1001-819521.html.

105. John Schwartz, "Year After 9/11, Cyberspace Door Is Still Ajar," *The New York Times,* September 9, 2002, p. 9.

106. Michelle Delio, "MS Refocuses on Software Pirates," *Wired News,* January 22, 2002, http://www.wired.com/news/print/0,1294,49856,00.html.

107. Joshua Dean, "Nation Unprepared for Cyber War, Experts Say," *Government Executive Daily Briefing* (December 19, 2001), http://www.govexec.com/dailyfed/1201/121901jl.htm.

108. Church of Scientology International, "Statement Regarding Copyright Infringers and Google," April 2002, http://www.politechbot.com/p-03917.html.

109. See Marc Rotenberg in this volume.

110. Quoted after Bill Wallace, "Terrorism Over the Internet is an Unlikely Scenario," *San Francisco Chronicle,* July 8, 2002.

3. Beyond the American Fortress: Understanding Homeland Security in the Information Age

1. Section 3(c)(1), Homeland Defense Bill, H.R. 1158, introduced to the United States House of Representatives (1st Session of the 107th Congress) on March 21, 2001, by Representative William Thornberry.

2. Ibid., Section 2(1).

3. I have followed the example of the Center for Strategic and International Studies (CSIS) in using "CBRN (chemical, biological, radiological, nuclear) attacks" as opposed to the more common "WMD" (weapons of mass destruction). "CBRN attack" is more precise in specifying the kinds of weapons under discussion without conflating the means with an assumed end. Mass destruction may not be the outcome of every CBRN attack. Likewise, it may be achieved by means other than CBRN weapons.

4. A particularly engaging account of these events can be found in Katie Hafner and Matthew Lyon, *Where Wizards Stay Up Late: The Origins of the Internet* (New York: Simon & Schuster, 1996).

5. See Sun Tzu's *The Art of War.* Though the date of this work remains contested, most authorities now agree that the main body of the text was produced by a single individual during the Warring States Period (c. 453–221 BC). The assertion of Chinese scholar Ralph Sawyer that ". . . in every sphere, Sun Tzu's *Art of War* predominates, eclipsing all the other [ancient Chinese] military writings combined" is indicative of the widely held view that *The Art of War* is the most influential strategic text ever written. One particularly well-prepared translation for the nonspecialist (and the source of the preceding quote) is Ralph D. Sawyer, *Sun Tzu: Art of War* (Boulder, Col.: Westview Press, 1994).

6. See Peter J. Hugill, *Global Communications Since 1844: Geopolitics and Technology* (Baltimore: The Johns Hopkins University Press, 1999), and Christopher R. Gabel, *Railroad Generalship: Foundations of Civil War Strategy* (Washington, D.C.: Government Printing Office, 1997).

7. By "security-related sector" I mean each of the five security spheres associated with the twentieth-century conception of total war—namely, the territorial sphere, the infrastructural sphere, the economic sphere, the societal sphere, and the transatmospheric/space sphere. For additional discussion regarding the implications of contemporary IT and security debates for these sectors as traditionally understood, see the Introduction to this volume.

8. Colin S. Gray, "Thinking Asymmetrically in Times of Terror," *Parameters* (Spring 2002), pp. 5–14.

9. Section 2 of the bill, titled "Definitions," notes that ". . . for the purposes of this Act . . . 'American homeland' or 'homeland' means the United States, in a geographic sense."

10. The three additional budget priorities are allocated 45% of the homeland security expenditure requested by the Bush Administration for FY2003 and represent those initiatives that are to be managed outside the Department of Homeland Security. They are broadly defined as follows: 1) Department of Defense Homeland Security (outside initiatives); 2) Other non–Department of Defense Homeland Security; and 3) Aviation Security.

11. Not addressed in the following section is the "insider threat." The insider threat refers to the risks associated with individuals who have internal access to targeted systems due to their membership with or employment by the organization that owns or operates said systems. The insider threat is of considerable significance to this debate. It has far-reaching implications for each form of cyber-aggression described here, as internal knowledge of a system and the possibility of internally implemented attacks heighten the likelihood of successfully executed tactics while lowering the probability that breaches will be detected. Though undoubtedly important, the numerous variations of the insider threat and the corresponding consequences for each form of cyber-aggression prevent comprehensive treatment of the topic within the purview of this chapter. Rather, I have chosen to focus upon the primary forms of cyber-aggression, each of which might be rendered more robust and effective through the integration of insider elements. For more detailed information on the insider threat, please refer to Dorothy Denning's chapter in this volume.

12. The vast range of meanings associated with the term "information warfare" precludes exhaustive treatment here. While some commentators treat "information warfare" as synonymous with "cyber-war," others consider it to be a broad umbrella term encompassing all tactics that make use of information exchange. For instance, though the coalition forces have targeted ele-

ments of Iraq's information infrastructure, such as the Information Ministry and television broadcasting facilites, most explicit references to "information warfare" in the coverage of the 2003 Gulf War allude to varieties of psychological warfare intended to win over the hearts and minds of Iraqi people through the distribution of leaflets and humanitarian aid. The breadth of meaning renders the term rather vague and difficult to deploy in any meaningful way.

13. Arnaud de Borchgrave, et al.'s, *Cyber Threats and Information Security: Meeting the 21st Century Challenge* (Washington, D.C.: Center for Strategic and International Studies, December 2000), cites a series of probes into various United States governmental, academic, and corporate systems as one such example. The sustained security breaches, which appear to have been administered from Russia, were undertaken successfully for an entire year before being detected in 1999.

14. Joel C. Willemssen, "Computer Security: Critical Federal Operations and Assets Remain at Risk." GAO Testimony (GAO/T-AIMD-00-314), September 11, 2000.

15. Borchgrave, et al., *Cyber Threats and Information Security.*

16. The contemporary Greek historian Herodotus (c. 484 BC–?) remains the principal source of information for these events.

17. See, for example, the writings of Chinese historian Ssu-ma Ch'ien (c. 145?–85 BC), who describes the mounted warfare tactics of the Hsiung-nu in terms almost identical to those invoked by Herodotus in his writings about the Scythian nomadic tribes that threatened ancient Greece.

18. Elaine C. Kamarck, "Applying 21st-Century Government to the Challenge of Homeland Security," *The New Ways to Manage Series* (New York: Price Waterhouse Coopers Endowment for the Business of Government, June 2002), p. 19.

19. Ibid., p. 17.

20. Message to the Congress of the United States from President George W. Bush introducing the proposed legislation to create a new Department of Homeland Security (June 18, 2002).

4. Toward a Theory of Border Control

1. The largest source of emergent diseases is likely to be the tropics. Granted, the threat from multiple-drug-resistant tuberculosis is probably greater from the former Soviet Union, and many disease vectors such as the mosquitoes that carry dengue disease cannot survive temperate climates. However, U.S. populations are more likely to carry resistance to temperate-climate diseases, and doctors know what to look for; the same cannot be said for tropical diseases.

2. Border control may require inspecting what comes in as well as what comes out. One purpose is to ensure that people who have *already* done harm cannot escape interrogation or prosecution by fleeing. Similarly, although the more lurid threats from cyber-intrusions are couched in terms of loss of control or corrupted information, it is often more cost-effective to exploit illicit entry by copying and exporting sensitive files. Detecting exploitation often requires knowing what leaves the system. On the other hand, in the case of war, killing an enemy on the way in or the way out can often be a negligible distinction.

3. Bad guys have also been kept out by questioning and then searching those who exhibit suspicious behavior; the terrorist who tried to bomb LAX airport in late 1999 was caught that way.

5. The Transformation of Global Surveillance

1. David Kahn, *The Codebreakers: The Comprehensive History of Secret Communication from Ancient Times to the Internet* (New York: Scribners, 1996), p. 3.

2. The significant piece of this communication is the date and time requested for a diplomatic meeting: 1 P.M. on a Sunday afternoon. That is an unusual time to schedule a diplomatic meeting. Lieutenant Commander Alwin Kramer, who headed the translation section of the Navy, which had intercepted the communication, realized that the odd time of the requested meeting

was significant and quickly discerned that 1 P.M. in Washington would be early morning in Hawaii (Kahn, pp. 3–4).

3. During Christmas 1994, hijackers sought to fly Air France flight 8969, a fuel-laden A300 Airbus, into the Eiffel Tower. Another terrorist talked about crashing a plane into the CIA building. During the summer of 2001, there had been "lots of chatter in the system" and the U.S. government alerted U.S. airlines of general hijacking threats. In August 2001, Zacharias Moussaoui had been arrested in Minneapolis for visa violations after a flight instructor alerted the FBI because of his concern about Moussaoui's attitude and behavior. An FBI agent in Phoenix was disturbed by the number of Arab men training at U.S. flight schools and wrote a memo describing the possibility that Al Qaeda operatives were training to pilot passenger planes. The dots were not connected until afterward. (Indeed, it was not until late May 2002 that FBI Director Robert Mueller acknowledged that the September 11 attack might have been preventable had the FBI put the information at its disposal together [Neil Lewis, "F.B.I. Chief Admits 9/11 Might Have Been Detectable," *The New York Times,* May 30, 2002, A1].)

4. A system for anonymous e-mail; see <http://www.obscura.com/~loki/remailer/remailer-essay.html; source code is at http://sourceforge.net/projects/mixmaster/>.

5. A system for anonymous web surfing; see http://www.anonymizer.com.

6. A system to prevent electronic eavesdropping and traffic analysis; see <http://www.onion-routing.net>.

7. William Broad, "A Nation Challenged: Domestic Security; U.S. Is Tightening Rules on Keeping Scientific Secrets," *The New York Times,* February 17, 2002, p. A1.

8. Tim Weiner, "How a Spy Left Taiwan in the Cold," *The New York Times,* December 20, 1997, p. A7.

9. William Broad, "Evading the Soviet Ear at Glen Cove," *Science,* vol. 217 (3), September, pp. 910–911.

10. The plane that was intercepted and made an emergency landing in Hainan, China, in March 2001 was on just such a surveillance mission.

11. Whitfield Diffie and Susan Landau, *Privacy on the Line: The Politics of Wiretapping and Encryption* (Boston: MIT Press, 1998), p. 89.

12. Duncan Campbell, *Interception Capabilities 2000.* "Report to the Director General for Research of the European Parliament (Scientific and Technical Options Assessment Programme Office) on the Development of Surveillance Technology and Risk of Abuse of Economic Information," PE 168.184/Part 3/4, Luxembourg (April 1999), p. 7.

13. Seymour Hersh, "The Intelligence Gap," *The New Yorker,* November 29, 1999, pp. 58–76.

14. Patrick Beesley, *Very Special Intelligence: The Story of the Admiralty's Operational Intelligence Center* (London: Hamilton, 1977).

15. Diffie and Landau, *Privacy on the Line,* p. 90.

16. Peter Wright, *Spy Catcher: The Candid Autobiography of a Senior Intelligence Official* (New York: Viking, 1987), pp. 52–53.

17. Diffie and Landau, *Privacy on the Line,* p. 259.

18. Seymour Hersh, "The Intelligence Gap," p. 59.

19. The *Liberty* was strafed by Israeli warplanes during the 1967 Six-Day War in what was claimed to be an accident and has never been fully explained. Thirty-four men were killed. The *Pueblo* was captured by the North Koreans while on an intelligence mission off the Korean peninsula; one American was killed, and the remaining eighty-two members of the *Pueblo*'s crew were held by the North Koreans for eleven months.

20. COCOM's membership included the United States, most Western European nations, Australia, New Zealand, and Japan.

21. Jeffrey Richelson and Desmond Ball, *The Ties that Bind: Intelligence Cooperation between the*

UKUSA Countries—the United Kingdom, the United States of America, Canada, Australia, and New Zealand (North Sydney: Allen and Unwin, 1985), pp. 4–5.

22. Ibid, p. 143.

23. Nicky Hager, *Secret Power: New Zealand's Role in the International Spy Network* (New Zealand: Craig Potton Publishing, 1996).

24. Duncan Campbell, "Interception Capabilities 2000."

25. European Parliament, Temporary Committee on the ECHELON Interception System, "Draft Report on the existence of a global system for the interception of private and commercial communications (ECHELON Interception System)," May 18, 2001.

26. Isambard Wilkinson, "U.S. Wins Spain's Favour with Offer to Share Spy Network Material," *Sydney Morning Herald,* June 18, 2001.

27. Whitfield Diffie and Susan Landau, "September 11th Did Not Change Cryptography Policy," *Notices of the American Mathematical Society,* April 2002, pp. 450–454, p. 453. A longer version of this paper, "The Export of Cryptography in the 20th Century and the 21st," appeared in Jeanie Treichel and Mary Holzer, eds., *Sun Microsystems Laboratories: The First Ten Years,* 2001, Technical Report 2001-102, http://www.research.sun.com/research/tenyears/volcd/papers/diffie.htm.

28. James Bamford, *Body of Secrets: Anatomy of the Ultra-Secret National Security Agency* (New York: Doubleday, 2001), pp. 409–411.

29. Ibid, pp. 414–415.

30. Ibid, pp. 421.

31. James Woolsey, "Why We Spy on Our Allies," *The Wall Street Journal,* March 17, 2000.

32. Diffie and Landau, *Privacy on the Line,* p. 87.

33. Campbell, "Interception Capabilities 2000," p. 7.

34. In the summer of 2000, Americans discovered that there was also domestic surveillance of the Internet, when the FBI revealed that it had developed a system named "Carnivore" for wiretapping the Net (Neil King Jr. and Ted Bridis, "FBI Wiretaps to Scan E-Mail Spark Concern," *The Wall Street Journal,* July 11, 2000, p. A3). The FBI argued that it was empowered to do such searches under the various wiretapping laws (see next section). This was a matter of some dispute, since the laws to which the FBI was referring make a distinction between content and transactional information, a distinction that is inherent in telephone technology but not in Internet packet-switching technology. Congress considered addressing these issues, perhaps with new legislation, and then September 11 intervened. The USA PATRIOT Act includes provisions for electronic surveillance of the Internet, establishing a legal basis for Carnivore-like systems.

35. Diffie and Landau, *Privacy on the Line,* p. 200.

36. William Broad, "Evading the Soviet Ear at Glen Cove."

37. Campbell, "Interception Capabilities 2000," p. 1.

38. United States, Senate Select Committee to Study Governmental Operations with Respect to Intelligence Activities, *Supplementary Staff Reports on Intelligence Activities and the Rights of Americans,* Book II, Report 94-755, Ninety-fourth Congress, Second Session, April 23, 1976, p. 12.

39. Foreign Intelligence Surveillance Court, United States, "In Re All Matters Submitted to the Foreign Intelligence Surveillance Court: Memorandum Opinion," May 17, 2002, p. 12.

40. Al Webb, " 'Spy' Cameras vs. Villains in Britain," *UPI* (March 8, 2002).

41. Stephen Bailey, David Harris, and B. L. Jones, *Civil Liberties: Cases and Materials* (London: Butterworths, 1991).

42. Command 9438, paragraph 10, as cited in Ibid, p. 148.

43. Duncan Campbell, *Signals Intelligence and Human Rights—the ECHELON Report* (draft), (August 8, 2000), p. 77.

44. Ibid.

45. Ibid.

46. Nicky Hager, *Secret Power,* p. 8.

47. Campbell, "Interception Capabilities 2000," p. 3.

48. Ibid.

49. If an encryption algorithm is properly designed, then the difficulty of unauthorized decryption is determined by the number of bits in the key; an increase of one bit doubles the cost to the intruder. It is often taken for granted that cryptosystems are as strong as their keys suggest and thus it is common to speak of forty-bit cryptography, meaning both that the keys are forty bits long and that breaking the system takes approximately a trillion encryptions. See Diffie and Landau, "September 11th Did Not Change Cryptography Policy," p. 451.

50. Susan Landau, "Standing the Test of Time: The Data Encryption Standard," *Notices of the American Mathematical Society,* March 2000, pp. 341–349.

51. Campbell, "Interception Capabilities 2000."

52. Australia, Canada, Czech Republic, Hungary, Japan, Norway, New Zealand, Poland, Switzerland, and the United States.

53. The EU change was not the only reason that the U.S. government finally loosened controls on encryption policy. There was also the increasing untenability of the controls. There was the lawsuit by Daniel Bernstein, which threatened to lead to a court decision that export control impinged on free speech. There was the government need to be able to purchase commercial off-the-shelf technology that already had strong encryption embedded in it. The EU change, however, was instrumental in the change in United States policy occurring at that particular time.

54. Nonmembers can sign Council of Europe treaties. Canada, Japan, South Africa, and the United States were involved in the drafting of the cyber-crime convention, and it is likely that some of these nations will sign.

55. Seymour Hersh, "The Intelligence Gap."

56. Another particularly interesting example of this is the reconstruction of Timothy McVeigh's time in Junction City, Kansas, where he rented the Ryder truck that he used to bomb the Murrah Building in Oklahoma City. See Diffie and Landau, *Privacy on the Line,* p. 119.

57. Seymour Hersh, "The Intelligence Gap." One example: On September 10, NSA intercepted two Al Qaeda messages that the agency translated on the twelfth to "Tomorrow is zero day," and "The match begins tomorrow." See Josh Meyer, Janet Hook, and Eric Lichtblau, "September 11 Alerts Translated Too Late," *Los Angeles Times,* June 21, 2002. However, it is not clear that translation on September 10 would have had any effect on the events of eleventh.

58. Foreign Intelligence Surveillance Court, United States, "In Re All Matters Submitted to the Foreign Intelligence Surveillance Court: Memorandum Opinion," May 17, 2002. Foreign Intelligence Surveillance Court, United States, "In Re All Matters Submitted to the Foreign Intelligence Surveillance Court: Order (docket number 02-249)," May 17, 2002.

59. Foreign Intelligence Surveillance Court, United States, "In Re All Matters Submitted to the Foreign Intelligence Surveillance Court: Memorandum Opinion," p. 11.

60. Ibid., p. 15.

61. Ibid.

62. Philip Shenon, "Court Comes to Life Over Ruling on Post 9/11 Police Powers," *The New York Times,* August 27, 2002, p. A12.

63. United States Foreign Intelligence Court of Review, "On Motions for Review of Orders of the United States Foreign Intelligence Surveillance Court (Nos. 02-622 and 02-968)," November 18, 2002.

64. Andrews, *Privacy and Human Rights 2002,* p. 282.

65. Stuart Millar, "Europe Votes to Sweep Away Data Privacy," *Manchester Guardian Weekly,* June 6–12, 2002, p. 7.

66. Ibid.

6. Privacy and Secrecy After September 11

1. Executive director, Electronic Privacy Information Center (EPIC), and adjunct professor, Georgetown University Law Center. Former counsel, Senate Judiciary Committee (Senator Patrick Leahy). This article originally appeared in the *Minnesota Law Review,* vol. 86, no. 6, pp. 1115–1135 (June 2002). Thanks to Mikal J. Condon for research assistance, and to Matthew Wegner and the *Minnesota Law Review* for organizing this symposium. Thanks also to Professor Paul Schwartz for his encouragement and Professor Daniel Soloye for his dedication.

2. See, e.g., "ABC News/Washington Post Terrorist Attack Poll #3," *ABC News/Washington Post,* September 29, 2001 (indicating high levels of public support for expanded government surveillance, use of wiretap authority, and ID cards in the wake of the September 11 attacks); Robert O'Harrow Jr. and Jonathon Krim, "A Changing America: National ID Cards Gaining Support," *The Washington Post,* December 17, 2001, p. A1 (indicating nearly 70% support for some form of national ID). But see "E-Government Poll," *The Washington Post,* February 27, 2002, p. A21 (finding that Americans are sharply divided on the issue of national ID cards, with only 47% in support of a national ID, and 44% viewing it as "an invasion of people's civil liberties and privacy"); Roper Center for Public Opinion Research, *Bureau of Justice Sourcebook of Criminal Justice Statistics* (1994) (illustrating long-standing public opposition [by three to one] to use of electronic surveillance as an acceptable investigative technique).

3. See, e.g., National Defense Authorization Act for Fiscal Year 2002, Pub. L. No. 107-107, 115 Stat. 1654 (2001); Defense Appropriations Act, 2002, Pub. L. No. 107-117, 115 Stat. 2230 (2002); Departments of Commerce, Justice, and State, the Judiciary, and Related Agencies Appropriations Act, 2002, Pub. L. No. 107-77, 115 Stat. 748 (2001): Uniting and Strengthening America by Providing Appropriate Tools Required to Intercept and Obstruct Terrorism Act (USA PATRIOT Act) of 2001, Pub. L. No. 107-56, 15 Stat. 272 (2001).

4. See Barnaby J. Feder, "A Surge in Demand to Use Biometrics," *The New York Times* December 17, 2001, p. C21, available at http://www.nytimes.com/2001/12/17/technology/17IRIS.html; O'Harrow and Krim, "A Changing America."

5. See United States v. Scarfo, 180 F. Supp. 2d 572 (D.N.J. 2001) (upholding the use of the Classified Information Procedures Act in a case involving a low-level mobster).

6. Communications Assistance for Law Enforcement Act (CALEA) of 1994. Pub. L. No. 103-414, 108 Stat. 4279 (codified at 47 U.S.C. §§ 1001-1010 [1995]).

7. The law-enforcement provision in the Subscriber Privacy provision in the Cable Communications Policy Act of 1984 (the Cable Act) provides a good example:

> Except as provided in subsection (c)(2)(D) of this section, a governmental entity may obtain personally identifiable information concerning a cable subscriber pursuant to a court order only if, in the court proceeding relevant to such court order—
>
> (1) such entity offers clear and convincing evidence that the subject of the information is reasonably suspected of engaging in criminal activity and that the information sought would be material evidence in the case; and (2) the subject of the information is afforded the opportunity to appear and contest such entity's claim.
>
> Pub. L. No. 98-549, 98 Stat. 2779 (1984) (codified as amended at 47 U.S.C. § 551(h) [2002]).

8. Title III of the Omnibus Crime Control and Safe Streets Act of 1968, Pub. L. No. 90-351, 82 Stat. 197 (1968) (codified as amended at 18 U.S.C. §§ 2510–2522 [1994]); *Olmstead* v. *United States,* 277 U.S. 438 (1928); *Katz* v. *United States,* 389 U.S. 347 (1967).

9. 425 U.S. 435 (1976).

10. 416 U.S. 21 (1974).

11. The Cable Act, 47 U.S.C. § 551(h) (2002). See also Right to Financial Privacy Act. Pub. L. No. 95-630, 92 Stat. 3697 (1978) (codified at 12 U.S.C. § 3401 [1994]); Electronic Communications Privacy Act (ECPA), Pub. L. No. 99-508, 100 Stat. 1848 (1986) (codified as amended at 18 U.S.C. §§ 2510-2522 [1994]); Privacy Protection Act, Pub. L. No. 96-440, 94 Stat. 1879 (1980) (codified as a amended at 42 U.S.C. § 2000aa-2000aa-12 [1994]).

12. See note 10; see also Video Privacy Protection Act, Pub. L. 100-618, 102 Stat. 3195 (1988) (codified as amended at 18 U.S.C. §§ 2710-2711 [2000]); Family Educational Rights & Privacy Act (FERPA), Pub. L. No. 93-380, 88 Stat. 571 (1974) (codified as amended in scattered sections of 47 U.S.C.).

13. See Health Insurance Portability and Accountability Act (HIPAA) of 1996, Pub. L. No. 104-191, 110 Stat. 1936 (1996) (codified in various provisions in 42 U.S.C. and 29 U.S.C.).

14. See Gramm-Leach-Bliley Act of 1999, Pub. L. No. 106-102, 113 Stat. 1338 (1999).

15. Elementary and Secondary Education Act Authorization Bill, Pub. L. No. 107-110 § 1061, 115 Stat. 1425 (2002).

16. Among the statutes amended by the USA PATRIOT Act are The Right to Financial Privacy, 12 U.S.C. § 3414; Consumer Credit Protection Act, 15 U.S.C. § 1681u; The Computer Fraud and Abuse Act, 18 U.S.C. § 1030; Additional Grounds for Issuing Warrant under Title II, 18 U.S.C. §3103; ECPA, 18 U.S.C. §§ 2510, 2511, 2516, 2517, 2520, 2702, 2703, 2707, 2709, 2711, 3066, 3121, 3124, 3127; FERPA, 20 U.S.C. §§ 1232g, 9007; The Cable Act, 47 U.S.C. § 551; The Foreign Intelligence Surveillance Act (FISA), 50 U.S.C. §§ 1803, 1804, 1805, 1806, 1823, 1824, 1842, 1843, 1861–1863 (1994 and Supp. 1998). See generally USA PATRIOT Act, Pub. L. No. 107-56, 15 Stat. 272 (various provisions amending language in each of the aforementioned statutes).

17. USA PATRIOT Act. Pub. L. No. 107-56, §§ 206, 216, 218, 115 Stat. 272 (2001).

18. Ibid. §§ 206–208, 214–215, 218, 225.

19. Ibid. § 213.

20. See U.S. Bureau of Prisons Special Administrative Measure for the Prevention of Acts of Violence and Terrorism, 66 Fed. Reg. 55,062 (2001) (to be codified at 28 C.F.R. pts. 500–501).

21. See Federal-Local Information Sharing Partnership Act of 2001, S. 1615, 107th Cong. (2001).

22. Peter Slevin, "Ashcroft Blocks FBI Access to Gun Records; Critics Call Attorney General's Decision Contradictory in Light of Terror Probe Tactics," *The Washington Post*, December 7, 2001, p. A26.

23. See, e.g., "E-Government Poll," supra note 2: Bill Miller, "Ridge to Brief Senators About Border Security; Session Conflicts With Byrd Hearing," *The Washington Post*, May 2, 2002, p. A2; O'Harrow and Krim, supra note 2: Robert O'Harrow Jr., "Facial Recognition System Considered for U.S. Airports, Reagan National May Get Scanning Device," *The Washington Post*, September 24, 2001, p. A14.

24. See Harris Poll, "Overwhelming Public Support for Increasing Surveillance Powers and, Despite Concerns about Potential Abuse, Confidence that the Powers Will be Used Properly," http://www.harrisinteractive.com/news/all-newsbydate.asp?NewsID=370 (October 3, 2001) (indicating that 68% of the public polled supports national identification cards).

25. Elise Ackerman and Paul Rogers, "ID Card Idea Attracts High-level Support: Top executives, lawmakers back national identification card proposal," *San Jose Mercury News*, October 16, 2001, p. 1A; Alan M. Dershowitz, "Why Fear National ID Cards?" *The New York Times*, October 13, 2001, p. A23; Press Release, "Senator Feinstein Identifies Weaknesses of U.S. Visa System," October 12, 2001, http://feinstein.senate.gov/releases01/s-visas.htm.

26. See *Oversight Hearing on "National Identification Card" Before the Subcomm. on Government Efficiency, Financial Management, and Intergovernmental Relations of the House Committee on Gov't Reform, 107th Cong.* (2001) [hereinafter *Oversight Hearing*] (statement of Representative Horn, chairman, House Committee on Government Reform); see also O'Harrow and Krim, supra note 2. ("[T]he political hurdles to a national ID card remain huge. President Bush has publicly downplayed their benefits, saying they're unnecessary to improve security. Bush's new cyberspace security chief, Richard Clarke, recently said he does 'not think it's a very smart idea.' ")

27. See *Oversight Hearing*, supra note 26 (statement of Ben Schneiderman, professor of Computer Science, University of Maryland), "We must ask whether there is now a secure data base that consists of 300 million individual records that can be accessed in real time? The government

agencies which come close are the Internal Revenue Service and the Social Security Administration, neither of which are capable of maintaining a network that is widely accessible and responsive to voluminous queries on a 24 hour by 7 days a week basis." Peter G. Neumann and Lauren Weinstein, "Risks of National Identity Cards," 44 Committee of the ACM 176 (2001); Bruce Schneier, "National ID Cards," *Crypto-gram Newsletter,* <http://www.counterpane.com/crypto-gram-0112.html#1> (December 15, 2001).

28. See Donna Leinwand, "National ID in Development, But Enthusiasm for the System Appears to be Fading, Poll Says," *USA Today,* January 22, 2002, p. 2A; Julia Scheeres, "Support for ID Cards Waning," *Wired News,* March 13, 2002, <http://www.wired.com/news/business/0,136,51000,00.html>.

29. See American Association of Motor Vehicle Administrations, "Special Task Force on Identification Security Report to the AAMVA Board," at <http://www.aamva.org/documents/private/idsecuritytaskforce/drvidsecuritytaskforcerecommendations.pdf> (January 2002); see also Robert O'Harrow Jr., "States Devising Plan for High-Tech National Identification Cards," *The Washington Post,* November 3, 2001, p. A10.

30. See "E-Government Poll," supra note 1; EPIC, "Your Papers, Please: From the State Drivers License to a National Identification System," <http://www.epic.org/privacy/id_cards/yourpapersplease.pdf> (opposing the AAMVA plan); Shane Ham and Robert D. Atkinson, "Progressive Policy Institute Report: Modernizing the State Identification System," <http://www.ppionline.org/documents/Smart_Ids_Feb_02.pdf> (February 7, 2002).

31. See Robert O'Harrow Jr., "Facial Recognition System Considered for U.S. Airports," *The Washington Post,* September 23, 2001, p. A14; Robert O'Harrow Jr., "D.C. Plans ID Card for Students; Aim of DMV Database is Missing Children," *The Washington Post,* August 15, 2001, p. A1; Bob Hirschfeld. "Security Is Watching," *TECH TV* (January 11, 2002), at <http://www.techtv.com/news/culture/story/0,24195,338-7924,00.html>.

32. See Karen Alexander, "Airport to Get Facial Recognition Technology" *L.A. Times,* October 29, 2001, p. B1; O'Harrow, "Facial Recognition System Considered for U.S. Airports," supra note 31; see also "Interest in face scanning grows: Makers of technology struggle to meet demand since attacks," Reuters (September 18, 2001), http://www.msnbc.com/news/630735.asp. ("'Right now what we need to do is build our defenses, as we need to protect innocent lives and prevent this from happening again,' said Visionics CEO Joseph Attick.")

33. See Liz Anderson, "At the Assembly—About Face," *The Providence Journal-Bulletin,* January 17, 2002, p. B1 (reporting that T.F. Green International Airport in Providence, Rhode Island, one of the first airports to consider facial recognition technology, decided in January 2002 that they would not install it after all, citing the possibility of false matches and other technological shortcomings of facial-recognition systems).

34. Amitai Etzioni, *The Limits of Privacy* (New York: Basic Books, 1999), p. 107.

35. Ibid.

36. Jennifer Lee, "Putting Parolees on a Tighter Leash," *The New York Times,* January 31, 2002, p. G1.

37. Ibid.

38. USA PATRIOT Act, Pub. L. No. 107-56, §§ 206, 216, 218, 115 Stat. 272 (2001).

39. Katz v. United States, 389 U.S. 347, 363–64 (1967) (White, J., concurring) (noting that the Katz holding does not preclude a national security exception to the warrant requirement for wiretapping). But see id. at 359 (Douglas and Brennan, JJ., concurring) (objecting to Justice White giving a "green light for the Executive Branch to resort to electronic eavesdropping without a warrant in cases which the Executive Branch itself labels 'national security' matters").

40. Ibid., p. 359.

41. Ibid.

42. FISA, 50 U.S.C. §§ 1801–1829, 1841–1846 (2002).

43. Compare 18 U.S.C. § 2518 with 50 U.S.C. § 1803.

44. See generally Patrick S. Poole, "Inside America's Secret Court: The Foreign Intelligence Surveillance Court," http://fly.hiwaay.net/~pspoole/fiscshort.html.

45. "Memorandum from John Ashcroft, Attorney General, to Heads of all Federal Departments and Agencies re: The Freedom of Information Act" (October 12, 2001) [hereinafter "Ashcroft FOIA Memorandum"], available at http://www.usdoj.gov/04foia/011012.htm.

46. See "Memorandum from Janet Reno, Attorney General, to Heads of all Federal Departments and Agencies re: The Freedom of Information Act 3" (October 4, 1993), available at <http://www.usdoj.gov/oip/foia_updates/Vol_XIV_3/page3.htm> (urging agencies toward greater openness under FOIA, with an overall "presumption of disclosure," establishing a new "foreseeable harm" standard governing the application of FOIA exemptions, and promoting "discretionary" FOIA disclosures as a means of achieving the goal of "maximum responsible disclosure" under the act).

47. See Tom Beierle and Ruth Greenspan Bell, "Don't let 'right to know' be a war casually," *The Christian Science Monitor,* December 20, 2001, p. 9; editorial, "On the Public's Right to Know; The Day Ashcroft Censored Freedom of Information," *San Francisco Chronicle,* January 6, 2002, p. D4; editorial, "Ashcroft sends a chilling message FOIA: Memo urging caution over freedom of information requests needs to be reviewed," *Ventura County Star-Free Press,* January 11, 2002, p. B6; Helen Thomas, "President Bush and John Ashcroft Trample the Bill of Rights," *Seattle Post-Intelligencer,* November 16, 2001, p. B6.

48. See "Ashcroft FOIA Memorandum," supra note 45; see also "Testimony of Attorney General John Ashcroft before the Senate Committee on the Judiciary" (December 6, 2001), available at http://www.usdoj.gov/ag/speeches/2001/1206transcriptsenatejudiciarycommittee.htm.

49. E.g., CBS News, *Face the Nation* (CBS television broadcast, September 16, 2001), available at http://www.cbsnews.com/stories/2001/09/17/ftn/main311563.shtml. (Senator Shelby, ranking minority member of Senate Intelligence Committee, referred to the terrorist attacks as "a massive intelligence failure.")

50. USA PATRIOT Act, Pub. L. No. 107-56, § 213, 115 Stat. at 285-86 (amending the U.S. Code to allow for delayed notification of the execution of a warrant).

51. Former CIA director R. James Woolsey alleged in a *Wall Street Journal* editorial in mid-October that the use of "weapon-grade" made clear that Saddam Hussein was responsible for the dissemination of anthrax in the nation's capitol. R. James Woolsey, "The Iraq Connection," *The Wall Street Journal,* October 18, 2001, at http://opinionjournal.com/editorial/feature.html?id=95001338. Subsequent reporting by *The Washington Post* and other newspapers established that the anthrax was almost certainly obtained from a U.S. lab. See also the report of the Federation of American Scientists on the profile of the likely perpetrator, a U.S.-trained scientist at http://www.fas.org/bwc/news/anthraxreport.htm. Rick Weiss and Susan Schmidt, "Capitol Hill Anthrax Matches Army's Stock: 5 Labs Can Trace Spores to Ft. Detrick," *The Washington Post,* December 16, 2001, p. A1; Rick Weiss and Dan Eggen, "US Says Anthrax Germ in Mail is 'Ames' Strain: Microbe is of Type Commonly Used in Research," *The Washington Post,* October 26, 2001, in A8.

52. See generally Etzioni, *The Limits of Privacy.*

53. Amitai Etzioni, "You'll Love Those National ID Cards," *The Christian Science Monitor,* January 14, 2002, p. 11.

54. Ibid.

55. See generally David Brin, *The Transparent Society: Will Technology Make Us Choose Between Freedom and Privacy?* (Reading, Mass.: Perseus Books, 1998).

56. David Brin, "Some Notes About Calamity and Opportunity," at <http://www.futurist.com/911/notes_about_calamity.htm>.

57. See David Streitfeld and Charles Piller, "Response to Terror, A Changed America: Big Brother Finds Ally in Once-Wary High Tech," *L.A. Times,* January 19, 2002, p. A1; Larry Ellison, "Digital Ids Can Help Prevent Terrorism," *The Wall Street Journal,* October 8, 2001, p. A23, available at http://www.oracle.com/corporate/index.html?digitalid.html.

58. See Ellison, "Digital Ids Can Help Prevent Terrorism."

59. Marc Rotenberg, "Privacy and Transparency: The Paradox of Information Policy" (2001), at http://www.rlg.org/annmtg/rotenberg01.html.

60. Samuel D. Warren and Louis D. Brandeis, "The Right of Privacy," *Harvard Law Revew:* 193 (1890).

61. 277 U.S. 438, 478 (1928) (Brandeis, J., dissenting).

62. Louis D. Brandeis, *Other People's Money, and How the Bankers Use It* (New York: F.A. Stokes, 1914), p. 92. ("Sunlight is said to be the best of disinfectants; electric light the most efficient policeman.")

63. See Abrams v. United States, 250 U.S. 616, 626 (1919) (Holmes, J., dissenting and Brandeis, J., concurring in the dissent). Cf. Schaefer v. United States, 251 U.S. 466, 482 (1920) (Brandeis and Holmes, J.J., dissenting) ("The constitutional right of free speech has been declared to be the same in peace and in war."): Whitney v. California, 274 U.S. 357, 372 (1927) (Brandeis, J., concurring).

> [The founding fathers] knew order cannot be secured merely through fear of punishment for its infraction; that it is hazardous to discourage thought, hope, and imagination; that fear breeds repression; that repression breeds hate; that hate menaces stable government; that the path of safety lies in the opportunity to discuss freely supposed grievances and proposed remedies; and that the fitting remedy for evil counsels is good ones.

64. See generally Philippa Strum, *Brandeis: Beyond Progressivism* (Lawrence, Kan.: University Press of Kansas, 1993); Philippa Strum, *Louis D. Brandeis: Justice for the People* (Cambridge, Mass.: Harvard University Press, 1984); cf. Int'l News Serv. v. Associated Press, 248 U.S. 215, 263 (1918) (Brandeis, J., dissenting) (suggesting that, given the vast public interest in news stories, such information should not be copyrightable, because to do so would "effect an important extension of property rights and a corresponding curtailment of the free use of knowledge and of ideas").

65. See Privacy Act of 1974, 5 U.S.C. § 552 (2000), reprinted and discussed in Marc Rotenberg, *Privacy Law Sourcebook 2001* (Washington, D.C.: Electronic Privacy Information Center, 2001), [hereinafter *Privacy Law Sourcebook,*] p. 39.

66. See *Privacy Law Sourcebook,* pp. 39, 60.

67. See, e.g., Freedom of Information and Protection of Privacy Act, R.S.B.C. 1996, ch. 165 (1993) (Can.).

68. See "OECD, Guidelines on the Protection of Privacy and Transborder Flows of Personal Data" (1980) [hereinafter "OECD Privacy Guidelines"], reprinted in *Privacy Law Sourcebook,* pp. 268–96.

69. See, e.g., David Banisar and Simon Davies, "Global Trends in Privacy Protection: An International Survey of Privacy, Data Protection, and Surveillance Laws and Developments," *J. Marshall J. Computer and Information Law* 1:11 (1999), p. 18.

70. See "OECD Privacy Guidelines."

71. See Federal Trade Commission, "Privacy Online: Fair Information Practices in the Electronic Marketplace: A Report to Congress" (May 2000), available at <http://www.ftc.gov/reports/privacy2000/privacy2000.pdf>. See also Daniel J. Solove, "Access and Aggregation: Public Records, Privacy, and the Constitution," 86 *Minnesota Law Review,* 1137 (2002) p. 86; Daniel J. Solove, "Privacy and Power: Computer Databases and Metaphors for Information Privacy," *Stanford Law Review,* 1393, 1461 (2001) p. 53; Paul Schwartz, "Beyond Lessig's Code for Internet Privacy: Cyberspace Filters, Privacy-Control, and Fair Information Practices," 2000 *Wisconsin Law Review,* 743, pp. 781–86 (2000).

72. "The right of individuals to access and challenge personal data is generally regarded as perhaps the most important privacy protection safeguard." *Privacy Law Sourcebook,* p. 290 (citing "OECD Privacy Guidelines").

73. Department of Health, Education and Welfare, *Records, Computers and the Rights of Citizens* (1973).

74. Florida Star v. B.J.F., 491 U.S. 524 (1989), which held a rape shield statute unconstitutional, is clearly one such case.

75. 532 U.S. 514 (2001).

76. See Bartnicki, 532 U.S. 514; Florida Star, 491 U.S. 524; Doe v. Otte, 259 F.3d 979 (9th Cir. 2001), cert. granted, Otte v. Doe, 70 U.S.L.W. 3514 (U.S. Feb. 19, 2002) (No. 01-729). Similar issues have arisen with public access to court records. See generally EPIC's Public Records Page at http://www.epic.org/privacy/publicrecords/.

77. See EPIC, CNS v. DOJ, at http://www.epic.org/open_gov/foia/cnss_v_doj.html.

78. For example, in EPIC's 1993 litigation seeking the release under FOIA of Secret Service records pertaining to the search and seizure of *2600* employees, EPIC obtained signed statements from targets of investigation to go forward with the FOIA request for relevant records held by the Secret Service. See EPIC. *2600 Archive,* at http://www.epic.org/security/hackers/2600/.

79. So much is made clear in the congressional findings and statement of purpose for the Privacy Act of 1974:

(a) The Congress finds that—

(1) the privacy of an individual is directly affected by the collection, maintenance, use, and dissemination of personal information by Federal angencies;

(2) the increasing use of computers and sophisticated information technology, while essential to the efficient operations of the Government, has greatly magnified the harm to individual privacy that can occur from any collection, maintenance, use or dissemination of personal information;

(3) the opportunities for an individual to secure employment, insurance, and credit, and his right to due process, and other legal protections are endangered by the misuse of certain information systems;

(4) the right to privacy is a personal and fundamental right protected by the Constitution of the United States; and

(5) in order to protect the privacy of individuals identified in information systems maintained by Federal agencies, it is necessary and proper for the Congress to regulate the collection, maintenance, use, and dissemination of information by such agencies.

(b) The purpose of this Act is to provide certain safeguards for an individual against an invasion of personal privacy by requiring Federal agencies, except as otherwise provided by law, to—

(1) permit an individual to determine what records pertaining to him are collected, maintained, used, or disseminated by such agencies;

(2) permit an individual to prevent records pertaining to him obtained by such agencies for a particular purpose from being used or made available for another purpose without his consent;

(3) permit an individual to gain access to information pertaining to him in Federal agency records, to have a copy made of all or any portion thereof, and to correct or amend such records;

(4) collect, maintain, use, or disseminate any record of identifiable personal information in a manner that assures that such action is for a necessary and lawful purpose, that the information is current and accurate for its intended use, and that adequate safeguards are provided to prevent misuse of such information;

(5) permit exemptions from the requirements with respect to records provided in this Act only in those cases where there is an important public policy need for such exemption as has been determined by specific statutory authority; and

(6) be subject to civil suit for any damages which occur as a result of willful or intentional action which violates any individual's rights under this Act.

Privacy Law Sourcebook, pp. 40–41.

80. Raymond Shih Ray Ku, "The Founders' Privacy: The Fourth Amendment and the Power of Technological Surveillance," *Minnesota Law Review* 86 (2002), pp. 1325, 1326.

81. See supra notes 52, 56, 57 and accompanying text.

82. [J]ust as our political life is free and open, so is our day-to-day life in our relations with each other. We do not get into a state with our next-door neighbor if he enjoys himself in his own way, nor do we give him the kind of black looks which, though they do no real harm, still do hurt people's feelings. We are free and tolerant in our private lives. . . .

Thucydides, *History of the Peloponnesian War* (431 B.C.E.) (New York: Penguin Books, 1972) p. 145 (quoting Pericles's Funeral Oration before the Athenians); see also Donald Kagan, *Pericles of Athens and the Birth of Democracy* (New York: The Free Press, 1991) pp. 146–47. (In Pericles's speech to the Athenians, he compares the absence of any privacy in Sparta to the Athenian regime, which "leaves considerable space for individualism and privacy, free from public scrutiny.")

83. For example, the American Bar Association created a new committee, the Cyberspace Committee Task Force, to examine the legal issues surrounding electronic surveillance, security, and privacy in the wake of September 11. The task force was developed to formulate guidelines in the face of "[t]he new frontier forged by the intersection of data protection, electronic communications and Cybercrimes, including CyberTerrorism, [which raise] novel business problems, particularly in light of new laws and standards related to the privacy of customer information." See "New ABA Cyberspace Committee Task Force to Examine Legal Issues Surrounding Electronic Security & Privacy," press release (January 30, 2002) (on file with author). In particular, the task force "will work to identify and interpret the ramifications of new laws, such as the antiterrorism USA PATRIOT Act of 2001."

84. See Anthony Jay, ed., *The Oxford Dictionary of Political Quotations* (New York: Oxford University Press, 1996) p. 141.

85. See, e.g., Judy Mann, "It's a Changed World, and We Will Adapt to It," *The Washington Post*, October 3, 2001, p. C12; Robin Toner, "Some Foresee a Sea Change in Attitudes on Freedoms," *The New York Times*, September 15, 2001, <http://www.nytimes.com/2001/09/15/national/15CIVI.html>.

86. Alexis de Tocqueville, *Democracy in America* (New York: Random House, 1945, 1835) p. 290.

Exhibit: Observing Surveillance

1. Joseph Stiglitz, "Quis Custodiet Ipsos Custodes: Corporate Governance Failures in Transition," in Annual World Bank Conference on Development Economics, Paris, June 21–23, 1999.

2. See Jeremy Bentham, "Panopticon or the Inspection-House: Containing the Idea of a New Principle of Construction Applicable to Any Sort of Establishment, in which Persons of Any Description are to be Kept Under Inspection," in Miran Bozovic, ed., *The Panopticon Writings* (London: Verso, 1995). See also University College London, "Bentham Project, Panopticon," http://www.ucl.ac.uk/Bentham-Project/info/panopticonhtm.htm.

3. Michel Foucault, *Discipline and Punish: The Birth of the Prison* (New York: Vintage Books, 1979).

4. Samuel Warren and Louis D. Brandeis, "The Right to Privacy," *Harvard Law Review* (1890).

5. See generally EPIC, EPIC Video Surveillance page, http://www.epic.org/privacy/surveillance/.

6. Harry A. Hammitt, David L. Sobel, and Mark Zaid, eds., *Litigation Under the Federal Open Government Laws* (Washington, D.C.: EPIC, 2002).

7. EPIC, Observing Surveillance (http://observingsurveillance.org/protest_zoom.html).

8. See also "Rhetorics of Surveillance from Bentham to Big Brother," http://ctrlspace.zkm.de/e/.

9. See "Surveillance and Society," http://www.surveillance-and-society.org/journalv1i1.htm.

7. Social and Electronic Networks in the War on Terror

1. This chapter is a modified version of a lengthier article by the same authors titled "Hacking Networks of Terror," currently under review for publication in a refereed journal.

2. With the exception of the frontier wars in North America, in which American natives lost their land and lives to an expanding European settler population, American citizens have been largely immune to conflict on their own soil.

3. Samuel Huntington, *The Clash of Civilizations and the Remaking of World Order* (New York: Simon and Schuster, 1996).

4. Steve Smith, "The Increasing Insecurity of Security Studies: Conceptualizing Security in the Last Twenty Years," in *Contemporary Security Policy* 20 (March 1999), pp. 72–101.

5. Jeffrey W. Legro and Andrew Moravcsik, "Is Anybody Still a Realist?" *International Security* 24 (February 1999), pp. 5–55.

6. Kenneth Waltz, *Theory of International Politics* (New York: Random House, 1979).

7. Keith Krause and Michael C. Williams, eds., *Critical Security Studies: Concepts and Case* (Minneapolis: University of Minnesota Press, 1997).

8. Robert Cox, "Social Forces, States, and World Order: Beyond International Relations Theory," *Neorealism and Its Critics,* Robert O. Keohane, ed. (New York: Columbia University Press, 1986), pp. 204–54.

9. Janet Tai Landa, *Trust, Ethnicity, and Identity* (Ann Arbor: University of Michigan Press, 1994).

10. Avner Greif, "Cultural Beliefs and the Organization of Society: A Historical and Theoretical Reflection on Collectivist and Individualist Societies," in *Journal of Political Economy* 102 (May 1994), pp. 912–50.

11. Beth V. Yarbrough and Robert M. Yarbrough, "Governance Structures, Insider Status, and Boundary Maintenance," in *Journal of Biometrics* (January 1999), pp. 289–310.

12. A. R. Radcliffe-Brown, "On Social Structure," *Journal of the Royal Anthropological Institute* 70 (1940), pp. 1–12.

13. John Burton, *World Society* (Cambridge: Cambridge University Press, 1972).

14. Margaret A. Keck and Kathryn Sikkink, *Activists Beyond Borders: Advocacy Networks in International Politics* (Ithaca, N.Y.: Cornell University Press, 1998).

15. Manuel Castells, *The Rise of the Network Society. Vol. 1 of The Information Age: Economy, Society, and Culture* (Oxford: Blackwell, 1996), p. 469; Jessica Lipnack and Jeffrey Stamps, *The Networking Book: People Connecting with People* (New York: Routledge and Kegan Paul, 1986); and Barry Wellman and S. D. Berkowitz, eds., *Social Structures: A Network Approach* (Cambridge: Cambridge University Press, 1988).

16. See Paul Baran, *On Distributed Communications* (Santa Monica, Calif.: Rand, 1964); and Katie Hafner, *Where Wizards Stay Up Late* (New York: Simon and Schuster, 1996).

17. Ronald J. Deibert, "Dark Guests and Great Firewalls: Chinese Internet Security Policy," in *Journal of Social Issues* 58 (January 2002) pp. 143–58.

18. Ronald J. Deibert, "International Plug N' Play: Citizen Activism, the Internet, and Global Public Policy," in *International Studies Perspectives* (January 2000), pp. 255–72.

19. Janice Gross Stein, Richard Stren, Joy Fitzgibbon, and Melissa MacLean. *Networks of Knowledge: Collaborative Innovations in International Learning* (Toronto: University of Toronto Press, 2001).

20. Nige Thrift, "On the Social and Cultural Determinants of International Financial Centres: The Case of the City of London," Nigel Thrift and Ron Martins, eds. *Money, Power, and Space,* (Oxford: Blackwell, 1994), pp. 327–55.

21. Ronald J. Deibert, "Wars of the Wide-Area Networks." Info Tech WarPeace 9-11 website, http://www.watsoninstitute.org/infopeace/911/deibert_wide.html.

22. Don Von Natta Jr., "Running Terrorism as a New Economy Business," *The New York Times,* November 11, 2001, p. WK5.

23. John Arquilla and David Ronfeldt, "Fighting the Network War," *Wired,* December 2001, pp. 150–61.

24. James Risen and Dexter Filkins, "Qaeda Fighters Said to Return to Afghanistan," *The New York Times,* September 10, 2002.

25. John Arquilla and David Ronfeldt, *Networks and Netwars: The Future of Terror, Crime, and Militancy* (Santa Monica, Calif.: Rand, 2001).

26. A good example mentioned earlier is the "regeneration" of corporate activity that took place after the attacks on the World Trade Center. Even though the main offices (nodes) of some corporations were destroyed, they could continue their operations from remote locations. Many announced on their websites immediately following September 11 that they were operating "business as usual." Likewise, after the Afghanistan bombing campaign and the fall of the Taliban, many Al Qaeda have reportedly taken root in areas of Pakistan and Iran, as will be discussed in more detail later in the chapter.

27. Ronald S. Burt, "Decay Functions," *Social Networks* 22 (2000), pp. 1–28.

28. Mary Kaldor, "Wanted: Global Politics," *The Nation* (October 18, 2001), <http://www.thenation.com/>.

29. Deibert, "Wars of the Wide-Area Networks."

30. For an elaboration of trust and its functional equivalents, see Jaz Gill and Richard Butler, "Cycles of Trust and Distrust in Joint-Ventures, *European Management Journal* 41 (January 1996), pp. 81–89; Vincent Buskens, "The Social Structure of Trust," *Social Networks* 20 (1998), pp. 265–289; and S. P. Shapriro, "The Social Control of Impersonal Trust," *American Journal of Sociology* (November 3, 1987), pp. 623–58.

31. For some of the special problems relating to covert action, see Richard Betts, "Fixing Intelligence," *Foreign Affairs* 81 (January 2002), pp. 43–59.

32. See Kaldor, "Wanted: Global Politics."

33. John Borland and Lisa M. Bowman, "E-Terrorism: Liberty vs. Security," *ZDNET* (August 27, 2002), http://zdnet.com.com/2001-11-0.

34. For a country-by-country overview, see the Electronic Privacy Information Center/Privacy International's "Privacy and Human Rights: An International Survey of Privacy," 2002, <http://www.privacyinternational.org/survey/phr2002>.

35. Douglas Farah, "Al Qaeda Gold Moved to Sudan—Iran, U.A.E. Used as Transit Points," *Washington Post,* September 3, 2002.

36. The most consistent critic along these lines is cryptologist and security expert Bruce Schneier. His commentary is collected at http://www.counterpane.com/.

37. See especially Robert Lemos, "What are the Real Risks of Cyberterrorism," *ZDNET* (August 26, 2002), http://zdnet.com.com/2100-1105-955293.html.

38. Arquilla and Ronfeldt, *Networks and Netwars,* p. 364.

39. Ashton Carter, "The Architecture of the Government in the Face of Terrorism," *International Security* 26, 3 (2001/2002), pp. 5–23.

40. Ibid., p. 10.

8. Programming Theaters of War: Gamemakers as Soldiers

1. Among the numerous reviews, see Kyle Ackerman and Rob de los Reyes, "Frictionless Insight's First Annual E3 Awards" (March 24, 2002), http://www.frictionlessinsight.com/Articles/E3_2002/E3_2002Awards.htm. Also see the Best of E3 Gamespy award for "best action game," http://www.gamespy.com/e32002/awards/index15.shtml, and Amer Ajami, "America's Army Operations," *Gamespot PC Reviews* (July 7, 2002), <http://gamespot.com/gamespot/stories/previews/0,10869,2873293,00.html>.

2. Fred Hapgood, "Simnet," *Wired Magazine* 5:4 (April 1997), <http://www.wired.com/wired/archive/5.04/ff_simnet_pr.html>.

3. J.A. Thorpe, "Future Views: Aircrew Training 1980–2000," unpublished concept paper at the Air Force Office of Scientific Research, 15 September 1978, discussed in Richard H. Van Atta, Sidney Reed, and Seymour J. Deitchman. *DARPA Technical Accomplishments: An Historical Overview of Selected DARPA Projects,* 3 Volumes, Institute for Defense Analysis, IDA Paper P-2429, 1991: vol. 2, chapter 16, p. 10; and M. Harris, "Entertainment Driven Collaboration," *Computer Graphics* 28:2 (May 1994), pp. 93–96, argues that SIMNET was inspired by the Atari game *Battlezone.*

4. Van Atta, et al., note 50, chapter 16, p. 10.

5. The training concept was to provide a means of cueing individual behavior, with the armored vehicle being part of the cueing. When individuals and crews reacted, they would provide additional cues to which others would react. Thus, the technology was to play a subservient role in the battle-engagement simulations, making no decisions for the crews, but rather simply and faithfully reproducing battlefield cues.

6. Van Atta, et al., chapter 16, p. 13.

7. See J.A. Thorpe, "The New Technology of Large Scale Simulator Networking: Implications for Mastering the Art of Warfighting," *Proceedings of the 9th Interservice Industry Training Systems Conference, November 30–December 2, 1987.* American Defense Preparedness Association, 1987, 492501.

8. R.J. Lunsford Jr., *U.S. Army Training Systems Forecast, FY 1990–1994,* Project Manager for Training Devices (U.S. Army Materiel Command), Orlando, Florida, October 1989, p. 14. Cited in Van Atta, chapter 16, p. 31.

9. F. Clifton Berry, Jr., "Re-creating History: The Battle of 73 Easting," *National Defense* (November 1991).

10. Ibid. Also see the discussion of the Battle of 73 Easting in Bruce Sterling, "War Is Virtual Hell," *Wired Magazine* 1:1 (January 1993), <http://www.wired.com/wired/archive/1.01/virthell.html?topic=&topic_set=>. See especially pp. 6–7 of the online article.

11. Berry, "Re-creating History." Also discussed in Kevin Kelly, "God Games: Memorex Warfare" in *Out of Control* (New York: Addison Wesley, 1994), <http://panushka.absolutvodka.com/kelly/ch13-e.html>.

12. Personal communication.

13. William D. Hartung, "Military Monopoly," *The Nation* (January 13/20, 1997).

14. See the discussion by Jeffrey Potter of Real3D in *Modeling and Simulation: Linking Entertainment and Defense* (Washington, D.C.: National Academy Press, 1997) pp. 164–65.

15. Real3D went out of business in October 1999. See WAVE Report, Issue 9099, October 20, 1999, http://www.wave-report.com/1999%20Wave%20issues/wave9099.html#anchor27942.

16. For Steven Woodcock's bio, see http://www.cris.com/-swoodcoc/stevegameresume.html. Also see Steven Woodcock interview on the future of AI technology and the impact of multiplayer network-capable games in *The Wall Street Journal Interactive Edition* (May 19, 1997). Also see Donna Coco, "Creating Intelligent Creatures: Game Developers are Turning to AI to Give Their Characters Personalities and to Distinguish Their Titles from the Pack," *Computer Graphics World* 20:7 (July 1997), pp. 22–28, <http://www.cgw.com/cgw/Archives/1997/07/07story1.html>.

17. General Charles C. Krulak, Marine Corps Order 1500.55, "Military Thinking and Decision Making Exercises," http://www.tediv.usmc.mil/dlb/milthink/.

18. For the PC-Wargames Catalog, see <http://www.tediv.usmc.mil/dlb/milthink/catalog/title.html>.

19. On *Doom* and the open source movement, see Eric S. Raymond, "The Magic Cauldron," (June 1999), <http://www.tuxedo.org/~esr/writings/magic-cauldron/magic-cauldron-10.html#ss10.3>.

20. For an interesting discussion of *Marine Doom,* see Rob Riddell, "Doom Goes to War: The Marines Are Looking for a Few Good Games," *Wired Magazine* 5:4 (April 1997), <http://www.wired.com/wired/archive/5.04/ff_doom.html?topic=&topic_set=>.

21. Michael Macedonia reports that perhaps the most successful use of commercial games for training has been with *Microsoft Flight Simulator.* The Navy issues a customized version of the software to all student pilots and undergraduates enrolled in Naval Reserve Officer Training Courses at sixty-five colleges. The office of the Chief of Naval Education and Training has also installed *Flight Simulator* at the Naval Air Station in Corpus Christi, Texas, and plans to install it at two other bases in Florida. See J.C. Herz and Michael Macedonia, "Computer Games and the Military: Two Views," *Defense Horizons* 11 (April 2002), pp. 1–8, especially p. 7.

22. MÄK's products use technologies called Distributed Interactive Simulation (DIS) and High-Level Architecture (HLA). Both technologies efficiently connect thousands of 3-D simulations together on a computer network. Replacing the DIS standard for net-based simulations, HLA has been designated as the new standard technical architecture for all DOD simulations. All simulations must be HLA-compatible by the end of 1999. The transition to HLA is part of a DOD–wide effort to establish a common technical framework to facilitate the interoperability of all types of models and simulations, as well as to facilitate the reuse of modeling and simulation components. This framework includes HLA, which represents the highest priority effort within the DOD modeling and simulation community. MÄK intends to leverage its technology for both the military and commercial markets by taking advantage of the nearly $500 million a year spent by the U.S. government on optimizing the speed and capabilities of DIS and HLA. State-of-the-art military DIS systems are now capable of running over 10,000 simulations simultaneously, networked together across far-ranging geographies. As low-cost commercial data services (bidirectional cable TV, ADSL, etc.) become more widely available to consumers, industry analysts projected the market for online, 3-D, multiuser simulations to reach $2 billion in the year 2000.

23. Warren Katz, "Networked Synthetic Environments: From DARPA to Your Virtual Neighborhood," in Clark Dodsworth Jr., ed., *Digital Illusion: Entertaining the Future with High Technology,* (New York: ACM Press, 1998), pp. 115–128.

24. Michael Macedonia, "Why Digital Entertainment Drives the Need for Speed," *Computer* 33:3 (2000), http://www.computer.org/computer/co2000/r3toc.htm.

25. *Modeling and Simulation: Linking Entertainment and Defense,* <http://www.nap.edu/readingroom/books/modeling>.

26. Andrew Pollack, "Trying to Improve Training, Army Turns to Hollywood," *The New York Times,* August 18, 1999. Online at http://www.isi.edu/nyt_uarc.html.

27. See note 16.

28. For the history and context, see the *Castle Smurfenstein* website, <http://evlweb.eecs.uic.edu/aej/smurf.html>.

29. On the development of mods and the shareware movement in gaming, two invaluable sources are Wagner James Au, "Triumph of the mod: Player-created additions to computer games aren't a hobby anymore—they're the lifeblood of the Industry," in *Salon* (April 16, 2002), http://www.salon.com/tech/feature/2002/04/16/modding/; J.C. Herz, "Gaming the System: Social Ecology, Cultural Dynamics, and Networked Innovation in the Computer Game Industry," paper presented in the Institute for Creative Technologies Inside Games Workshop, May 22, 2002, available online at: http://www.ict.usc.edu/%7Einsidegames/. J.C. Herz and Michael Macedonia, chief scientist for STRICOM, engaged in an extremely interesting and provocative discussion on user communities, game design, and the military in "Computer Games and the Military: Two Views," *Defense Horizons* (April 2002), pp. 1–8, <http://www.ndu.edu/inss/DefHor/DH11/DH11.pdf>. Another outstanding discussion of the mod phenomenon is provided in Sue Morris, "Online Gaming Culture: An examination of emerging forms of production and participation in first-person-shooter multiplayer gaming" (June 1999), online at Gamegirlz: http://www.gamegirlz.com/articles/gameculture.shtml.

30. Ben Morris's career is discussed on many game websites. One of the most helpful interviews was done by Vangie "Aurora" Beal, "The Past, Present & Future of Worldcraft—An interview with Ben Morris" (1999), http://www.gamegirlz.com/articles/wc_001.htm.

31. Marc Laidlaw, "My World and Welcome to It," *Wired* 5:3 (March 1997), <http://www.wired.com/wired/archive/5.03/streetcred.html?pg-5>. Laidlaw has subsequently joined Valve Software as a writer and game designer.

32. On *Counter-Strike* creator Minh "Gooseman" Le, see Bruce Rolston, "The Secret Life of Gooseman: Minh Le may be the most influential designer you know nothing about," *The Adrenaline Vault* (December 30, 2000), http://www.avault.com/articles/getarticle.asp?name-gooseman.

33. See the brief bios of the CS Team at the official *Counter-Strike* site, <http://www.counter-strike.net/csteam.html>.

34. "Beta version" refers to the final test version of software released for public testing prior to the final commercial release of a software product.

35. See the event announcement page of the *Cyberathlete's Professional League* at <http://www.thecpl.com/index.html?p-sc2002>. The Summer Event took place at the Dallas Hyatt Regency and was primarily sponsored by Intel and co-sponsored by Plantronics, Micro Exchange, BAWLS, SoundMax, Xabre, and NetFire.com. Merchandise sponsors include: Logitech, Altec Lansing, Belkin, Hercules, and Netgear.

36. See the announcement by James Fudge, "Half-Life Mod Expo July 29," *Computer Games Magazine* (July 28, 1999), http://www.cdmag.com/articles/021/139/hl_mod_expo.html, for the mod expo that took place in San Francisco (July 29, 1999); and the Sierra Games (Valve parent company) announcement: <http://www.sierra.com/games/half-life/official-releases.html#modexpo>.

37. See the press release on the *Steam* website: <http://www.steampowered.com/HTML/Press_Release.html>.

38. Quoted in Wagner James Au, "Triumph of the Mod: Player-created additions to computer games aren't a hobby anymore—they're the lifeblood of the Industry," *Salon* (April 16, 2002), p. 1, http://www.salon.com/tech/feature/2002/04/16/modding/.

39. J.C. Hertz and Michael Macedonia, "Computer Games and the Military," p. 2.

40. Ibid. In his response to Hertz's similar argument in *Defense Horizons* (April 2002), Michael Macedonia acknowledged the importance of the commercial sector as the leading element in contemporary gaming and simulation, a point he has made numerous times as chief scientist at STRICOM. He did not, however, take up the interesting challenge about what it would mean for the military to throw itself completely into the globally networked, self-organizing and distributed networks driving game innovation.

41. "Bots" are the characters and actions in a game controlled by artificial intelligence. In this chapter, the term "bot culture" is often substituted for the term "mod culture," which refers to the ways in which some sophisticated users access the artificial intelligence files of the game and modify them.

42. Discussed by J.C. Hertz, "For Game Makers, There's Gold in the Code," *The New York Times*, December 2, 1999. Archived at <http://www.nytimes.com/library/tech/99/12/circuits/articles/02game.html>—requires registration but no fee.

43. The superior AI of the Reaper allowed it to learn the gamer's particular style of play and adapt to take advantages of his or her weaknesses. The Reaper is difficult to kill because it is excellent at avoiding shots, but is then deadly accurate with the placement of its own shots. On Steven Polge's career, see the interview on *Planet Quake*, <http://www.planetquake.com/interviews/steve.shtm>. Polge worked on network protocols at IBM for seven years before joining the gaming industry full time.

44. http://www.planetunreal.com/fightforfreedom/introduction.htm

9. Perpetual Revolution in Military Affairs, International Security, and Information

1. Mark Helprin, "Revolution or Dissolution," *Forbes* 161:4 (February 23, 1998), pp. 86–102, quote from p. 98. Helprin is a well-known novelist and is also a veteran of the Israeli Self-Defense Forces.

2. For a discussion of the Clausewitz-Foucault dialogue on war and politics see Chris Hables Gray, *Postmodern War: The New Politics of Conflict* (New York: Guilford; London: Routledge, 1997), pp. 258–259.

3. The "institutionalization of innovation" comes from Martin Van Creveld, *Technology and War* (New York: Free Press, 1989). "Moore's Law" is the prediction in computerdom that computing power will increase geometrically. Originally Gordon Moore predicted that it would be in eighteen month cycles but it is closer to twelve now. See, Gordon Moore, "Cramming More Components Onto Integrated Circuits," *Electronics* 38:8 (April 19, 1965), pp. 114–117.

4. Michael O'Hanlon, "Can High Technology Bring U.S. Troops Home?" *Foreign Policy* (Winter 1998), pp. 72–84, quote from p. 72.

5. Andrew Krepinevich, "Cavalry to Computer: The Pattern of Military Revolutions," *National Interest* (Fall 1994); reprinted in *Foreign Policy* (Winter 1998), pp. 82–83.

6. Mikkel Vedby Rasmussen, "The Acme of Skill: Clausewitz, Sun Tzu and the Revolutions in Military Affairs" (Copenhagen: Dansk Udenrigspolitsk Institut [DUPI, 2001]), report no. 12, p. 1.

7. On the real reasons for the Bush space program, see Chris Hables Gray, "Star Wars 2001," *CPSR Newsletter* 19:2 (Spring 2001), pp. 1, 3. The problems of this approach are described in Jonathan S. Lockwood, "Space Control Versus Space Denial in 21st Century Warfare: Achilles heel of the RMA?" *Defense & Foreign Affairs Strategic Policy* 28:8 (August 2000), pp. 4–6.

8. O'Hanlon, "Can High Technology Bring U.S. Troops Home?" pp. 2, 3, 12.

9. Chris Hables Gray, "The Crisis of Infowar," in Gerfield Stocker and Christine Schopf, eds. *Infowar* (New York: Springer Wien/New York, 1998), pp. 130–137.

10. Brian Cantrell Smith, "The Limits of Correctness in Computers," from the Center for the Study of Language and Information, report No. CSLI-85-36 (Palo Alto: Stanford University, 1979). This very important article is also in Charles Dunlop and Rob Kling, eds., *Computerization and Controversy: Value Conflicts and Social Choices* (New York: Academic Press, 1985).

11. Ilya Prigogine, *Order Out of Chaos* (New York: Bantam Doubleday Dell, 1989). "Out of control systems" are described at length in Kevin Kelly, *Out of Control: The New Biology of Machines, Social Systems, and the Economic World* (New York: Addison-Wesley, 1994).

12. Quoted in David Lamb, "Reflections of 'Norman of Arabia,' " *San Jose Mercury News*, February 26, 1991, p. 14A. A detailed analysis of the Kuwait 1991 war is in chapter 2 of Gray, *Postmodern War*, pp. 36–50.

13. An extensive discussion of these incidents and many others is in Gray, *Postmodern War*, pp. 19–69.

14. Mark Bowden, *Black Hawk Down: A Story of Modern War* (New York: Penguin, 1999).

15. Gray, *Postmodern War*, p. 37.

16. Eric Schmitt, "U.S. Blames Taliban for Civilian Deaths in an American Raid," *The New York Times*, September 7, 2002, p. A7.

17. *The Washington Post* staff, "U.S. role in Afghanistan unclear," *The Great Falls-Tribune* (August 4, 2002), p. 2A.

18. For an argument that the current situation is a second cold war, see Chris Hables Gray, "September 11: Not a New War," in *Teleopolis* (2001), <http://www.heise.de/tp/english/inhalt/co/9826/1.html>.

19. David J. Rothkopf, "Cyberpolitik: The Changing Nature of Power in the Information Age," in *The Journal of International Affairs* 51:2 (Spring 1998), pp. 325–59.

20. Colin S. Gray, "Thinking Asymmetrically in Times of Terror," *Parameters* (Spring 2002), pp. 5–14.

21. Edward Herman, *The Real Terror Network* (Boston: South End Press, 1982).

22. In Gray, *Postmodern War,* there is an extended discussion of these elements of postmodern war, most notably on pp. 168–194.

23. Gregory D. Foster, "The Postmodern Military: The Irony of 'Strengthening' Defense," *Harvard International Review* 23:2 (Summer 2001), pp. 24–29.

10. Bullets to Bytes: Reflections on ICTs and "Local" Conflict

1. I would like to thank Deirdre Collings for her invaluable editorial comments, which added greatly to the substance of this chapter.

2. It is interesting to note that even in countries that prohibit their population's access to satellite stations—such as Iran—the receivers are now so small that individuals can and do easily hide the dish antenna, or pay off local officials to turn a blind eye. Post-Taliban Afghanistan has experienced somewhat of a satellite-dish craze, as owners have dusted off old and reinstalled dishes that have in some cases remained hidden for years. See Abdul Rahman Oman Niazi, "Satellite TV Craze" (Afghan Recovery Report), Institute for War & Peace Reporting, 2002, <http://www.iwpr.net>.

3. Interwave, "Barakaat Telecommunications Selects Interwave for Network Expansion in Somalia," press release, February 27, 2001, Peter Maass, "Ayn Rand Comes to Somalia," *The Atlantic Monthly* 5 (May 2001).

4. Afghan Media Resource Center (1999) cited by Internews, August 24, 2002, <http://www.internews.org/regions/centralasia/afghanistan.htm>.

5. See, for example, Mats Berdal and David Malone, *Greed & Grievance: Economic Agendas in Civil Wars* (Boulder, Colo.: Lynne Rienner Press, 2000).

6. See, for example, Mary Kaldor, *New Wars and Old Wars: Organized Violence in a Global Era* (Stanford, Calif.: Stanford University Press, 1999).

7. Mark Duffield, *Global Governance and the New Wars* (London: Zed Books, 2001).

8. See, for example, United Nations Development Plan, *Creating a Digital Dynamic: Final Report of the Digital Opportunities Initiative* (New York: UNDP, 2001).

9. Christianthi Avgerou, "Recognizing Alternative Rationalities in the Deployment of Information Systems," *Electronic Journal on Information Systems in Developing Countries* 3:7 (2000).

10. I served as the chief technical adviser responsible for UN ICT systems in Rwanda between 1998 and 2000. During that time, I prepared a survey of UN information and communications systems security in Rwanda, Burundi, and Angola.

11. For an excellent analysis of information conflict in the Great Lakes region see Nik Gowing, "New Challenges and Problems for Information Management in Complex Emergencies: Ominous Lessons from the Great Lakes and Eastern Zaire in late 1996 and early 1997." This paper was prepared through funding provided by the European Community's Humanitarian Office and was presented at a conference examining the role of media reporting in zones of conflict ("Dispatches From Disaster Zones": The Reporting of Humanitarian Emergencies, London, May 27–28, 1998).

12. See, for example, Helmut Anheir, Marlies Glasius, and Mary Kaldor, eds., *Global Civil Society 2001* (Oxford: Oxford University Press, 2001).

13. See, for example, http://www.advocacynet.org.

14. Georges Corm, "Militia Hegemony & Reestablishment of the State," Deirdre Collings, ed., *Peace for Lebanon; from War to Reconstruction* (Boulder: Lynne Rienner Press, 1994).

15. HINA, "IMV Set up as Bosnia's License Regulator" (BBC Monitoring Media, 1998).

16. Scott Peterson, *Me against My Brother: At War in Somalia, Sudan and Rwanda* (New York: Routledge, 2000).

17. Activists and "hacktivists" in the industrialized countries were quick to pick up on the potential of this technology, and in recent years independent and alternative media have started to take advantage of these inexpensive technologies to build networks of news gathering that shadow the large-scale operations of media Goliaths such as CNN, BBC, and others. However, the lack of professionalism (in production) and colorful mosaic of ideologies and issues that characterize these large loose coalitions has hampered their ability to move beyond a hard-core of true believers and establish a more mainstream presence.

18. Al-Manar Television, 2002, http://www.manartv.com.

19. In recent years these kinds of self-produced streaming music video–cum–reportages have become popular with resistance groups worldwide. In the Caucasus, for example, websites using similar techniques are operated by Chechen groups fighting against Russian federal forces.

20. Friedman goes on to write, "I would like to say the footage was out of context, but there was no context. There were no words. It was just pictures and martial music designed to inflame passions." Thomas J. Friedman, "Global Village Idiocy," *The New York Times,* May 12, 2002.

21. Martin Woollacott, "Arab Eyes Travel to Jerusalem Every Day: Like Vietnam for the U.S., TV Brings the War Home," *The Guardian Weekly,* May 9, 2002, p. 12.

22. James Bamford, *Body of Secrets: Anatomy of the Ultra-Secret National Security Agency: From the Cold War through the Dawn of a New Century* (New York: Doubleday, 2001).

23. For excellent accounts of the battle of Grozny from the military and journalistic points of view, see Timothy Thomas, "The Battle of Grozny: Deadly Classroom for Urban Combat," *Parameters* 29:2 (Summer 1999); Sebastian Smith, *Allah's Mountains: The Battle for Chechnya* (London: I.B. Tauris, 2001); Carlotta Gall and Thomas De Waal, *Chechnya: Calamity in the Caucasus* (New York: New York University Press, 2000).

24. Good accounts of the U.S. mission to Somalia can be found in the following sources: Scott Peterson, *Me against My Brother;* Mark Bowden, *Blackhawk Down: A Story of Modern War* (New York: Atlantic Monthly Press, 1999); and Vernon Leob, "The CIA in Somalia," 2000, <http://www.nomadnet.com/somcia.html>.

25. Perhaps ironically, both of their concepts were initially sketched out in research supported by the RAND Corporation. See John Arquilla and David Ronfeldt, "Cyberwar Is Coming!," *Comparative Strategy* 12:2 (Spring 1993), and John Arquilla and David Rondfeldt, *In Athena's Camp: Preparing for Conflict in the Information Age* (Santa Monica: RAND, 1997).

26. James Adams, "Virtual Defense," *Foreign Affairs* 80:3 (2001).

27. During the struggle over East Timor, for example, Portuguese hackers were blamed for defacing and hacking several key Indonesian government websites. In retaliation, Indonesian government hackers were accused of having taken down the East Timor country domain by a sophisticated attack against a server located in Ireland. Similar engagements have occurred between Azeri and Armenian hackers against each other's systems and infrastructures, mirroring the now stagnant conflict over Nagorno-Karabah, and earlier this year individuals aligned with the banned Falun Gong movement were said to have been responsible for temporarily hijacking the satellite feed broadcasting China's main TV channel. Sources: Tedjabayu, "Indonesia: The Net as a Weapon," *Cybersociology* 5:5 (1999); Richard Rogers, " 'Internet & Society' in Armenia and Azerbaijan? Web Games and a Chronicle of an Infowar," *First Monday* 5:9 (2000); and Jonah Greenberg, "China TV on Red Alert after Satellite Hijacks," *Reuters.com* (2002).

28. Some sources pinpoint the moment of "attack" to a message circulated by Israeli hackers over Internet ICQ calling for a coordinated "ping" attack against the main Hizbollah website. Sources: Reuters, "Israeli-Arab Warfare, Web-Style," *Wired News* (2001); and Zeid Nasser, "Interface: Digital Warriors of Arabia," *The Star: Jordan's Political, Economic and Cultural Weekly* 20 (December 6, 2000).

29. In the tit for tat that followed, Israeli hackers were credited with taking down thirty-four pro-Palestinian websites. Giles Trendle, "Cyberwars: The Coming Arab E-Jihad," *Middle East* 322 (April, 2002); Carmen Gentile, "Israeli Hackers Vow to Defend," *Wired News* (2000); Ellis Shu-

man, "The Mideast Turns to Cyberwar," *About.com* (2001); Cletus Nelson, "Hacker Holy Wars," Disinformation, (2000) http://www.disinfo.com.

30. iDefense, "Middle East Cyber Conflict Update: Cyber War Could Spill Over to Other Regions of the World," iDefense Intelligence Service (2000).

31. Giles Trendle, "Cyberwars: The Coming Arab E-Jihad," *Middle East* 322 (April, 2002); and Carmen Gentile, "Israeli Hackers Vow to Defend," *Wired News* (2000).

32. Giles Trendle, "Cyberwars: The Coming Arab E-Jihad."

33. iDefense, "Middle East Cyber Conflict Update: Cyber War Could Spill-over to Other Regions of the World," and Cletus Nelson, "Hacker Holy Wars."

34. Carmen Gentile, "Palestinian Crackers Share Bugs," *Wired News* (2000[b]).

35. Avi Machlis, "Middle East Foes Byte the Bullet in Cyberwar: Israelis and Arabs around the World Are Conducting a Virtual Intifada by Sabotaging Websites," *Financial Times,* October 28, 2000, p. 3.

36. See, for example, http://www.pita-palestine.org/damage.html, and also, Al-Ayyam, "Palestinian Ministers Detail Damage Caused by Israel; Face Deputies' Criticism," *BBC Monitoring—Middle east—Economic* (2002); Alfred Hermida, "Palestinian Websites Knocked Off-Line," *BBC News Online* (2002); and Rema Hammami, Sari Hanafi, and Elizabeth Taylor, "Destruction of Palestinian Institutions: Preliminary Report April 13 2002," <http://www.amin.org/eng/uncat/2002/apr/apr133.html> (Palestinian NGO Emergency Initiative in Jerusalem, 2002).

37. Alfred Hermida, "Palestinian Websites Knocked Off-Line."

38. Rema Hammami, Sari Hanafi, and Elizabeth Taylor, "Destruction of Palestinian Institutions: Preliminary Report April 13 2002."

39. Daoud Kuttab, "Forced Off the Air in Ramallah," *The New York Times,* April 6, 2002.

40. John Arquilla and David Rondfeldt, *In Athena's Camp: Preparing for Conflict in the Information Age* (Santa Monica: RAND, 1997); and John Arquilla and David Rondfeldt, eds., *Networks and Netwars: The Future of Terror Crime and Militancy* (Santa Monica: Rand, 2001).

41. John Arquilla, David Ronfeldt, Graham Fuller, and Melissa Fuller, *The Zapatista Social Netwar in Mexico* (Santa Monica: Rand—Arroyo Center, 1998).

42. Harry Cleaver, "The Zapatistas and the International Circulation of Struggle: Lessons Suggested and Problems Raised," (INET, 1998).

43. For excellent accounts of the second Russo-Chechen war, see Anne Nivat, *Chienne De Guerre: A Woman Reporter Behind the Lines of the War in Chechnya* (New York: Public Affairs, 2001); Emil Pain, "The Second Chechen War: The Information Component," *Military Review* LXXX: 4 (July–August, 2000); John Dunlop, *The Second Russo-Chechen War Two Years On* (Stanford, Calif.: Hoover Institution, 2001); Timothy L. Thomas, *Manipulating the Mass Consciousness: Russian and Chechen 'Information War' Tactics in the 2nd Chechen-Russian Conflict* (Fort Leavenworth: Foreign Military Studies Office, US Army, 2001); and Anna Politkovskaya, *A Dirty War: A Russian Reporter in Chechnya* (London: Harvill Press, 2001).

44. Between the two phases of the conflict from 1996 to 1999, Chechnya saw the development of two rival cell phone providers and at least one wireless Internet provider (in Grozny). There are also unsubstantiated reports that cell phone towers were built throughout the republic and interconnected by satellite circuits, creating somewhat of a national network. Regardless of the accuracy of these latter reports, it is clear that communications and communications security was a major preoccupation of the Chechens in both phases of the war.

45. Some analysts have even suggested that the Russian government took a page out of a NATO playbook. During intervention in Bosnia (and later Kosovo), NATO forces ran a comprehensive campaign of information warfare controlling the informational as well as physical battlespace. Serbian Radio communications were systematically jammed, and the entry of troops was facilitated by a wide-ranging public relations campaign.

46. The Internet has become an important channel for Palestinians to circumvent what they perceive as Israeli barriers over their ability to communicate their aspirations and hopes to the

world, as well as a vital organizing tool for most organizations. In 2001, Paltel adopted "Tell the World" as their new slogan. See Elizabeth Biddlecombe, "Internet 'Sole Technological Outlet' for Palestinians, Says Paltel," *Total Telecom* (2001), http://www.paltel.net/articles/art5.html, and Nigel Parry, *The Past and Future of Information Technology in Palestine: An Introduction for the Palestinian NGO Community* (Birzeit: Birzeit University, 1997).

11. ICT and the World of Smuggling

1. As I research globalized commodity and service flows that take place outside of legal channels, I am dealing with more than the unquestionably illegal. Goods and services may be illegal, illicit, informal, unrecorded—all of which have different relationships to legality; many goods and services that move outside of the clearly legal cross a number of il/legal designations. For this reason, I find the term "extralegal" most useful, and the term xlegal a convenient designator.

2. This research was conducted in southern Africa and Europe in 2001–2002 with a grant from the John T. and Catherine C. MacArthur Foundation.

3. Carolyn Nordstrom, "Shadows and Sovereigns," *Theory, Culture and Society,* vol. 17[4] (August 2000) pp. 35–54.

4. United Nations Research Institute, *States of Disarray: The Social Effects of Globalization* (London: UNRISD, 1995).

5. Gary Slapper and Steve Tombs, *Corporate Crime* (London: Longman, 1999).

6. Suraj Gupta, *Black Income in India* (New Delhi: Sage, 1992).

7. Donald Rutherford, *Dictionary of Economies* (New York: Routledge, 1992), p. 42.

8. Susan Pozo, *Price Behavior in Illegal Markets* (Aldershot, U.K.: Avebury, 1996); Avner Greif, "Contracting, Enforcement, and Efficiency: Economics Beyond the Law," in M. Bruno and B. Pleskovic, eds., *Annual World Bank Conference on Development Economics 1996* (Washington, D.C.: The World Bank, 1996) pp. 239–265.

9. Ed Ayers, "The Expanding Shadow Economy," *World Watch,* vol. 9[4] (1996), pp. 11–23.

10. George Lopez and David Cortwright, "Making Targets 'Smart' From Sanctions," paper delivered at the International Studies Association meetings, Minneapolis, Minn., March 18–22, 1998; Bureau for International Narcotics and Law Enforcement Affairs, *International Narcotics Control Strategy Report 1996* (Washington, D.C.: U.S. Department of State, March 1997).

11. Tony Hodges, *Angola from Afro-Stalinism to Petro-Diamond Capitalism* (Oxford: James Currey, 2001); Jakkie Cilliers and Christian Dietrich, eds., *Angola's War Economy* (Pretoria: Institute for Security Studies, 2000).

12. Global Witness, *A Rough Trade: The Role of Companies and Governments in the Angolan Conflict* (London: Global Witness, 1998), p. 11.

13. Carolyn Nordstrom, "Out of the Shadows," in Thomas N. Callaghy, Roben Latham, and Ronald Kassimir, eds., *Intervention and Transnationalism in Africa* (Cambridge: Cambridge University Press, 2002).

14. Suraj Gupta, *Black Income in India.*

15. Federal Communications Commission, *FCC Release Study on Telephone Trends* (Washington, D.C.: FCC, May 22, 2002).

16. International Telecommunications Union, *Key Global Indicators for the World Telecommunication Service Sector* (Geneva: United Nations/ITU, 2002).

17. David Gunzerath, *Radio and the Internet,* 2002, http://www.nab.org/Research/Reports/RadioandInternet/index.htm.

18. Interviews with Hewlett Packard, IBM, and the computer association of South Africa.

19. Carolyn Nordstrom, "Shadows and Sovereigns."

20. Manuel Castells, *End of Millennium* (London: Blackwell, 1998); Susan Strange, *The Retreat of*

the State: The Diffusions of Power in the World Economy (Cambridge: Cambridge University Press, 1996).

21. John McDowell and Gary Novis, "The Consequences of Money Laundering and Financial Crime," in *The Fight Against Money Laundering Economic Perspectives* (U.S. Department of State: Office of International Information Programs, 2001), pp. 4–6.

22. Ibid., pp. 4–5.

12. Information Technology and the Web Activism of the Revolutionary Association of the Women of Afghanistan (RAWA)—Electronic Politics and New Global Conflict

1. There are also smaller groups of Aimaks, Turkmens, and Balochis, according to 1999 figures.

2. CIA, *The World Factbook 2000,* <http://www.cia.gov/cia/publications/factbook/geos/af.html people>.

3. December 1979 to February 5, 1989.

4. According to the *Annual Report for the Year 2000* by the International Campaign to Ban Land mines, the situation in Afghanistan has improved: "an estimated five to ten people were injured or killed by mines every day in 1999, compared to an estimated ten to twelve people in 1998 and an estimated twenty to twenty-four people in 1993."

5. "UNHCR's Contribution to a Special Inter-agency Briefing on Pakistan/Afghanistan—Urgent Need for Camp Sites for Afghan Refugees in Pakistan" (February 8, 2001), <http://www.unhcr.ch/news/cupdates/0101afg.htm>, accessed August 15, 2001.

6. UNICEF, "A Humanitarian Appeal for Children and Women, January–December 2001—Afghanistan," http://www.unicef.org.

7. At 1,700 per 100,000 births. Ibid.

8. GDP per capita in 1999 was $800. Ironically, the $2.3 million (1996) external debt is an economic bright spot. CIA, *The World Factbook 2000,* <http://www.cia.gov/cia/publications/factbook/geos/af.html>.

9. CIA, *The World Factbook 2000,* http://www.cia.gov/cia/publications/factbook/geos/af.html.

10. China, Iran, Pakistan, Tajikistan, Turkeminstan, and Uzbekistan plus the United States and Russia.

11. "A Regional Action Plan adopted by 'Six plus Two' Group in New York on 13 September 2000." UN ODCCP, http://www.odccp.org/uzbekistan/actionplan.html.

12. "Afghanistan ends opium poppy cultivation," in *ODCCP Update* (June 2001), <http://www.odccp.org/newsletter_2001-06-30_1_page002.html>.

13. There is much evidence that the Taliban were heavily involved in opium cultivation. For example, just before the ban, "on 17 April [2000] Taliban militiamen arrested Shujaat Ali Khan, a journalist with the Pakistani daily *Frontier Post,* in his hotel room in Kabul. He was taken to a police station near the presidential palace where he was interrogated at length and accused of being an American spy. He was eventually released three days later after a friend intervened on his behalf, but was arrested again by the Taliban the next day, for no apparent reason. He was kept for nine days in a filthy cell 'crawling with scorpions and all kinds of insects,' threatened with death, questioned daily about his alleged ties with the U.S. Central Intelligence Agency and accused of manipulating other journalists at the *Frontier Post.* Shujaat Ali Khan had come to Afghanistan with a convoy from the United Nations High Commission for Refugees bringing dozens of Afghan families from Pakistan. He said he had angered the Taliban by taking photographs of fields of opium poppies." *Reporters Sans Frontiers Annual Report 2001,* <http://www.rsf.fr/uk/home.html>. Similar evidence has appeared in international press reports, see "The Taliban's drug dividend," Kate Clark, *BBC News,* June 14, 2000, <http://news.bbc.co.uk/hi/english/world/south_asia/newsid_783000/783268.stm>.

14. Forcing the international community to recognize Taliban entailed obliging it to deal with the regime. In 2001, the Taliban arrested foreign workers for Relief Now (two Americans, two Australians, and four Germans) on charges of propagating Christianity, which effectively forced the three governments concerned to send diplomatic representatives to Kabul.

15. Human Rights Watch, "Afghanistan: Crisis of Impunity—The Role of Pakistan, Russia, and Iran in Fueling the Civil War," July 2001, Vol. 13, No. 3 (C), <http://www.hrw.org/reports/2001/afghan2/>.

16. The government overthrown by the Taliban, the ISA, is supported by the United Front. The United Front is mainly made up of the Jamiat-i Islami-yi led by Burhanuddin Rabbani. The United Front's main military leader is Ahmad Shad Massood, who is the ISA minister of defense. See HRW, "Afghanistan: Crisis of Impunity."

17. In its report for 2000, HRW noted that "on April 21, United Front faction Hizb-i Wahdat took control of Bamiyan City, only to lose it after heavy fighting in early May. Following the Hizb-i Wahdat victory, relief workers reported that its forces beat and detained residents suspected of supporting the Taliban, and burned their houses. When Taliban forces retook the city, they reportedly took reprisals by shooting suspected Hizb-i Wahdat supporters, primarily ethnic Shi'a Hazaras, burning hundreds of homes and deporting men to unknown locations." *HRW World Report 2000,* http://www.hrw.org/wr2k/Asia.htm#Afghanistan. HRW also noted that the United Front has targeted specific ethnic groups: "the United Front has been on the defensive in its home territories, but there have nevertheless been reports of abuses, including summary executions, burning of houses, and looting, principally targeting ethnic Pashtuns and others suspected of supporting the Taliban. The ethnicization of the conflict in the north raises grave concerns about further reprisal attacks on civilians by both sides," in "Afghanistan: Crisis of Impunity—The Role of Pakistan, Russia, and Iran in Fueling the Civil War," July 2001, vol. 13, no. 3 (C), http://www.hrw.org/reports/2001/afghan2/Afghan0701.htm.

18. Amnesty International, *Annual Report 2001—Covering events from January–December 2000 Afghanistan.*

19. Under Taliban, men were hanged, women stoned, and homosexuals crushed beneath collapsing walls. See Amnesty International, *Annual Report 2001—Covering events from January–December 2000 Afghanistan.*

20. See *The World Factbook 2000,* http://www.cia.gov/cia/publications/factbook/geos/af.html.

21. Reporters Sans Frontières, *Annual Report 2001,* http://www.rsf.fr/uk/home.html.

22. See "Taliban Smash TVs," *BBC News* (July 30, 1998), <http://news.bbc.co.uk/hi/english/world/south_asia/newsid_142000/142352.stm>.

23. "Taliban rules out lifting TV ban," *BBC News,* July 23, 2000, <http://news.bbc.co.uk/hi/english/world/south_asia/newsid_847000/847408.stm>.

24. The UF claimed that 30,000 people watched the station each evening.

25. Reporters Sans Frontières, *Annual Report 2001,* http://www.rsf.fr/uk/home.htm.

26. Ibid. BBC correspondent Owen Bennett-Jones provided glimpses into Afghan life from Pakistan. He reported on a Pakistani soccer team in Kandahar arrested for wearing shorts during a match, which Taliban officials said violated the Islamic dress code. Twelve players were arrested and their heads shaved. Five other players managed to escape. (*BBC News,* July 17, 2000).

27. http://www.afghan-ie.com

28. http://www.Taliban.com

29. A message at http://www.Taliban.com with a photo of bin Laden said, "Taliban was again fucked by RyDen. FuckZ: Usama Bin Laden, Ibn Al Khatab Maskadov and all Chechen terrorists. BASTARD STILL WANTED DEAD OR ALIVE: 5,000,000$ for direct info. (it's not joke, its an official info from FBI). You can become a MILLIONAIRE, do it for yourself! Additional info about this you can find at www.fbi.gov. No more messages here, all people around the world already inform that are only stupid monkeys Contact: ry_den@land.ru."

30. The URL http://www.rawa.org/ was current when research on the RAWA website was conducted in July–August 2000. By July–August 2001, the website had migrated to <http://www.afghan.rawa.org/rawa>.

31. Activities included distributing food, blankets, and medicine in refugee camps; organizing home-based classes for women in Afghanistan; attempts to foster global awareness of the issue via the UNCHR; visits to Washington, D.C., New York City, Canada, and Japan; and interviews with beggars and prostitutes in Kabul.

32. The website has received three awards: "Best of '97" at *ZDNet,* http://www.zdnet.com, "Hot Site," http://www.stpt.com, and "Political Site of the Day," http://www.aboutpolitics.com.

33. See Michael Dartnell, "Insurgency Online: Elements for a Theory of Anti-government Internet Communication," in *Small Wars and Insurgencies,* vol. 10, no. 3 (London: Frank Cass & Co., Ltd., Winter 1999), pp. 117–136.

34. "About RAW A . . ." http://www.rawa.org.

35. Ibid.

36. See Amnesty International, http://www.amnesty.se/women/23ea.htm.

37. See http://rawa.fancymarketing.net/goals.htm.

38. See http://pz.rawa.org.

39. In August 2001, both of these publications, which sell for about $10 U.S. each, were listed as out of stock at http://songs.rawa.org/rawa/burst.htm.

40. The translated reports available at http://songs.rawa.org/rawa/ai.htm are: "Afghanistan: International Responsibility for Human Rights Disaster"; "Afghanistan: Grave Abuses in the Name of Religion"; "Afghanistan: Cruel, Inhuman or Degrading Treatment or Punishment"; "Human Rights Defenders in Afghanistan: Civil Society Destroyed"; "Afghanistan: The Human Rights of Minorities"; "Women in Afghanistan: Pawns in Men's Power Struggles"; "Children Devastated by War: Afghanistan's Lost Generations"; and, "Refugees from Afghanistan: The World's Single Largest Refugee Group." A link to http://www.amnesty.org is also provided.

41. The documents here point out that, even prior to international outrage over destruction of ancient Buddhist sites in 2001, the conflict already resulted in destruction of Kabul's renowned national museum and sale of many surviving priceless artifacts abroad.

42. The restrictions are found at http://songs.rawa.org/rawa/rules.htm. RAWA has provided translations in Spanish, Italian, French, and German.

43. RAWA has reproduced the report at http://songs.rawa.org/rawa/channel4.htm.

44. See http://rawa.fancymarketing.net/help.htm.

45. See http://rawa.fancymarketing.net/petition.htm.

46. See *North County Times,* December 19, 2000, http://www.nctimes.com/news/121900/y.html.

47. In August 2001, http://www.Taliban.com became unavailable, having been hacked by an individual who posted a strong anti-Islamic denunciation and left an e-mail address apparently based in Russia. The site of the Islamic Emirate at http://www.afghan-ie.com is now also unavailable. RAWA clearly won the electronic civil war.

48. Source: RAWA at http://songs.rawa.org/rawa/rules.htm.

13. The Internet's Mediation Potential in Protracted Conflicts: The Case of Burundi

1. I would like to express deep appreciation for BYC members who gave me formal authorization to refer to BYC's website for research purposes; BYC members who are setting a great example by remaining focused on a return to lasting peace in Burundi and for all whose messages continue to be a source of inspiration for me. Without great insights from this volume's editor, Robert Latham, challenging me to push the question of Internet's role in conflict resolution even further in my analysis, I would probably not have taken on the task of contributing this chapter

at a time when, as a novice at a new nonacademic research position, I lost the freedom of managing my time, a privilege I never took for granted in academic settings. I am also grateful for the various discussions I had with Paul Kaiser, prior to and through the writing process, and for being my most reliable critic and editor.

2. See http://umuco.community.everyone.net/community/scripts/thread.pl.

3. Ahmedou Ould-Abdallah, *Burundi on the Brink 1993–95: A UN Special Envoy Reflects on Preventive Diplomacy* (Washington, D.C.: United States Institute of Peace, 2000), p. 119.

4. Ibid., p. 119.

5. According to John Paul Lederach, a facilitator is also referred to as a moderator who plays the intermediary role of mediation by fulfilling the "range of functions during proximity or face-to-face talks between adversaries (e.g., chairing meetings, interpreting positions and responses etc. . . .)." John Paul Lederach, *Building Peace: Sustainable Reconciliation in Divided Societies* (Washington, D.C.: United States Institute of Peace, 1997), p. 68.

6. See Ed Garcia in "People's Participation in Peace Processes: Reflecting on Selected Experiences from Asia, Africa and Latin America," available online at <http://www.dse.de/ef/disarmnt/garcia-d.htm>.

7. According to Chandra Sriram, there are four phases of conflict. At the "potential conflict" phase, a variety of sources of stress may be identified that may provoke conflict at the very beginning of the conflict life cycle. The "gestation of conflict" phase refers to when mobilizing factors and flashes of low-intensity violence and/or repression may become increasingly apparent. The "trigger/mobilization of conflict" refers to the phase when there may be a high degree of tension and confrontation between conflicting parties, and some force or threat of use of force may be deployed. The "post-conflict" phase refers to when there has been a cessation of hostilities, but the risk of conflict flaring anew is high. See Chandra Lekha Sriram and Karin Wermester, eds., *From Promise to Practice: Strengthening UN Capacities for the Prevention of Violent Conflict* (Boulder: Lynne Reinner, 2003), for detailed case studies that examine these phases in greater detail.

8. Kofi Annan, "The Prevention of Armed Conflict: Report of the Secretary General," A/55/985-S/2001/574 (June 7, 2001).

9. John G. Cockell, "Planning Preventive Action," in *From Reaction to Prevention: Opportunities for the UN System* (Boulder: Lynne Reinner, 2001).

10. My italics to highlight the importance of communication and hence, indirectly, the medium of communication.

11. Chester A. Crocker, Fen Osler Hampson, and Pamela Aall, "Multiparty Mediation and the Conflict Cycle," in Chester A. Crocker, Fen Osler Hampson, and Pamela Aall, eds., *Herding Cats: Multiparty Mediation in a Complex* (Washington D.C.: United States Institute of Peace, 1999), p. 26.

12. Paul J. Kaiser, "Zanzibar: a Multilevel Analysis of Conflict Prevention," in Chandra Lekha Sriram and Karin Wermester, eds., *From Promise to Practice: Strengthening UN Capacities for the Prevention of Violent Conflict* (Boulder: Lynne Reinner, 2003).

13. John Keane, "Structural Transformation of the Public Sphere," in Kenneth L. Hacker and Jan van Dijk, eds., *Digital Democracy: Issues of Theory and Practice* (London: Sage, 2000), p. 70.

14. Russel Spears and Martin Lea, "Panacea or Panopticon? The Hidden Power in Computer-Mediated Communication," *Communication Research* 21:4 (1994), pp. 427–459.

15. Vitaly Dubrovsky, Sara Kiesler, and N. Sethna Beheruz, "Equalization Phenomenon: Status Effects in Computer-Mediated and Face-to-Face Decision-Making Groups," *Human-Computer Interaction* 6 (1991), p. 122.

16. Spears and Lea, p. 430.

17. Ibid. p. 437.

18. Anna Malina, "Perspectives on Citizen Democratization and Alienation in the Virtual Public Sphere" in Barry N. Hague and Brian D. Loader, eds., *Digital Democracy: Discourse and Decision Making in the Information Age* (London: Routledge, 1999), p. 30.

19. Keane, p. 70.

CONTRIBUTORS

Ralf Bendrath is a political scientist and a doctoral candidate at the Free University of Berlin. He is the co-founder and executive director of the German-Austrian Research Group Information Society and Security Policy (Forschungsgruppe Informationsgesellschaft und Sicherheitspolitik/FoG:IS) in Berlin and maintains the e-mail discussion list Infowar.de. His work covers information warfare, critical infrastructure protection, arms control in cyberspace, the connection between war and technology, and the information revolution in general. Recent publications include *Arms Control in Cyberspace, Perspectives of Peace Policy in the Age of Computer Network Attacks* (Berlin: Heinrich Böll Foundation, 2002; ed. with Olga Drossou and Olivier Minkwitz) and "The Cyberwar Debate: Perception and Politics in U.S. Critical Infrastructure Protection," *Information & Security* 7 (2001).

Michael Dartnell is Assistant Professor of Political Science and Information and Communication Studies at the University of New Brunswick in Saint John, Canada. His publications include the book *Action Directe: Ultra-Left Terrorism in France, 1979–1987* as well as the articles "The Electronic Starry Plough: The eNationalism of the Irish Republican Socialist Movement (IRSM)" (2001), "Hyperterrorism: A New Form of Globalized Conflict" (2001), "The Belfast Agreement: Peace Process, Europeanization, Fragmentation, and Legitimacy" (1999), and "Insurgency Online: Elements for a Theory of Anti-government Internet Communication" (1999). He is now finishing the book *Insurgency Online: Web Activism and Global Conflict.*

Ronald J. Deibert is associate professor of political science and director of the Citizen Lab at the University of Toronto. He is the author of *Parchment, Printing, and Hypermedia: Communications in World Order Transformation* (New York: Columbia University Press, 1997) as well as numerous articles and book chapters on the Internet and world politics.

Dorothy E. Denning is a professor in the Department of Defense Analysis at the Naval Postgraduate School. Her research over the past thirty years has spanned the areas of information security and the impact of the Internet on crime and terrorism. She is the recipient of the August Ada Lovelace Award, the National Computer Systems Security Award, and several other awards. Her 130 publications include *Information Warfare and Security* (Reading, Mass.: Addison-Wesley, 1999) and "Is Cyber Terror Next?" in *Understanding September 11* (New York: The New Press, 2002).

Chris Hables Gray is an associate professor of the Cultural Studies of Science and Technology and of Computer Science at the University of Great Falls in Montana. He is also core faculty in the Graduate School of The Union Institute and University and is a professor at Goddard College. He is the author of *Postmodern War* (New York: Guilford Press, 1997) and *Cyborg Citizen* (New York: Routledge, 2000). He is currently working on a book about terror and peace and, with a collective, on a collection about anarchism.

Rose M. Kadende-Kaiser is currently a research analyst at Geneva Global INC, an organization that seeks to enhance philanthropic investment through evaluative research. Prior to her current position, she was a visiting scholar at the Solomon Asch Center for Study of Ethnopolitical Conflict at the University of Pennsylvania, and assistant professor of anthropology and director of the Women's Studies Center at Mississippi State University. Her research interests include gender and development, grassroots peace-building, and the role of the Internet in conflict transformation.

Susan Landau is senior staff engineer at Sun Microsystems Laboratories. She is co-author, with Whitfield Diffie, of *Privacy on the Line: The Politics of Wiretapping and Encryption* (Cambridge, Mass.: MIT Press, 1998), and she is also primary author of the 1994 Association for Computing Machinery report "Codes, Keys, and Conflicts: Issues in US Crypto Policy." Before becoming involved in policy, Landau worked in symbolic computation and algebraic algorithms. She is a fellow of the American Association for the Advancement of Science.

Robert Latham is director of the Social Science Research Council Program on Information Technology and International Cooperation. He has taught at New York–area schools such as Columbia University and is the author of *The Liberal Moment: Modernity, Security, and the Making of Postwar International Order* (New York: Columbia University Press, 1997) and co-editor of *Intervention and Transnationalism in Africa: Global/Local Networks of Power* (Cambridge, Mass.: Cambridge University Press, 2001). He is currently co-editing *Digital Formations: Information Technology and New Architectures in the Global Realm.* Dr. Latham has written numerous articles on topics such as global affairs and information technology, international security, liberalism, human rights, and sovereignty for a variety of journals and edited volumes.

Timothy Lenoir is professor of history and chair of the Program in History and Philosophy of Science at Stanford University. He has published several books and articles on the history of biomedical science from the nineteenth century to the present, and is currently engaged in an investigation of the introduction of computers into biomedical research from the early 1960s to the present, particularly the development of computer graphics, medical visualization technology, the development of virtual reality and its applications in surgery, and other fields. Two current projects include a web documentary project to document the history of bioinformatics funded by the Alfred P. Sloan Foundation, and "How They Got Game," a history of interactive simulation and video games.

Martin C. Libicki has been a Senior Policy Researcher at RAND since 1998. He works on the relationship between information technology and national security. He received his PhD from the University of California–Berkeley (1978), writing on industrial economics. He also received a master's degree in City Planning from U.C. Berkeley (1974), and a bachelor's degree in Mathematics from MIT (1972). Prior employment includes twelve years at the National Defense University, three years on the Navy Staff as program sponsor for industrial preparedness, and three years as a policy analyst for the GAO's Energy and Minerals Division. For more information, http://www.rand.org/personal/libicki/.

Carolyn Nordstrom is associate professor of anthropology at the University of Notre Dame. Her books include *A Different Kind of War Story* as well as several edited volumes. The most recent book, funded by the MacArthur Foundation, is *War and Its Shadows: The Legal, the Illicit, and the Invisible* (forthcoming, University of California Press, 2003). She has also written numerous articles on globalization and illicit economies.

Rafal Rohozinski works as a senior adviser to the UN and other international organizations on information and communication technology and conflict issues. During the past ten years his work has taken him to conflict zones in the CIS, sub-Saharan Africa, and Middle East. He is presently a Ford Foundation/SSRC scholar researching the nexus between ICTs and local conflict in the developing world.

Marc Rotenberg is executive director of the Electronic Privacy Information Center in Washington, D.C., a public interest research organization in Washington, D.C., and adjunct professor at Georgetown University Law Center. He is the editor, with Philip Agre, of *Technology and Privacy: The New Landscape* (Cambridge: MIT Press, 1998) and author, with Daniel J. Solove, of *Information Privacy Law* (New York: Aspen Publishing, 2003).

Janice Gross Stein is Belzberg Professor of Conflict Management in the Department of Political Science and director of the Munk Centre for International Studies at the University of Toronto. She is a fellow of the Royal Society of Canada. Her most recent publications include *Networks of Knowledge: Innovation in International Learning* (Toronto: University of Toronto Press, 2001); *The Cult of Efficiency* (Toronto: House of Anansi Press, 2001); and *Street Protests and Fantasy Parks* (Vancouver: UBC Press, 2002). She is currently writing a book on local and global challenges to accountability.

Rachel Yould is a Rhodes and Fulbright scholar currently completing her doctorate at the University of Oxford. Government roles have included service as Acting Japan Desk Officer and, later, Consultant to the United States Department of Defense. Ford Foundation funding made possible Rachel's recent participation in a Social Science Research Council Summer Collegium as a Fellow of the SSRC's Program on Information Technology, International Cooperation and Global Security. She is now a Research Fellow at Japan's Keio University in association with the World Wide Web Consortium (W3C).

INDEX